Praise for Linda Goodnight and her novels

"*In the Spirit of…Christmas* joyfully portrays the true spirit of the holiday season… The ultimate result is heartwarming."
—*RT Book Reviews*

"Linda Goodnight does her protagonists justice with her sensitive writing in *A Season for Grace*."
—*RT Book Reviews*

"*The Heart of Grace*, by Linda Goodnight, is a wonderfully poignant story with excellent character development."
—*RT Book Reviews*

"From its sad, touching beginning to an equally moving conclusion, *A Touch of Grace* will keep you riveted."
—*RT Book Reviews*

New York Times Bestselling Author
Linda Goodnight

IN THE SPIRIT OF...
CHRISTMAS

and

A SEASON
FOR GRACE

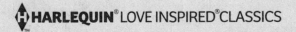

HARLEQUIN® LOVE INSPIRED®CLASSICS

Recycling programs
for this product may
not exist in your area.

ISBN-13: 978-0-373-60183-7

In the Spirit of…Christmas & A Season for Grace

Copyright © 2015 by Harlequin Books S.A.

The publisher acknowledges the copyright holder
of the individual works as follows:

In the Spirit of…Christmas
Copyright © 2005 by Linda Goodnight

A Season for Grace
Copyright © 2006 by Linda Goodnight

Printed in U.S.A.

CONTENTS

Linda Goodnight, a *New York Times* bestselling author and winner of a RITA® Award in inspirational fiction, has appeared on the Christian bestseller list. Her novels have been translated into more than a dozen languages. Active in orphan ministry, Linda enjoys writing fiction that carries a message of hope in a sometimes dark world. She and her husband live in Oklahoma. Visit her website, lindagoodnight.com, for more information.

Books by Linda Goodnight

Love Inspired

The Buchanons

Cowboy Under the Mistletoe
The Christmas Family

Whisper Falls

Rancher's Refuge
Baby in His Arms
Sugarplum Homecoming
The Lawman's Honor

Redemption River

Finding Her Way Home
The Wedding Garden
A Place to Belong
The Christmas Child
The Last Bridge Home

Visit the Author Profile page
at Harlequin.com for more titles.

IN THE SPIRIT OF...
CHRISTMAS

You will go out in joy and be led forth in peace,
the mountains and hills will burst into song
before you, and all the trees of the field
will clap their hands.
—*Isaiah* 55:12

Dedicated with love to my aunts and uncle:
Bonnie, Pat, Carmalita and Robert.
I'll never forget how you stood, a wall of family,
supporting me at my first book signing
and at every signing since. You're the best!

Chapter One

Leaning over the steering wheel of his blue-and-gray Silverado, Jesse Slater squinted toward the distant farmhouse and waited. Just before daybreak the lights had come on inside, pats of butter against the dark frame of green shutters. Still he waited, wanting to be certain the woman was up and dressed before he made his move. She had an eventful day ahead of her, though she didn't know it.

Aware suddenly of the encroaching autumn chill, he pulled on his jacket and tucked the covers around the child sleeping on the seat beside him, something he'd done a dozen times throughout the night. Sleeping in a pickup truck in the woods might be peaceful, but it lacked a certain homey comfort. None of that mattered this morning, for no matter how soul-weary he might be, he was finally back home. *Home*—a funny word after all these years of rambling. Even though he'd lived here only six years after his mother had inherited the farm, they were formative years in the life of a boy. These remote mountains of southeastern Oklahoma had been the only real home he'd ever known.

Peace. The other reason he'd come here. He remembered the peace of lazy childhood days wading in the creek or fishing the ponds, of rambling the forests to watch deer and squirrel and on a really lucky day to spot a bald eagle soaring wild and regal overhead.

He wanted to absorb this peace, hold it and share it with Jade. Neither of them had experienced anything resembling tranquility for a long time.

The old frame house, picturesque in its setting in the pine-drenched foothills of Oklahoma's Kiamichi Mountains, was as it had always been—surrounded by green pastures and a dappling of scattered outbuildings. Somewhere a rooster heralded the sun and the sound sent a quiver of memory into Jesse's consciousness.

But his memory, good as it was, hadn't done justice to the spectacular display of beauty. Reds, golds and oranges flamed from the hills rising around the little farm like a fortress, and the earthy scent of pines and fresh air hovered beneath a blue sky.

"Daddy?"

Jesse turned his attention to the child, whose sleepy green eyes and tangled black hair said she'd had a rough night too.

It was a sorry excuse of a father whose child slept in a pickup truck. And he was even sorrier that she didn't find it unusual. His stomach knotted in that familiar mix of pain and joy that was Jade, his six-year-old daughter.

"Hey, Butterbean. You're awake."

Reaching two thin arms in his direction, she stretched like a kitten and yawned widely. "I'm hungry."

Jesse welcomed the warm little body against his, hugging close his only reason to keep trying.

"Okay, darlin'. Breakfast coming right up." With one

eye on the farmhouse, Jesse climbed out of the truck and went around to the back. From a red-and-white ice chest he took a small carton of milk and carefully poured the contents into a miniature box of cereal.

Returning to the cab, he handed the little box to Jade, consoling his conscience with the thought that cereal was good for her. He didn't know much about that kind of thing, but the box listed a slew of vitamins, and any idiot, no matter how inept, knew a kid needs milk.

When she'd eaten all she wanted, he downed the remaining milk, then dug out a comb and wet wipes for their morning ablutions. Living out of his truck had become second nature for him during fifteen years on the rodeo circuit, but in the two years since Erin had died, he'd discovered that roaming from town to town was no life for a little girl. She'd been in and out of so many schools only her natural aptitude for learning kept her abreast of other children her age. At least, he assumed she was up to speed academically. Nobody had told him different, and he knew for a fact she was smart as a tack.

But she needed stability. She deserved a home. And he meant for her to have one. He lifted his eyes to the farmhouse. This one.

A door slammed, resounding like a gunshot in the vast open country. A blonde woman came out on the long wooden porch. Of medium height, she wore jeans and boots and a red plaid flannel jacket that flapped open in the morning air as she strode toward one of the outbuildings with lithe, relaxed steps. No hurry. Unaware she was being watched from the woods a hundred yards away.

So that was her. That was Lindsey Mitchell, the modern-day pioneer woman who chose to live alone and raise Christmas trees on Winding Stair Mountain.

Well, not completely alone. His gaze drifted to a monstrous German shepherd trotting along beside her. The animal gave him pause. He glanced over at Jade, who was dutifully brushing her teeth beside the truck. She hadn't seen the shepherd, but when she did there would be trouble. Jade was terrified of dogs. And for good reason.

Running a comb through his unruly hair, he breathed a weary sigh. Dog or not, he had to have this job. Not just any job, but *this* one.

When his daughter had finished and climbed back into the cab, he cranked the engine. The noise seemed obscenely loud against the quiet noises of a country morning.

"Time to say hello." He winked at the child, extracting an easy grin, and his heart took a dip. This little girl was his sunshine. And no matter how rough their days together had been, she was a trooper, never complaining as she took in the world through solemn, too-old eyes. His baby girl had learned to accept whatever curves life threw her because it had thrown so many.

Putting the truck into gear he drove up the long driveway. Red and gold leaves swirled beneath his tires, making him wonder how long it had been since anyone had driven down this lane.

The woman heard the motor and turned, shading her eyes with one hand. The people in the nearby town of Winding Stair had warned him that she generally greeted strangers with a shotgun at her side. Not to worry, though, they'd said. Lindsey was a sweetheart, a Christian woman who wouldn't hurt a flea unless she had to. But she wasn't fool enough to live alone without knowing how to fire a rifle.

He saw no sign of a weapon, though it mattered little.

A rifle wouldn't protect her against the kind of danger he presented. Still, he'd rather Jade not be frightened by a gun. The dog would be bad enough.

He glanced to where the child lay curled in the seat once again, long dark eyelashes sweeping her smooth cheeks. Guilt tugged at him. He'd been a lousy husband and now he was a lousy father.

As he drew closer to the house, the woman tilted her head, watching. Her hair, gleaming gold in the sun, lifted on a breeze and blew back from her shoulders so that she reminded him of one of those shampoo commercials— though he doubted any Hollywood type ever looked this earthy or so at home in the country setting. The dog stood sentry at her side, ears erect, expression watchful.

Bucking over some chug holes that needed filling, Jesse pulled the pickup to a stop next to the woman and rolled down the window.

"Morning," he offered.

Resting one hand atop the shepherd's head, Lindsey Mitchell didn't approach the truck, but remained several feet away. Beneath the country-style clothes she looked slim and delicate, though he'd bet a rodeo entry fee she was stronger than her appearance suggested.

Her expression, while friendly, remained wary. "Are you lost?"

He blinked. Lost? Yes, he was lost. He'd been lost for as long as he could remember. Since the Christmas his mother had died and his stepdaddy had decided he didn't need a fourteen-year-old kid around anymore.

"No, ma'am. Not if you're Lindsey Mitchell."

A pair of amber-colored eyes in a gentle face registered surprise. "I am. And who are you?"

"Jesse Slater." He could see the name held no meaning for her, and for that he was grateful. Time enough to spring that little surprise on her. "Calvin Perrymore sent me out here. Said you were looking for someone to help out on your tree farm."

He'd hardly been able to believe his luck when he'd inquired about work at the local diner last night and an old farmer had mentioned Lindsey Mitchell. He hadn't been lucky in a long time, but nothing would suit his plan better than to work on the very farm he'd come looking for. Never mind that Lindsey Mitchell raised Christmas trees and he abhorred any mention of the holiday. Work was work. Especially here on the land he intended to possess.

"You know anything about Christmas-tree farming?"

"I know about trees. And I know farming. Shouldn't be too hard to put the two together."

Amusement lit her eyes and lifted the corners of her mouth. "Don't forget the Christmas part."

As if he could ever forget the day that had changed the direction of his life—not once, but twice.

Fortunately, he was spared a response when Jade raised up in the seat and leaned against his chest. She smelled of sleep and milk and cereal. "Where are we, Daddy?"

The sight of the child brought Lindsey Mitchell closer to the truck.

"You're at the Christmas-tree farm." She offered a smile that changed her whole face.

Though she probably wasn't much younger than his own thirty-two, in the early-morning light her skin glowed as fresh as a teenager's. Lindsey Mitchell was not a beautiful woman in the Hollywood sense, but she had a clean, wholesome, uncomplicated quality that drew him.

Something turned over inside his chest. Indigestion,

he hoped. No woman's face had stirred him since Erin's death. Nothing stirred him much, to tell the truth, except the beautiful little girl whose body heat warmed his side just as her presence warmed the awful chill in his soul.

"A Christmas-tree farm. For real?" Jade's eyes widened in interest, but she looked to him for approval. "Is it okay if we're here, Daddy?"

The familiar twinge of guilt pinched him. Jade knew how her daddy felt about Christmas. "Sure, Butterbean. It's okay."

In fact, he was anxious to be here, to find out about the farm and about how Lindsey Mitchell had come to possess it.

"Can I get out and look?"

Before he had the opportunity to remember just why Jade shouldn't get out of the truck, Lindsey Mitchell answered for him. "Of course you can. That's what this place is all about."

Jade scooted across the seat to the passenger-side door so fast Jesse had no time to think. She opened the door, jumped down and bounded around the pickup. Her scream ripped the morning peace like a five-alarm fire.

With a sharp sense of responsibility and a healthy dose of anxiety, Jesse shot out of the truck and ran to her, yanking her shaking body up into his arms. "Hush, Jade. It's okay. The dog won't hurt you."

"Oh, my goodness." Lindsey Mitchell was all sympathy and compassion. "I am so very sorry. I didn't know Sushi would frighten her like that."

"It's my fault. I'd forgotten about the dog. Jade is terrified of them."

"Sushi would never hurt anyone."

"We were told the same thing by the owner of the

rottweiler that mauled her when she was four." Jade's sobs grew louder at the reminder.

"How horrible. Was she badly hurt?"

"Yes," he said tersely, wanting to drop the subject while he calmed Jade. The child clung to his neck, sobbing and trembling enough to break his heart.

"Why don't you bring her inside. I'll leave Sushi out here for now."

Grateful, Jesse followed the woman across the long front porch and into the farmhouse. Once inside the living room, she motioned with one hand.

"Sit down. Please. Do you think a drink of water or maybe a cool cloth on her forehead would help?"

"Yes to both." He sank onto a large brown couch that had seen better days, but someone's artistic hand had crocheted a blue-and-yellow afghan as a cover to brighten the faded upholstery. Jade plastered her face against his chest, her tears spotting his chambray shirt a dark blue.

Lindsey returned almost immediately, placed the water glass on a wooden coffee table and, going down on one knee in front of the couch, took the liberty of smoothing the damp cloth over Jade's tear-soaked face. The woman was impossibly near. The clean scent of her hair and skin blended with the sweaty heat of his daughter's tears. He swallowed hard, forcing back the unwelcome rush of yearning for the world to be normal again. Life was not normal, would never be normal, and he could not be distracted by Lindsey Mitchell's kind nature and sweet face.

"Shh," Lindsey whispered to Jade, her warm, smoky voice raising gooseflesh on his arms. "It's okay, sugar. The dog is gone. You're okay."

The sweet motherly actions set off another torrent

of reactions inside Jesse. Resentment. Delight. Anger. Gratitude. And finally relief because his child began to settle down as her sobs dwindled to quivering hiccups.

"There now." Adding to Jesse's relief, Lindsey handed him the cloth and stood, moving back a pace or two. She motioned toward the water glass. "Would you like a drink?"

Jade, her cheek still pressed hard against Jesse's chest, shook her head in refusal.

"She'll be all right now," Jesse said, pushing a few stray strands of damp hair away from the child's face. "Won't you, Butterbean?"

Like the trooper she was, Jade sat up, sniffed a couple of times for good measure, and nodded. "I need a tissue."

"Tissue coming right up." Red plaid jacket flapping open, Lindsey whipped across the room to an end table and returned with the tissue. "How about some juice instead of that water?"

Jade's green eyes looked to Jesse for permission.

He nodded. "If it wouldn't be too much trouble."

"No trouble at all." Lindsey started toward a country-kitchen area opening off one end of the living room. At the doorway, she turned. "How about you? Coffee?"

The woman behaved as if he were a guest instead of a total stranger looking for work. The notion made him uncomfortable as all get out, especially considering why he was here. He didn't want her to be nice. He couldn't afford to like her.

Fortunately, he'd never developed a taste for coffee, not even the fancy kind that Erin enjoyed. "No thanks."

"I have some Cokes if you'd rather."

He sighed in defeat. He'd give a ten-dollar bill this morning for a sharp jolt of cold carbonated caffeine.

"A Coke sounds good." He shifted Jade onto the couch. Her hair was a mess and he realized he'd been in such a hurry to get here this morning, he hadn't even noticed. Normally, a headband was the best he could do, but today he'd even forgotten that. So much for first impressions. Using his fingers, he smoothed the dark locks as much as possible. Jade aimed a wobbly grin at him and shrugged. She'd grown accustomed to his awkward attempts to make her look like a little girl.

He glanced toward the kitchen, saw that Lindsey's back was turned. With one hand holding his daughter's, he took the few moments when Lindsey wasn't in sight to let his gaze drift around the house. It had changed— either that or his perception was different. Eighteen years was a long time.

The wood floors, polished to a rich, honeyed glow, looked the same. And the house still bore the warm, inviting feel of a country farmhouse. But now, the rooms seemed lighter, brighter. Where he remembered a certain dreariness brought on by his mother's illness, someone—Lindsey Mitchell, he supposed—had drenched the rooms in light and color—warm colors of polished oak and yellow-flowered curtains.

The house looked simple, uncluttered and sparkling clean—a lot like Lindsey Mitchell herself.

"Here we go." Lindsey's smoky voice yanked him around. He hoped she hadn't noticed his intense interest. No point in raising her suspicions. He had no intention of letting her know the real reason he was here until he had the proof in his hands.

"Yum, Juicy Juice." Jade came alive at the sight of a cartoon-decorated box of apple juice. "Thank you."

Lindsey favored her with another of those smiles that

set Jesse's stomach churning. "I have some gummy fruits in there too if you'd like some—the kind with smiley faces."

Jade paused in the process of stabbing the straw into the top of her juice carton. "Do you have a little girl?"

Jesse was wondering the same thing, though the townspeople claimed she lived alone up here. Why would a single woman keep kid foods on hand?

If he hadn't been watching her closely to hear the answer to Jade's questions, he'd have missed the cloud that passed briefly over Lindsey's face. But he had seen it and wondered.

"No." She handed him a drippy can of Coke wrapped in a paper towel. "No little girls of my own, but I teach a Sunday-school class, and the kids like to come out here pretty often."

Great. A Sunday-school teacher. Just what he didn't need—a Bible-thumping church lady who raised Christmas trees.

"What do they come to your house for?" Jade asked with interest. "Do you gots toys?"

"Better than toys." Lindsey eased down into a big brown easy chair, set her coffee cup on an end table and leaned toward Jade. Her shoulder-length hair swept forward across her full mouth. She hooked it behind one ear. "We play games, have picnics or hayrides, go hiking. Lots of fun activities. And—" she smiled, pausing for effect "—I have Christmas trees year-round."

Christmas trees. Jesse suppressed a shiver of dread. Could he really work among the constant reminders of all he'd lost?

Jade smoothly sidestepped a discussion of the trees,

though he saw the wariness leap into her eyes. "I used to go to Sunday school."

"Maybe you can go with me some time. We have great fun and learn about Jesus."

Jesse noticed some things he'd missed before. A Bible lay open on an end table near the television, and a plain silver cross hung on one wall flanked by a decorative candle on each side. Stifling an inner sigh, he swallowed a hefty swig of cola and felt the fire burn all the way down his throat. He could work for a card-carrying Christian. He had to. Jade deserved this one last chance.

"We don't go anymore since Mama died."

Jesse grew uncomfortably warm as Lindsey turned her eyes on him. Was she judging him? Finding him unfit as a father because he didn't want his child growing up with false hopes about a God who'd let you down when you needed Him most?

He tried to shrug it off. No way he wanted to offend this woman and blow the chance of working here. As much as he hated making excuses, he had to. "We've moved a lot lately."

"Are you planning to be in Winding Stair long?"

"Permanently," he said. And he hoped that was true. He hadn't stayed in one spot since leaving this mountain as a scared and angry teenager. Even during his marriage, he'd roamed like a wild maverick following the rodeo or traveling with an electric-line crew, while Erin remained in Enid to raise Jade. "But first I need a job."

"Okay. Let's talk about that. I know everyone within twenty miles of Winding Stair, but I don't know you. Tell me about yourself."

He sat back, trying to hide his expression behind another long, burning pull of the soda. He hadn't expected her to ask that. He thought she might ask for references or about his experience, but not about him specifically. And given the situation, the less she knew the better.

"Not much to tell. I'm a widower with a little girl to support. I'm dependable. I'll work hard and do a good job." He stopped short of saying she wouldn't regret hiring him. Eventually, she would.

Lindsey studied him with a serene expression and a slight curve of a full lower lip. He wondered if she was always so calm.

"Where are you from?"

"Enid mostly," he answered, naming the small town west of Oklahoma City that had been more Erin's home than his.

"I went to a rodeo there once when I was in college."

"Yeah?" He'd made plenty of rodeos there himself.

With a nod, she folded her arms. "What did you do in Enid? I know they don't raise trees in those parts."

He allowed a smile at that one. The opening to the Great Plains, the land around Enid was as flat as a piece of toast.

"Worked lineman crews most of the time and some occasional rodeo. But I've done a little of everything."

"Lineman? As in electricity?"

"Yes, ma'am. I've helped string half the power lines between Texas and Arkansas."

His answer seemed to please her, though he had no idea what electricity had to do with raising Christmas trees.

"How soon could you begin working?"

"Today."

She blinked and sat back, taking her coffee with her. "Don't you even want to know what the job will entail?"

"I need work, Miss Mitchell. I can do about anything and I'm not picky."

"People are generally surprised to discover that growing Christmas trees takes a lot of hard work and know-how. I have the know-how, but I want to expand. To do that I need help. Good, dependable help."

"You'll have that with me. I don't mind long hours, hard work or getting dirty."

"The pay isn't great." She named a sum barely above minimum wage. He wanted to react but didn't. He'd made do on less. Neither the job nor the money was the important issue here.

"The hours are long. And I can be a slave driver."

Jesse couldn't hold back a grin. Somehow he couldn't imagine Lindsey as much of a slave driver. "Are you offering me the job or trying to scare me off?"

She laughed and the sound sent a shiver of warmth into the cold recesses of Jesse's heart. "Maybe both. I don't want to hire someone today and have him gone next week."

"I'm not going anywhere. Jade's already been in two schools this year, and it's only October."

Her eyes rested on Jade as she thought that one over. One foot tapping to a silent tune while she munched gummy faces, his daughter paid little attention to the adults.

"I have about twenty acres of trees now but plan to expand by at least another ten by next year. Would you like to have a look at the tree lot?"

"Not now." Not at all, ever, but he knew that was out of the question. Once he took possession the Christmas trees would disappear. "Just tell me what I'll be doing."

For the next five minutes, she discussed pruning and

replanting, spraying and cutting, bagging and shipping. All of which he could do. No problem. He'd just pretend they were ordinary trees.

"I'll need character references before I make a final decision."

Jesse reached in his jacket pocket and pulled out a folded paper. He'd been prepared for that question. "Any of these people will tell you that I'm not a serial killer."

"Well, that's a relief. I'd hate to have to shoot you."

He must have looked as startled as he felt because she laughed. "That was a joke. A bad one, I'll admit, but I can shoot and I do have a gun."

Was she warning him to tread lightly? "Interesting hobby for a woman."

"The rifle was my granddad's. He had quite a collection."

"Is he the one who taught you to shoot?"

"Mostly. But don't worry about safety." She glanced at his adorable little girl with the missing front tooth. "I have a double-locked gun safe to protect the kids who come out here. Owning a firearm is a huge responsibility that I don't take lightly."

Rising from the overstuffed armchair, she took the sheet of references from his outstretched fingers. The clean scent of soap mixed with the subtle remnants of coffee drifted around her. The combination reminded him way too much of Erin.

"I'll give some of these folks a call and let you know something this afternoon. Will that be all right?"

"Sure."

"I'll need your telephone number. Where can I reach you?"

Jesse rubbed a hand over the back of his neck. "Hmm. That could be a problem. No phone yet."

"Where are you living? Maybe I know someone close by and could have them bring you a message."

"That's another problem. No house yet either."

She paused, a tiny frown appearing between a pair of naturally arched eyebrows. Funny that he'd notice a thing like a woman's eyebrows. "You don't have a place to live?"

Jade, who'd been as quiet as a mouse, happily sipping her juice and munching green and purple smiley faces, suddenly decided to enter the conversation. "We live in Daddy's truck."

Great. Now he'd probably be reported to child welfare.

But if Lindsey considered him a poor parent, she didn't let on in front of Jade. "That must be an adventure. Like camping out."

"Daddy says we're getting a house of our own pretty soon."

Jesse was glad he hadn't told the child that he'd been talking about *this* house.

Lindsey's eyes flickered from Jade to him. "Have you found anything yet?"

Oh, yes. He'd found exactly the right place.

"Not yet. First a job, then Jade and I have a date with the school principal. While she's in school I'll find a place to stay."

"Rental property is scarce around here, but you might check at the Caboose. It's an old railroad car turned into a diner on the north end of town across from the Dollar Store. Ask for Debbie. If there is any place for rent in the area, she'll know about it."

"Thanks." He stood, took Jade's empty juice carton and looked around for a trash can.

"I'll take that." Lindsey stretched out a palm, accepting the carton. No long fancy nails on those hands, but the short-clipped nails were as clean as a Sunday morning.

"Come on, Jade. Time to roll." Jade hopped off the couch, tugging at the too-short tail of her T-shirt. The kid was growing faster than he could buy clothes.

Stuffing the last of the gummy fruits into her mouth, she handed the empty wrapper to Lindsey with a shy thank-you smile, then slipped her warm little fingers into his.

"How about if I give you a call later this afternoon," Jesse asked. "After you've had a chance to check those references?"

"That will work." She followed him to the door.

Jade tugged at him, reaching upward. "Carry me, Daddy."

He followed the direction of her suddenly nervous gaze. From the front porch the affronted German shepherd peered in through the storm door, tail thumping hopefully against the wooden planks.

Jesse swept his daughter into his arms and out the door, leaving behind a dog that terrified his daughter, a house he coveted and a woman who disturbed him a little too much with her kindness.

He had a very strong feeling that he'd just compounded his already considerable problems.

Chapter Two

Uncertainty crowding her thoughts, Lindsey pushed the storm door open with one hand to let the dog inside though her attention remained on the man. He sauntered with a loose-limbed gait across the sunlit yard, his little girl tossed easily over one strong shoulder like a blanket.

Jesse Slater. The name sounded familiar somehow, but she was certain they'd never met. Even for someone as cautious of the opposite sex as she was, the man's dark good looks would be hard to forget. Mysterious silver-blue eyes with sadness hovering at the crinkled corners, dark cropped hair above a face that somehow looked even more attractive because he hadn't yet shaved this morning, and a trim athletic physique dressed in faded jeans and denim jacket over a Western shirt. Oh, yes, he was a handsome one all right. But looks did not impress Lindsey. Not anymore.

Still, she couldn't get the questions out of her head. Why would a man with no job and a child to raise come to the small rural town of Winding Stair? It would be different if he had relatives here, but he'd mentioned none. Something about him didn't quite ring true, but she was loath to turn him away. After all, if the Christmas Tree Farm was to survive, she needed help—immediately. And Jesse Slater needed a job. And she'd bet this broad-shouldered man was a hard worker.

The child, Jade, hair hanging down her father's back like black fringe, looked up and saw that Sushi was now inside, then wiggled against her father to be let down. She slid down the side of his body then skipped toward the late-model pickup.

At the driver's-side door, Jesse boosted the little girl into the cab and slid inside behind her. Then for the first time he looked up and saw Lindsey standing inside the storm door, watching his departure. He lifted a hand in farewell, though no smile accompanied the gesture. Lindsey, who smiled—and laughed—a lot, wondered if the darkly solemn Jesse had experienced much joy in his life.

The pickup roared to life, then backed out and disappeared down the long dirt drive, swirling leaves and dust into the morning air.

Lindsey, who preferred to think the best of others, tried to shrug off the nagging disquiet. After months of seeking help, she should be thankful, not suspicious, to have a strong, healthy man apply for the job. But the fact that she'd almost given up hope that anyone would be willing to work for the small salary she could afford to pay was part of what raised her suspicions.

She wrestled with her conscience. After all, the poor man had lost his wife and was raising a small daughter alone. Couldn't that account for his air of mysterious sadness? Couldn't he be seeking the solitude of the mountains and the quiet serenity of a small town to help him heal? Even though she knew from experience that only time and the Lord could ease the burden of losing someone you love, the beautiful surroundings were a comfort. She knew that from experience too.

Stepping back from the doorway, she stroked one hand across Sushi's thick fur. "What do you think, girl?"

But she knew the answer to that. Sushi was a very fine judge of character and she hadn't even barked at the stranger. Nor had she protested when the man had come inside the house while she was relegated to the front porch.

Looking down at the sheet of paper still clutched in one hand, Lindsey studied the names and numbers, then started for the telephone.

"If his references check out, I have to hire him. We need help too badly to send him away just because he's too good-looking."

Later that afternoon, Lindsey was kneeling in the tree lot, elbow-deep in Virginia pine trimmings, when Sushi suddenly leaped to her feet and yipped once in the direction of the house.

A car door slammed.

Pushing back her wind-blown hair with a forearm, Lindsey stood, shears in hand, and strained her eyes toward the house. A blue Silverado once more sat in her driveway and Jesse Slater strode toward her front door.

Quickly, she laid aside the shears and scrambled out of the rows of pine trees.

Hadn't the man said he'd call for her decision? What was he doing out here again? Her misgivings rushed to the fore.

"Hello," she called, once she'd managed to breech the small rise bordering the tree lot. The house was only about fifty yards from the trees, and Sushi trotted on ahead.

Jesse spun on his boot heel, caught sight of her and lifted a hand in greeting.

"No wonder you didn't answer your phone," he said when she'd come within speaking distance.

With chagrin, Lindsey realized that it had happened again. While working in the trees, she frequently lost track of time, forgot to eat, forgot about everything except talking to the Lord and caring for the trees. Maybe that's why she loved the tree farm so much and why she'd been so reluctant to take on a hired hand. While among the trees, she carried on a running conversation with God, feeling closer to Him there than she did anywhere—even in church.

"I'm sorry. I didn't realize it was so late." Holding her dirty hands out to her sides, she said, "Why don't you come on in while I wash up? Then we can talk."

Jesse, who'd managed to shave somewhere since she'd seen him last, hesitated. "I hate to ask this, but would you mind putting the dog up again? My daughter is with me."

Lindsey pivoted toward the truck, aware for the first time that a small, worried face pressed against the driver's-side window. "I don't mind, but that is something else we need to discuss. If you're going to work for me, we have to find a way for Jade and Sushi to get along."

A ghost of a grin lit the man's face. "Does that mean none of my references revealed my sinister past?"

"Something like that." In fact, his references had been glowing. One woman had gone beyond character references though, and had told Lindsey about Jesse's wife, about the tragic accident that had made him a widower, and about his raw and terrible grief. Her sympathy had driven her to pray for the man and his little girl—and to decide to hire him.

"If you'll carry Jade inside again, I'll hold Sushi and leave her outside while we talk."

Jesse did as she asked, galloping across the lawn with the child on his back, her dark hair streaming out behind like a pony's tail. Dog forgotten in the fun, Jade's giggle filled the quiet countryside.

"Would you like some tea? Or a Coke?" Lindsey asked once the child and man were seated inside on the old brown sofa. "I've been in the trees so long I'm parched as well as dirty."

"A Coke sounds great, although we don't intend to continue imposing on your hospitality this way."

"Why not?"

He blinked at her, confused, then gave a short laugh. "I don't know. Doesn't seem polite, I suppose."

She started into the kitchen, then stopped and turned around. "If you're going to work for me, we can't stand on ceremony. You'll get hungry and thirsty, so you have to be able to come up here or into the office down at the tree patch and help yourself."

"So I have the job." With Jade glued to his pants leg, he followed Lindsey into the kitchen, moving with a kind of easy, athletic grace.

Lindsey stopped at the sink to scrub her hands. The smell of lemon dishwashing liquid mingled with the pungent pine scent emanating from her skin and clothes. It was a good thing she loved the smell of Christmas because it permeated every area of her life. Even when she dressed up for church and wore perfume, the scent lingered.

"If you want it. The hours are long. The work is not

grueling, but it is physical labor. You can choose your days off, but between now and Christmas, things start hopping."

An odd look of apprehension passed over Jesse's face. He leaned against the counter running alongside the sink. "What do you mean, *hopping?*"

"Jesse, this is a Christmas Tree Farm. Though I'm mostly a choose-and-cut operation, I also harvest and transport a certain number of trees to area city lots, grocery stores, etc., about mid-November." She dried her hands on the yellow dishtowel hanging over the oven rail.

"Do you do that yourself or have someone truck them?" He followed her to the refrigerator, where she handed him two colas. He popped the lids and gave one to Jade, then took a long pull on the other, his silver eyes watching her over the rim.

"Right now I'm delivering them myself, but long-range I want a large enough clientele to ship them all over the country." Her shoulders sagged. "But that takes advertising and advertising takes money—which I do not have at present." Taking a cola for herself, she waved a hand. "But I'm getting off topic here. Let's go sit down and discuss your job. Jade," she said, glancing down toward the child, "I have some crayons and a coloring book around here somewhere if you'd like to color while your dad and I talk."

The child's eyes lit up, so Lindsey gathered the materials she kept stashed in a kitchen drawer and spread them on the table.

The child eyed the table doubtfully and clung tighter to her father's leg. She pointed toward the living room, not ten feet away. "Can I go in there with you and Daddy?"

The poor little lamb was a nervous wreck without her daddy.

"Of course you can." Lindsey swept up the crayons and book and proceeded into the living room, settling Jade at the coffee table.

All the while, she was aware of the handsome stranger's eyes on her. His references were excellent. She could trust him. She *did* trust him. She even felt a certain comfort in his presence, but something about him still bothered her.

Was it because he was too good-looking? She had been susceptible to good looks once before and gotten her heart broken.

No. That had happened a long time ago and, with the Lord's help, she had put that pain behind her.

Hadn't she?

The sharp tang of Coke burned Jesse's throat as he watched the play of interesting emotions across Lindsey's face. She was not a woman who hid her feelings particularly well. If he was to pull this off, he would have to win her confidence. And right now, from the looks of her, she was worried about hiring him.

"I'm a hard worker, Miss Mitchell. I'll do a good job."

"Lindsey, please. There can't be that much difference in our ages."

"Okay. And I'm Jesse. And this lovely creature is Jade." He poked a gentle finger at Jade's tummy.

His little girl beamed at him as though he'd given her a golden crown and, as usual, his heart turned over when she smiled. That one missing front tooth never failed to charm him. "Daddy's silly sometimes."

"I guess I'll have to learn to put up with that if he's

going to work out here. What about you? What are we going to do about you and my dog?"

"I don't like dogs. They're mean." When Jade drew back against the couch, green eyes wide, Jesse sighed.

What in the world was he going to do about this stand-off between dog lover and dog hater? He'd give anything to see Jade get over her terrible fear of dogs, but the trauma ran so deep, he wondered if she ever would. In fact, since Erin's death, her fear had worsened, and other fears had taken root as well. She didn't want him out of her sight, she was terrified of the dark, and her nightmares grew in intensity.

He took a sip of cola, thinking. "Could we just play it by ear for a while and see how things go? Jade will be in school most of the time anyway."

"I work long, sometimes irregular hours, especially this time of year."

"I don't mind that." The more hours he worked the more money he'd make. And the more time he'd have to question Lindsey and check out the farm.

"Then I have a suggestion. The school bus runs right by my driveway. Why not have Jade catch the bus here in the morning and come back here after school?"

Jesse breathed an inward sigh of relief. He'd hoped she'd say that. Otherwise he would have to take off work twice a day to chauffeur his child to and from school.

"That would be a big help."

"Yes, but coming here will also put her in contact with Sushi morning and night."

"Hmm. I see your point." Pinching his bottom lip between finger and thumb, he considered, but came away empty. "Any ideas?"

"Yes, but fears like that don't disappear overnight.

We'll need some time for Jade to acclimate and to realize that Sushi is one of the good guys." She smiled one of those sunshine smiles that made him feel as though anything was possible—even Jade accepting the dog.

"In the meantime, while Jade is here, Sushi can remain outdoors or in one of the bedrooms with the door closed. When we're working in the field, sometimes she hangs out in the office anyway. She won't like being left out, but it will only be until Jade feels more comfortable with her around."

There she went again, tossing kindness around like party confetti. He had to stop setting himself up this way. Liking Lindsey Mitchell could not be part of the deal. "I'm sorry about this. Sorry to be so much trouble."

"Don't worry about it. Jade's fear isn't your fault, and she certainly can't help it." She shot a wink toward Jade, who looked up, green eyes wide and solemn. "Not yet, anyway."

The child was poised over a drawing of the Sermon on the Mount, red crayon at the ready. Jesse swallowed hard.

"Daddy, I want to see the Christmas trees."

The knot tightened in Jesse's chest. Pictures of Jesus. Christmas trees. What was next? "How about tomorrow?"

Jade didn't fuss, but disappointment clouded her angelic face. She resumed coloring, trading the red crayon for a purple one.

"Come on, Jesse." Lindsey rose from the armchair. "You may as well see where you'll be spending most of your time. While we're down there, I'll show you the little office where I keep the equipment and explain my plans for this Christmas season."

He'd have to do it sooner or later. Feeling as if he

were being led to the gallows, Jesse swigged down the remainder of his Coke and stood.

"Where are the Christmas trees?" Gripping Jesse's hand, Jade took in rows and rows of evergreens, swiveling her head from side to side plainly searching for something more traditionally Christmas.

She might be disappointed, but Jesse inhaled in relief, feeling the pungent pine-scented coolness in his nostrils. They were just trees. Plain ordinary pine trees, no more Christmassy than the thousands of evergreens lining the woods and roads everywhere in this part of Oklahoma. The only differences were the neat rows and carefully tended conical shapes of a specific variety. Nothing to get all worked up over.

"Where are the decorations? And the presents?" Jade was as bewildered as she was disappointed.

Kneeling in the rich dirt, Lindsey clasped one of Jade's small hands in hers. "Listen, sweetie, don't fret. Right now, the lot doesn't look like anything but green pine trees, but just you wait another month. See that little building over there?"

After turning to look, Jade nodded. "Are the Christmas trees in there?"

Lindsey laughed, that warm, smoky sound that made Jesse's stomach clench. "Not yet. But the decorations are in there. Lights, and Santas, and angels. Even a nativity set and a sleigh."

"Yeah?" Jade asked in wonder.

"Yeah. And with your daddy to help me this year, we'll set out all of the decorations, string lights up and down these rows, hook up a sound system to pipe in Christmas carols. Maybe you and I can even decorate one special tree up near the entrance where cars pull in. Then every night and day we'll have a Christmas party. People will come to choose a tree and we'll give them wagon rides from the parking area through the tree lot."

The woman fairly glowed with excitement and the effect was rubbing off on Jade. Pulling away from her dad for the first time, she clapped her hands and spun in a circle.

"Let's do it now."

"Whoa, Butterbean, not so fast." He laid a quieting hand on her shoulder. "Lindsey already told you that part comes later." The later the better as far as he was concerned.

"But soon, though, sweetie." Lindsey couldn't seem to bear seeing Jade disappointed. She motioned toward an open field where a large brown horse grazed on the last of the green grass. "See that horse down there? He loves to pull a wagon, does it all the time for hayrides— but at Christmas he gives visitors rides from the parking area through the tree lot."

"What's his name?"

"Puddin'. Don't you think he looks like chocolate pudding?"

Jade giggled. "No. He's big."

"Big, but very gentle. He likes kids, especially little girls with green eyes."

"I have green eyes."

Lindsey bent low, peering into Jade's face. "Well, how about that? You sure do. You'll be his favorite."

Jesse watched in amazement as Lindsey completely captivated his usually quiet daughter. If he wasn't very careful, he'd fall under her spell of genuine decency too. Given his mission, he'd better step easy. Common sense said he should discourage Jade from this fast-forming friendship, but she'd had so little fun lately, he didn't have the heart to say a word.

"Can I go see the Christmas in your building?"

"Sure you can." Popping up, Lindsey dusted her knees and looked at Jesse. His reluctance must have shown because she said, "If we can convince your daddy there are no monsters in there."

Mentally shaking himself, Jesse forced a smile he didn't feel. Santas and angels and horse-drawn wagons. Great. Just great. He wanted no part of any of it. But he wanted this job. And he wanted this farm. To get them both he'd have to struggle through a couple of months of having Christmas shoved down his throat at every turn. It was more than he'd bargained for, but he'd have to do it.

Somehow.

Chapter Three

Delighted to see Jade so excited and to find a fellow Christmas lover, Lindsey clasped her small hand and started toward the storage building. Jesse's voice stopped her.

"You two go ahead. I'll get busy here in the trees."

Lindsey turned back. A crisp October breeze had picked up earlier in the afternoon, but the autumn sun made the wind as warm as a puppy's breath. "Work can wait until tomorrow."

"You have plenty of trimmings here to get rid of. I'll start loading them in the wheelbarrow."

If reluctance needed a pictorial representation, Jesse Slater had the job. Hands fisted at his side, the muscles along his jawbone flexed repeatedly. Lindsey's medical training flashed through her head. Fight or flight—the adrenaline rush that comes when a man is threatened. But why did Jesse Slater feel threatened? And by what? She was the woman alone, hiring a virtual stranger to spend every day in her company. And she didn't feel the least bit threatened.

"Don't you want to see all my Christmas goodies?"

His expression was somewhere between a grimace and a forced smile. "Some other time."

He turned abruptly away and began gathering trimmed pine branches, tossing them into the wheelbarrow. Lindsey stood for a moment, observing the strong flex of muscle beneath the denim jacket. His movements were jerky, as though he controlled some deep emotion hammering to get loose.

Regardless of his good looks and his easy manner, something was sorely missing in his life. Whether he realized it or not, Jesse was a lost and lonely soul in need of God's love.

Ever since coming to live on her grandparents' farm at the age of fifteen, Lindsey had brought home strays, both animal and human. She'd been a stray herself, healed by the love and faith she'd found here in the mountains. But there was something other than loneliness in Jesse. Something puzzling. Maybe even dangerous.

Then why didn't she send him packing?

"Could we go now?" A tug from Jade pulled her attention away from the man and back to the child.

"Sure, sweetie. Want to race?"

The storage and office buildings, which looked more like old-time outhouses than business buildings, were less than fifty feet from the field. Lindsey gave the child a galloping head start, her short, pink-capri-clad legs churning the grass and leaves. When enough distance separated them, Lindsey thundered after her, staying just far enough behind to enjoy the squeals and giggles.

When Lindsey and Jade returned sometime later, Jesse had shed his jacket and rolled back his shirtsleeves.

The work felt good, cleansing somehow, and he wanted to stay right here until nightfall.

"That was fun, Daddy." Jade pranced toward him with a strand of shiny silver garland thrown around her neck like a boa. "Lindsey let me bring this to decorate a tree."

"Little early for that isn't it?" He tried not to react, tried to pretend the sight of anything Christmassy didn't send a spear right through his heart. But visions of gaily-wrapped gifts spilled out around a crushed blue car still haunted him.

Lindsey shrugged. "It's never too early for Christmas. Looks like you've been busy."

He'd filled and emptied the wheelbarrow several times, clearing all the rows she'd trimmed today.

"Impressed?"

She rested her hands on her hipbones and smiled. "As a matter of fact, I am."

"Good." Yanking off his gloves, he resisted returning the smile. "What's next?"

"Nothing for now. It will be dark soon."

She was right. Already the sun bled onto the trees atop the mountain. Darkness would fall like a rock, hard and fast. He'd run away once into the woods behind the farm and darkness had caught him unaware. He'd spent that night curled beneath a tree, praying for help that never came.

"Guess Jade and I should be heading home then."

Knocking the dust off his gloves, he stuffed them into a back pocket, letting the cloth fingers dangle against his jeans.

"Did you find a house to rent today?"

"Your friend Debbie hooked me up. Sent me to the mobile-home park on the edge of town."

She picked up his jacket, swatted the pine needles away and handed him the faded denim. "Is it a nice place?"

He repressed a bitter laugh and tossed the jacket over one shoulder. Anything was nice after living in your truck. When Jade had seen the tiny space, she'd been ecstatic.

"The trailer will do until something better comes along." He couldn't tell her that the something better was the farm she called home.

By mutual consent they fell in step and left the tree lot, Jade scampering along between them, deliberately crunching as many leaves as possible.

Before they reached his truck, Lindsey said, "I have extra linens, dishes and such if you could use them."

Don't be so nice. Don't make me like you.

He opened the door and boosted Jade into the cab. "We're all right for now."

"But you will let me know if you discover something you need, won't you?"

Grabbing the door frame, he swung himself into the driver's seat.

"Sure." *Not in a hundred years.* What he needed was somewhere in the courthouse in Winding Stair and she didn't need to know a thing about it—yet. He'd planned to start his investigation today, but finding a place to live had eaten up all his time. Soon though. Very soon he would have the farm he'd coveted for the past eighteen years.

Lindsey wiped the sticky smear of Jade's maple syrup off the table, trying her best not to laugh at the father-and-daughter exchange going on in her kitchen. In the week since she'd hired Jesse Slater, he and Jade had become a comfortable part of her morning routine. As many times as she'd offered, Jesse refused to take his meals with her, but he hadn't objected when she'd taken to preparing breakfast for his little girl.

Now, as she cleaned away the last of Jade's pancakes, Jesse sat on the edge of a chair with his daughter perched between his knees. Every morning he made an endearingly clumsy attempt to fix the child's beautiful raven hair. And every day Lindsey itched to do it for him. But she said nothing. Jade was, after all, Jesse's child. Just like all the other children she loved and nurtured, Jade was not hers. Never hers.

Normally, he smoothed her hair with the brush, shoved a headband in place, and that was that. This morning, however, Jesse had reached his limit when Jade announced she wanted to wear a ponytail like her new best friend, Lacy. Lindsey suppressed a smile. From the expression on his face, Jesse considered the task right next to having his fingernails ripped out with fencing pliers.

A pink scrunchie gritted between his teeth, he battled the long hair into one hand, holding it in a stranglehold. He'd once let slip that he'd ridden saddle broncs on the rodeo circuit and, Lindsey thought with a hidden smile, that he must have done so with this same intense determination.

Finally, with an audible exhale, he dropped back against the chair. "There. All done."

"Jess..." Lindsey started, then hushed. As much as she longed to see the little girl gussied up like the princess she could be, she wouldn't interfere.

Jade touched a hand tentatively to her head. The lopsided ponytail resided just behind her left ear. A long strand of unbound hair tumbled over the opposite shoulder and the top of her head had enough bumps and waves to qualify as an amusement-park ride.

"Daddy, I don't think Lacy wears her ponytail like this."

Lindsey couldn't hold back the laughter bubbling up inside her. Dropping the dishtowel over the back of a chair, she covered her face and giggled.

Jesse heaved an exasperated moan and rolled his silver eyes. "What? You don't appreciate my talent?"

Lindsey could barely get her breath. "It isn't that— It's just, just—" She took one look at the child's hair and started up again.

Jesse had never joked with her before, didn't smile much either, but this time a reluctant half smile tugged at one corner of his mouth and kicked up, setting off laugh crinkles around his eyes. "If I were a hairdresser in LA, this would be all the rage."

"If you were a hairdresser in LA, I'd stay in Oklahoma."

"All right, boss lady, if you think you can do better—" He bowed toward Jade, extending his arm with a flourish. "She's all yours."

"I thought you'd never ask. I have been itching to get my hands on that gorgeous hair." She grabbed the hairbrush and guided the grinning child back into the chair, then stood behind her. As she'd suspected, the dark hair drifted through her fingers like thick silk. In minutes she had the ponytail slicked neatly into place.

"Impressive," Jesse admitted, standing with his head tilted and both hands fisted on his hips.

"I love playing hairdresser."

"No kidding?" His gaze filtered over her usual flannel and denim. "You don't seem the type."

"I think I should be insulted." She smoothed her hand down Jade's silky ponytail. "Just because I dress simply and get my hands dirty for a living doesn't mean I'm not a girl, Jesse."

He held up both hands in surrender. "Hey, no offense meant. You are definitely a girl. Just not frilly like some."

Like your wife? she wondered. Was she frilly? Is that the type you prefer?

As soon as the thoughts bounded through her head, Lindsey caught them, shocked to even think such things. Once she'd dreamed of marrying a wonderful man and having a houseful of children, but after her fiancé's betrayal, trusting a man with her heart wasn't easy. Add to that the remote, sparsely populated area where she'd chosen to live, and she'd practically given up hope of ever marrying. Besides, she had a farm to run. She didn't want to be interested in Jesse romantically. He was her hired hand and nothing more.

She turned her attention to Jade, handing the child a mirror. "There, sweetie. See what you think."

Jade touched her hair again. Then a smile bright enough to light a room stretched across her pretty face. "I'm perfect!"

Both adults laughed.

Jade flopped her head from side to side, sending the ponytail into a dance. "How did you make me so pretty?"

"My Sunday-school girls come out for dress-up parties sometimes. We do hair and makeup and wear fancy play clothes. It's fun."

"Can I come sometime?"

"Sure. If it's okay with your dad. In fact, tonight is

kids' night at church if you'd like to come and meet some of my Sunday-school students."

"Daddy?" Jade asked hopefully, her eyebrows knitted together in an expression of worry that made no sense given the harmless request.

Some odd emotion flickered over Jesse, but his response was light and easy. He pecked the end of her nose with one finger. "Not this time, Butterbean. You and I have to work on those addition facts."

The child's happiness faded, but she didn't argue. Head down, ponytail forgotten, she trudged to the couch and slid a pink backpack onto her shoulders. Her posture was so resigned, so forlorn that Lindsey could hardly bear it.

"Hey, sweetie, don't worry. My Sunday-school class comes out here pretty often. Maybe you can come another time."

The child gave a ragged sigh. "Okay." She hugged her father's knees. "Bye, Daddy."

He went down in front of her, drawing her against his chest.

Lindsey's throat clogged with emotion. The man was a wonderful dad, the kind of father she'd always dreamed of having for her own children someday. But someday had never come.

"I'll get the dog," she said, going to the door in front of Jade as she had every morning this week. She brought Sushi inside, watching through the glass storm door as the little girl headed to the bus stop, a small splash of pink and white against the flaming autumn morning. In the distance, Lindsey heard the grinding gears of the school bus.

As a teenager she'd ridden that bus to high school

and home again, and in the years since she'd watched it come and go year after year carrying other people's children. But this morning she watched a child make the journey down her driveway to the bus stop, and, for the first time, felt a bittersweet ache in her throat because that child was not her own.

By noon the damp October morning had given way to blue skies and the kind of clouds Jade called marshmallows. A bit of breeze swirled down from the north, promising a frost soon, but Jesse wasn't the least bit cool. As he sat on the top step, leaning backward onto the front porch, he enjoyed what had become his usual lunch, a Coke and a ham sandwich, and pondered how one little woman had ever done all this work by herself.

Besides the routine weeding and spraying, he'd helped her clear several acres of land in preparation for planting another thousand or so trees next week. And from her description of November's chores, October was a vacation.

He had to admit, however reluctantly, that he admired Lindsey Mitchell. She never complained, never expected him to do anything she wasn't willing to do herself. As a result he worked twice as hard trying to lift some of the load off her slim shoulders, and her gratitude for every little thing he did only made him want to do more.

She was a disconcerting woman.

Twisting to the left so he could see her, he said, "Mind if I ask you a question?"

Wearing the red flannel and denim that seemed so much a part of her, Lindsey sat in an old-fashioned wooden porch swing sipping her cola. A partially eaten ham sandwich rested at her side. Sushi lay in front of her, exercising mammoth restraint as she eyed the sandwich longingly.

"Ask away." With dainty movements, Lindsey tore off a piece of ham and tossed it to the dog.

"What would entice a pretty young woman to live out here all alone and become a Christmas-tree farmer?"

The corners of her eyes crinkled in amusement as she wiped her fingers on her jeans. Jesse's stomach did that clenching thing again.

"I didn't exactly plan to be a Christmas-tree farmer. It just happened. Or maybe the Lord led me in this direction." One hand gripping the chain support, she tapped a foot against the porch and set the swing in motion. "My parents are in the military so we moved around a lot. When I was fourteen—" she paused to allow a wry grin. "Let's just say I was not an easy teenager."

Surprised, Jesse swiveled all the way around, bringing one boot up to the top step. Lindsey was always so serene, so at peace. "I can't see you causing anyone any trouble."

"Believe me, I did. Dad and Mom finally sent me here to live with my grandparents. They thought stability, the same school, the country atmosphere and my grandparents' influence would be good for me. They were right."

"So you didn't grow up here?" Now he was very interested.

Lindsey shook her head, honey-colored hair bouncing against her shoulders, catching bits of light that spun it into gold. Odd that he would notice such a thing.

"Actually none of my family is originally from around here. My grandparents bought this farm after they retired. Gramps began the Christmas Tree Farm as a hobby because he loved Christmas and enjoyed sharing it with others."

Jesse decided to steer the conversation toward her grandparents and their purchase of the farm, feeling somewhat better to know Lindsey had not been involved in what had happened eighteen years ago.

"How long did your grandparents own this place?"

"Hmm." Her forehead wrinkled in thought. "I'm not sure. They'd probably been here three or four years when I came. I've lived here nearly fifteen years."

Jesse did the math in his head. The time frame fit perfectly. He rotated the Coke can between his palms then tapped it against his upraised knee. So her grandfather had been the one.

"Did you have any idea who your grandfather bought this place from?" As soon as he asked, Jesse wanted his words back. The question was too suspicious, too far off the conversation, but if Lindsey noticed she said nothing.

"I haven't a clue. All I know is after Granny passed away, Gramps put the farm and everything on it into my name. By then, I wanted to live here forever, so other than bringing me to a faith in Jesus, this was the greatest gift they could have given me."

The too-familiar tug of guilt irritated Jesse. He had no reason to feel bad for her. She'd enjoyed the benefit of living here for years while he'd wandered around like a lost sheep. Only during his too-short time with Erin had he ever found any of the peace that hovered over Lindsey like a sweet perfume. And he was counting on this farm to help him find that feeling again.

"So you became a tree farmer like your grandfather."

Stretching backward, Lindsey ran both hands through the top of her hair, lifted the sides, and let them drift back

down again. Jesse found the motion as natural and appealing as the woman herself.

"I tried other things. Went to college. Became a lab
tech. Then Sean and I—" She paused, and two spots of
color stained her cheekbones. "Let's just say something
happened in my personal life. So, when Gramps passed
away three years ago, I couldn't bring myself to let the
tree farm go. After that first year of doing all the things
he'd taught me and of watching families bond as they
chose that perfect Christmas tree, I understood that this
was where my heart is."

Though curious about the man she'd mentioned, Jesse
decided to leave the subject alone. Knowing about her
love life would only make his task more difficult. "So
you gave up your job to dedicate all your time to the
farm."

"I still take an occasional shift at the hospital and fill
in for vacations in the summer to keep my skills sharp
or to put a little extra money in the bank. But this is my
life. This is what I love. And unless economics drive me
out of business, I'll raise Christmas trees right here on
Gramps' farm forever."

Though she couldn't possibly know his thoughts, to
Jesse the announcement seemed like a challenge. Averting his eyes, he ripped off a piece of sandwich and tossed
the bit of bread and ham to the dog.

Sushi thumped her tail in thanks.

"You spoil her more than I do."

"Yeah." He pointed his soda can toward the north.
"We have visitors."

A flock of geese carved a lopsided V against the sky,
honking loudly enough to rival a rush-hour traffic jam.

"They're headed to my pond."

"And then to a vacation in Florida."

Lindsey laughed and drew her knees up under her chin. "Watching them makes me feel lazy."

"What's on for this afternoon now that we've cleared that new plot of land?"

"Tomorrow we'll need to go over to Mena and pick up the saplings I've ordered. So this afternoon I thought we'd get ready for the wienie roast."

"Who's having a wienie roast?"

"I am. Well, my church actually, but since I have such a great place for it, complete with a horse to give wagon rides, I host the party out here every fall. I hope you and Jade will come."

"I wouldn't want to impose." In truth, the idea of hanging out with a bunch of church people made him sweat. He'd played that scene before, for all the good it had done him in the end.

"Trust me, after you drag brush for the campfire, whittle a mountain of roasting sticks and set up tables, chairs and hay bales, you will have earned a special place at this function."

"I don't know, Lindsey. I'm not sure I would fit in."

Dropping her feet to the porch floor, Lindsey leaned forward, face earnest, hair swinging forward, as she reached out to touch his arm.

"Please, Jesse. Jade would have so much fun. And having a little fun now and then wouldn't hurt you either."

He was beginning to weaken. A wienie roast was not the same as going to church. And Jade would love roasting marshmallows over a campfire. More than that, it was high time he got moving on his mission.

Lindsey's words echoed his thoughts. "Winding Stair

is full of good people. The party would be a great opportunity for you to get acquainted with some of them."

She was right about that. He needed to get friendly with the townsfolk. But not for the reasons she had in mind. He gulped the rest of his cola, taking the burn all the way to his stomach.

Somebody in this town had to know what had happened eighteen years ago. The more people trusted him, the sooner he could have his answers—and the sooner he and Jade could take possession of this farm.

Likely no one would remember him. Les Finch had not been a friendly man, and they'd kept to themselves up here in the mountains. As a boy, Jesse had been a quiet loner, preferring the woods to school activities. And his name was different from his mom and stepdad. His secret was, he believed, safe from the unsuspecting folk of Winding Stair.

He didn't like playing the bad guy, but right was right. This was his home…and he intended to claim it.

Chapter Four

"Think this will be enough?"

At Jesse's question, Lindsey dumped an armload of firewood into a huge oval depression in the ground. Dusting bark and leaves from the front of her jacket, she evaluated the stack of roasting sticks Jesse had piled next to a long folding table.

"How many do you have there? Fifty, maybe?"

He hitched one shoulder, distant and preoccupied as if whittling enough roasting sticks was the last thing on his mind. "Close."

"That should do it." She knelt beside the campfire pit and began to arrange the wood. "Some of the older boys like to make their own—especially when they have a girlfriend to impress."

"It's a man thing." Jesse tossed the last stick onto the pile and snapped shut a pocketknife, which he then shimmied into his front jeans' pocket. "I think we're about set. What time will the guests arrive?"

"Sevenish. Some will meet at the church and bring the bus. Others will drift in at will throughout the evening." Leaning back on her heels, she gazed up at him.

The look on his face said he wanted to be a thousand miles away by then. "It'll be fun, Jesse."

Jade, who resided less than five feet from her daddy at all times, sat on a bale of hay munching an apple with childish contentment. One tennis-shoed foot was curled beneath her while the other beat a steady rhythm against the tight rectangle of baled grass.

"I never went to a wienie roast before," she said.

She'd been ecstatic, hopping and dancing around her father like a puppy when he'd told her of the plans. Lindsey wished Jesse showed half that much enthusiasm.

"You'll like it. We'll play games and take a ride in the wagon and roast marshmallows." Playfully bumping the child's hip with her own, Lindsey sat down next to her. "You'll need your coat. The temperature gets pretty cool after the sun goes down."

Jesse propped a booted foot on the end of the bale next to Jade. He rubbed at his bottom lip, pensive. "We better head home and get cleaned up."

Jade frowned at one palm and then the other. Apple juice glistened on her fingers. "I'm clean."

Jesse shot Lindsey a wry glance. "Well, I'm not." Scooping his daughter up into strong arms, he rubbed her nose with his. "And we'll stop by the store for some marshmallows."

The gap-toothed smile appeared. "Okay!"

He tossed Jade over his shoulder the way Lindsey had seen him do a dozen times. After a thoughtful pause, he said, "I guess we'll see ya at seven then."

Watching the enigmatic man and his child cross the yard, Lindsey experienced an uncomfortable sense of loss and loneliness. Given the number of times she'd asked him or Jade to church functions, she'd been pleasantly surprised when Jesse had agreed to come to the party. He'd been more than clear on a number of occasions that spiritual issues were on his no-call list.

Still, she had a funny feeling about Jesse's decision to join tonight's festivities. He'd been almost grim all afternoon while they'd made the preparations, as if the party was a nasty medicine to take instead of a pleasure to be enjoyed.

Going to release a resentful Sushi from her office confinement, Lindsey heard the roar of Jesse's pickup truck fading into the distance and wondered if he would return at all.

By seven-thirty, friends of every age milled around the clearing along the back side of Lindsey's farm, but there was no sign of Jesse and Jade. Disappointment settled over Lindsey like morning fog on a pond as she watched the driveway for the familiar silver-and-blue truck. The party would have been good for father and daughter. That's why her disappointment was so keen, not because she missed their company, although she was too honest to deny that fact completely. Still, she had plenty of other friends around, and the party, as always, was off to a roaring start.

Beneath a full and perfect hunter's moon, the scent of hickory smoke and roasting hotdogs circled over a crackling campfire. The night air, cool and crisp, meant jackets and hooded sweatshirts, many of which lay scattered about on hay bales or on the short browning grass as their owners worked up a sweat in various games.

A rambunctious group of teenagers and young adults played a game of volleyball at the nets she and Jesse had strung up. Smaller children played tag by lantern light or crawled over the wagonload of hay parked at an angle on the north end of the clearing. Most of the adults chatted and laughed together around the food table and a huge cattle tank filled with iced-down soda pop and bottled water.

"Where's that hired hand of yours, Lindsey?" Pastor Cliff Wilson, standing with a meaty arm draped over the shoulder of his diminutive wife, was only a few years older than Lindsey. She still had difficulty believing that this gentle giant had once spent more time in the county jail for drinking and disturbing the peace than he did in church. Just looking at him reminded Lindsey and everyone else of the amazing redemptive power of Jesus's love. "I thought we'd get to meet him tonight."

"I did, too, Cliff," she said. "But it looks like he backed out on coming. Jade will be so disappointed." So was she. Jade needed the interaction, and though Jesse held himself aloof, he needed to mingle with people who loved and served God.

"Jade?" Cliff's wife, Karen, spoke up. "What a pretty name. Is that his little girl?"

Karen and Cliff had yet to conceive and every child held special interest for the pastor's wife.

"Yes. She's adorable. A little shy at first, so if they do come, give her some time to warm up." Lindsey took a handful of potato chips from a bag on one of the long folding tables and nibbled the salt from one. "Aren't you two going to eat a hotdog?"

Karen laughed and hugged her husband's thick shoulder. "Cliff's already had three."

The pastor rubbed his belly. "Just getting started."

Downing a sizable portion of cola, the minister slid

two franks onto the point of a stick and poked it into the flames. "One for me, and one for my lady friend here."

Lindsey smiled, admiring the open affection between the pastor and his wife.

"Come on, Lindsey." Debbie Castor, the waitress at the Caboose Diner and one of Lindsey's closest friends, had joined the volleyball game. "We need someone who can spike the ball. Tom's team is waxing us."

Tom was Debbie's husband, and they loved competing against each other in good-natured rivalries.

"Okay. One game. I still haven't had my hotdog yet." To shake off her disappointment at Jesse's absence, Lindsey trotted to the makeshift court. She was in good shape from the physical aspect of her job and was generally a good athlete, but tonight her mind wasn't on the game. Up to now, Jesse had always kept his word, and she experienced a strange unease that something was amiss.

When Tom's team easily defeated Debbie's, she stood with hands on her knees catching her breath. "Sorry, guys. I wasn't much help tonight. I must be losing my touch."

"Maybe after you eat you'll regain your former glorious form, and we'll play another game."

With a laugh, she said, "No deal, Tom. You just want to beat us again."

"Right on, sister," Tom teased, bringing his arms forward to flex like a body builder. Balding and bespectacled, the fireman fooled everyone with his small stature and mischievous nature. Only those who knew him understood how strong and athletic he really was.

Still grinning, Lindsey fell in step beside Debbie and headed back to the campfire. "Have you eaten yet?"

"Half a bag of Oreos," Debbie admitted. "All I want

lately is chocolate." Leaning closer she whispered, "I think I'm pregnant again."

Lindsey's squeal was silenced by Debbie's, "Shh. I don't want Karen to hear until I'm sure. I wouldn't want to hurt her."

"Ah, Deb. She's not like that. Karen will be happy for you."

"But to see someone like me have an unplanned pregnancy when she can't even have an intentional one must be difficult for her."

Lindsey knew the pain of wanting, but never having children, and yet her joy for her friends was genuine.

"Does Tom know yet?"

Debbie nodded, her orange pumpkin earrings dancing in the firelight. "He's still a little shell-shocked, I'm afraid. Finances are so tight already with the three we have, but he'll come around."

"You and Tom are such great parents. This baby will be the darling of the bunch, you wait and see. God always knows what He's doing."

"You're right, I know, but it's still a shock." Looking around, she spotted Tom across the way. "I think I'll go over and let the daddy-to-be pamper me awhile."

Lindsey watched her friend snag another cookie as she sashayed around to the opposite side of the campfire where her husband waited. A twinge of envy pinched at her as she gazed at the group gathered on her farm. They were mostly couples and families, people who shared their lives with someone else. Even the teenagers paired up or hung together in mixed groups going through the age-old ritual of finding a partner.

Lindsey loved these people, liked attending functions

with them, but times such as these made her more aware than ever of how alone she was.

To shake off the unusual sense of melancholy, Lindsey found a roasting stick and went in search of a frankfurter to roast. She had too much to be thankful for to feel sorry for herself. She'd chosen to live in this remote place away from her family where there were few unattached men her age. If the Lord intended for her to have a mate, He'd send one her way.

An unexpected voice intruded on her thoughts.

"Could you spare two of those for a couple of fashionably late strangers?"

A pair of solemn silver eyes, aglow in the flickering firelight, met hers.

Her heart gave a strange and altogether inappropriate lurch of pleasure.

Jesse was here.

Jesse stared into Lindsey's delighted eyes and wished he was anywhere but here. From the minute he'd left the farm, he had struggled with a rising desire not to return. Except for his promise to Jade, he wouldn't have. He no more belonged with Lindsey and her holy church friends than he belonged in Buckingham Palace with the queen.

Jade gripped his leg, eyes wide as she watched children running in wild circles outside the perimeter of the firelight.

"You didn't think we were coming, did you?" he said to Lindsey.

She handed him a roasting stick, eyebrows lifted in an unspoken question. "I was beginning to wonder if something had happened."

The open-ended statement gave him the opportunity

to explain, but he let the moment pass. His life was his business. Lindsey's gentle way of pulling him in, including him, was already giving him enough trouble.

"We brought marshmallows." Jade's announcement filled the gap in conversation. She thrust the bag toward Lindsey.

"Cool. Let's eat a hotdog first and then we'll dig into these." Lindsey placed the bag on the table and took a wiener from a pack. "Do you want to roast your own?"

Jade pulled back, shaking her head. "Uh-uh. The fire might burn me."

"How about if I help you?" Lindsey slid the hotdog onto the stick and held it out.

Jesse could feel the tension in his child's small fingers. Her anxiety over every new experience worried him. He squatted down in front of her. "It's okay. Lindsey won't let you get hurt."

Indecision laced with worry played over his daughter's face. Lindsey, with her innate kindness, saw the dilemma. Jade wanted the fun of roasting the hotdog, but couldn't bring herself to trust anyone other than him. Jesse hid a sigh.

"This hotdog will taste better if Daddy cooks it. Isn't that right, sugar?" Lindsey said, handing him the loaded stick. "I'll grab another."

Squatting beside Lindsey with Jade balanced between his knees, Jesse thrust the franks into the flames. Jade rested a tentative hand just behind his.

More than anything Jesse longed to see Jade as confident and fearless as other six-year-olds. Deep inside, he was convinced that regaining his inheritance, giving her a stable home environment and surrounding her with familiar people and places would solve Jade's problem. Tonight he hoped to take another step in that direction.

Letting his gaze drift around the campfire, Jesse studied the unfamiliar faces. Somebody here must have known Lindsey's grandparents and probably even his stepfather. Some self-righteous churchgoer standing out there in the half darkness sucking down a hotdog might have even been involved in the shady deal that had left him a homeless orphan.

"Everyone here is anxious to meet you," Lindsey said, her voice as smoky and warm as the hickory fire.

Given the train of his thoughts, Jesse shifted uncomfortably. "Checking out the new guy to make sure you're safe with me?"

The remark came out harsher, more defensive than he'd planned.

Serene brown eyes probing, Lindsey said, "Don't take offense, Jesse. This is a small town. They only want to get acquainted, to be neighborly."

He blamed the fire and not his pinch of guilt for the sudden warmth in his face. She was too kind and he wished he'd followed his gut instinct and stayed at the cramped little trailer.

"Here you go, Butterbean." Taking the hotdog from the flames, he went to the table for buns and mustard. Lindsey and Jade followed.

One of the biggest men he'd ever seen handed him a paper plate. "You must be Jesse."

Lindsey made the introductions. "This is my pastor, Cliff Wilson."

Jesse's surprise must have shown because the clergyman bellowed a cheerful laugh. "If you were out killing preachers, you'd pass me right up, wouldn't you?"

Cliff looked more like a pro wrestler than a preacher. A blond lumberjack of a man in casual work clothes and tennis shoes with blue eyes as gentle and guileless as a child's and a face filled with laughter.

"Good to meet you, sir," Jesse said stiffly, not sure how to react to the unorthodox minister.

"Everyone calls me Pastor Cliff or just plain Cliff." The preacher offered a beefy hand which Jesse shook. "You from around this area?"

"Enid." Giving his stock answer, Jesse concentrated on squirting mustard onto Jade's hotdog. No way he'd tell any of them the truth—that he'd roamed this very land as a youth.

"Lindsey says you're heaven-sent, a real help to her."

"I'm glad for the work." He handed the hotdog to Jade, along with a napkin. "Lindsey's a fair boss."

By now at least a half dozen other men had sidled up to the table for introductions and food refills. Jesse felt like a bug under a magnifying glass, but if he allowed his prickly feelings to show, people might get suspicious. He needed their trust, though he didn't want to consider how he'd eventually use that trust against one of their own.

"A fair boss? Now that's a good 'un." A short, round older man in a camouflage jacket offered the joking comment. "That girl works herself into the ground just like her grandpa did. I figure she expects the same from her hired help."

Jesse stilled, attention riveted. This fellow knew Lindsey's grandparents and was old enough to have been around Winding Stair for some time. He just might know the details Jesse needed to begin searching the courthouse records.

"Now Clarence." Eyes twinkling a becoming gold

in the flickering light, Lindsey pointed a potato chip at the speaker. "You stop that before you scare off the only steady worker I've ever had."

"Ah, he knows I'm only kidding." Clarence aimed a grin toward Jesse. "Don't you, son?" Before Jesse could respond, the man stuck out his hand. "Name's Clarence Stone. I live back up the mountain a ways. If you ever need anything, give me a holler."

A chuckle came from the man in a cowboy hat standing next to Clarence. His black mustache quivered on the corners. "That's right, Jesse. Give Clarence a holler. He'll come down and talk your ears off while you do all the work."

Clarence didn't seem the least bit offended. He grinned widely.

"This here wise guy is Mick Thompson," he said with affection. "Mick has a ranch east of town, though if it wasn't for that sweet little wife of his, he'd have gone under a long time ago."

Mick laughed, teeth white in his dark face. "I have to agree with you there, Clarence, even if Clare is your daughter. I wouldn't be much without her."

Jesse's mind registered the relationship along with the fact that Mick owned a ranch. Now that was something Jesse understood.

"You raise horses on that ranch of yours?" he asked, making casual conversation while hoping to turn the conversation back to Lindsey's grandparents.

"Sure do. You know horses?" Mick sipped at his plastic cup.

"I've done a little rodeo. Bronc-riding mostly."

"No kidding?" Mick's eyebrows lifted in interest. "Ever break any colts?"

"Used to do a lot of that sort of work." Before Erin died. But he wouldn't share that with Mick.

"Would you like to do it again?"

"I wouldn't mind it." He missed working with rough stock, and breaking horses on the side would put some much-needed extra money in his pocket.

"Don't be trying to hire him away from Lindsey, Mick," the jovial Clarence put in. "She'll shoot you. And I'll be left to support your wife and kids."

"You'd shoot me yourself if you thought Clare and the kids would move back up in those woods with you and Loraine."

Both men chuckled, and despite himself, Jesse enjoyed their good-natured ribbing.

Lindsey, having drifted off in conversation with a red-haired woman, missed the teasing remark. Without her present, Jesse wanted to turn the conversation back to her grandfather, but wasn't sure how to go about it without causing suspicion.

"Tell you what, Jesse," Mick said, stroking his mustache with thumb and forefinger. "When you have some time, give me a call. I have a couple of young geldings that need breaking, and I can't do it anymore. Bad back."

Were all the people of Winding Stair this trusting that they'd offer a man a job without ever seeing him work?

"How do you know I can handle the job?"

Mick's mustache quirked. "Figure you'd say so if you didn't think you could."

"I can."

"See?" Mick clapped him on the back and clasped his hand in a brief squeeze. "My number's in the book. And I pay the going rate."

"Appreciate the offer, but I doubt I can get loose from here until after the holidays."

The familiar sense of dread crawled through his belly. He'd much rather be tossed in the dirt by a bucking horse than spend one minute in Lindsey's tree lot. He'd counted on the old adage that familiarity breeds indifference. So far, that hadn't proven true. If anything, he dreaded the coming weeks more than ever.

Mick sipped at his soda before saying, "After Christmas is fine with me. Those colts aren't going anywhere. Meantime, if you need help hauling these trees, let me know. I got a flatbed settin' over there in my barn rustin'."

"He sure does," Clarence teased. "And it would do him good to put in a full day's work for a change."

An unbidden warmth crept through Jesse. Offers of help from friends didn't come too often, but this offhand generosity of strangers was downright unsettling.

"Jade, Jade." Two little girls about Jade's age came running up and interrupted the conversation. One on each side, they grabbed her hands and pulled. "Come play tag."

She looked to Jesse for approval. "Can I, Daddy?"

"Don't you want to finish your hotdog?"

"I'm full." She handed him the last bite of the squeezed and flattened sandwich.

He downed the remains and wiped the mustard off her face. "Go on and play."

She grabbed his hand and tugged. "Come with me."

Jesse shook his head, standing his ground for once. "I haven't finished my own hotdog. I'll be here when you get back. Promise."

After a moment of uncertainty, the desire to play with her friends won out.

Jesse's heart gladdened to see his little girl race away with the other children for once instead of clinging to his leg like a barnacle.

Biting into his smoky hotdog, Jesse watched and listened, hoping for an opportunity to casually probe for information. His attention strayed to the gregarious preacher.

Pastor Cliff seemed to be everywhere, laughing, joking and making sure everyone had a great time. The teenagers flocked around him as though he was some football star, begging him to join their games, occasionally pelting him with a marshmallow to gain his attention. Punctuating the air with a few too many "praise the Lords" for Jesse's comfort, the preacher nonetheless came across like a regular guy. He'd even overheard Cliff promise to help repair someone's leaky roof next week. The big man sure wasn't like any minister Jesse had ever encountered.

"When are we taking that wagon ride, Lindsey?" Cliff bellowed, indicating a small boy perched on his shoulders. "Nathaniel says he's ready when you are."

"Do you kids want the tractor or the horse to pull us?" Lindsey called back.

"The horse. The horse," came a chorus of replies from all but the preacher.

Jesse knew the big, powerful horse stood nearby inside a fenced lot, his oversized head hanging over the rails, waiting his opportunity. The animal liked people and was gentle as a baby.

"How about you, Cliff? What's your preference?" a man called, his face wreathed in mischief.

The oversized preacher waved his upraised hands in mock terror. "Now, Tom, you know I don't mess with any creature that's bigger than me."

"Which wouldn't be too many, Cliff," came the teasing answer.

Everyone laughed, including Cliff, though the joke was on him. Grudgingly, Jesse admired that. The minister he'd known would have seen the joke as an offense to his lofty position.

"You're out-voted, preacher," Lindsey called, starting toward the gate. "I'll get Puddin'."

Shoving his hands into the pockets of his jean jacket, Jesse fell into step beside her. Though mingling with the church crowd provided opportunities to gather information, he needed some distance. He hadn't expected their friendliness, the ease with which they accepted him, and most of all, he'd not expected them to be such everyday, normal people. Lindsey's church family, as she called them, was fast destroying his long-held view of Christians as either stiff and distant or pushy and judgmental.

"Need any help?" he asked.

She withdrew a small flashlight from inside her jacket, aimed the beam toward the gate, and whistled softly. "I put his harness on earlier. All I need to do is hook the traces to the wagon."

Jesse stepped into the light and raised the latch. In seconds the big horse lumbered up to nuzzle at his owner while she snapped a lead rope onto his halter. Together they led him toward the waiting wagon.

"He's a nice animal." Jesse ran a hand over the smooth, warm horseflesh, enjoying the feel again after too much time away from the rodeo. "What breed is he?"

"Percheron mostly." She smiled at the horse with affection. "Although I'm not sure he's a full-blood since I have no papers on him, but he has the sweet temperament and muscular body the breed is known for. And he loves to work."

"Percheron." Jesse rolled the word over in his head. He knew enough about horses to know the name, but that was about it. "Different from the quarter horses I'm used to."

"Certainly different from the wild broncs. Puddin' doesn't have a buck anywhere in him." One on each side of the massive horse, they headed back toward the heat and light of the bonfire. "Every kid within a ten-mile radius has ridden him, walked under him, crawled over him, and he doesn't mind at all." She turned toward him, her face shadowed and pale in the bright moonlight. "What about you? Do you still have horses?"

He shook his head. "No. After Erin died, I—" He stopped, not wanting to revisit the horrible devastation when he'd sold everything and hit the road, trying to run from the pain and guilt. He'd told Lindsey more about his past than he'd ever intended to, but talking about Erin was taboo. "I'd better find Jade."

He stalked off toward the circle of squealing children, aware that he'd been abrupt with Lindsey and trying not to let that bother him. He'd intentionally sought her company, and now he was walking away.

Ruefully, he shook his head. What a guy.

In the distance he spotted Jade, her long hair flying out behind her as she ran, laughing. With a hitch beneath his rib cage, he watched his daughter, grateful for the rare display of playful abandon. Letting the shadows absorb him, he stood along the perimeter of children, hoping this place would ultimately heal them both.

"Hey, Jesse." A hand bigger than Puddin's hoof landed on his shoulder. The preacher. "Great party, huh?"

"Yeah." Though he didn't belong here, he had to admit the party was a success. Just seeing Jade carefree was worth a few hours discomfort on his part.

"Lindsey's a great gal."

Jesse followed the minister's gaze to where Lindsey, surrounded by too many youthful helpers, attached the patient horse to the wagon. Silently, he agreed with Cliff's assertion. Lindsey *was* a good woman. Her decency was giving his conscience fits. "You known her long?"

"A few years. Ever since coming here to minister." Cliff nodded at the rowdy crowd around the fire. "Most of these folks have known her and each other much longer, but God really blessed me when he sent me to Winding Stair. I feel as if Lindsey and all the others out there are my family now."

Clarence approached, this time accompanied by a small, gray-haired woman with rosy cheeks, who carried a plate of homemade cookies. "That's the way it's supposed to be, ain't it, preacher?"

Cliff reached for the cookies. "Yep."

"How about you, Jesse?" Clarence motioned toward the plate.

Out of courtesy Jesse accepted the dessert, taking a bite. He liked the mildly sweet flavor of the old-fashioned cookie. "These are good."

"Course they are," Clarence said. "Loraine makes the best oatmeal cookies in the county. And if you don't believe me, just ask her."

"Oh, Clarence, you old goof." The smiling little woman flapped a hand at him. "Jesse, don't pay any mind to my husband. This isn't my recipe and he knows it. Lindsey's grandma gave it to me. Now that woman could cook."

Blood quickening, Jesse saw the opportunity and took it. "You knew Lindsey's grandparents?"

"Sure did. Better folks never walked the earth, as far as I'm concerned." She paused long enough to dole out more cookies to passersby. Jesse kept his mouth shut, waiting for her to go on, blood humming with the hope that he was about to learn something.

"Betty Jean—that was her grandma—could do about anything domestic. A country version of Martha Stewart, I guess you'd say." She chuckled softly at her own joke. "And she wasn't stingy about it either. Would share a jar of pickles or a recipe without batting an eye. A fine neighbor, she was. A real fine neighbor."

She looked a little sad and Jesse shifted uncomfortably. He needed to keep Loraine and Clarence talking but he didn't want to think of the Mitchells as decent folks. There was nothing decent about stealing from an orphan.

Keeping his tone casual, Jesse said, "Lindsey's a good cook too."

"Betty Jean would have made sure of that." Loraine thrust the nearly empty plate toward him. "Another cookie?"

"Might as well take one, Jesse," Clarence put in with a chortle. "She ain't happy unless she's feeding someone."

Jesse hid a smile. It was hard not to like Loraine and Clarence Stone. "Thanks."

He accepted the cookie, mind searching for a way to gain more information. He'd suffered through an hour of stilted conversation to get this far. He wasn't about to let this chance slip away.

"What about Lindsey's grandpa? I guess he's the one who taught her to use that rifle...."

"Yep," Clarence said. "That was Charlie, all right. Me and him used to hunt and fish together, and he liked to brag about Lindsey's shooting. Called her his little Annie Oakley."

Jesse's stomach leaped.

Charlie.

His patience had paid off. At last, he had someone to blame along with his stepfather. Lindsey's grandfather, the man who'd stolen this eighty-acre farm from a teenage boy, was named Charlie Mitchell.

In the shadowy distance, snatches of conversation and laughter floated on the night air. One particular laugh—a throaty, warm sound that sent shivers down his spine— stood out from the rest.

Lindsey.

He wanted to put his hands over his ears, to block out the sound. He'd finally discovered some information, and nobody, no matter how sweet and kind, was going to stop him from using it.

Chapter Five

Lindsey draped her jacket over the back of a kitchen chair and went to the sink. She'd had a long afternoon without Jesse there to help, but she couldn't complain. In the weeks he'd worked on the farm, this was the first time he'd asked for time off. So she had spent the afternoon marking the trees they'd soon cut and bale for delivery.

Ever since the night of the cookout, she'd noticed a shift in him. He worked harder than ever on the farm, putting in long hours and cutting himself no slack. But he seemed to be bothered by something—not that there was anything new about that—but this was a subtle mulling as though he had something heavy on his mind.

With a sigh, Lindsey acknowledged how much she'd come to depend upon the mysterious Jesse. She needed him, and regardless of his inner demons, she liked him. He was a good man with a heavy burden. If only she could find a way to help him past that burden—whatever it was.

Two or three times today she'd turned to ask Jesse's advice about something before remembering he was gone. Funny how she'd never needed anyone before other than Sushi and the Lord, but Jesse had changed all that. And she wasn't sure becoming dependent on her hired hand was such a good idea.

Turning the water tap, she filled a glass and drank deeply, thirsty even though the early November weather was cloudy and cool with the promise of rain hanging like a gray veil over the land. In the back of her mind, she faintly registered a rumbling in the distance but paid little mind. After washing and drying her hands, she headed to the refrigerator.

She had one hand on last night's chicken and rice when the screaming began.

An adrenaline rush more powerful than an electric shock propelled her into action. Faster than she thought possible, Lindsey bounded into the bedroom, unlocked the gun case, removed her rifle and rushed out into the yard, loading the weapon as she moved. An occasional mountain lion roamed these hills.

Peering in the direction of the screams, Lindsey stopped...and lowered the gun.

Jade stood halfway down the gravel driveway, frozen in fear, screaming her head off. Directly in front of her, Sushi lay on her back, feet in the air, groveling for all she was worth.

With a feeling somewhere between relief and exasperation, Lindsey stashed the rifle on the porch and loped down the driveway.

What was Jade doing here? Where was Jesse? And when would the child realize that Sushi was her friend?

"Sushi, come," she called. The German shepherd leaped to her feet, shook off the dust and leaves and trotted to Lindsey's side. Pointing to a spot several yards away from the terrified child, she commanded, "Stay."

The dog obeyed, plopping her bottom onto the dirt, tongue lolling, while she watched Jade with worried eyes.

Jade's screaming subsided, but the harsh sobs continued as Lindsey went down on her knees and took the little girl into her arms. She had a dozen questions, but now was not the time to ask them. Soon enough she could discover why Jesse had not picked up Jade at school as he'd planned.

"Jade, listen to me." Pushing the tangled hair, damp with tears, back from Jade's face she said gently, "Stop crying and listen. We need to talk like big girls."

Jade gave several shuddering sobs, scrubbing at her eyes with her fingertips. "The dog was going to get me."

"That's what we have to talk about. Sushi will not hurt you. Look at her. She's sitting down there begging for you to like her, but she won't even come near you unless I tell her to."

"She ran at me. I saw her teeth."

"She was smiling at you. You're part of her family now and she was excited to see you. That's how she behaves when I come home from someplace, too."

"It is?" Wary and unconvinced, Jade glanced from Lindsey to Sushi and back again.

"Sure. Every time you come home, she whines to be let out so she can play with you. It makes her very sad that you don't like her."

Jade's expression said she was thinking that over, but still she clung tightly to Lindsey.

"Where's my daddy?"

"I'm not sure, sweetie. He was supposed to pick you up at school."

The little girl's small shoulders slumped. "He's probably dead." And she burst out crying again.

"No, Jade, no." Please God, let me be right. Don't let anything else happen to this child. The loss of her mother had completely destroyed her sense of safety. "Your daddy is running late and didn't get back in time. He'll be here soon, and while we wait, you and I can have a dress-up tea party."

Lindsey could see she scored some points with the idea so she pressed the advantage. "Sushi wants to come, too. She even has some dress-up clothes."

Jade found that amusing. A hesitant smile teetered around her mouth. "Really?"

"Absolutely. All my Sunday-school kids invite Sushi to their tea parties because she's such a nice dog, so she has a hat, a boa and a fancy vest to wear."

"She might bite me."

"No," Lindsey said firmly. "She will not." Sliding Jade to the ground, she took the child's hand. "Come on. I'll show you."

Sushi waited right where she'd been told to stay, eagerly thumping her tail at the first sign of movement in her direction.

Jade pulled back. "Uh-uh."

Lindsey sighed, but relented and swept the little girl into her arms. "Okay, then. I have another idea."

She carried Jade to the house. A bewildered Sushi remained in the driveway as commanded.

"Stand here inside the house where you can see Sushi and me through the glass door." Lindsey took a piece of leftover chicken from the fridge. She'd planned to have the meat for supper, but helping Jade begin the process of overcoming this phobia was far more important. "Watch what a good girl Sushi is and how she loves to play, but she always minds me when I tell her to do something. Okay?"

Nodding and wide-eyed, Jade stood inside the door, her face pressed to the glass while Lindsey stepped onto the porch and called the dog. When Sushi arrived, skidding to a stop at her owner's command, Lindsey spent several minutes putting the animal through all her obedience commands. Extremely well disciplined, Sushi even resisted the piece of baked chicken, though Lindsey knew the meat was her favorite treat.

Then she played with Sushi, petting her, tossing sticks that the dog retrieved, scratching her belly.

Finally, Lindsey lay down on the porch to show her total trust of the dog. Sushi responded by plopping her big head onto Lindsey's chest with a delighted sigh that made Jade laugh.

Sitting up, Lindsey rotated toward Jade. "See what a good girl she is?"

"Uh-huh."

"Would you like to pet her?"

"Uh-uh." But Lindsey could see that, for once, she wanted to.

Confident they'd made progress, Lindsey relented. "Maybe next time?"

Leaving Sushi on the porch, Lindsey dusted her clothes and came inside. She peeked at the yellow teapot clock hanging over the cook stove. Jade had been here at least thirty minutes and still no sign of Jesse. Refusing to worry, she internalized a little prayer, and turned her attention to occupying Jade. The little girl didn't need to fret about her daddy even if Lindsey was.

"I'm starved."

"Me, too."

Using her best imitation of an English lady, Lindsey said, "Shall we prepare tea and dine?"

Jade giggled. "Can we dress up too? And you can be the princess and I'll be the queen?"

"Lovely idea, my queen. Right this way, please." Nose in the air as befit royalty, she led the way to the huge plastic storage bin in her bedroom closet, where she kept a variety of thrift-shop and novelty-store play clothes. Jade, getting into the spirit of the game, followed suit. She fell upon the container, carefully lifting out one garment after another, exclaiming over each one as if the clothes came from Rodeo Drive.

In no time, she'd chosen outfits for both of them and they traipsed on plastic high heels, boas trailing, into the kitchen to prepare the Oklahoma version of high tea.

"Let's make fancy sandwiches first. Later, we'll do cookies."

"Do you have Christmas cookie cutters?" Jade shoved at her sun hat, repositioning the monstrosity on her head. Bedecked with more flowers than Monet had ever painted, the hat tied with a wide scarf under the child's chin. Lindsey thought she looked adorable.

"A bunch of them. We can use them on the sandwiches if you want to."

"Cool. Do you gots sprinkles too?"

"Oh, yeah. I have tons of sprinkles. All colors. But let's not put those on the sandwiches."

Jade giggled. "For the cookies, silly. I want to make

Daddy a big red cookie." Her face fell. "I wish my daddy would come. I'll bet he's getting hungry."

"He'll be here soon," Lindsey said with more confidence than she felt as she spread the sandwich fixings on the table. "Tell you what. Let's say a little prayer asking Jesus to take care of him and bring him safely home."

She hardly noticed that she'd referred to her own house as home for Jesse and Jade. Semantics didn't matter right now.

"Okay." To Lindsey's surprise, Jade closed her eyes and folded her little hands beneath her chin. Even though Jesse shied away at the mention of God, someone had taught this child to pray.

Closing her own eyes, Lindsey said a short but heartfelt prayer.

"Amen."

Jade's shoulders relaxed. "Jesus will take care of Daddy, won't He?"

"Yes, He will. And He'll take care of you too." She smeared mayo on a slice of bread, handing it to Jade to layer on the meat and cheese. "Did you know you have a guardian angel who is always with you?"

Shaking her head, Jade licked the mayo off one finger.

"Well, you do. Everybody does. But God has very special guardian angels that take care of children. Jesus loves you so much He tells your very own angel to keep watch over you day and night."

"Even when I'm asleep?"

"Yes." She chose an angel from the pile of cookie cutters. "That's why you don't need to be afraid of anything—ever. Your angel is always here, looking after you."

Jade took the metal angel, studied it, and then pressed

the shape into a sandwich. "Does Daddy have a guarding angel?"

Lindsey smiled at the mispronunciation. "He sure does."

"Can I save this angel sandwich for my daddy?"

"Of course you can. We'll make enough of everything so he can eat, too, when he gets here."

That seemed to satisfy Jade, and Lindsey wished she were as easily comforted. Where was Jesse? Leaving Jade alone was so uncharacteristic of him. Had something happened? In the weeks of their acquaintance she'd grown fond of him, fonder than was comfortable, and the thought of something happening to him was unspeakable.

Agitated and filled with self-recriminations, Jesse stormed across Lindsey's yard, hoping with everything in him that Jade was here. He couldn't believe he'd gotten so busy, so deeply enmeshed in the stacks of court records that the time had slipped away and he'd forgotten to pick Jade up from school until she was long gone. What kind of lousy father was he anyway?

Sushi bounded out to meet him, a good sign. His spirits lifted somewhat, though he'd feel better if the German shepherd bit him. He deserved to be punished. For all his searching, he hadn't found a bit of useful information; not one single reference to any transaction between Charles Mitchell and Les Finch.

The day as gray as his mood, Jesse mounted the porch—and heard singing. A husky adult voice that sent an unexpected shiver of pleasure dancing along his nerve endings blended sweetly with a higher, childish melody.

Relief flooded him. Jade was here. Pausing at the

open door, he could see the two through the glass. They were in the kitchen at the table, their backs turned, singing "Mary Had a Little Lamb" while they worked at something.

He squinted, leaning closer. What kind of get-ups were they wearing?

With an inner smile, he waited until they finished their song before pecking lightly on the door. Two heads swiveled in his direction.

"Daddy!" Jade dropped something onto the table and clambered off her chair. She ran toward him, nearly tripping over a long, white dress that looked suspiciously like a well-used wedding gown. Taking a moment to hike the yards of wrinkled satin and lace into one hand, she stumbled onward, lime-green high heels clunking against the wooden floor.

Mood elevating with every step his baby took, Jesse opened the door and stepped inside the living room.

"My, don't you look beautiful," he said.

But Jade was having none of his compliments. She got right to the point. "The teacher made me ride the bus 'cause you didn't come."

"I'm sorry I was late, Butterbean. Your teacher did the right thing sending you to Lindsey, where you would be safe and happy."

"Where were you? I got scared. I thought you were dead like Mommy."

A searing pain cut off Jesse's windpipe. Of course she'd think that. That's why he always made a point of being exactly where she expected—to allay her well-founded fears.

Lindsey appeared in the living room. "Your daddy is here now, Jade, and he's just fine."

"Jesus took care of him the way you said."

A serene smile lit Lindsey's eyes. "Yes, He did."

Jesse didn't know what was going on with their talk of Jesus and decided not to ask. He looked to Lindsey, grateful for her care of Jade, but not wanting to tell her where he'd been. Wearing a hat with peacock feathers sticking out the top, and a rather bedraggled fake fur stole over someone's old red prom dress, she looked ridiculously cute. If he hadn't felt so guilty, he would have laughed.

"I'm sorry for putting you out this way."

"Jade is no problem. But we were a little concerned about you."

Exactly what he didn't need—Lindsey's concern, although he knew it was there, felt it day in and day out as she carefully avoided subjects she'd discovered were painful or taboo. Always, that gentle aura of peace and inner joy reached out to him.

"I had some personal business to handle, which took much longer than I'd planned. Somehow the time got away from me, and by the time I rushed over to the school…" He lifted his hands and let them fall.

"Well, you're here now." Lindsey smiled that sweet, tranquil smile that changed her face to a thing of beauty. Jesse tried, but failed, to resist the pleasure that one motion gave him.

And then she made things worse by asking, "Are you hungry?"

An unbidden rush of warmth filled him from the inside out. Coming to this house and this woman was starting to feel far too natural and way too good.

"Come on, Daddy. Come see. We're making a tea party, and I'm the queen." Skirts sweeping the floor, Jade led the way into the kitchen and lifted an odd-shaped bit of bread from the table, thrusting it at him. "I made this guarding angel for you."

"Tea, huh? And an angel sandwich." He took the offering, examining the small figure with all due seriousness. "Sounds delicious. Anything I can do to help?"

Lindsey nodded toward a plate of fresh fruit. "You could slice up the apples if you'd like."

"Lindsey." Jade's plaintiff protest drew both adults' attention. She eyed her father skeptically. "He can't come to the tea party without dress-up clothes."

An ornery gleam flashed in Lindsey's brown eyes. "She's right, Dad. Tea requires formal attire."

Before he could object on purely masculine grounds, Jade rushed off, returning with a purple boa, a tarnished tiara, and a yellow-and-black satin cape. "Here, Daddy, you can be king."

Lindsey laughed at the pained expression on Jesse's face and in return, received his fiercest glare of wry humor.

"I'll get you for this," he muttered under his breath as Jade dressed him, carefully twining the boa around his neck before placing the crown on his head with a triumphant—if somewhat crooked—flourish.

Lindsey wrinkled her nose at him and adjusted her stole with a haughty toss of her head. "Mess with me, mister, and I'll find you a pair of purple plastic high heels to go with that dashing feather boa."

Jesse surprised himself by tickling her nose with the aforementioned boa. "I'm the king, remember. Off with your head."

She laughed up at him, and he realized how much smaller she was than he, and how feminine she looked in a dress, even a silly outfit like this one. Out of her usual uniform of jeans and flannel, she unsettled him. Lindsey was a pretty woman as well as a nice one.

One more reason he needed to find the answer to his questions and get out of here. He couldn't get attached to a woman he'd eventually have to hurt.

For all his searching today, he'd found no record of this farm or the transaction between his stepfather, Les Finch, and Charles Mitchell. If he didn't find something next time, he'd be forced to ask the clerk for information, a risk he hadn't wanted to take. Asking questions stirred up suspicion. Someone was bound to want to know what he was up to. Sooner or later, word would filter back to Lindsey and he'd be out of a job and out of luck. Discretion made for a slow, but safer, search.

Lindsey whacked his shoulder with her boa. "Are you going to slice that fruit or stand there and stare at my glorious hat?"

Her humor delighted him. "The hat does catch a man's eye."

Lindsey and Jade both giggled at his silliness. Even he wondered where the lightheartedness came from. He'd had a rotten afternoon, but the warmth of this house and the company of these two females lifted his spirits.

Taking up the stainless-steel knife, he sliced an apple into quarters. "What kind of sandwiches are we making?"

"Baloney and cheese."

"Ah, a gourmet's delight." Placing the apple slices on a plate in as fancy a design as he could manage, he plucked a few grapes and arranged them in the center.

Lindsey clapped a slice of wheat bread on top of the

meat and cheese. "And afterward, we'll make sugar cookies."

"With sprinkles," Jade chimed in, her face a study in concentration as she pushed the metal cutters into the sandwiches.

"Jesse, why don't you arrange the fancy sandwiches on this plate while Jade finishes cutting them. Then we'll be ready to eat."

They were only sandwiches. Bread, baloney, cheese and mayonnaise. He could do this. Looking at his beaming child instead of the Christmas shapes, Jesse made a circle of sandwiches on the platter.

"What about the tea?" Jade asked.

"Oh. The tea!" Lindsey clattered across the floor in her high heels, opened a cabinet and removed a quart fruit jar. "I hope the two of you like spiced tea."

"Hot tea?" Jesse asked doubtfully.

She dumped a healthy amount of the mixture into a blue ceramic teapot. With a twinkle in her eye, she admitted, "Spiced tea tastes a lot like apple cider. Grandma taught me to make it. It's a conglomeration of tea, orange drink mix, lemonade and a bunch of yummy spices."

"Sounds better than hot tea," he admitted, pointing an apple slice at her before popping it into his mouth. "Maybe I can stand it."

Lindsey sailed across the floor and tapped his hand with the spoon. "Even the king has to wait until we all sit down together."

"Meanie." He snatched a grape. At her look of playful outrage, he laughed and snitched another.

She stopped dead, spoon in one hand, silly hat tilted to one side in rapt attention. "Jesse," she said, her smoky voice breathy and soft.

"What? Am I drooling grape juice?"

"You laughed."

He opened his mouth once, closed it and tried again. Sure he laughed. People laughed when they were happy. The realization astonished him. He'd laughed because he was happy. When was the last time he'd felt anything even close to happiness?

"I won't do it again."

"Oh, yes, you will." All business and smiles, she shouldered him out of the way. "Go get that little card table in the laundry room and set it up. Jade will put on the table cloth and centerpiece while I finish our tea fixin's."

"Yes, ma'am." He saluted, slung his cape over his face in a super-hero imitation and did as he was told.

By the time the table was ready and they'd sat down to dine on the odd little meal, Jesse had gotten into the swing of the tea party. Wearing a get-up that would make his rodeo buddies howl, knees up to his chin, he reached for one of Jade's raggedy cookie-cutter sandwiches.

"Let's bless the food," Lindsey said, folding her hands in front of her.

A worried expression replaced the glow on Jade's face, and nearly broke Jesse's heart. Seated across from him at the small square table, she looked from Lindsey to him, waiting. Jesse did the only thing he could. He bowed his head, closed his eyes, and listened to Lindsey's simple prayer. When he looked back into his daughter's face, he knew he'd done the right thing. Playing the hypocrite for fifteen seconds hadn't killed him.

Stunned to realize he not only hadn't been bothered by the prayer or the other Christian references, Jesse chewed thoughtfully on the most delicious baloney and cheese sandwich he'd ever tasted and watched Lindsey do the same. He wondered at how time spent with her had changed him, easing the prickly sensation that usually came at the mention of God. Most of all he wondered at how easily Lindsey Mitchell, the lone pioneer woman, had become a part of his and Jade's lives. Considering how dangerous that was for him, he should toss down his Santa sandwich and run. But he knew he wouldn't. Lindsey's gentle female influence was so good for Jade. He tried to be a decent dad, but there were things a little girl needed that a man never even thought of.

"Tea, your highness?" Lindsey said to Jade, holding the pretty teapot over a dainty cup.

"Yes, your princess-ness. Tea, please." Pinky finger pointed up—he didn't know where she'd learned that—Jade lifted the poured tea and sipped carefully. "Delicious. Try it, Daddy."

"That's 'your daddy-ness' to you, queenie." Taking a sip of the surprisingly tasty tea, Jesse relished the sound of his child's giggle.

Yes, Lindsey was good for her. And as disturbing as the thought was, she was good for him, too.

Taking a sandwich from the serving dish, Jade said, "I think Sushi wants this one." She handed the food to Lindsey. "Will you give it to her so she won't be sad?"

Jesse couldn't believe his ears. Jade was worried about upsetting the dog? Capturing Lindsey's glance, he asked a silent question with his eyes.

Brown eyes happy, Lindsey only shrugged and said, "We're gaining ground." Getting up from her chair, she started toward the door. "Come with me, Jade. You can watch from inside."

When Jade followed, Jesse couldn't be left behind. He

had to see this with his own eyes—if he could keep his tiara from falling down over them. Sure enough, Jade stood inside the glass door, a tentative smile on her face, while Lindsey stepped out on the porch and fed the dog.

If Jade overcame her fear of dogs, he'd almost believe in miracles.

Lindsey must have noticed his bewildered expression because she laughed.

"Doubting Thomas," she said to him, then leaned toward Jade. "Did you see the way Sushi wagged her tail? That means thank you."

Holding on to her flowered hat, Jade pressed against the glass and whispered to the dog. "You're welcome."

When Sushi licked the door, Jade jumped back, almost stumbling over her skirts, but at least she didn't scream.

"Sushi gave you a kiss, Butterbean," Jesse offered after he'd swallowed the thickness in his throat.

"Uh-huh. I saw her, but I didn't want a doggy kiss. I'm the queen." Resuming her air of royalty, she lifted the tail of her dress and clomped to the kitchen. "Can we make cookies now? It's almost Christmas."

Lindsey, satin skirts rustling, peacock feather flopping, followed behind Jade like a cartoonist's version of a royal lady-in-waiting. "You're right. Christmas will be here before we know it. Guess what your daddy and I are doing tomorrow?"

Jesse had a sneaky feeling he didn't want to know.

The gap in Jade's mouth flashed. "What?"

"We're going to put up the decorations and get the Christmas-tree lot ready for visitors."

"Yay! Can I help? Can I decorate a tree? Can I put up the angel?" Jade wrapped her arms around Lindsey's red-satin-covered knees and hopped up and down. "Please, please, please."

Jesse's stomach sank into his boots. The day he'd dreaded had come. The Christmas season was upon him.

Chapter Six

"It Came Upon a Midnight Clear" blared from a loud-speaker positioned over the gate that opened into the Christmas-tree lot. The smell of pine mingled with the musty scent of Christmas decorations brought out of storage this morning. Though the temperature was in the high thirties, Jesse stripped away his jean jacket and hung the worn garment on the fence next to Lindsey's red plaid one.

He didn't have to look around to find the jacket's owner. Every cell in his body knew she was near—a sensation he found singularly disconcerting, to be sure. Last night, in the midst of a costumed tea party, some subtle shift in their boss/employee relationship had occurred. And Jesse didn't know if the change was a good thing or a very dangerous one.

From his spot stringing lights on staked poles, he turned to find her just inside the entrance, rubbing dust from a large wooden nativity scene. She'd shared her plans with him for the lot, and though the overwhelming dose of Christmas wasn't his idea of a good time, Lindsey's customers would come for this very atmosphere of holiday cheer.

Shoppers would park outside the gate then ride in the horse-drawn wagon down a lane aglow with Christmas lights and dotted with various lighted holiday ornaments: the nativity, a sleigh with reindeer, angels, snowmen. Jesse couldn't imagine anything she'd forgotten.

Chest tight, whether from watching Lindsey or thinking too much, he turned his concentration to the electrical part of his job. Electricity he knew. Lights he knew. The rest he'd ignore. And as soon as the opportunity arose, he'd kill that music.

"Jesse, could you put more speakers along the drive and down into the lot? I'm not sure we can hear the music all the way."

His shoulders slumped. So much for killing the tunes. After twisting two wires together, he rose from his haunches and asked, "Wouldn't my time be better spent cutting and baling those trees we marked this morning?"

She paused, pushed back her hair with one hand and studied him. When those eyes of hers lasered into him he couldn't do anything but wait until she finished speaking. She had pretty eyes, golden-brown and warm and slightly tilted at the edges like almonds.

"Why do you dislike Christmas?"

He blinked, squeezing hard on the pliers in his fist. "Never said I didn't like Christmas."

"Okay, then," She gave a saucy toss of her head. "Why do you dislike Christmas *decorations?*"

If the subject weren't so problematic, he'd have smiled. Lindsey's way of injecting humor into everything could lift anybody's mood.

Sushi chose that moment to insinuate her furry self

against his legs, almost knocking him into the row of linked-together stakes.

Squatting, he took refuge in the dog, scuffing her ears with both hands. "Did I remember to thank you last night?"

"You just changed the subject."

He gave a little shrug. "So I did."

"Okay, I'll let you off the hook—for now." She lifted the hair off her neck, a habit of hers that Jesse liked. The movement was so utterly female. Erin had done that. Jade did it sometimes too.

"What are you thanking me for? Or was that just a ruse you use to avoid answering my question?"

He shook his head. "No ruse. I owe you big-time."

"For what?"

She really didn't know?

"About a dozen things. Looking after Jade until I got here. For supper."

"Such as it was." She laughed, letting her hair tumble down. Even without the sunlight, her hair looked shiny and clean.

"I've eaten worse than baloney sandwiches and sugar cookies."

"Don't forget the fruit." She tilted a wise man backwards and washed his ancient face. "Last night was fun, Jesse."

"Yeah." No point in denying the truth. Rising, he gave Sushi one final stroke. "Most of all, I appreciate your patience with Jade about the dog. I know leaving her outside is a pain."

Lindsey captured him with her gaze. "I don't want thanks for that, Jesse. I just want to see Jade confident and unafraid."

Taking up the next strand of lights waiting to be hung, he sighed. "Me, too."

"She'll get there." The wise man satisfactorily cleaned, she left him and the rest of the nativity. Coming up beside Jesse, she took one end of the lights, holding them in place while he secured them to the poles. "She's already less fearful than when she first came."

"I noticed. She didn't even fuss when I put her to bed last night. She said her guarding angel would watch her sleep." He glanced toward her, noticed the curve of her cheek and the tilt of her lips, then quickly looked away. "She talked a lot about that."

"I hope you didn't mind me telling her."

He hitched a shoulder, not wanting to go there. "It's okay. Whatever works."

Lindsey laid a hand on his arm. "The Bible works cause it's true, Jesse," she said, her smoky voice soft. "Aren't you comforted knowing your own special angel watches over you?"

The warmth of her fingers spread through his shirt sleeve. He tried to concentrate on twisting plastic fasteners.

"Can't say I've given it much thought."

"Maybe you should." She dropped her hand and went back to straightening the tangle of lights, but her touch stayed with him like a promise made.

Could Lindsey be right? Was there more to this Christian thing than he'd ever realized? Being around her and her church friends, witnessing her steadfast faith and the way she handled the bumps in her life with a certain assurance had him thinking about God with a fresh perspective. As a boy he'd believed, had even accepted Jesus as his savior at church camp when he was twelve.

And then life had turned him upside down, and the God of the universe had seemed so far away.

But why would a caring God, a God who assigned each person an angel, take a man's wife and leave a little girl motherless? Why would He allow a vicious drunk to steal a boy's home and toss him out on the streets to fend for himself? Where was God in that?

He didn't know. But more and more lately, he wanted to reconcile Lindsey's God with the one in his head.

"Silent Night" drifted into his awareness. Lindsey moved away, back to the nativity. Other than the floodlights she'd asked him to rig up, the set looked ready to him. As she adjusted the sheep and fluffed the hay inside the manger, joy practically oozed from her.

Sure she was happy. Why shouldn't she be? Other than losing her elderly grandparents, Lindsey had probably never had a moment's heartache in her life. Loving God and exuding tranquility was easy for her.

Frustrated at his line of depressive thinking, he yanked hard on a tangled cord, and turned his mind to more important matters—his search.

They had trees to haul this week which would give him the time and opportunity to ask questions in town. Yesterday at the courthouse he'd slipped up once, expressing to the clerk his interest in the transaction that gave Lindsey's grandfather ownership of the Christmas Tree Farm. When the woman had looked at him curiously, he'd covered his tracks with vague remarks about Lindsey's plans for expansion. If only he could talk freely with someone like Clarence or Loraine Stone, the couple who claimed to have known Charlie Mitchell so well. Sooner or later, by biding his time and listening, he'd have his opportunity.

* * *

After dusting and organizing the main pieces of the nativity, Lindsey went back to the storage shed for the final figure—the eight-foot-tall animated camel that blinked long-lashed eyes and mooed. She tugged and pulled, careful not to damage the heavy object in the journey across the rough field. Stopping to readjust, she saw Jesse leap the fence and trot in her direction.

"Why didn't you say something?"

"I can get it."

With a look of exasperation, he hoisted the camel into his strong arms. "You shouldn't have to. That's why you hired me."

Oddly touched and feeling more like a helpless female than she'd ever felt in her life, Lindsey traipsed along beside him. How could she not admire this man? Every time she turned around, he was lifting work from her shoulders, both literally and figuratively. She'd never seen anyone work so hard for so little pay. And for all his silences and secrets, Jesse had a way of making her feel special.

Lindsey wasn't sure if that was such a good idea, given the spiritual differences between them, but she liked Jesse Slater. And she loved his little girl.

As if he'd heard her thoughts of Jade, Jesse spoke. His voice came from the opposite side of the camel's hump.

"Jade will be excited when she sees all this."

"You don't think she'll be disappointed that we did so much without her?" She'd worried about that all day. After the way Jade had begged to take part, Lindsey didn't want her hurt. But setting up the farm for Christmas took time.

"I explained to her last night that we'd have to do most

of the work today. She was okay with it as long as she gets to do something."

A jingle bell came loose from the saddle and Lindsey ducked beneath the camel's neck to retrieve it.

"I promised to save the 'best stuff' until she gets here. She and I are going to put up the wreaths and decorate that tree up front." She pointed toward the entrance, the bell in hand jingling merrily. "And she can flip on the lights as soon as the sun sets. I hope that's enough."

Jesse's silver eyes, lit by an inner smile, slanted toward her. "You're amazing with her, you know it?"

Buoyed by the compliment, Lindsey shook the bell at him and grinned. "I cheat. I use Christmas."

The teasing admission moved the smile from Jesse's eyes to his lips, changing his rugged, bad-boy expression into a breathtaking sight. That solitary action shot a thrill stronger than adrenaline through Lindsey. Someday, she'd break all the way through the ice he'd built around himself and make him smile all the time.

Startled at such thinking, Lindsey rushed ahead to open the gate. Where had that come from? Jesse was her employee and maybe her friend. But that was all he could be.

Heart thudding in consternation, she analyzed the thought. As a Christian, she wanted to see him happy. She wasn't falling for him. Was she? She'd been in love with a man like Jesse before—a devastatingly handsome man filled with secrets. And Sean had betrayed her so completely she'd come home to the farm and promised never to fall for a pretty face again.

Jesse eased the camel into place alongside the rough wooden building that sheltered the baby Jesus and his earthly parents. He'd already positioned bales of hay around the site and spread straw on the ground. Later, he'd rig up the spotlights and the Star of Bethlehem to bring the scene to life.

In minutes, he had the camel bellowing and blinking.

With a grimace, he shut off the mechanism. "Jade will love that monstrosity."

With laughter and a clap of her hands, Lindsey put aside her troubled thoughts. "I thought as much. We'll let her turn it on as soon as she gets home from school."

Jesse dusted his hands down the sides of his jeans, one corner of his mouth quirking ever-so-slightly. "What's next? Singing Santas? Yodeling elves?"

"Nothing quite that fun. We'd better begin cutting and baling. I'd like to haul the first load tomorrow if we have enough ready."

"So soon?"

"The rush begins on Thanksgiving. That's only a week away. Stores and lots like to have their trees ready to sell."

Switching off the last strains of "Silent Night," he gestured in the direction of the trees. "Lead on, boss lady."

Though disappointed to lose the beautiful music, Lindsey hummed Christmas carols as they began the process of cutting the marked and graded trees. Jesse manned the chain saw and as each tree toppled, Lindsey slid a rolling sled-like device beneath the pine and pulled it to the waiting baler.

Accustomed to lifting the heavy trees, Lindsey manhandled each one into the cone-shaped baler to be compressed into a tight bundle and secured with netting.

Saw in one gloved hand, Jesse poked his head around a tree. "Leave those for me to lift and bale."

"We'd never get finished that way. I'm used to the work, Jesse. Stop fretting."

But pleasure raced through her blood when he laid aside the saw long enough to lift the baled tree onto the flatbed truck. She might be accustomed to heavy work, but being treated like a girl was a novel and somewhat pleasant, if misguided, occurrence.

Following him back into the wide row, and lost in thought, Lindsey never saw the danger coming. One minute, she was examining a hole in her glove and the next she heard the crack and whine of falling timber.

"Lindsey, look out!"

She looked, but all she saw was green blocking the gray-blue sky and rapidly closing in on her.

Then all the air whooshed from her lungs as Jesse came flying and knocked her to the ground, taking the brunt of the felled pine across his back and head.

She tasted dust and pine sap. Prickly needles poked over Jesse's shoulders and scratched the side of her face. Her pulse pounded and her knees trembled as if she'd done jumping jacks for the last hour.

One arm flung protectively over her head, his chest lying across her back, Jesse's warm breath puffed against her ear. "Are you okay?"

He sounded scared.

"Fine." She struggled to draw air into her lungs. "You?"

"Yeah." Jesse's heart raced wildly against her shoulder blades. The situation was anything but intimate, and yet Lindsey was aware of him in an entirely new way.

"You're crushing me," she managed.

"Sorry." He shoved the tree to one side before rolling to a sitting position.

Offering a hand, he pulled Lindsey up to sit beside him. Breath coming in rapid puffs, his concerned gaze checked her over.

With a tenderness usually reserved for Jade, he stroked one calloused finger down her cheek. "You have a scratch."

She studied his face, but resisted the urge to touch him. Already her skin tingled from his simple gesture, and her insides were too rattled from the accident to think straight. Her throat felt tight and thick. "So do you."

He flicked one shoulder, tossing off her concern like an unwanted gum wrapper.

"I'll heal." He took a deep breath and blew out a gusty sigh. "Man, that scared me. I can't believe I let that tree get away from me."

"Not your fault. I heard the saw. I knew you were harvesting, but I was…distracted." She wasn't about to tell him that he'd been the distracting element. And now she was more discombobulated than ever. Jesse had put himself in harm's way to protect her. And she liked the feeling of having a man—of having Jesse—look after her.

Oh, dear. She could be in real trouble here if she didn't watch her step. There was no denying Jesse's attractiveness, but the idea of letting another handsome face turn her head was worrisome. Jesse's secretiveness and his resistance to the Lord bothered her, too. But as a Christian, she wanted to provide a shining example of Christ's love; to share the incomprehensible peace of mind the Lord had given her.

Somewhere there had to be a midway point between being Jesse's friend in Christ and falling for him.

She only wished she knew how to find it.

Chapter Seven

"Are you sure you don't mind?" Jesse asked the moment he and Jade arrived on Thanksgiving Day. "We can still head down to the Caboose and grab a bite to eat."

A sharp wind, the likes of which rip and tear across Oklahoma with the energy of wild, vicious dogs, swept a draught of cold air into the farmhouse.

Though the oven had warmed the place considerably, Lindsey wasn't one to fritter away expensive heating fuel. She plucked at the quilted sleeve of Jesse's coat and pulled him inside.

"And waste this feast I've been cooking all morning? Not a chance, mister. You are stuck with my home cooking. No arguments."

Ducking beneath her daddy's arms, Jade slipped into the house and started shedding her outerwear. She wore a red wool coat Lindsey had never seen before over a plaid jumper, black tights and patent-leather shoes. Lindsey's heart did a funny stutter-step. Jesse had dressed her up for Thanksgiving dinner.

"You guys toss your coats in the bedroom. I need to check on the dressing and sweet potatoes."

Hands on the snaps of his jacket, Jesse stood in the kitchen doorway sniffing the air. "Candied sweet potatoes?"

She nodded. "With marshmallows and brown sugar."

He let out a low groan. "Forget the Caboose. I wouldn't leave now even if you chased me with that shotgun of yours."

Lindsey couldn't hold back the rush of pleasure. She knew she was blushing and quickly bent over the oven door to blame her increased color on the heat.

Asking Jesse and Jade to Thanksgiving dinner made perfect sense. They had no other place to go, and she had no family living close enough to cook for. In fact, she'd been as energetic as that silly bunny for the three days since Jesse had agreed to share the holiday with her.

"So," Jesse said, coming back into the kitchen from putting away his wraps. "What can we do to help?"

The foil-covered turkey was nicely basted and already out of the oven. The dressing and sweet potatoes were almost ready as were the hot rolls. Though she didn't want to admit as much to Jesse, she'd gotten up earlier than normal to bake everything the way her grandmother always had.

"We'll be ready to eat soon." She turned with a smile, wiping her hands on her bib apron. "You could set the table if you'd like."

"Come on, Butterbean," he said to Jade. "The slave driver is putting us to work."

He was in high spirits today, a rare occurrence to Lindsey's way of thinking. And she liked seeing him this way, without the load of care he usually wore like an anvil around his neck.

Jade's dress shoes clicked on the kitchen floor as she

helped her daddy spread the white lacy tablecloth and set out three of Granny's best Blue Willow place settings.

After carefully positioning a knife and fork on top of paper napkins, she looked up. A small frown puckered her brow. "Where's Sushi going to eat?"

"Sushi?" Lindsey hesitated, a potholder in one hand. "I put her in the extra bedroom."

"Oh." Turning back to her job, Jade said nothing more about the dog. The adults exchanged glances.

Jesse mouthed, "Don't ask me."

Jade seemed unmindful that she'd raised adult eyebrows with her concern for a dog she supposedly despised. Letting the subject drop, Lindsey returned to the task of getting the food on the table. In her peripheral vision, she caught the red flash of Jade's plaid jumper and gleaming shoes.

"You sure look pretty today," she said.

"Well, thank you, ma'am." Jesse's teasing voice had her spinning toward him. "You look pretty, too."

Jade burst into giggles. "Daddy! She meant me. I'm pretty."

On tiptoes, the little girl twirled in a circle.

Jesse slapped a hand against one cheek in mock embarrassment. "Do you mean to tell me that I don't look pretty?"

Gap-tooth smile bigger than Dallas, Jade fell against him, hugging his legs. "You're always pretty."

Lindsey had to concur, even though she'd never before seen Jesse in anything but work clothes. Seeing him in polished loafers, starched jeans, and a light blue dress shirt that drew attention to his silvery eyes took her breath away.

Considering how decked-out the Slaters were, she was

glad she'd taken the time to dress up a bit herself. Though her clothes were still casual, she'd chosen dark brown slacks instead of jeans and a mauve pullover sweater. And she'd put on earrings, something usually reserved for church. They were only small filigree crosses, but wearing them made her feel dressed-up.

With a wry wince of remembrance, she glanced down. If only she'd exchanged her fluffy house shoes for a snazzy pair of slides... Ah, well, she was who she was. As Granny used to say, you can't make a silk purse out of a sow's ear.

Delighted to have guests on Thanksgiving Day, she didn't much care what anyone wore. Just having them here was enough.

After sliding a fragrant pan of yeast rolls from the oven, she slathered on melted butter, and dumped the rolls into a cloth-covered basket.

Without waiting to be told, Jesse put ice in the glasses and poured sweet tea from the pitcher Lindsey had already prepared.

"What's next?" he asked, coming to stand beside her at the counter. He brought with him the scent of a morning shower and a manly cologne that reminded Lindsey of an ocean breeze at sunrise.

She, on the other hand, probably smelled like turkey and dressing with a lingering touch of pine.

"I think we're about ready." She handed a bowl of cranberry sauce to Jade. "If you'll put this beside the butter, your daddy and I will bring the hot stuff."

Jade took the bowl in both her small palms, carefully transferring the dish to the table. Jesse and Lindsey followed with the rest and settled into their places.

The trio sat in a triangle with Jesse taking the head

of the table and the two ladies on either side of him. Lindsey, out of long habit, stretched out a hand to each of them.

Jade reacted instantly, placing her fingers atop Lindsey's. After a brief, but noticeable interval, Jesse did the same, and then joined his other hand to his daughter's.

The moment Jesse's hand touched hers, Lindsey recognized her error. She hoped with all her might that the Lord would forgive her, because she was having a hard time concentrating on the prayer with Jesse's rough, masculine skin pressing against hers.

Somehow she mumbled her way through, remembering to thank God for her many blessings during the past year, including the blessing of Jesse and Jade.

Jesse tensed at the mention of his name. At the closing "amen," he cleared his throat and shifted uncomfortably. Jade, on the other hand, beamed like the ray of sunshine she was.

"Guess what?" she offered, with the usual scattered thought processes of a six-year-old. "I have a loose tooth."

"Let's see." Lindsey leaned forward, pretending great interest as Jade wiggled a loosening incisor. "Maybe it will fall out while you're eating today."

Jade's eyes widened in horror. "What if I swallow it?"

The poor little child was afraid of everything.

"Well, if you do," Jesse said, helping himself to the sweet potato casserole, "it won't hurt you."

"But I can't swallow it. I have to show it to my teacher so she can put my name on the tooth chart."

Doing her best to suppress a laugh, Lindsey placed a hot roll on her plate and passed the basket to Jesse. His eyes twinkled with his own amused reaction. Swallowing the tooth wasn't the problem. Jade was afraid of being left out, a perfectly healthy, normal worry for a first-grader.

"I don't think you'll swallow the tooth, Jade, but if you do, the teacher will still put your name on the chart."

Green eyes blinked doubtfully. "How will she know?"

"She can look at the new empty place in your mouth."

The little girl's face lit up. She wiggled the tooth again. "Maybe it will come out today."

"We have corn on the cob. That's been known to do the trick."

"Okay." Jade reached eagerly for the corn Lindsey offered. "Eat one, Daddy."

Jesse quirked an eyebrow in teasing doubt. "I don't know, Butterbean. Your old dad can't afford to lose any of his teeth."

"Oh, Daddy." She pushed the platter of steaming corn in his direction. "It's good."

"Okay, then. I just hope you don't have to go home with a toothless daddy."

Jade grinned around a huge bite of corn as her daddy filled his plate.

"This all looks terrific, Lindsey." Jesse added a hearty helping of turkey and dressing. "You've worked hard."

"Cooking was fun. I haven't had a real Thanksgiving dinner since Gramps died."

He spread butter on the golden corn, his surprised attention focused on Lindsey. "Why not? Don't you usually visit your family for holidays?"

"Some holidays, but not this one. I can't. Thanksgiving begins my peak season, and lots of families want their tree the weekend after Thanksgiving."

"Then your family should come here."

"Oh." She gestured vaguely, then scooped up a bite of green bean casserole. "They're all pretty busy with their own lives. Kim, my sister, is expecting a baby early next year. She's in Colorado near her husband's family so naturally, they have their holidays there."

Chewing the creamy casserole, Lindsey had to admit the food tasted incredible. Could she credit the home cooking? Or the company?

Jesse absently handed Jade a napkin. With a sweet smile filled with yellow corn, she swiped at her buttery face.

Having a child—and a man—at her dinner table gave Lindsey an unexpected sense of fulfillment.

"What about your parents?" Jesse asked, coming right back to the conversation.

"Like Kim, they want me to come to them. Right now they're in Korea, so that wasn't possible this year."

"You wouldn't leave the trees anyway."

"I might sometime if I could find the right person to run the place for a couple of days."

He chewed thoughtfully, swallowed and took a drink of tea before saying, "I would have done it this year if you'd said something."

Lindsey's insides filled, not with the sumptuous Thanksgiving meal, but with the pleasure of knowing Jesse meant exactly what he'd said. She mulled over the statement as she watched him eat with hearty male abandon.

"I never would have considered asking you."

Fork in hand, he stiffened. His silver eyes frosted over. "You don't trust me to do a good job?"

"Of course, I trust you." Almost too much, given how little she knew about him. "I only meant that leaving you to do all the work while I vacationed would be a huge imposition."

His tense jaw relaxed. "Oh."

He studied the rapidly disappearing food on his plate, some thought process that Lindsey couldn't read running amok inside his head.

A vague unease put a damper on Lindsey's celebratory mood. Why had Jesse reacted so oddly?

She bit into the tart cranberry-and-sage-flavored dressing, pondering. Had she offended him? Or was the problem deeper than that?

Jade, who'd been busily doing damage to the ear of corn, stopped long enough to take a huge helping of turkey.

"You won't eat that," Jesse said, reaching for the meat.

Jade slid the plate out of his reach. "It's for Sushi. She's hungry and lonely. She might be crying."

Lindsey couldn't believe her ears. Jade worried about the dog without any encouragement from the adults? Was this the break she'd been praying for?

Jesse seemed to recognize the moment, too, for he tossed down his napkin and said, "Can't have Sushi crying." Chunk of dark meat in hand, he pushed back from his chair. "Let's take her this."

Lindsey thrilled when Jade slipped down from her chair to follow her dad. She took his outstretched hand, her own tiny one swallowed up in the protective size of her father's.

Unable to avoid the parallel, Lindsey thought of her heavenly Father, of how His huge, all-powerful hand is always outstretched in protection and care. The comparison brought a lump to her throat. She'd messed up a lot in her life, but the Father had never let her down. Even when she'd sequestered herself here on Winding Stair to hide from the hurts of this world, He'd come along with her, loving her back to joy, giving her this farm in place of the things she'd lost.

Jesse and his daughter took three steps across the sun-drenched kitchen before Jade stopped and turned. She stretched out a hand.

"Come on," she said simply as though Lindsey was an expected presence, a part of her life.

The lump in Lindsey's throat threatened to choke her. How long had she hungered for a child? A family? And now, on this Thanksgiving Day she felt as if she had one—if only for today.

Dabbing at her mouth with a napkin, she rose and joined the pair, asking tentatively, "Would you like Sushi to come out and play?"

"I don't want to play."

Before Lindsey had time to express her disappointment, Jade went on. "But she can come out and sit by you."

At the bedroom door, Lindsey went down in front of the child. "You are such a big girl. I'm so proud of you for being nice to Sushi. She *is* lonely in there all by herself and she doesn't understand why she's locked up."

Dark hair bouncing, Jade nodded. "I know."

"We'll give her this turkey." She indicated the meat in Jesse's hand. "And then I'll pet her a little before letting her out. She might be excited and jump because she's happy to see us."

Jade reached both arms toward her father. "Hold me up, Daddy."

With a sigh that said he didn't consider this progress,

he hoisted his daughter. Lindsey opened the door and commanded, "Sushi, stay."

The German shepherd, already spring-loaded, wilted in disappointment, but she followed her owner's command. Tail swishing madly, ears flicking, she waited while Lindsey stroked and murmured encouragements. Once convinced that Sushi's self-control was intact, she gazed up at Jade.

"She's all ready for that turkey. Hold it by your fingertips and give it to her."

Heart thudding with hope, Lindsey told the dog to sit and be gentle.

Worried green eyes shifting from the dog to Lindsey, Jade gathered her courage. When she looked to Jesse, he winked and gave her an encouraging nudge. "Go ahead."

Taking the poultry, Jade strained forward. Jesse held on tight, face as tense and hopeful as Lindsey's heart.

As if she understood the child's dilemma, Sushi waited patiently, and then daintily took the meat between her front teeth.

Jade's nervous laugh broke the anxious moment. Lindsey hadn't realized she was holding her breath. As casually as she could while rejoicing over this huge step, she turned back to the kitchen. Sushi's toenails tapped the floor as she followed. She pointed to a spot far away from Jade, and the dog collapsed in ecstasy.

To her delight, Jade slithered out of Jesse's arms, unafraid to be on even ground with the animal.

"How about some pecan pie?" Lindsey asked, tilting the pie in their direction.

Jade shook her head. "Can I play with your playhouse?"

She indicated the extra room where Lindsey kept toys and games for her Sunday-school girls.

"Sure. Go ahead."

As Jade skipped off into the other room, Lindsey lifted an eyebrow toward Jesse. "Pie?"

Jesse patted his flat, muscled stomach. "Too full right now. Later maybe?"

"Later sounds better to me, too. I'm sure there are plenty of football games on if you'd like to watch television while I clean the kitchen."

"No deal. You cook. I wash."

Lindsey was shocked at the idea. "You're my guest. You can't wash dishes."

Already rolling up his shirtsleeves, Jesse argued. "Watch me."

"Then I'm helping, too." She tossed him an apron, the least frilly one she owned.

He tied it around his slender middle, and in minutes they had the table cleared and water steaming in the old-fashioned porcelain sink.

As Lindsey stacked the dishes on the counter, Jesse washed them. The sight of his strong dark arms plunged into a sink full of white soapsuds did funny things to her insides.

They were down to the turkey roaster when the crunch of tires on gravel turned their attention to visitors.

"Who could that be?" Lindsey asked, placing a dried plate into the cabinet before pushing back the yellow window curtain. "I don't recognize the vehicle."

Jesse came up beside her. A hum of awareness prickled the skin on Lindsey's arms.

"I'll go out and check." Her breath made tiny clouds on the cool window. "Could be an early customer."

Her prediction proved true, and though she normally didn't open until the day after Thanksgiving, she was too kindhearted to turn them away.

Upon hearing their story, she was glad they'd come.

"Thank you for letting us interrupt your holiday," the woman said as she watched her children traipse happily through the thick green pines. "We thought decorating the tree before their dad shipped out for the Middle East tomorrow would help the kids. They've never had Christmas without him."

Lindsey placed a hand on the woman's arm. "It's us who owe you—and your husband—thanks."

As they went from tree to tree, discussing the perfect shape and size, Lindsey realized that Jesse and Jade had disappeared. In moments, she knew why. Red and green lights, dim in the bright November sun, flicked on all over the lot. Then the gentle strains of "Away in a Manger" filtered from the stereo speakers Jesse had stretched from the gate into the trees.

When he returned, coming up beside Lindsey with Jade in tow, she couldn't hold back her gratitude. "Thank you for thinking of that."

He shrugged off the compliment. "Some people like this stuff."

But you don't. What could have happened to turn Jesse into such a Scrooge? She wanted to ask why again, to press him for information, but now, with a customer present, was not the moment.

The family found the perfect tree and Jesse set to work. In no time, the tree was cut, baled, and carefully secured on top of the family's car. Three exuberant children piled inside the four-door sedan, faces rosy with excitement and cold. The soldier reached for his wallet, but Lindsey held out a hand to stop him.

"No way. The tree is a gift. Enjoy it."

The man argued briefly, but seeing Lindsey's stubborn stance, finally gave in. "This means a lot to my family."

He got inside the car and started the engine.

"Merry Christmas," Lindsey said, leaning down into the open window. "You'll be in my prayers."

With more thanks and calls of Merry Christmas, the family drove away, the Virginia pine waving in the wind.

"That was a real nice thing you did," Jesse said, his arm resting against hers as they watched the car jounce down the driveway.

"I love to give trees to people like that. What a blessing."

"You don't make money giving them away."

"No, but you create joy, and that's worth so much more."

Jade, who'd been listening, rubbed her hand across the needles of a nearby pine and spoke in a wistful voice. "I wish I could have a Christmas tree."

"What a grand idea!" Lindsey clapped her hands. The sound startled several blackbirds into flight. "Let's pick one right now. You and your daddy can decorate it tonight."

Beside her, Jesse stiffened. A warning sounded in Lindsey's head, but she pushed it away, intent upon this latest happy project.

"Come on." She gestured toward the smaller trees. "You can choose your very own tree. Any one you want."

Jade held back, her face a contrast of longing and reluctance.

The warning sound grew louder. "What's wrong, sweetie? Don't you want a tree?"

Small shoulders slumping with the weight, Jade wagged her head, dejected. "Daddy won't let me."

"Sure he will."

But one look at Jesse told her she was wrong.

"Jesse?" With a sinking feeling, she searched his face. What she found there unnerved her.

"Leave it alone, Lindsey," he growled, jaw clenching and unclenching.

"Daddy hates Christmas." Tears shimmered in Jade's green eyes. "Mommy—"

"Jade!" Jesse's tortured voice stopped her from saying more. He stared at his daughter, broken and forlorn.

Jade's eyes grew round and moist. Biting her lower lip, she flung her arms around Jesse's knees.

Expression bereft, Jesse stroked his daughter's hair, holding her close to him.

Heart pounding in consternation, Lindsey prayed for wisdom. Whatever had happened was still hurting Jesse and this precious little girl. And avoiding the issue would not make the pain go away.

She touched him, lightly, tentatively. "Let me help, Jesse. Talk to me. Tell me what's wrong."

"Talking doesn't change anything." His face was as hard as stone, but his eyes begged for release.

She hesitated, not wanting to toss around platitudes, but knowing the real answer to Jesse's need. "I don't know if you want to hear this, but there's nothing too big for the Lord. Jesus will heal all our sorrows if we let Him."

"I wish I could believe that. I wish…" With a weary sigh, he lifted Jade into his arms and went to the little bench along the edge of the grove and sat down. With a deep, shivering sigh, he stared over Jade's shoulder into the distance, seeing something there that no one else could.

Unsure how to proceed, but knowing she had to help this man who'd come to mean too much to her, Lindsey settled on the bench beside him and waited, praying hard that God would give her the words.

Something terrible had broken Jesse's heart and her own heart broke from observing his pain.

After an interminable length of silence disrupted only by the whisper of wind through pine boughs, Jade climbed down from her daddy's lap.

Her dark brows knit together. "Daddy?"

"I'm okay, Butterbean." He clearly was not. "Go play. I want to talk to Lindsey."

"About Mommy?"

Jesse dragged a hand over his mouth. "Yeah."

Lindsey saw the child hesitate as though she felt responsible for her father's sorrow. Finally, she drifted away, going to the parked wagon where she sat anxiously watching the adults.

When Jesse finally began to speak, the words came out with a soft ache, choppy and disconnected.

"Erin looked a lot like Jade. Black hair and green eyes. Pale skin. She was a good woman, a Christian like you." He hunched down into his jacket, though the afternoon air wasn't cold. "I tried to be one, too, when she was alive."

So that explained how Jade had learned to pray and why she knew bits and pieces about Jesus. Jesse and his wife had known the Lord, but something had driven him away from his faith.

"Christmas was a very big deal to her. She loved to shop, especially for Jade and me. We didn't have a lot of money." He kicked at a dirt clod, disintegrating the clump into loose soil. "My fault, but Erin made the best of it. We always had a good Christmas because of her. She could make a ten-dollar gift seem worth a million."

Something deep inside told Lindsey to be quiet and let him talk. Letting the pain out was the first step to healing, and the cleansing would give the Lord an opportunity to move in. Granny had taught her that when she'd wanted to curl into a ball and disappear from the pain of Sean's betrayal.

"Two years ago—" He stopped, sat up straight and tilted his head backward, looking into the sky.

"What happened?" she urged gently.

"Christmas Eve. Erin had a few last-minute gifts to buy. One present she'd had in layaway for a while, though I didn't know it at the time. She'd been waiting to have enough money to pick up that one gift." He swallowed hard and scrubbed a hand across his eyes. "Jade and I stayed at the house, watching Christmas cartoons and munching popcorn balls. We were waiting for Erin to get home before we hung the stockings. We never hung them because Erin never came home."

Biting at her lower lip, Lindsey closed her eyes and prayed for guidance.

"Oh, Jesse," she whispered, not knowing what else to say. "I'm so sorry."

He shifted around to look at her. "I'm not telling you this for sympathy."

But sympathy wasn't the only emotion rushing through her veins.

She was starting to care about Jesse. Not only the

way a Christian should care about all people, but on a personal level too. Every day she looked forward to the minute the blue-and-silver truck rumbled into her yard, and he swung down from the cab and ambled in that cowboy gait of his up to the front porch. She relished their working side by side. She enjoyed looking into his silvery eyes and listening to the low rumble of his manly voice. She appreciated his strength and his kindness.

She cared, and the admission unsettled her. He was too wounded, too broken, and too much in love with a dead wife for her to chance caring too much. She could be a friend and a shoulder to cry on, but that was all she could let herself be.

Jesse gripped the edge of the bench, needing Lindsey's compassion and afraid of flying apart if he accepted it. Now that he'd begun the awful telling, there was no way he could stop. Like blood from a gaping wound, the words flowed out.

"Three blocks from our house a drunk driver hit her, head-on."

He'd been sitting in his recliner, Jade curled against him watching Rudolph when the sirens had broken the silent night. He'd never forget the fleeting bit of sympathy he'd felt for any poor soul who needed an ambulance on Christmas Eve. Safe and warm in his living room, he had no way of knowing the holiday had chosen him— again—for heartache.

"A neighbor came, pounding on the door and yelling. She'd seen the wreck, knew it was Erin's car. I ran." He didn't know why he'd done that. A perfectly good truck sat in the driveway, but he hadn't even thought of driving to the scene. "Like a fool, I ran those three blocks, thinking I could stop anything bad from happening to my family."

He relived that helpless moment when he'd pushed past policemen, screaming that Erin was his wife. He recalled the feel of their hands on him, trying to stop him, not wanting him to see.

"She was gone." Stomach sick from the memory, he shoved up from the bench, unable to share the rest. Lindsey was perceptive. She'd understand that he'd witnessed a sight no man should have to see. His beautiful wife crushed and mangled, the Christmas gifts she'd given her life for scattered along the highway, a testament to the violence of the impact.

Back turned, he clenched his fists and told the part that haunted him still.

"The present she'd gone after was mine." He'd wanted the fancy Western belt with his name engraved on the back, had hoped she'd order it for him. Now the belt remained in its original box, unused, a reminder that Erin had died because of him.

"Now you know why I feel the way I do about Christmas." He spoke to the rows and rows of evergreens, though he knew Lindsey listened. He could feel her behind him, full of compassion and care. When she laid a consoling hand on his back, he was glad. He needed her touch. "Jade and I both have too many bad memories of Christmas to celebrate anything."

Jesse looked toward the wagon which had already been outfitted for hauling visitors through the grove. Jade had crawled beneath the down quilt and lay softly singing along with the music, waving her hands in the air like a conductor. He'd somehow tuned out the carols until then.

Lindsey's hand soothed him, making small circles on his back. "Don't you want Jade to remember her mother?"

"Of course I do. How could you ask me that?"

"You said Erin loved Christmas and wanted the holiday to be special for you and Jade. Those times with her mother are important to Jade, and Christmas is one of the best memories of all."

Not for him. And not for Jade either.

"I'd never take away her memories of Erin," he said gruffly.

"When you refuse to let her have a Christmas tree, you're telling her child's mind to forget her mother and to forget all those wonderful times with her."

"That's not true," he denied vehemently. "I'm protecting her. I don't want her to relive that terrible night every Christmas."

"Are you talking about Jade? Or yourself?"

He opened his mouth to refute the very idea that he was protecting himself instead of Jade. But words wouldn't come.

"You can't allow your own pain to keep Jade from having a normal childhood." Her warm, throaty voice implored him.

"I'd never do that," he said, but the denial sounded weak. With growing angst, he realized Lindsey could be right. In his self-focused pain, he'd hurt his little girl, denying her the right to remember her mother laughing beneath the tree on Christmas morning, the three of them dancing to "Jingle Bell Rock."

He squeezed his eyes closed as memories washed over him.

"Not intentionally, but don't you realize that she reads

everything you do or don't do, interpreting your actions in her childish understanding? She wants to have Christmas, but she worries about you."

A great blue heron winged past, headed to the pond. Out in the pasture, the black horse grazed on an enormous round bale of hay, summer's green grass a memory.

"I don't want her worrying about me."

"You can't stop her. She wants you to be happy. She loves you. God loves you, too, Jesse, and He wants to help you get past this."

"I don't know how." And even if he did, he wondered if "getting past" Erin's death wouldn't somehow be disloyal.

"Erin's death wasn't your fault. Start there."

"I can't help thinking she would be alive if she hadn't gone shopping."

"Those are futile thoughts, Jesse. You would be better served to wonder how you can honor her life."

He turned toward her then. She'd hit upon the very thing he longed for. "I don't know how to do that either."

"You already are in one way. You're raising Jade to be a lovely child. But God has more for you. He wants you to have a life free of guilt and anger. Full of peace."

Jesse felt the tug of that peace emanating from his boss lady. A fierce longing to pray, something he hadn't done in two years, gnawed at him.

"Let's go choose a tree," Lindsey urged, holding out a hand. "For Jade."

He took a breath of clean mountain air and blew it out, his chest heavy and aching. He could do this for his baby. A Christmas tree wasn't that big a deal, was it? He'd worked in the things for a couple of months now without dying.

His eyes drifted over the acres of pines, noting one major difference. These were bare. If he took a Christmas tree back to the trailer, Jade would want to decorate it.

He turned his attention to the wagon where his brave little trooper no longer sang and conducted. Huddled down into the quilt, her black hair tousled, she lay sleeping.

Last Christmas, the first anniversary of Erin's death, he'd done his best to ignore the holiday altogether. Erin's family, far away in Kentucky had sent gifts, but he'd tossed them in the garbage before Jade had seen them. The few times she'd mentioned presents, he'd reacted so harshly she'd quickly gotten the message that the subject of Christmas was off limits.

But she'd cried, too. And that forgotten memory of her tears tormented him.

Fighting down a rising sense of dread, Jesse took Lindsey's hand. "Let's go wake her."

Lindsey's quiet eyes studied him. "Are you okay with this?"

Though uncertain, he nodded.

They went to the wagon where Jade lay sleeping like an angel, her black hair a dark halo around her face. Sooty lashes curved upon her weather-rosy cheeks. One arm hugged the covers, rising and falling with the rhythm of her silent breath.

"Look at her, Jesse. You have so much to be thankful for. I know people who'd give anything to have a child like Jade." Her voice grew wistful. "Including me."

Her soft-looking lips turned down, one of the rare times he'd seen her unhappy. He didn't like seeing her sad.

"I thought you were perfectly content up here alone." They spoke in hushed tones so as not to startle the sleeping child. But the quiet created an intimacy that made him feel closer to Lindsey than he had to anyone in a long time.

"I'm learning to be content in the Lord, but that doesn't mean I don't think about having a family someday."

Something stirred inside Jesse. Lindsey would make a great mother—and a good wife to the right man. Someday one of those holy churchgoers who'd never committed a sin in his life would marry her.

Already miserable with the forthcoming Christmas tree, he didn't want to think about Lindsey with some other man.

Fighting off the uncomfortable thoughts, he stroked a knuckle down Jade's cheek. "Hey, Butterbean. Wake up. Ready to get that Christmas tree?"

His little girl blinked, her green eyes sleepy and confused, but filled with a hope that seared him. "Really?"

With a nod, he swallowed hard and helped her down from the wagon. As if she expected the offer to be rescinded at any moment, Jade wasted no time. She grabbed each adult by the hand and pulled them toward the grove.

An hour later, laden with lights and tinsel and lacy white angel ornaments Lindsey had given Jade from a box in her Christmas building, they'd headed back to the trailer. Jade had been ecstatic over the three-foot tree, raising the level of Jesse's guilt as well as his anxiety. All the way into town he'd wondered if he could actually go through with it, if he could spend a month staring at a reminder of all he'd lost.

In the end he'd been a coward, placing the small, shining tree in Jade's bedroom where he wouldn't have to see it. His child had been so thrilled with the thing, she hadn't questioned the reason. He'd nearly broken, though, when she'd crawled exhausted beneath her covers, the sweetest smile on earth lifting her bow mouth. "Is it okay if I say a prayer and thank Jesus for my tree and all my guarding angels?"

"Sure, baby, sure."

Long after she'd fallen asleep, he'd sat in the trailer's tiny living room, staring blindly at the paneled wall.

What had he gotten himself into? Lindsey Mitchell with her sweetness and overwhelming decency was tearing him apart. His frozen heart had begun to thaw. And like blood-flow returning to frost-bitten fingers, the sensation was pure torture.

Chapter Eight

Jesse was tired, bone-weary. A basket of laundry at his feet, he sat on the plastic couch in his mobile home folding clothes. Jade was in her tiny excuse of a bedroom playing with a small dollhouse borrowed from Lindsey.

After the busy Thanksgiving weekend, he'd worked half of last night, and even though the tree farm was jumping this morning, he'd knocked off at noon. He felt bad about leaving Lindsey alone with the customers, but he had business to attend to.

Then he'd spent hours in the courthouse and on the telephone, leaking out bits of himself to strangers in exchange for information about his stepfather. One conversation had given him the name of a backwoods lawyer who'd been around eighteen years ago. A lawyer with a drinking problem who'd been known to do "buddy deals." Trouble was, no one remembered where the man had gone when he'd left Winding Stair years ago.

His stomach growled and he tried to remember if he'd eaten today. Probably not. Lindsey usually forced lunch on him, but he'd left too early for that.

He needed answers worse than he needed food. Day

after day in Lindsey's company was starting to scare him. And for all the good she'd done his child, Jade was getting too attached. He had to bring this situation to an end soon.

A sudden knock rattled the entire trailer. Tossing aside a worn towel, he went to answer the door, bristling at the sight of his oversized visitor. Preacher Cliff whatever-his-name-was. No wonder the trailer had shaken under the pounding. So Lindsey had betrayed his confidence and sicced her minister on him. Preparing for an on-slaught of unwanted advice, pat answers and sympathy for his loss, he opened the door.

"Hey, Jesse, how are you doing?"

Jesse accepted the warm handshake and exchanged greetings. "Come on in."

Not that he really wanted the preacher in his house, but he didn't want to upset Lindsey either.

"No, no. I can't stay. The men are working on the church Christmas display tonight, and Karen threatened not to feed me if I was late to supper." He gave a hearty laugh and tapped his belly. "Can't be starving the skinny little preacher."

In spite of himself, Jesse smiled. It was hard not to like Lindsey's pastor.

"I hate to bother you with this," Cliff went on, "but Lindsey tells me you're a whiz with electrical hook-ups. Brags to everyone about you. We're having a bit of trouble at the church getting our display to work right, and she thought you might be willing to have a look."

Jesse's first impulse was to say no and slam the door, but the preacher's words soaked through first. Lindsey bragged about him to other people?

In spite of himself he asked, "Any idea what's gone wrong?"

"Aw, I don't know. Clarence and Mick seemed to think the problem is in the breaker box, but we can't fix it."

Jesse squinted in contemplation. "Clarence and Mick will be there?"

"They're at the church right now. That's why I came by to talk to you. They're at their wits' end with this thing."

Clarence Stone was a man who'd been around awhile, a man who might know more about the lawyer, Stuart Hardwick. Spending time in his company, even at a church, could be worth the effort. And he'd seen Mick Thompson several times since the cookout weeks ago and liked the guy. He wasn't one of those preachy kind of Christians who didn't know how to get his hands dirty. And their common interest in horses might someday lead to friendship. He'd need a friend when he regained the land that Lindsey now called home.

Ignoring the pinch of regret that grew worse each time he thought of Lindsey's reaction to losing the farm, he looked at his watch. "I'll head over there now, see what I can do."

Cliff clapped Jesse on the shoulder. "Great. I'll meet you in the parking lot."

Jesse knew where Winding Stair Chapel was located and, after collecting Jade and her dolls and making sure his tools were in the truck, drove to the church.

Three other pickups were parked outside the native-rock building. Their owners were scattered around the outside of the church at various projects. They'd set up a life-sized nativity and lined the railed walkway from the parking area to the entrance with luminaries. The two huge evergreens standing sentry on each corner of the lot had been draped with lights, and the outline of an enormous star rose high over the chapel. A man wearing a leather tool belt balanced on the roof, labored over the star.

The men had gone to a lot of trouble, and from the looks of things, they were far from finished.

He was surprised to find himself here, at a church. Not that he didn't believe in God, but part of him wondered if God believed in him. He'd felt empty for such a long time.

"Man, are we glad to see you," Mick Thompson called as soon as Jesse and Jade exited the pickup. "Help's on the way, boys," he bellowed to the remaining men. "Lindsey's expert is here."

Lindsey's expert? The friendly greeting buoyed Jesse. As tired as he was, he wanted to help if possible. "I'll do what I can. What's the main trouble?"

Clarence Stone waved his arms at a latticework of electrical circuitry spread over the churchyard. "Everything. We're all hooked up, cords and wires are run, but the angels won't flutter and Baby Jesus won't shine."

Jesse squelched his amusement at the old man's joking manner.

"Show me your electrical setup and where all the breakers are. I have my tester and tool pouch in the truck. Maybe we can find the source of the problem and work from there."

Boots crunching across the gravel drive, Mick motioned toward the lighted building. "My wife is in the Sunday school preparing next week's lesson. Your little girl can play with my kids if she wants to. Clare will keep an eye on her while you're busy."

Jade jumped at the chance and was taken inside by the giant preacher who'd wheeled in behind Jesse. It did Jesse's heart good to see Jade willing to be out of his sight for a few minutes.

"Breaker box is in the church office," Clarence said and led Jesse down the long hall to the back of the church. To Jesse, the older man's presence and eager conversation was a stroke of good luck.

"The tree farm hopping yet?" Clarence asked as Jesse stepped up on a ladder to examine the box that housed the breakers. He unscrewed four screws and removed the face plate.

Jesse nodded, concentration riveted more on testing the voltage to the breakers than on the conversation. "We've been real busy since Thanksgiving."

Clarence peered upward, leaning an arm against the rock wall below Jesse. "I reckon Lindsey's in her element. Never seen a child love Christmas the way she does. Been that way ever since I knew her."

"How long has that been?" Jesse said the words casually, never taking his eyes off the readings. The breakers had power. The problem was likely in the attic.

"Ever since she moved in with Charlie and Betty Jean. Before that really. I'd see her now and again when she and her folks came to visit."

"Lindsey thought a lot of her Grandma and Grandpa Mitchell." He flipped the main breaker to the off position.

"Mitchell?" Clarence stared up at him, puzzled for a moment. "You mean Baker, not Mitchell. Mitchell was the other side of the family. I never knew them. Now Charlie and me, we was good friends. Hauled hay with each other. Things like that."

As Clarence rattled on about his friendship with Lindsey's grandfather, the light came on inside Jesse's head. The volt meter trembled in his fingers as adrenaline zipped through him. No wonder he'd had such a hard time finding data. He'd been looking under the wrong name.

"I suppose the Bakers have owned that farm for generations." He knew better, but figured tossing the idea out in the open would keep Clarence talking.

"Nah. Charlie bought the place when he retired from the phone company. Let's see..." Clarence squinted at the ceiling, rubbing his chin. "'Bout twenty years ago, I reckon. Before that a man name of Finch owned it, if memory serves. I didn't know him too well. Not a friendly sort. Charlie started the tree farm."

Les Finch. Jesse's gut clenched. No, his stepfather wasn't a friendly sort unless a man had a bottle of whiskey or something else he wanted. And he had never owned the farm, either, but he'd wanted everyone to think he did.

Carefully, he guided the subject away from Les Finch. No use helping Clarence remember the boy who'd lived on that farm with the unfriendly Finch.

"I have an idea what the problem is, but I need to get up in the attic." He looked around, saw the opening and moved the ladder beneath.

Clarence followed along, eager to help and full of chatter, but otherwise basically useless. "Think you can fix it?"

Taking his flashlight from his tool pouch, Jesse shoved the attic door open and poked his head into the dark space above. The problem was right in front of him. "Should have the power up and running in no time."

Clarence clapped his hands. "Lindsey said you would. She sure thinks highly of you, and that means something to us around here. Lindsey's like her grandma. Has a heart of gold and will do about anything for anybody. But she don't trust just everyone. Kinda got a sore spot where that's concerned."

A sore spot? Lindsey? Tilting his face downward at the old farmer, curiosity piqued, he asked, "Why do you say that?"

"Well, I reckon you'll hear it if you stay around here long enough, though I'm not surprised Lindsey didn't tell you herself. Some things are kinda painful to discuss."

Jesse concentrated on repairing a ground wire that had been chewed in half by some varmint, likely a squirrel, but every fiber of his being was tuned in to Clarence.

"Some college fella without a lick of sense or decency broke her heart a few years back. Poor little thing come crying home all tore up and hasn't left that farm for more than a day or two since. Sometimes I think she's hiding out up there so no one can hurt her again."

Jesse wrestled with the need to punch something but used his energy to splice the line and wrap the ends with insulated tape. His blood boiled to think of Lindsey crying over some snot-nosed college boy.

"I've never noticed anything wrong." But that wasn't exactly true. Hadn't he seen the shadows in her eyes when she talked about wanting a child like Jade? "She seems happy enough."

"Naturally. She's got the Lord. I don't know how folks that don't know the Lord get by when hard times come."

Jesse was beginning to wonder that himself.

"I figure she's over the guy by now." At least, he

hoped so. He collected his tools, placing each one in his pouch.

"No doubt about that. She's a strong young woman, but the heartache of having her fiancé get some other girl pregnant while she was away making money for the wedding, won't ever leave her. That's why I say trust don't come easy."

Jesse's pliers clattered to the tile below. He clenched his fists as anger, swift and hot, bubbled up in him. What kind of low-life would do such a thing? Gentle, loving Lindsey, who gave and helped and never asked for anything in return, shouldn't have been treated so cruelly. She must have been crushed at such betrayal from the man she loved and trusted.

Clumping down the ladder, he went to the breaker box, insides raging at the injustice. A good woman like Lindsey deserved better.

As he flipped the breaker switch, illuminating the darkening churchyard, the awful truth hit him like a bolt of electricity. Lindsey trusted him, too. And he was going to hurt her almost as much.

Lindsey was happy enough to sing—and so she did—inside the Snack Shack, as she liked to call the small building where she and Jade served hot apple cider and Christmas cookies to their "guests." Gaily bedecked with holiday cheer, the cozy room boasted a long table, where customers could warm up and enjoy the music and atmosphere while Jesse baled their chosen tree and Lindsey rang up their sale.

At present, a family of five occupied the room, admiring Lindsey's miniature Christmas village while they munched and waited. They'd had their ride through the grove, all of them singing at the top of their lungs, the children so full of excited energy they kept hopping off the wagon to run along beside. Their unfettered cheer delighted Lindsey and had even brightened Jesse's usually serious countenance.

Jade, catching the good mood, had agreed to let Sushi roam free as long as Jesse was within sight.

Yes, Lindsey's life was full. Not since before Gramps died had the holidays seemed so merry.

The door flew open and Jesse stepped inside, rubbing his gloveless hands together. A swirl of winter wind followed him. The collar of his fleece-lined jacket turned up, framing his handsome face.

An extra jolt of energy shot through Lindsey. More and more lately, Jesse's presence caused that inexplicable reaction. With a simple act like walking into a room, he made her world brighter.

Two nights ago he'd solved a problem with the electricity at the church, and she'd been so proud of him. He was smart and resourceful and the hardest, most honest worker anyone could ask for.

"Daddy!" Jade charged from behind the homemade counter, where she'd been doling out gingerbread men. "Want a cookie?"

Lindsey grinned. Jade had forced the sweets on him every time he'd entered the building. He never stayed long, just grabbed the cookie and ran. Even though he had been busy with a steady stream of customers all night, she suspected that the holiday atmosphere still bothered him.

"I'm stuffed, Butterbean." Absently patting her head, he said to the eagerly waiting family, "Your tree's ready to go. It's a beauty."

After giving the kids a few more cookies and the man a set of tree-care instructions, she, Jade and Jesse escorted the family out into the clear, cold night. Together they stood, Jade between them, watching the car pull away. For a moment, as cries of "Merry Christmas" echoed across through the crisp air, Lindsey had the fleeting thought that this is what it would be like if the three of them were a family bidding goodbye to friends after a fun-filled visit.

A gust of wind, like an icy hand, slapped against her.

Flights of fancy were uncharacteristic of someone as practical as she. And yet, here she stood, in the nippy, pine-scented night, behaving as if Jesse and Jade belonged to her. The need for family had never weighed as heavy nor had the longing been so great.

Wise enough to recognize the symptoms, Lindsey struggled to hold her emotions in check, to fight down the rising ache of need. She loved the dark-haired child clinging to her hand. And she had feelings for Jesse, though she refused to give those feelings a name.

Jesse was good help, and he was great company, but they were too different. His grief for his late wife, coupled with his ambivalence toward God, were all the roadblocks the Lord needed to put in her way. She had ignored the signs before. She wouldn't let herself be that foolish again.

The evening's pleasure seeped away. Maybe she wasn't meant to have a family. Maybe the Lord intended her to be alone, growing trees for other families to enjoy, and sharing her maternal love with the children from her church. After the foolish mistakes she'd made with Sean, perhaps the Lord didn't trust her to make that kind of decision.

* * *

Jesse pulled Jade against him to block the wind and tugged her coat closed, though his mind was on Lindsey. He felt her sudden withdrawal as if she'd turned and walked away. When the customers pulled out of the drive she'd been laughing and happy, but now her shoulders slumped, and she stared into the distance like a lost puppy.

"Are you okay?"

"Tired, I guess." She pulled the hood of her car coat up and snapped the chin strap.

Sure she was tired. Had to be after the long days of hard work they'd been putting in. Though things would settle down after the holidays, this was the busiest time of year for the farm. He knew for a fact she was up every morning with the sun and worked on the books long after he went home. He'd tried to take more of the physical labor on himself, but when he did she added something else to her own chore list. Still, he had a feeling more than exhaustion weighed her down tonight.

"Let's close up. It's nearly ten anyway." They normally locked the gates and cut the lights at ten.

Solemn-faced, she nodded. "I'll unharness Puddin' and get him settled."

As she turned to go, Jesse reached out and caught her elbow. He had the sudden and troublesome yearning to guide her against his chest and ask what was wrong. Not a smart idea, but an enticing one.

"You and Jade take care of things inside," he said. "I'll tend to Puddin' and the outdoor chores."

The wind whipped a lock of hair from beneath her hood and sent it fluttering across her mouth. Tempted to catch the wayward curl, to feel the silky softness against his skin, Jesse shoved his hands into his pockets.

"Come inside and warm up first," she said, tucking the stray hair back in place. "You've been out in this wind all evening."

So had she for the most part, but he didn't argue. A warm drink and a few minutes of rest wouldn't hurt him and it would please her. Funny how pleasing Lindsey seemed important tonight.

Inside the building, Jesse stood amidst the cheery knickknacks breathing in the scents of cinnamon and pine and apples. The room reeked of Lindsey and the things she enjoyed. If he wanted to stop thinking about her—and he did—here among her decorations was not the place to do it.

Normally, the Snack Shack and all the holiday folderol depressed him, but depression plagued him less and less lately. He'd figured he was just too busy and tired to notice, but now he worried that Lindsey and not fatigue had taken the edge off his sorrow.

To avoid that line of thinking, he gazed around the room at the lighted candles, the holly rings, and all the other festive things that Lindsey loved. Looking at them didn't hurt so much anymore.

"You ought to put a little gift shop in here." He didn't know where that had come from.

"I've thought about it, but never had enough help to handle gifts and the trees." Lindsey was behind the counter helping Jade seal leftover cookies into zip-up bags.

"You should consider the idea."

"Too late this year. Maybe next."

Jesse could see the notion, coming from him, pleased her. He had other ideas that would please her, too. Some he'd shared, like the concept of developing a website for the farm and using the internet for free marketing. He'd even volunteered to start tinkering with designs after the rush season.

Lifting a glass angel, he turned the ornament in his hands. What was happening to him? Why was he thinking such ridiculous, useless thoughts?

Lindsey didn't need a website or advertising or even a gift shop. This time next year she and her Christmas trees would be long gone. That's the way it had to be. Justice would be served. He'd have his home…and his revenge.

The tender, loving expression on the angel's face mocked him. Discomfited, he put the ornament back on the shelf.

Lindsey bustled around the counter, carrying a steaming cup. "Cider?"

Her inner light was back on, and he was glad. Taking the warm mug, he smiled his thanks and waited like a child expecting candy for her to return the smile.

His fingers itched to touch her smooth skin, and this time, before he could change his mind, he cupped her cheek. A question sprang to her eyes—a question he couldn't answer because he didn't understand himself.

Dropping his hand, he avoided her gaze and pretended to sip the warm drink. Ever since Clarence had told him of Lindsey's cheating fiancé, he'd struggled against the need to take her in his arms and promise that no one would ever hurt her that way again. The reaction made no sense at all.

A strange energy pulsed in the space between them and he knew she waited for him to say something, to explain his uncharacteristic behavior. But how could he explain what he didn't understand?

He felt her move away, wanted to call her back, wanted to say...what? That he liked her? That he was attracted to her?

He heard her murmuring to Jade, but his head buzzed so much he couldn't make out the conversation. He sipped the sweet cider, hoping to wash away his deranged thoughts. Attracted? No way. Couldn't happen.

He looked up to find Lindsey gathering his drowsy daughter into her arms. Most nights Jade fell asleep long before closing and Lindsey put her to bed on an air mattress behind the counter. Tonight being Friday, Jade had stayed awake as long as possible, but a few moments of quiet stillness had done her in.

His baby girl snuggled into Lindsey's green flannel, eyes drooping as she relaxed, contented and comfortable. Expression tender, his boss lady brushed a kiss onto Jade's peaceful forehead. They looked so right together, this woman and his child.

Something dangerous moved inside Jesse's chest. A thickness lodged in his throat. Lindsey Mitchell was slowly worming her way into his heart.

A war raged within him. He couldn't fall in love with Lindsey. He couldn't even allow attraction. To do so would betray Erin's memory and interfere with his plans for restitution and revenge. He was within arm's reach of everything he'd dreamed of for years. He and Jade deserved this place. No matter how sweet Lindsey Mitchell might be, he would not be distracted.

Once he'd discovered Lindsey's grandfather's real name, he had easily found the information he needed. Sure enough, Stuart Hardwick, the crooked lawyer, had done the deal. When he'd told the court clerk this morning that he'd been searching under the wrong name, she'd curled her lip in reproach. "Coulda told you that if you'd asked."

Now that a clerk knew he was searching Lindsey's farm records, it was only a matter of time before word lcakcd out and Lindsey knew his intent. He thought about going to the sheriff with what he knew, but a confession from Hardwick would settle matters more quickly. He needed to find Stuart Hardwick first—and fast.

He took one last glance at Lindsey.

He was too close to the truth to let anything—or anyone—stop him now.

Hardening his heart, he went out into the cold night.

Chapter Nine

Waving a paper, Jade barreled down the lane, pink backpack thumping against her purple coat.

"Lindsey. Lindsey! Can you make a costume?"

On her knees, clearing away the remains of a tree stump, Lindsey braced as Jade tumbled against her. Mother love too fierce to deny rose inside her. Jade needed her love and attention, regardless of the sorrow Lindsey would someday suffer when the child was gone. She wasn't foolish enough to think a man of Jesse's talents would always work for minimum wage.

"What kind of costume, sweetie?"

"An angel. An angel." Jade's excitement had her fluttering around waving her arms like wings. "I'm the guarding angel for Jesus."

Every year the elementary school put on a Christmas program. The conclusion of the play was traditionally a nativity scene with the singing of "Silent Night" by the entire audience. Once there had been talk of removing the religious scene from the school, but such an outcry arose that the tradition remained. The town loved it, expected it, and turned out en masse to see the little ones dressed in sparkly, colorful costumes. Jade, with her milky skin and black hair, would be a beautiful angel.

Jesse came around the end of a row where he'd been cutting trees for a grocer who had requested a second load.

"What's all the noise about?" he demanded, his expression teasingly fierce. "I can't even hear my chain saw with you two carrying on this way."

Jade threw her arms around his legs and repeated her request for an angel costume. The fun drained out of Jesse's face.

"Lindsey's too busy with the farm," he said shortly.

Jade's happy expression fell, and Lindsey couldn't bear to see her disappointment.

Jesse had behaved strangely all day, his manner brusque and distant. He'd even refused their usual lunch break of sandwiches in the Snack Shack, saying he'd eat later. But there was no reason for him to dim Jade's happiness.

"Making a costume for Jade would be my pleasure. You know that."

"Don't bother yourself." Jesse spun away and started back into the trees.

"Jesse." She caught up to him, touched his arm. "I'd love to make the costume for Jade. What's wrong with you today?"

"You're not her mother. Stop trying to be."

Stricken to the core, Lindsey cringed and pressed a shaky hand to her lips. Was that what he thought? That she wanted to take Erin's place?

Jesse shoved both hands over his head. "Look. I shouldn't have said that. I'm sorry. It's just that—" His expression went bleak. He squeezed his eyes closed. "No excuses. I'm sorry."

"Daddy." Jade, whom they'd both momentarily forgotten, slipped between them, tears bright in her green eyes. "It's okay. I don't have to be in the play."

Lindsey thought her heart would break—for the child, for herself and even for the troubled man.

Jesse fell to his knees in front of Jade and gripped her fiercely to him, his face a mask of regret. "Daddy didn't mean it, Butterbean. You can be in the play."

Over her dark head, he gazed at Lindsey desolately. "Make the costume. It would mean a lot to both of us."

Throat thick with unshed tears, Lindsey nodded, confused and hurt. She'd never intended to touch a nerve. She'd only wanted to see the little girl happy.

Pushing Jade away a little, Jesse smoothed her dark hair, leaving both hands cupped around her face. "You'll be the prettiest angel in the program. Lindsey will make sure of that." He raised pleading eyes. "Won't you, Lindsey?"

Like the Oklahoma weather, Jesse had changed from anger to remorse. Bewildered and reeling from his sharp accusation, Lindsey's stomach churned. But not wanting Jade to suffer any more disappointment, she swallowed her own hurt and agreed. "Jade and I can shop for materials tomorrow after school if that's okay."

She felt tentative with him in a way she never had before. What had brought on this vicious outburst in the first place?

"Whatever you decide is fine. Anything." Rising, he turned Jade toward the Snack Shack. Lindsey knew their conversation wasn't over, but he didn't want the little girl to hear any more. "Better head up there and do your homework. You and Lindsey can talk about the costume later."

With the resilience of childhood, Jade started toward the building, but froze when the German shepherd bolted from the trees to follow.

"Sushi!" Lindsey commanded. "Come." The disappointed dog obeyed, coming to flop in disgust at Lindsey's feet. Jade was making progress, but not enough to be alone in the building with the animal.

As soon as the door closed behind his daughter, Jesse said, "You have been nothing but good to Jade and me. I had no right to snap at you, to say such an awful thing."

"I'm not trying to replace Erin," she said quietly.

"I know. I'm sorry." Absently, he stroked the adoring dog, his body still stiff with tension. "How can I make it up to you?"

"Forget it ever happened." She smiled, perhaps a bit tremulously, although she felt better knowing he hadn't intended to hurt her. "And I'll do the same."

His jaw tightened. Her forgiveness seemed to anger him. "Don't be so nice all the time, Lindsey. When someone treats you like dirt, take up for yourself."

She wanted to disagree. Arguing over small injustices and taking offense served no good that she could see, but Jesse seemed bent on picking a fight. And she refused to play into his bad mood. "I don't understand you today."

"Welcome to the club." He shoved his hands in his pockets and looked up at the gray-blue sky. "I'm a jerk, Lindsey. You should fire me."

She longed to comfort him, though she was the wounded party. Normally, Jesse was easygoing and pleasant company. More than pleasant company, if she admitted the truth. But something was terribly wrong today, and getting her back up wasn't the solution.

"Your job is safe. I can't get along without you."

The Freudian slip resounded in the chilly afternoon air. She not only couldn't get along without him, she didn't want to. He'd become too important.

Resisting the urge to smooth her fingers over the rigid line of his jaw and tell him that, another wayward notion drifted through her mind. Jesse Slater, even in a bad mood, was a better man than her former fiancé would ever be. Her stomach hurt to make the comparison, but the ache cleared when she realized that no matter what torment beat inside Jesse, he was too honorable to do the kind of things Sean had done. Jesse knew when he was wrong and apologized. Sean never had.

His gaze riveted on the sky, Jesse's quiet voice was filled with repressed emotion. "Do you think God plays favorites?"

Lindsey blinked. Where had that come from? And what did it have to do with sewing an angel costume? "Do you?"

"Sure seems that way."

"Is that what's bothering you today? You think God doesn't care about you as much as He does other people?"

"I've wondered." A muscle twitched along one cheekbone. "But maybe I don't deserve it."

She ran her fingertips over the soft needles of the closest tree, praying for the right words to help her friend. "Jesus loved us—all of us—so much He died for us."

"I've been giving that a lot of thought lately." He studied the ground as if the Oklahoma dirt held the answers to the mysteries of the universe. "But not everyone is as good as you are, Lindsey. Definitely not me."

Lindsey's pulse did a stutter-step.

"I'm not perfect, Jesse," she said. "I've done things I'm not proud of, too."

Picking up her shears, she clipped at a wayward branch, unable to look at Jesse but compelled to share. "I was engaged once."

Snip. Snip. She swallowed, nervous. "And I did things I regret. I trusted the wrong man, telling myself that love made our actions all right." She snipped again, saw the shears tremble. "But that was a mistake. He was a mistake."

Jesse's work-hardened hand closed over hers, gently taking the clippers. "Lindsey."

Her gaze flew to his face.

She wondered if she had disappointed him, but Jesse needed to understand that she had made her share of wrong choices—and yet God loved her.

Fire flashed in Jesse's silvery eyes. "The man," he said, "was a moron."

Sweet relief washed through Lindsey. Jesse wasn't angry *at* her. He was angry *for* her.

"So was I. Then. But God forgave me, and eventually I forgave myself." She reached for the cutters, her fingers grazing his. "He'll do the same for you."

"Yeah. Well…" Jesse let the words drift away.

She knew he'd tried to serve God in the past, but had drifted away when Erin died. Understandable, but so backwards. She'd learned the hard way to run *to* the Lord when trouble struck instead of away from Him.

They stood in silence, contemplative for a bit until Jesse bent to retrieve the chain saw.

"Guess we better get back to work if I'm going to haul that load in the morning."

For all the conversation, trouble still brooded over him like a dark cloud.

"Jesse."

He paused.

"Is there anything else bothering you?" she asked, certain that there was. "Anything I can help with?"

Silver eyes studied her for several long seconds. He took her hand and squeezed it. "I'm grateful to you, Lindsey. No matter what happens. Remember that."

Puzzled by the strange declaration, Lindsey waited for him to say more, but before he could, a truck rumbled through the gate, and the moment was gone. As if relieved by the interruption, Jesse hurried to greet the customer.

She'd seen so much change in Jesse since the day he'd first driven into her yard asking for a job. She'd watched him grow more comfortable with her talk of God. He was easier around the Christmas decorations too, and since telling her of Erin's death, he'd opened up some about his feelings of guilt in that department. And he smiled more too.

But today, regardless of his denial, Jesse battled something deep and worrisome. And given his peculiar behavior, she had a bad feeling that his troubles had something to do with her.

Heat from the farmhouse embraced Jesse as he came through the door. The dog, curled beside the living-room furnace, lifted her head, recognized him, and lay down again with a heavy sigh. Jesse stood for a moment in the doorway, taking in the warm, homey comfort of this place. A sense of déjà vu came over him, a subconscious memory of long ago when the world had been right.

The aroma of roast beef tickled his nose and made his hungry stomach growl. The tree patch was quiet, only one buyer since noon, and Lindsey had knocked off early to make Jade's costume and cook supper for them all. After his behavior the other day, he found it hard to refuse her anything.

Jade's giggle blended with Lindsey's rich laugh in a sweet music that had Jesse longing to hear it again and again. They were at the table, happily laboring over some kind of gauzy white material and yards of sparkly gold tinsel.

He'd been wrong to jump on Lindsey about making the costume and even more wrong to accuse her of trying to take Erin's place. No one could do that. But Lindsey's love and motherly care was changing Jade for the better. Only a fool would deny or resent the obvious.

And he'd almost told Lindsey the truth. He'd yearned to admit that her farm was his and that he wanted it back. The torment was eating him alive because, to get what he wanted, he had to break Lindsey's heart. He'd tried praying, as she had suggested, but his prayers bounced off the ceiling and mocked him.

Lindsey spotted him, then, standing in the doorway, watching. Her full mouth lifted. "You look frozen."

He gave a shiver for effect. The temperature had plummeted into the twenties, unusual for this part of the country. Working outside in the Oklahoma wind proved a challenge.

"I thought you could make that costume in an hour?"

"I can. But I'm teaching Jade."

Stripping off his heavy coat, he came on into the kitchen. "Isn't she too little for sewing?"

"Daddy!" Insulted, Jade jammed a saucy hand onto

a hip. "I have to learn sometime. Besides, I'm the tryer-on-er."

Amused, he tilted his head in apology. "I stand corrected."

"We'll have the body of the gown finished in a few minutes. Coffee's on and Cokes are in the fridge. Whichever you want."

No matter how cold the weather, Jesse liked his cola. Going to the refrigerator, he took one, popped the top and turned to watch the womenfolk do their thing.

Patiently, Lindsey held the gauzy fabric beneath the sewing-machine needle, demonstrating how to move the gown without sewing her own fingers. She looked so pretty with her honey hair falling forward, full lips pursed in concentration. He'd been right the first time he'd seen her. Lindsey, beneath her flannel and denim, was very much a woman.

He sipped his cola, wanting to look away, but he couldn't. Watching Lindsey gave him too much pleasure.

When the seam was sewn, Jade took the scissors and proudly clipped the thread.

"There you go, Miss Angel." Lindsey held the white flowing garment against Jade's body. "Perfect fit."

Jade looked doubtful. "Where's the wings?"

"We'll do those after supper. Jesse, if you'll move the machine, we can set the table."

"Anything to hurry the food." He unplugged the old Singer that must have belonged to her grandmother, and hefted it into Lindsey's spare room.

"Tell me your part again," Lindsey was saying as he came back into the kitchen.

"Below the angel's shining light, love was born on Christmas night," Jade recited, slowly and with expression.

"You're going to be the very best speaker." Scooping the remaining materials off the table, Lindsey spoke to Jesse. "Isn't she, Dad?"

"No doubt about it." He hooked an arm around Jade's middle and hoisted her up. Her giggle made him smile. "And the prettiest angel, too."

"Are you going to come watch me?"

The question caught him by surprise. Slowly, he eased her down into a chair. "Well… I don't know, Jade. I'm awfully busy here at the tree farm."

Whipping around, a steaming bowl in one hand, Lindsey refused to let him use that excuse. "We'll be closed that night."

Jade was getting too involved with all this Christmas business. Next thing he knew, she'd be talking about Santa Claus and wanting to hang up stockings.

"I'm not much on Christmas programs. You two can go without me."

Both females looked at him with mild reproach. The room grew deafeningly quiet until only the tick of the furnace was heard.

Finally, Lindsey slapped a loaf of bread onto the table and turned on him. Her golden-brown eyes glowed with a hint of anger. "The program is important to Jade, and you need to be there. You might actually enjoy yourself."

He doubted that, but he didn't want Lindsey upset with him again. He was still battling guilt over the last time.

With a defeated sigh, he followed her to the stove,

took the green peas from her and carried the bowl to the table.

"All right, Butterbean," he said, tapping Jade on the nose. "If the tree lot is closed, I'll be there."

"Really, Daddy?" The hope in her eyes did him in.

"Really."

Her beauteous smile lit the room and illuminated his heart.

As he drew his chair up to the table, the familiar gnaw of dread pulled at his stomach. A Christmas program. What had he gotten himself into?

The atmosphere at the Winding Stair Elementary School was one of controlled chaos. After dropping an angelic Jade at her classroom with a gaggle of lambs and ladybugs, Jesse followed Lindsey down the long hall to the auditorium. The noise of a community that knew each other well filled the place with cheer. Everyone they passed spoke to Lindsey and many, recognizing him, stopped to shake his hand and offer greetings.

He hadn't been to a school Christmas program since he was in grade school himself, but the buzz of excitement was the same.

At the door, a teenage girl in a red Santa hat offered him a program and a huge flirtatious smile.

"Hi, Lindsey," she said, though her eyelashes fluttered at him. He ignored her, staring ahead at the milieu of country folks gathered in this one place.

Lindsey greeted the girl warmly, then began the slow process of weaving through the crowd toward the seats. She'd been right. The program was a community event. Everyone was dressed up, the scent of recent showers and cologne a testament to the importance of Winding Stair's Christmas program.

"I think you have an admirer," Lindsey teased when they were seated.

He knew she meant the teenager at the door, but the idea insulted him. "She's a kid."

Lindsey laughed softly. "But she's not blind or stupid."

Surprised, he turned in the squeaky auditorium seat. What had she meant by that? But Lindsey had taken a sudden interest in studying the photocopied program.

"Look here." She pointed. "Jade is on stage for a long time."

"No kidding?" He looked over her shoulder with interest. The sweet scent of jasmine rose up from the vicinity of her elegant neck and tantalized his senses. From the time she'd climbed into his truck, he'd enjoyed the fragrance, but up close this way was even nicer.

She looked pretty tonight, too. He'd never seen her in a real dress and when she'd opened the front door, he'd lost his breath. Surprise, of course, nothing more. In honor of the occasion, she wore red, a smooth, sweater kind of dress that looked pretty with her honey-colored hair.

The lights flickered, a signal he supposed, for the crowd hushed and settled into their seats. The doors on each side of the auditorium closed and the principal stepped out in front of the blue velvet curtain to welcome everyone.

In moments, the curtains swooshed apart, and Jesse waited eagerly for the moment his baby would come on stage.

The program was festive and colorful and full of exuberant good will if not exceptional talent. Most of the children were animals of some sort and each group sang to the accompaniment of a slightly out-of-tune piano.

When two ladybugs bumped heads, entangling their antenna, Jesse laughed along with the rest of the crowd. A teacher scuttled from backstage, parted the antenna and with a smiling shrug, disappeared again. The children seemed unfazed.

Another time, one of the fireflies dropped his flashlight and the batteries came clattering out. To the delight of the audience, the little boy crawled through legs and around various other insects until he'd retrieved all the scattered parts of his illumination.

Despite his hesitancy to come tonight, Jesse was having a good time. None of the awful, tearing agony of loss overtook him as he'd expected. He had to credit Lindsey and his little angel for that.

"There she is," Lindsey whispered and pushed at his shoulder as if he couldn't see for himself the vision moving onto the stage.

Beneath the spotlight, his angel glittered and glowed in the costume Lindsey had so lovingly created. Her halo of tinsel shimmered against the shining raven hair as she bent to hover over the manger. Even from this distance, he could see her squinting into the crowd, looking for him.

In a sweet, bell-like voice, she spoke her lines, and Jesse reacted as if he hadn't heard them a thousand times in the past two weeks.

"Beneath the angel's shining light, love was born on Christmas night."

Tenderness rose in his throat, enough to choke him.

As he watched Jade, angel wings outstretched, join her class in singing "Silent Night," he thought his heart would burst with pride. Such sweetness. Such beauty. And he'd almost missed it.

Erin should have been here, too.

He waited for the familiar pain to come, and was surprised when it didn't.

Jade caught sight of him somehow and her entire face brightened. Had she thought he wouldn't stay?

With a start, he realized how wrong he'd been to let his own loss and pain affect his child's happiness and well-being. Huddled in his darkness, he'd let two years of Jade's life pass in a blur while he nursed his wounds and felt sorry for himself.

As the program ended and Jade was swept away in the thundering mass of first-graders, Jesse looked down. At some point during the play, he'd taken hold of Lindsey's hand and pulled it against his thigh. How had that happened? And why didn't he turn her loose now that the play was over? But with her small fingers wrapped in his, he was reluctant to let her go.

"She was wonderful," Lindsey said, eyes aglow as she turned to him.

"The best one of all."

"Of course." And they both laughed, knowing every parent in the room thought the same thing about his or her own child.

And even though she wasn't Jade's parent, Jesse knew Lindsey loved his daughter unreservedly.

Still holding her hand, and bewildered by his own actions, Jesse rose and began the shuffle out of the jammed auditorium and down the hall to the classrooms. There they collected Jade from the rambunctious crowd of first-graders and headed out the exit.

"Excuse me." A man about Jesse's age stopped them

as they started down the concrete steps. A vague sense of recognition stirred in Jesse's memory. "I saw you earlier and couldn't help thinking that I should know you? Did you ever go to school here?"

Jesse stiffened momentarily before forcing his shoulders to relax. No use getting in a panic. Play it cool. "Sorry. I'm a newcomer. Moved here back in October."

The man tilted his head, frowning. "You sure remind me of a kid I went to junior high with. Aw, but that's a long time ago."

"Well, you know what they say." Jesse shrugged, hoping he sounded more casual than he felt. "Everybody looks like someone."

"Ain't that the truth? My wife says I'm starting to resemble my hound dog more and more every day."

They all laughed, and then using the excuse of the cold wind, Jesse led the way to the truck. He'd been expecting that to happen. Sooner or later, someone was bound to recognize him from junior high school. He glanced at Lindsey as she slid into the pickup. Still smiling and fussing over Jade, she hadn't seemed to notice anything amiss.

Cranking the engine, he breathed a sigh of relief. That was a close one.

Chapter Ten

"Ice cream, Daddy. Pleeease." Jade, who'd begged to keep her costume on, bounced in the seat of the Silverado. She was still hyper, wired up from her very first Christmas program. With every bounce, her angel wings batted against Lindsey's shoulder.

Lindsey awaited Jesse's reply, hoping he'd see how much Jade needed a few more minutes of reveling in the moment.

Jesse shook his head as he turned on the defrosters. "Too cold for ice cream."

The three of them had rushed across the schoolyard to the parking lot, eager to escape the cold wind after the brief, but chill-producing delay by the man who'd thought Jesse looked familiar. The truck was running and heat had begun to blow from the vents, but they still shivered.

"Hot fudge will counter the cold," Lindsey suggested, casting a sideways grin at Jesse. "We gotta celebrate."

"You're no help," he said, rolling his silver eyes. "But if you ladies want ice cream, ice cream you shall have. Let's head to the Dairy Cup."

A quiver of satisfaction moved through Lindsey. Jesse had enjoyed tonight, she was certain. But what had really stunned her was when he'd reached over and grasped her hand. For a second, she'd almost forgotten where she was, though she doubted Jesse had meant anything by it. Most likely, he'd reached for her in reaction to Jade's thrilling grand entrance. Still, those moments of her skin touching his while they shared Jade's triumph lingered sweetly in her mind.

As the truck rumbled slowly down Main Street, her legs began to thaw.

"I'll be glad when the weather warms up again," she said.

Jesse's wrist relaxed over the top of the steering wheel. "Supposed to tomorrow, isn't it?"

"Some. But there's a chance of snow too."

"Snow!" Jade exclaimed and started bouncing again. "Can we make a snowman?"

Lindsey patted the child's knee. "Wouldn't be any fun unless we did."

Jesse glanced her way. "I have a load of trees to haul to Mena tomorrow. I hope we don't get snow before that's done."

"If it snows, you can't haul those trees. These mountain roads can be treacherous in snow or ice."

"Might as well get the job done. I have some other business to take care of in Mena, too."

His personal business intrigued her, though she would never pry. Several times he'd taken off an afternoon for "business reasons." And just last Sunday at church someone had mentioned seeing him at the municipal building several times. What kind of business would require so many visits to the courthouse?

"Well, all right, stubborn. I'll just pray the snow holds off."

She managed to distract the wiggling Jade by pointing out the Christmas decorations visible everywhere. They drove past closed businesses gaily decorated with white stenciled greetings and flashing red and green lights. Fiber-optic trees rotated in some display windows, and attached to the light posts were giant candy canes that caught the reflection of car lights and wobbled with each gust of wind.

Winding Stair looked as lovely and quaint as always at Christmas.

"This town is like a step back in time," Jesse said, as though he'd read her mind.

"I love it."

"The place grows on you, that's for sure."

She wasn't certain what he meant by that, but at least he hadn't criticized her beloved town. Small, provincial and backwoods it might be, but Winding Stair took care of its own.

"There are a lot of good people here. Not fancy, but good to the bone."

He stared at her across Jade's head for so long she feared he'd run a stop sign.

"Yeah," he finally said. "There are."

What was that supposed to mean?

Her pulse was still thudding in consternation when they pulled into the graveled drive of the Dairy Cup and got out. From the number of cars around the café, other playgoers had also experienced a sudden need for celebration.

Jade raced to the door, black hair blowing wildly from beneath her tinsel halo. Her wings sparkled and jostled against her back. Lindsey had wanted to replace the wings with a coat, but Jade had pleaded to wear the costume awhile longer. They had compromised by sliding the coat onto her arms—backward.

The small, independently owned Dairy Cup boasted all of five booths and a short counter with three stools. Jesse took the only empty spot, a back booth next to the jukebox. Lindsey slid onto the green vinyl seat across from him while Jade rushed to the jukebox.

"Can we play a song, Daddy?"

Jesse fished in his pocket and handed over a quarter.

"The menu is up there," Lindsey said, pointing to a signboard above the cash register. "Tell me what you want and I'll go up and order for us."

"My treat," Jesse said. "I owe you for making me go to the play tonight."

She smiled, pleased at his admission. "So you really did have a good time?"

"Yeah. A real good time." He folded his hard-working hands on the tabletop. "So what will you have, Miss Mitchell?"

Jade's quarter clunked in the slot. A slow, romantic love song poured out of the machine.

You, Lindsey wanted to say. And the thought shocked her. She looked up at the menu so that Jesse couldn't read the answer in her eyes.

"Chili sounds good."

"I thought you were all for hot fudge."

She flopped her palms out to each side and grinned. "I'm female. I changed my mind."

"Chili sounds good to me too." He turned in the seat toward his daughter. She was twirling in a circle to the music, the glitter on her wings sparkling beneath the fluorescent lights. "Hey, Butterbean, what do you want?"

She twirled right on over to him and plopped onto the vinyl seat. She took his cheeks between her small hands and smooched him. "A hotdog."

"A hotdog! You wanted ice cream."

She shrugged small shoulders. The gossamer wings rose and fell, and then she scooted out of the booth and began twirling again. "A hotdog."

Lindsey pressed a hand to her mouth, suppressing a giggle.

Jesse shook his head, the edges of his mouth quivering. "Women. I'll never understand them."

Pretending exasperation, he rose and went to order. Lindsey watched him. In truth, she couldn't keep her eyes off him. Though the notion was ridiculous, she felt as if they were on a date. All evening, there had been small sparks between them. He'd even looked at her differently when she'd opened the door wearing a dress. Something had happened tonight, some subtle change in their relationship. And she knew without a doubt, this was something she'd better pray about.

The next afternoon, Jesse pulled the long flatbed truck next to the curb on a side street in the town of Mena. Lindsey's prayers must have worked because the snow had held off, although the sky had that shiny white glare that usually meant wintry weather. He was loaded down with trees, but the delivery stop would have to wait. This one couldn't.

A row of nicely appointed residences, all with wide lawns and wreaths on the doors, lined the street. He pulled the small scrap of paper from his jacket and read the number for the hundredth time. Yes, this was the place. According to his information, a retired lawyer lived here. Stuart Hardwick.

Heart racing, he strode to the door and knocked. He'd rehearsed his speech all the way from Winding Stair, but when the door opened, the words stuck in his throat.

An old man, with a bulbous nose and a shock of white hair, squinted at him. "Yes?"

"Mr. Hardwick?"

"I'm Hardwick. Who are you?"

"Jesse Slater." Placing a hand on the wooden door to keep it from being closed in his face, he said, "May I come in? We need to talk."

"I don't know you, Mr. Slater."

Using his free hand, Jesse fumbled for the copied document, drew it out and flipped it open beneath Hardwick's nose. "You knew my stepfather, Les Finch."

The old man peered at the paper, scratching his chin. "Maybe I did and maybe I didn't. I worked for a lot of folks over the years."

"Could we at least discuss it?"

Hardwick considered for a minute before stepping back. "Too cold to stand in the door. Come on in."

Passing through a small entry, they entered a musty-smelling, overheated living room. The man clicked on a lamp and shuffled to a table littered with glasses and papers.

"Care for a drink, Mr. Slater?" He lifted a half-empty whiskey bottle.

"No thanks." After living with Les Finch, strong drink had never tempted Jesse.

"You won't mind if I do then." After filling a glass to

the rim, he sipped, then sat down in a chair and waved for Jesse to do the same.

"Now what's this business of yours? Let me see that paper."

Jesse handed over the form his stepfather had signed, making the sale of Jesse's farm valid.

"Eighteen years ago my mother died, leaving her parents' farm to me. My stepfather, Les Finch, somehow managed to sell the place, claiming ownership."

"What's that got to do with me?"

"Someone smarter about legal and business affairs than Les had to do the paperwork."

"And you think I'm that man?"

"I know you are."

"Look, son, I'm an old man. Retired now. Eighteen years is a long time." His tone was soothing, compassionate, and Jesse figured he had perfected this tone in years of making deals. "Why don't you just let this thing go?"

"Because I have a little girl, and she deserves the home I never had. That farm belongs to me, and I want it back—for her."

Studying the paper, the lawyer took another sip of whiskey. "This document looks legal enough to me. How are you planning to prove the place is yours?"

"You. I want you to tell the truth. Confess that you helped Les Finch figure a way to forge my mother's name to forms that gave him ownership."

"Whoa now, boy. You're accusing me of a crime."

The old hypocrite. He *had* committed a crime, probably more than one. Anger hotter than the stifling room temperature rose in Jesse.

"What did he pay you, Hardwick?" he asked through

clenched teeth. "Part of the profits? A gallon of Kentucky bourbon?"

Jesse regretted his outburst immediately. Stuart Hardwick's bulbous nose flared in anger while his manner grew cool as the December day.

"I'm afraid I can't help you, Mr. Slater. Now if you will excuse me, it's time for my afternoon nap."

He tossed back the remaining liquor and pushed out of the chair.

Jesse leaped to his feet, unwilling to let the crooked lawyer off the hook. He squeezed his hands tight to keep from grabbing Hardwick by the shirt collar and wringing the truth out of him.

"Listen, old man, Les Finch stole everything I owned, moved me off to an unfamiliar city, and then tossed me out like a stray dog when I was barely fifteen. Scared, alone, heartbroken, hungry. Do you know what that's like?" He slammed his fists together. "That's never going to happen to my little girl. Never."

Hardwick turned away, went to the table and poured another drink. His hand trembled on the glass. "Any man who'd treat a kid so badly isn't worth much."

"No, he's not. He wasn't." The lawyer stood so long with his back turned, leaning on the table with shoulders slumped and the whiskey in front of him, that Jesse softened. "Maybe you didn't know that Finch would abandon me once he had his hands on the sale money. Maybe you would have done things differently if you'd known. Isn't that reason enough to help me now?"

Hardwick slowly shook his head. "I don't know, boy. Like I said, that was a long time ago." He took a deep pull of the liquor, shuddered, and backhanded his mouth.

"Tell you what. You write down where you can be contacted. If I remember anything, I'll get in touch."

There was nothing left for Jesse to do short of physical violence, and he wouldn't lower himself to that. Deflated and disheartened, he scribbled his address on the back of the paper and left the house.

By the time he reached the retailer who'd ordered the extra load of pines, he'd regained a splinter of hope. After all, Hardwick hadn't flatly refused to help him. If the old bird had any conscience left at all, maybe he'd still come through.

"Looks like a nice bunch of trees, Mr. Slater," the lot owner said as he inspected the pines piled high on Lindsey's flatbed.

Pride welled up inside Jesse as he slipped on his leather gloves and loosened the tie-down ropes to unload. "Miss Mitchell takes very good care of her lot. All her trees are in perfect condition like this."

"My customers have sure been happy with that first load you brought in. They sold fast." The owner waved his hand toward the Christmas trees remaining on his lot. "These you see out here now came in from out of state, but they're about gone too. Can't be running low on trees with Christmas still more than a week away."

To Jesse's way of thinking, the out-of-state pines weren't half as green and well-shaped as Lindsey's. The man should have bought all his stock from the Christmas Tree Farm.

The lot owner turned toward his office and bellowed, "Jerry, get out here and help get these trees in place."

A man, presumably Jerry, came out, buttoning his coat against the chill, and began moving the trees onto the lot. In minutes, the three had unloaded the truck.

As Jesse shouldered a final baled pine, an idea came to him. "Mr. Bailey, have you ever considered ordering all your trees from us? You can't get trees this fresh anywhere else."

The man stopped, thought a minute, then said, "You're right about that, but I like to offer more variety to my customers. You folks have nice trees, but all of them are Virginias."

"Look out there, Mr. Bailey." Jesse gestured to where the new Virginia pines were being erected alongside the less fresh trees. "Which do you think people will buy? Will they care if it's a Virginia instead of a Scotch, or will they want the freshest, prettiest tree available?"

"Got a point there, Slater. Tell you what." He dug in his pocket for a business card. "I own six lots in this part of the country. You have Miss Mitchell give me a call when the season ends, and we'll talk about it. Maybe we can work out a deal for next year."

Jesse's spirits soared. An exclusive sale to six area dealers would be a huge boost to Lindsey's business. They'd need to clear and plant more acres, but that was no problem. He could do it.

With a firm handshake and a hearty thanks, Jesse leaped into the truck and started back up the winding road toward home. He slapped the steering wheel and whistled "Jingle Bells" as the old truck bounced and chugged up the mountain. Visions of Lindsey's golden eyes, her tawny hair and her pretty smile danced before him sweeter than sugar plums.

Man, he couldn't wait to tell her the news and to feel her smoky laugh wrap around him like a warm hug. She'd be so happy.

And she'd think he was the biggest hero in town.

The cheerful thoughts no sooner filtered through his brain than reality crowded in.

His fingers tightened on the wheel.

For now he had to play the role of Mr. Nice Guy, helping Lindsey's business grow and prosper. For the sake of his child, he had to lie and deceive. He wasn't sure what that made him, but one thing was for sure—he was nobody's hero.

Chapter Eleven

Fat white flakes of snow began falling about an hour before closing time. The last customer, her tree in the back of an SUV, hurried away before the roads became troublesome.

Standing beneath the dark sky, snow swirling around her in the still cold, Lindsey knew they'd have no more business tonight. She stroked a hand over Sushi's pointed ears, smiling when the dog licked at a snowflake.

Jesse's news about a possible exclusive contract had been especially encouraging, given how slow the farm had been for the last several days. Her big days were always on the weekends, but with an employee's wages to pay, she needed cash coming in.

She'd tried not to worry, trying instead to pray and let the Lord handle everything. And the possibility of selling more trees locally was surely an answer to those prayers. The lot owner in Mena had paid cash for this last load, too, and that was doubly good news. She lifted her heart in silent gratitude.

Jesse had been, for him, almost animated when he'd arrived home that afternoon. She'd laughed with joy, restraining the urge to throw her arms around him. Lately, she wanted to do that every time she saw her hired hand.

"Might as well shut down for the night," she said, pulse accelerating as he came toward her. Crossing the short, shadowy distance between them, he looked lean and mysterious and incredibly attractive.

"Where's Jade?" His voice raised goose bumps on her arms.

She rubbed at them and hitched her chin toward the Snack Shack. "Inside."

His boots crunched as he twisted toward the building. "Let's get her and take a ride. Puddin's still harnessed."

"Are you serious?" Although she enjoyed driving families through the trees, she'd never taken a ride for her own personal pleasure. Riding alone had held no attraction. But riding with Jesse...

"Come on. It'll be fun." He paused, then frowned down at her in concern. "Unless you're too tired."

"No. No. Not at all." In fact, energy strong enough to run the Christmas lights suddenly zipped through her. "A ride sounds wonderful."

"You know what they say in this part of the country. Enjoy the snow fast." He rubbed his gloved hands together and smiled. "It will be gone tomorrow."

Lindsey's stomach went south. If she'd known a wagon ride would make him smile, she'd have suggested one sooner.

"Race ya to the shack," she said, eager to encourage his cheerful mood. "Last one to tell Jade is a rotten egg."

Before Jesse could react, she grabbed the advantage and took off in a hard run.

"Hey!" His boots thudded against the hard ground, and she watched his long shadow rapidly overtaking hers. Catching up in record time, Jesse nabbed her elbow. As if she'd reached the end of a bungee cord, Lindsey plummeted backward, banging into his chest.

He quickly righted her so that she wouldn't fall, and they stood staring at each other, smiling and panting. His strong, workman's hands held her by the upper arms. Bright Christmas lights around the window of the shack blinked off and on, bathing them in alternating shades of red and green.

Sushi leaped around their legs, barking in excitement.

"Cheater," he said, eyes twinkling an odd shade of blue in the rotating light.

He was inches away, his mouth so close and so tempting. She wanted him to kiss her.

The door to the Snack Shack opened behind them, and Jade called out in a worried voice. "Why is Sushi barking?" And then the child noticed the fluffy white flakes. "It's snowing!"

Coatless, she rushed outside and twirled around, grabbing for snowflakes, fear of the dog forgotten in her excitement.

Jesse dropped his hands and stepped away from Lindsey. A vague, but troubling disappointment crept over her. She had no business wanting more from Jesse than friendship. Crossing her arms, she hugged herself against the sudden cold.

"Get back inside and get your coat on," Jesse called, moving menacingly toward Jade.

The child yelped like a stepped-on pup and, giggling, bolted for the warm building. Jesse growled like a bear and gave chase.

Trying to forget that infinitesimal moment when she'd thought Jesse might kiss her, Lindsey followed them inside.

"Yay! Yay! Yay!" Jade cried, hopping and dancing and squealing in the wagon bed. She opened her mouth, trying to catch snowflakes on her tongue.

"Better get under those covers, Butterbean."

To Lindsey, the child's exuberance was a refreshing change from the frightened little girl of months ago. She still feared the dark and anything unfamiliar, but according to Jesse the nightmares had slowly disappeared, and she seemed so much easier in her own skin.

At her daddy's suggestion, though, Jade settled down and slid beneath the downy covers. She hummed happily.

After a double-check of Puddin's harness, Lindsey came around to step up into the wagon. Jesse appeared at her side, hand on her elbow, and guided her safely onto the bench. She felt both feminine and foolish, considering the number of times she'd boarded alone.

Sushi stood on the ground a few feet away, tail thumping madly, mouth open and smiling, begging to join the fun.

Lindsey twisted around. "Jade, Sushi wants to ride with us."

She let the suggestion hang in the air, waiting for the little girl to make the decision.

Jade levered up to peer over the side at the begging German shepherd who managed to look so pitiful Lindsey was hard-pressed not to laugh.

"Okay." Jade pointed toward the very end of the wagon. "Down there."

Lindsey rejoiced for the progress.

Jesse gave a quick look of gratitude and squeezed her hand.

Once the dog was safely ensconced, Jesse rattled the reins and Puddin' plodded forward. Jingle bells, attached to the sides, tickled the air and blended with Christmas carols still echoing from the sound system.

Jesse didn't complain about the carols anymore. Could he be healing?

Heart full and happy for reasons she hadn't yet considered, Lindsey clapped her hands and began singing at the top of her lungs.

Jesse laughed.

The beautiful, male sound thrilled her so much that she sang all the louder, standing in the wagon to throw her hands into the air.

"You're crazy, woman." And he laughed again.

Jade crawled from beneath her covers to join the rowdiness. Jesse shook his head. "Now you're corrupting my daughter."

Lindsey gave him a playful push. "Oh, come on, Scrooge, sing."

"You don't know what you're asking for." He guided the horse along the perimeter of the trees, turning down a wide alleyway. "For all you know, I can't carry a tune."

"You can't be that bad." When he only grinned, she taunted, "Can you?"

As she'd hoped, Jesse rose to the teasing challenge. In the next moment, all three were belting out a loud and energetic version of "Frosty the Snowman" with Jesse providing the "thumpety, thump, thump" at the appropriate time.

At the end of the song, they all laughed so hard, tears welled in Lindsey's eyes. Jade flopped onto the seat between the adults, pointing out every snowflake that landed on the horse's back, asking questions about angels and Jesus and Christmas. While the briskly refreshing air reddened noses and cheeks, the pleasure of a family feeling warmed Lindsey from the inside out. She loved this little girl as if she'd borne her.

At last, Jade's energy was exhausted, and she drooped against her daddy's side. He stopped the wagon.

"Looks like the princess is tuckered out," he said quietly.

Scooping her into his arms, he carried Jade to the wagon bed and gently placed her beneath the quilts.

Lindsey turned on the seat to watch them, heart overflowing as Jesse adjusted his daughter's covers, snugging them securely under her chin. When he bent to kiss the angel face, Lindsey knew what she'd been trying to deny for so long. She not only loved Jade.

She loved Jade's daddy.

She'd been building to this moment since the day he'd arrived. Over the weeks, he'd not only lightened her workload and given her great new ideas for the farm, he'd filled her with a new sense of purpose and joy.

Closing her eyes at the wonder and beauty of so tremendous an emotion, she felt the wagon give as Jesse returned to his seat.

"Ready to head for home?" he asked, his voice muted.

She turned to look at him and knew the light of love was there for him to see.

Snowflakes tumbled down and the ground resembled a sugar-sprinkled spice cake. Tips of tree branches were flocked white. Indeed, they needed to call it a night.

But she was reluctant to leave this cold cocoon that

had been spun around them here in the snowy, lighted grove.

"Whenever you are." The words came out in a whisper.

Shifting on the seat, he said, "You're snow-kissed," and rubbed his thumb across her lower lip.

He stared at her for two beats, then bent his head and brushed his lips over hers. Where her mouth was cold, his was warm and subtle and incredibly tender. So tender, tears sprang to her eyes.

When the kiss ended, their gazes held for the longest time.

"You're a very special lady, Lindsey Mitchell," he said at last and leaned his forehead against hers. His warm breath puffed softly against her skin, raising gooseflesh.

Pulse tripping madly, Lindsey caressed his cheek. "No more special than you—and that little girl back there."

Straightening, he took her hand and pulled her close beside him on the wagon seat. "We were both a mess when we met you. But you've changed us. And I'm grateful."

"I love her." She dare not say she loved him, too, though it was true. She'd never expected to trust enough to love again, but even with his faults and moods, Jesse had proven himself a thousand times over to be an honorable man.

She wanted to ask his feelings for her. He cared, yes, but love? She didn't know.

Lord, she thought, I need Your direction. I've waited so long to love someone again. But is Jesse the right one? Or have I been alone too long to see things clearly?

She loved Jesse. There was no doubt in her mind about

that, and real love was always from God. But as much as she loved him, Lindsey loved the Lord more. As long as Jesse had spiritual issues to resolve, she would do what she'd done for so long—wait upon the Lord, and pray that He would renew her strength. Because, if Jesse was wrong for her, it would take all the strength she had to get over him.

"Jade loves you too," Jesse replied. He gazed off into the dark woods. "I don't know what to do about that."

"Do?" His statement bewildered her. "Love is a good thing, Jesse, not a problem you have to fix."

"I don't want her to be hurt anymore. Erin—" He shifted in the seat, putting distance between them as if he'd somehow betrayed his dead wife by kissing Lindsey.

Suddenly, the hurtful words of days ago came back to her. "Are you afraid that if Jade cares for me, she'll forget her mother? That I'll replace Erin in Jade's life?"

He shook his head in denial, but Lindsey felt his withdrawal. Giving her hand a quick squeeze and release, he gathered the reins, shook them, and set the horse plodding forward.

The tinkling bells had lost their cheer.

Jesse had the strongest urge to grab his child, get in his truck and run. Instead, he guided the placid Puddin' out of the Christmas trees toward the barn.

The jingle of harness and the plod of hoofed feet were the only sounds to break the pristine night.

He could never run far enough to forget what had just happened between him and Lindsey.

Lindsey.

"She won't."

Jesse shifted his gaze to the parka-clad woman beside

him, mind too scattered to catch the drift of her conversation. "What?"

"Jade will remember Erin. Maybe not specifics, but she'll have memories. Most of all she'll remember the way her mother loved her."

"I hope so."

"She does. We've talked about it."

He blinked in surprise. "You and Jade talked about Erin?"

"She needs to talk about her mother, Jesse, to share her memories, to ask questions."

Discussing Erin had always hurt too much. He'd assumed Jade felt the same.

"What kind of questions could a six-year-old have?"

Lindsey blinked up at him. "Plenty. She asked me where her mama was now and if dying had hurt. Things like that."

"Oh, God." He squeezed his eyes closed. That his baby would worry about such things cut him to the quick.

"Yes. That's exactly what I told her. Because Erin was a Christian, she was with God now, in His big, wonderful house in Heaven."

"Did that upset her? Talking about her mother's death, I mean."

He'd never considered discussing such a horrible event with a child. And at the time, Jade had barely been four. Surely she couldn't remember that much.

"Just the opposite. She seemed happy, relieved. Her little mind had some things about that day very confused."

Jumping down from the wagon to open the barn door, Jesse frowned. "What kind of things?"

"For some reason, Jade thought she was to blame for her mother's death."

The old wooden door scraped back, clattering against the wall. Snow swirled up from the motion.

"Where would she get such a crazy idea?"

"Who knows? Children don't think like we do. They're egocentric. The world turns because of them. So when something bad happens, it must have been because they were bad."

"That's ridiculous."

"She said you were mad for a long time." She stuck a gloved hand out and caught a giant snowflake. "I tried to explain the difference between mad and sad."

Climbing back onto the cart, Jesse rattled the reins to send the horse into the barn.

"She was right. I was angry."

"That's normal, isn't it?"

"But I never dreamed Jade would take the blame on herself or think I was mad at her. She's my heart. My reason for going on."

"She's very secure in your love, Jesse. You're a good father." The lights from the barn reflected in her guileless eyes. "We're making a memory book. A Mama and Jade memory book."

Something turned over in Jesse's chest. "What's that?"

"Jade is drawing pictures of all the things she remembers about her mother. And I'm helping her write down other memories." She touched his arm. "She won't forget."

No. Jade wouldn't forget. Not with Lindsey around to gently, lovingly preserve those precious memories.

Wonder expanded inside him.

What kind of woman would nurture a dead woman's memory for the sake of a child? A woman she hadn't even known?

He had the overpowering desire to kiss her again. To hold her and tell her all that was in his heart.

Lindsey Mitchell was something special.

She was sweet and good. And loving.

Indecision warred within him. Feelings, long sublimated, rose to the surface. Falling for Lindsey Mitchell was the worst thing that could happen, for both of them. She deserved better. He cared about her. He cared a lot and didn't ever want to see her hurt. And hurting her would be the ultimate end of their relationship.

Part of him wanted to confess everything here and now and beg her forgiveness. But fear held him back. He'd enjoyed their sweet kiss. He'd seen the tenderness in her eyes, and he didn't want to replace that affection with loathing.

Lindsey valued honesty above everything, and he'd lied to her from the beginning. She'd never forgive him for his deceit.

And what about Erin? Being faithful to her was as important to him as remembering was to Jade. He'd made a promise at her funeral to take care of their little girl. Giving her this farm was the only way he knew how to keep that promise.

Oh, man. He was in a mess. For weeks, he'd envied Lindsey's easy way of praying, of turning troubles over to the Lord. More than anything, he wished he could do that now.

He'd known for a while that he wanted to kiss her. But tonight, she'd given him back his joy. He'd laughed and sung like a maniac—and enjoyed every crazy second.

Then when he'd looked around and had seen her surrounded by snowflakes, he'd no longer had the will to resist.

Long years from now when she was gone from this place, he'd recall the cold snow dissolving against her skin as he'd warmed her soft lips with his.

He drew the horse to a stop next to a stall, hopped to the ground and reached up for Lindsey. Swinging her down from the wagon, he stood with his hands on her waist. "I had fun."

"Me too." An ornery glint turned her eyes to gold. She poked a gloved finger into his chest. "And now that I know you can sing…"

He quirked a brow, glad they were still comfortable with one another. "Are you threatening blackmail?"

"Of course."

"A good Christian woman like you. What an example," he said mildly.

She whopped him on the arm and turned away to unharness the horse. Puddin' stood patiently waiting for his warm stall and extra feed.

"You didn't mind my talking to Jade about her mother, did you?"

"No. I'm glad." If he'd been a better father, he would have recognized the need.

"Good."

The barn grew silent. Outside, snow filtered down like feathers from angel wings. Jesse crossed to the feed bin. The rich scent of hay and sweet feed filled the shadowy barn.

"Jesse." Lindsey's hushed tone was serious again, warning him. His hand stilled on the galvanized feed bucket.

"Yeah?" He turned his head, but Lindsey stood with her back to him, her hands making absent circles on the horse's neck.

The bells on the harness jingled. Then another moment of silence passed. Jesse got a sinking feeling in the pit of his stomach.

Lindsey's shoulders rose and fell. The horse blew impatiently.

When she finally spoke, her smoky voice flowed out on a sigh. "I have feelings for you."

Jesse drew in a deep, sorrowful breath of horse-scented air and squeezed his eyes shut. He exhaled slowly, trying to control the riot inside his chest.

"I know," he said quietly. Dread, like a lead weight, pressed down on him. The last thing he needed right now was to get emotionally involved with a woman— especially this one. And yet, he was.

She gave a little self-deprecating laugh that hurt his heart. "Just wanted to get it out in the open. It won't affect our working together."

He'd never thought of Lindsey as anything but strong and capable. But she looked small and vulnerable beside the massive horse, her hair bunched around the neck of her coat in a child-like tangle.

What did he say without hurting her? The truth? That he'd come here under false pretenses. That he planned to take away the farm she worked so hard to hold on to? Did he tell her he felt something, too, but old grievances were too deeply engrained to turn back now?

He shook his head ruefully. No, the truth would hurt her most of all.

Pouring the sweet feed into the trough, he waited

for the noise to subside and then said the only thing he could. "Not a problem."

Liar, he thought, his insides rattling like hail on the tin roof of his trailer.

Lindsey's feelings were a major problem.

And so were his own.

Chapter Twelve

Desperation drove Jesse down the curvy mountain road on Sunday morning. Desperation also allowed Jade to attend Sunday school with Lindsey at Winding Stair Chapel. Jesse dare not take Jade where he was going.

The only way to avoid more suffering on the part of everyone involved was to bring the situation to its rightful end. He'd give Stuart Hardwick one more opportunity to come clean and then he'd find his own lawyer and go to the sheriff. The story could break out into the open soon and Lindsey could discover the truth about him.

His chest tightened. Both were bound to happen anyway.

He wished he'd never met Lindsey Mitchell.

No. That wasn't true. He wished she didn't live on the property that belonged to him.

He never should have kissed her. The memory of her sweetness stayed with him like the haunting lyrics of a bittersweet song.

Halfway down the mountain, he passed the turn to Clarence Stone's place and slowed the Silverado, bringing the truck to a stop in the middle of the muddy road.

A coyote leaped from the field and loped across in front of him. Jesse watched the wild, wily creature disappear.

He had taken a liking to the old farmer and had the strongest urge to drive up and talk to him.

He glanced at the clock on the dashboard.

"The guy's probably in church already," he muttered.

Just the same, he threw the truck into reverse, backed up and made the turn. All the way up the road, he questioned his own reasoning.

A talk with Stuart Hardwick was pressing. So why was he on his way to see a man he hardly knew? To talk? To somehow reassure himself that taking back the farm was the right thing to do?

The idea scared him. Nobody, but nobody was going to talk him out of that farm.

Mud splattered against the side of the truck as the road narrowed and curved sharply upward. In minutes, the lane dead-ended at a small frame house surrounded by a knee-high white fence. Two dogs of questionable heritage leaped from the front porch to loudly herald his arrival.

The front door, gaily decked with a holiday wreath, opened immediately. Jingle bells swayed merrily with the movement. Loraine Stone's face appeared, then disappeared as Jesse stepped down from the truck and slammed the door.

Clarence shoved the old-fashioned storm door open. "Come in here, boy. Good to see you."

The snow had disappeared almost as quickly as it had come, leaving behind wet, soggy ground.

Jesse picked his way across the spongy yard and carefully wiped his boots on the welcome mat before stepping into the warm living room. The scent of recently fried bacon hung in the air.

"Well, Jesse. What brings you down the mountain this morning?"

He was wondering the same thing himself.

Taking in Clarence's church attire, he shifted uncomfortably. "I guess you're about to leave for church. I don't want to delay you."

"Don't worry about that. Sit down and tell me what's on your mind." Clarence pushed a drowsy cat to one side and joined her in a big flowered easy chair, relaxing as if he had nothing better to do than sit and visit. "A feller doesn't drive back up in here on a muddy day for no reason."

Jesse took the couch opposite him, thinking he should be in Mena by now.

"I don't really know why I stopped by."

One corner of the old man's mouth twitched as if he knew why. The notion irritated Jesse somewhat.

"Anything to do with Lindsey?"

"No." But the denial came too quickly. Leaning his elbows on his thighs, he clarified. "Partly."

Clarence studied him for a minute while scratching the cat behind one ear. His wife appeared in the living room, dressed for church and carrying a shiny black purse.

"You want me to go on, hon?" she asked.

Jesse leaped to his feet. "No, I'll go. We can talk again some other time." Since he had no idea why he'd come here, he might as well leave. And he had no intention of coming back again.

Clarence gestured him down. "You stay put. The Lord has a reason for you showing up on my doorstep on Sunday morning."

The Lord? Not since coming to Winding Stair had

Jesse considered that God was interested in anyone's day-to-day activities. But according to Lindsey and her friends, God cared about everything.

Loraine Stone leaned down and pecked her husband on the cheek. "You might take a peek at that roast after a while."

Purse hooked over one elbow and a fabric-covered Bible in her hand, she left, acting neither upset nor surprised that her husband had stayed behind to talk to a virtual stranger. Clarence had once referred to himself as a good listener. Maybe others made this trek up the mountain to seek wisdom from the old guy.

Jesse wanted to laugh. Seeking wisdom sounded a bit too mystical for his comfort.

In minutes, the putter of a car engine sounded and then faded in the distance.

"You want some coffee, son?"

"No, thanks. I really should go. I have some business to attend to in Mena." But he didn't get up.

Clarence rose and got them both a cup of coffee anyway. Setting the mug on the polished coffee table in front of Jesse, he said, "Mind my asking what kind of business a man conducts on Sunday morning?"

As a matter of fact, Jesse did mind. "Personal."

Settling back into the chair, Clarence adjusted the cat before asking the same question again, "Have anything to do with Lindsey?"

"No." Jesse shook his head to clear away the lie. "Yes."

Clarence's grin gleamed in the sunlight that sliced a space between the drapes. "When your mind's made up, you're full of indecision, ain't ya, boy?"

The gentle jab brought a smile. "I have a problem, Clarence. And I don't know what to do about it."

"I don't either. But I know Someone who does."

Jesse knew what was coming. For once, he didn't mind. He was just grateful that Clarence hadn't asked for details about his problem.

"The Lord knows everything." Clarence paused to blow across the top of his coffee and sipped lightly before continuing. "He has the answer to every question and every problem every time."

"You make it sound easy."

"Nothing easy about living right in this crazy world. But letting God direct your path and trusting that He has everything under control is as easy as pie."

"I don't know how to go about that."

"Just start by talking to Him. He's like any other friend. The more you visit, the closer you get."

"I never thought of God as a friend." Jesse took the coffee from the table and studied the warm mug between his palms, pondering God as an approachable being. That wasn't the way he'd been taught, but he'd observed that kind of attitude in Lindsey.

"Well, He is. Jesus is the best friend you'll ever have. And He's always there to listen to your troubles and to help you work out the answers."

"Is that it? Just pray and the answer will come?"

"Most of the time. But remember that God ain't Santa Claus. He'll give you what you need, and that's not always what you want."

To Jesse the words seemed like a warning. A warning he didn't want to hear.

"But doesn't a man have a right to do what he believes is best?" The heat of the room coupled with his heavy jacket increased the pressure building inside him. He clinked the mug onto the table, shoulders bunching forward in tension. "Shouldn't I fight for what I know is rightfully mine?"

He caught himself and stopped, having almost said too much.

"Rights. We sure hear a lot about people's rights these days." Clarence's voice was conversational as if he hadn't noticed the edge in Jesse's words. "But when I get to thinking about Jesus and what He did for us, I know we've become a self-centered world, too stuck on our own desires. Jesus could have demanded His rights— and gotten them. But He chose to do what was best for others instead of what was easy for Himself."

Jesse thought about that, his chest tight with indecision. Clarence had something special in his life just as Lindsey did, but the old man couldn't possibly understand what he'd been through. Clarence had a home and stability and people who cared for him.

A small voice pecked at his conscience. Everyone had heartache. Just because he didn't know about theirs, didn't mean they hadn't suffered too.

"Anything you'd like me to pray with you about, Jesse?"

Jesse declined with a shake of his head. "No, thanks, but I appreciate the offer."

He stood to leave. Clarence pushed the lazy calico cat to one side and followed suit.

"Well, I'll be praying for you anyway. You'll make the right decision. Whatever that may be."

Jesse only hoped Clarence was right, because regardless of all that had been said, they'd solved nothing. Not that he'd expected to, but he'd had hope. He was as confused as he had been before. Only now, he'd wasted thirty minutes of precious time.

There was nothing left for him to do but resume the trip to Mena and try once more to change the mind of a certain crooked lawyer with a drinking problem.

The stars were bright that night—as bright, Lindsey imagined, as they had been on the first Christmas. The inky sky resembled diamonds on black velvet, sparkling and twinkling with such beauty, she wanted to stand forever here in the cold, hands in her coat, head tilted back to take in the wonder of God's creation.

"The sky does look pretty, doesn't it?" From behind her, Jesse's boots thudded softly against the hard ground.

It was closing time. He had turned off the music for the night and all but the security lights were now dark. Quiet lay over the land like a reverent prayer.

Turning, she smiled up at him. Her pulse bounded, reacting as it always did now that she knew she loved him. Having him here and near was enough, she'd told herself. Loving him was enough.

Jesse hadn't said a word about her admission that she cared for him. And she was grateful. Unless he could return her feelings, anything he might say would only embarrass them both.

At church, she'd prayed especially hard to understand the Lord's leading. Maybe Jesse and Jade had been sent for her to help them find the healing they needed. Maybe she'd been meant to love them back to health and then to let them go. She didn't know.

Pastor Cliff had preached on the scripture, "Trust in the Lord with all your heart and lean not unto your own understanding," and the message had seemed ready-made for her. But following through with the advice wasn't easy.

"I like to think about the days when God created the world. What an awesome thing to know He made all this beauty just for us to enjoy. He must love us so much more than we can ever understand."

"Pretty amazing, all right." Jesse stared into the distance, the line of his face pensive. "I'm going out to feed the horse. Want to come with me?"

Though they'd already taken Puddin' and his wagon to the barn, a belated customer had interrupted them. The horse hadn't been properly groomed or fed.

She shook her head, though the temptation to spend every minute in his company was great. "Jade's finishing up your Christmas present. I told her I'd help her wrap it before you left tonight. She wants it under her tree at home."

She waited for his eyes to frost over and his face to close up the way it always did when Christmas gifts were mentioned. But this time proved different. Though he looked serious, he nodded. "She's getting pretty fired-up about Christmas."

"Have you bought her a present yet?" She knew Jesse had ignored Christmas last year. And Jade remembered all too well.

"No." He jammed his hands into his pockets.

"I could go shopping for you if you'd like."

"I'll do it."

Happiness bubbled up inside her. "You will?"

He shrugged and a grudging grin tugged at his mouth.

Before she could think better of the action, Lindsey threw her arms round his waist and laughed. When she started to pull away, Jesse held on a moment longer before letting her go.

"I'll be back in a few minutes." He started off across the semi-darkened field toward the barn.

"Don't hurry. Jade and I need time to wrap a certain present."

His chuckle echoed back to her on the chilly night breeze.

Suddenly lighthearted, Lindsey rushed inside the Snack Shack. The warm scent of sugar cookies made her stomach growl. She snitched a broken one and took a bite.

"Where's Daddy?" Jade was at the table laboring over the specially designed and decorated candies Lindsey had helped her make. From the looks of them, the finishing touches were almost in place.

"Gone to feed Puddin'."

The child looked up, affronted. "He said I could help him."

"I'm sorry, sweetie. I guess he forgot." Lindsey took some wrapping paper from beneath the counter and laid the roll on the table.

"I can catch up." Jade rushed to the door and shouted into the darkness. "Daddy, wait! I'm coming."

"What about wrapping your daddy's present?"

"You do it. Please, Lindsey. I saved something 'specially for Puddin'." She struggled into her coat, small fingers fumbling with the zipper until Lindsey reached down to help.

Lindsey followed her to the door and watched as she ran across the grass in pursuit of Jesse, pleased that Jade had a treat for the horse she'd once considered too big and scary.

The barn was less than a hundred yards away and Lindsey spotted Jesse's shadowy form beneath the diffused security lights. Satisfied that Jade would overtake her daddy, she turned back inside.

With a heart filled with gladness, she set to work wrapping Jesse's gift. Using candy molds, Lindsey had helped Jade create hearts and angels and various other chocolate delights for her daddy. Tonight Jade had added sprinkles and nuts.

After wrapping each piece in plastic wrap, Lindsey placed the treats into a pretty decorated tin she'd saved from last year. She wrapped the present and placed a big red bow on top, then set about cleaning up the Snack Shack for the night.

She was washing the coffeepot when the door opened and Jesse stepped inside. A small draught of cold air snaked in with him.

Smiling, she opened her mouth to speak, but the words died in her throat.

He was alone.

"Where's Jade?"

He looked around the room as if he expected the child to jump from beneath the table or from behind a chair. "Isn't she here?"

Slowly, Lindsey replaced the glass carafe and shook her head. "No. She wanted to go with you. I watched her until she was almost caught up. Didn't you see her?"

"Yes, but she came back here. She gave me a piece of apple for the horse. Then she said she was coming back to help you."

Lindsey pressed a hand to her mouth and fought down fear. "Where is she?"

"I don't know," Jesse answered grimly. "But I aim to find out."

He yanked the door open with such force the Shack rattled.

Going into the yard, he cupped his hands around his mouth and bellowed. "Jade!"

Trembling, Lindsey threw on her coat and followed. "I'll check the house."

"I'll head back to the barn."

They took off in a dead run, both returning in minutes without Jade. Lindsey had taken the time to grab her rifle and a pocketful of ammunition. If they had to go into the woods, they'd need it. Jesse eyed the weapon but didn't comment.

Together they searched the other out-buildings and the tree lot, calling Jade's name over and over, but there was no sign of the little girl.

Lindsey had thought she was panic-proof, but anxiety knotted her stomach and the nerves in her neck.

"She's terrified of the dark. Where could she be?"

"We know she was between here and the barn, so let's walk a circle around that area. If we don't find her, we'll widen the circle until we do. She's out here somewhere."

And likely crying her eyes out. The night was cold and dark, except for the stars. And there were wild animals in the woods and mountains behind Lindsey's farm.

Taking flashlights from the Snack Shack, they searched the grounds and then the area around the barn until finally reaching the wooded treeline that led up into the mountain.

"Surely, she wouldn't have gone into the woods alone," Lindsey said.

"Unless she got confused or something scared her

and she ran without thinking." Suddenly, he stopped and shone his flashlight all around Lindsey. "Where is Sushi?"

"I don't know. She was outside earlier. I assumed she'd followed you to the barn." As soon as the words were out, she knew what Jesse was thinking. "Sushi wouldn't do anything to scare Jade. She knew Jade was easily frightened."

His jaw clenched, unconvinced. "Then where is she?"

"Maybe she went along with Jade, to protect her."

"Or maybe she chased her into the woods. Maybe she's the reason Jade ran away in the darkness."

"I don't believe that."

"Can you think of any other reason Jade would take off this way?"

She couldn't, but she also wouldn't believe the protective, loving German shepherd was responsible for Jade's disappearance. If anything, Sushi had followed Jade because she loved her and was worried about her. Convincing Jesse of that, however, was another matter.

"We'll find her, Jesse."

His jaw clenched and unclenched in barely controlled anger. "If that dog has hurt her, I'll kill it with my bare hands."

His assumption of the worst angered her. "You'd better be more concerned about the real dangers out there."

"The real danger is the one I know about."

"Sushi is not a danger. She wouldn't harm anyone unless they threatened me. Jade was even beginning to accept her company."

"And maybe that wasn't a good thing. If you hadn't forced the situation, Jade wouldn't have felt she had to accept the dog to please you."

Hurt pierced her like a sharp nail. "That's not true. Jade knew I was trying to help her."

"Yeah? Well, look where that got us." He jerked around and stalked off into the darkness, calling back over his shoulders. "I mean it, Lindsey. That dog is dead if she's harmed my daughter."

Lindsey felt as if he'd slapped her. Did he really believe she'd force Jade to do something that would ultimately harm her? Did he really believe she'd bring an animal into Jade's life that would turn on her?

She trembled, not from cold, but from the harshness of Jesse's accusations. Tears burned inside her throat. Stiffening her spine, she swallowed and shook them off. Her own heartache had to take a backseat to the current crisis. She would cry later. Right now, a scared little girl waited.

Take care of her, Lord. And help us find her safe and sound.

She hoisted the rifle onto her shoulder, aimed the flashlight into the cold night...

And started walking.

Chapter Thirteen

Sometime after midnight the wind died, and the temperature hovered in the upper thirties. Above the shadowy forest, the Milky Way smeared the indigo sky and stars danced and twinkled.

So beautiful…and so scary for a little girl alone.

Cold and more worried than he had ever been in his life, Jesse huddled deeper into his fleece jacket and thought about going back to the house to call the police. But Winding Stair was a small town manned by one police officer per shift. By the time the officer rounded up a search party, morning would be here. Surely, he'd find Jade before then.

Stomping on through the woods, twigs and branches snapping beneath his feet, he thought of how terrified Jade must be. Every sound magnified in the silence. For a child who feared the dark and suffered nightmares, the dark woods held unfathomable terrors.

He envisioned her as she'd been in the barn. Though warmly dressed in her coat and heavy jeans, her hood had been down. Would she think to put it up?

Was she cold? Was she crying? Was she hurt?

The torments of not knowing ate at him like hungry wolves.

For the first two hours he'd run on adrenaline. Now he was running on sheer determination.

From in front of him came a scratching, rustling noise.

A dark form loomed, and, with a swift surge of hope, he rushed forward. His boots snagged on twisted, twining tree roots growing above ground. He stumbled but managed to catch himself on the rough bark of an ancient blackjack, jarring his wrists in the process.

A startled possum drew back to hiss a warning, beady red eyes aglow in the flashlight beam. Jesse sagged in disappointment and hoped Jade didn't encounter any nocturnal animals.

He hoped she didn't encounter Sushi either.

Trudging onward, deeper into the thickening woods, he called her name over and over.

"Jade!"

The call was swallowed up in the dense trees. He paused to listen, longing for the answering call. Only the awful silence of a dark winter's night replied.

He had to find her. Soon. He was a grown man and the cold and fatigue was wearing on him. How could a child hold out for long?

Fear and dread pulled at him, much stronger than the weariness.

If anything had happened to his baby, he couldn't go on. He would have no reason.

Another hour passed with no sign of the dark-haired angel. He found himself murmuring half-formed prayers.

"Please help me find her. Please protect her."

The weight on his chest grew until he thought he'd smother. Finally, when he could bear the stress no longer, he cried out, half in anger, half in hope-filled despair. "God, are You listening? Do You care?"

An owl hooted in the distance and, had the situation not been so serious, Jesse would have laughed. Leave it to Jesse Slater to pray to God and be answered by an owl.

But he didn't know what else to do. Lindsey believed in prayer. Clarence said God always answered, one way or the other. The way he figured it, no one was out here to hear him anyway or to know that Jesse had lost his reason along with his daughter. Praying would keep his mind from considering all the terrifying possibilities. And it sure couldn't hurt anything.

His prayers began in desperation.

"Lord, I know You're up there watching. I've always believed You were real, but I don't know You very well. Not like Lindsey and Clarence do. I have no right to ask favors, but maybe You'll do this one thing for Jade. Help me find her, Lord. Show me where she is."

A tree branch sliced across his face. He jerked back, fingered the skin and dismissed the scratch as inconsequential.

"Take care of her, God. Don't let her be scared. I know she is. I promised Erin I'd take care of our baby. Now look what I've done. I've lost her." A cry of grief pushed at his windpipe. "Don't let anything happen to her. I beg You not to take her, too."

The words of his prayer became jumbled, tumbling out from a heart filled with fear and seasoned with suffering.

"Was it me, Lord? Have I done something so bad that everyone I love gets taken away? Mama and Erin are gone. Don't take Jade. I'll do anything. Anything."

Somewhere—far too close for comfort—coyotes yipped and howled, raising the hair on Jesse's neck.

Pausing next to an outcropping of boulders, he shouted, "Jade! Jade!" until his voice broke.

As he collapsed exhausted onto the rocks, tears gathered behind his eyelids. He hadn't let himself cry when Erin died, fearing his grief would be too terrible for Jade to witness. Truth be told, he hadn't cried in a long time.

"Oh, God, I don't know what to do. She's out there and she's scared." He buried his cold, damp face in gloved hands. "Please help me."

Clarence claimed God was a friend who cared, who longed for friendship in return. Could that be true? All these years, he'd assumed he was last on God's Christmas list. Could he have been wrong all this time?

He began to pray in earnest then, pouring out the sorrow and agony of his past as if God didn't already know his life story. And yet the telling cleansed him, released him from the torment and anger he'd harbored so long, as though God Himself took on the load and carried his sorrows away.

He didn't know how long he sat there talking, but when he raised his face to the star-sprinkled heavens he was a new man—still terribly afraid for his child, but renewed in a way he couldn't begin to explain or understand.

All these years he'd thought God had abandoned him. But now he saw as clearly as he saw the Milky Way above—he'd been the one to pull away and forget the Lord. Now he understood what Lindsey had meant when she'd said that God would never leave or forsake us. God didn't. But man did.

At the reminder of Lindsey, regret pushed into his

consciousness. Every time his own guilt started to eat at him, he lashed out at her, and he'd done it again tonight over the dog.

Maybe Jade had become frightened and run away from Sushi, but he couldn't blame Lindsey for that. She only meant good for Jade. She loved her.

And she loved him.

"Lord, I'm so unworthy. Of her. Of You. I hope she can forgive me." He raised his head and stared into the heavens. "I hope You will too."

A gentle warmth, startling in the cold, suffused him as if someone had draped an electric blanket over his shoulders.

With restored courage and a Friend to guide him, he pushed off the boulder and set out to find his daughter.

At the first gray promise of morning, Jesse turned back and headed out of the woods. All through the long night, he'd walked and searched and prayed. Twice he and Lindsey had crossed paths and then parted again to cover more ground. The wooded area expanded to the north and eventually became a state park. There were miles and miles to cover if Jade had gone in that direction. Now, he had little choice but to call in a search team.

Eyes scratchy and dry from cold and sleeplessness, he continued to strain at every shadow, hoping, praying. He was peering beneath a low-hanging cedar when a terrifying sound raised the hair on his neck.

Growling, snarling animal sounds—whether of dog or coyote or wolf, he couldn't tell—came from somewhere to his left. Breaking into a dead run, he headed toward the sound.

A gunshot ripped the morning quiet. Birds flapped

up from the trees, filling the air with rushing wings and frightened calls.

Jesse's heart jump-started. Though beyond weary, the rush of adrenaline propelled him faster.

Barking and snarling became louder, and he recognized the sound—a dog. Sushi.

Fear mixed with anger whipped through him.

Breaking through the dense growth of trees, he glimpsed a purple coat. A small form, black hair spilled out all around, lay curled on the ground. Sushi, hair raised and teeth bared, stood over her.

Heart in his throat, Jesse cried out. "Jade!"

The dog spun toward the voice just as Lindsey arrived from the opposite direction.

"Daddy, Daddy!" Jade sat up, gripping Sushi's neck as though the dog was a lifeline.

Everything was happening too fast. Jesse couldn't comprehend anything except the sight of his little girl on the ground and the dog standing over her. Rushing forward, he fell to the earth and yanked Jade into his arms, away from the animal.

"Are you all right? Did the dog bite you? Did she hurt you?" Pushing her a little away, he frantically checked her for injuries. Her cheeks were red and her face dirty, but otherwise she appeared all right.

Lindsey's smoky voice, strained with exhaustion came toward them. She still carried the flashlight and her gun. "Sushi didn't hurt her, Jesse. She protected her."

Pressing his child close to him for warmth and safety, he looked up into Lindsey's red-rimmed eyes.

"What do you mean? She was standing over Jade's helpless body, ready to attack."

"No, Daddy, no." Jade pulled his face around to gain

his full attention. "Sushi tried to fight the bad dogs that came."

Jesse blinked in bewilderment. "Bad dogs?"

He looked at the German shepherd sitting a few feet away, and then toward the woods from whence Lindsey had come.

His mind began to clear and reason returned. Lindsey had fired the shots and followed something into those woods. "Coyotes?"

Carefully placing her rifle on the ground, Lindsey knelt in front of him. With a soft smile, she stroked Jade's tangled hair. "Coyotes don't usually approach humans, but she was small and still and probably looked vulnerable. I heard Sushi's warning growl and arrived in time to chase them off. Thank God."

A shiver ripped through Jesse. He squeezed his eyes closed against the unthinkable image of Jade and a pack of coyotes. "Yes. Thank God."

Lindsey noticed the words of praise. Her eyes questioned him, but she made no comment. As naturally as if he'd done it forever, he pulled Lindsey against his other side and held her there. His girls, one on each side, where he wanted them.

"And Sushi, too, Daddy," Jade insisted. "She stayed the night with me. She snuggled me up and made me be warm. I cried, but she licked my face."

Jesse's heart ached at the image of his daughter alone and afraid and crying. But he was happy too, and relieved beyond words.

"Where were you, sweetheart? How did you get lost?"

Jade pointed at the sky. Her knit gloves were dirty and loaded with bits of grass and twigs.

"I wanted the star."

Lindsey appeared as puzzled as he. "What star, Jade?"

"The falling star. For Daddy." She cupped a hand over her mouth and leaned toward Lindsey. In a conspiratorial whisper, she said, "For a present. So he would like Christmas again."

A lump filled Jesse's throat. Jade had ventured into the dark and frightening night alone to capture a shooting star for him. To make him happy.

He pressed his face into her hair, chest aching enough to burst. "Oh, baby. Daddy's so sorry."

She patted his ears. "It's okay, Daddy. I didn't find the star, and I got lost. But my guarding angel was with me, just like Lindsey said. Sushi and me went to sleep, and I wasn't scared anymore."

The German shepherd sat on her haunches, tail sweeping the brown earth, eyes shining as if she knew she'd done a good thing. With a final hug, Jade pushed up from Jesse's lap and went to embrace the big furry dog.

"Sushi is my friend."

Who would think a guardian angel had a fur coat and four legs?

His gaze locked with Lindsey's.

Or had another kind of angel protected his daughter?

"I owe you an apology, and this dog a T-bone steak," he told Lindsey.

She shook her head, tangled, windblown hair swinging around her tired face. He thought she looked beautiful. "No apologies or steaks are needed. We can thank God He used Sushi to protect Jade when we couldn't."

"I was wrong about the dog." Now was his chance to tell her the rest. "I've been wrong about a lot of things. But last night, when I was scared out of my mind, God and I had a long talk."

Hope sprang into her expression. "You did?"

They were cold and tired and needed to get back to the house, but some things couldn't wait to be told.

"You were right. God was here all the time, waiting for me to make the first move. I'm only sorry I waited so long."

"Oh, Jesse." Lindsey threw her arms around his neck and kissed his rough, unshaven cheek. Then, as if she regretted the spontaneous act, she drew back, blushing.

Her golden eyes were inches away and the look of love was there for any fool to see. Suddenly all his reservations faded away as easily as the daybreak had chased away the night.

He loved Lindsey Mitchell. He wondered why he'd fought it so long. She was everything good and beautiful he wanted in his life.

He waited, expecting to be engulfed with guilt because of Erin. This time the feeling never came. Loving Lindsey in no way negated the love he'd had for his wife, but Erin was gone, and she would have handed him his head for not letting her go sooner. She would have expected him to take care of their daughter and to get on with living.

And that's exactly what he intended to do.

"Come back here, woman." Elbow locked around her neck, he drew Lindsey close again. He hardly noticed the cold ground seeping through his clothes. "A kiss on the cheek won't cut it."

Her eyes widened, but she didn't pull away.

With a silent prayer of thanks, Jesse bent his head and kissed Lindsey's sweet mouth.

"What was that?" she asked when they parted, her voice even huskier after a night in the cold.

"Something amazing has happened. Something I thought was impossible. I have a lot of things to tell you later, when we're rested and warm, but there's one thing that can't wait." He cupped her cheek, unable to take his eyes off her, now that he recognized the truth. "I love you, Lindsey."

A multitude of emotions played over her face.

"Oh, Jesse, I'm going to cry."

He winced in mock horror. "Don't even think about it. At least, not until you say you love me too."

Eyes glistening with unshed tears, she stroked a hand over his jaw. "I do. With everything in me."

Jesse's heart filled to the bursting point. This woman had done so much for him. She'd made him a better man than he'd ever dreamed of being. She'd loved him in a way that healed the gaping wound he'd carried around inside for so long. And most of all, she'd led him back to the Lord.

The morning sun broke over the eastern horizon, orange as a pumpkin, and as bright as the new light shining in Jesse's soul.

The increasing temperature was welcome, but the morning air was still cold enough to be uncomfortable.

"Time to get you and the butterbean back to the house."

"Time to go to work," she argued, but didn't move from her place in his arms. "Customers won't wait, no matter how tired we are."

Customers. All night, he'd been so preoccupied with finding his daughter that he hadn't thought of the long day ahead.

"I'll take care of the farm today." He kissed her on

the nose and then set her on her feet. "You and Jade will have a good breakfast and plenty of sleep."

"I'll argue with you later," she said. "Right now that breakfast sounds too tempting to pass up."

Jesse chuckled, shaking his head at this special woman. He'd have to lock her in the house to keep her away from the tree patch, no matter how much sleep she did or didn't get. As for himself, he felt as invigorated as if he'd slept for days.

Holding hands, they started toward Jade. The little lost angel jogged around in circles with Sushi, appearing unfazed by her eventful night.

"From the looks of her, Jade had a lot more sleep than either of us."

"Thanks to Sushi," Jesse admitted.

A soft smile curved Lindsey's mouth. The light in her eyes spoke volumes. "And her guardian angel."

The situation with the farm and his rightful ownership tried to press in, but Jesse shoved the thoughts away. Right now, he wanted to bask in all the good things that had come from this strange night. Today he was happy to love and be loved. He'd worry about his dilemma some other time.

Chapter Fourteen

"Hey, woman, get a move on." Eyes twinkling and step jaunty, Jesse burst through the front door of the farmhouse bringing the chill with him. "All work and no play—"

He stopped in his tracks when he spotted her.

"Whoa." A slow smile eased the perpetual sadness from his eyes. "If I'd known you'd look like that, I would have offered to take you Christmas shopping a long time ago."

Lindsey blushed, pleased but discomfited by the unaccustomed praise. "Slacks and a sweater aren't that impressive, Jesse."

He pumped his eyebrows. "Says who?"

Lindsey laughed, unable to resist this teasing, happy version of the man she loved. Since that anxiety-filled night of searching for the lost Jade, he'd been full of good humor and unbounded joy.

"I suppose after seeing me in pine-covered jeans and boots every day, anything is an improvement."

"What about me, Daddy? Am I pretty too?" Jade

preened, showing off the red bow holding back her black satin hair.

"You are stunning." He swooped the child into his arms and blew onto her neck. Her giggle filled the room and brought Sushi in to investigate the commotion.

Jesse eased Jade to the floor and scratched the dog's ears. "Tom and his boy are all set to handle everything while we're gone. Any last-minute instructions you want to give them?"

Tom's teenage son had worked part-time for Lindsey last year and knew how the tree farm operated. She had no qualms about leaving the pair from her church in charge while she, Jesse and Jade spent a few hours in Mena. She looked forward to an afternoon of shopping, having dinner, and spending quality time with this pair that had won her heart.

"Tom and Jeff can handle it." She reached for his rough hand and squeezed, grateful and so full of love she could hardly see straight. "Thanks for thinking of this. I know how you feel about crowds and shopping."

He shrugged off the idea that he'd done anything special. "Everyone needs time off, even the invincible pioneer woman on Winding Stair Mountain."

She laughed. "I don't feel too invincible sometimes." Most of the time, to tell the truth.

She'd never admitted until now that she had insulated herself here on the mountain. Pastor Cliff had tried to talk to her once, and his gentle assessment had been correct. She'd used the tree farm as an excuse to distance herself from everyone but her church family, afraid of being hurt, afraid to trust.

Two nights ago, during their search for Jade, when Jesse had declared his love, her own fears had evaporated like morning mist. She'd seen Jesse's hard work around the farm, experienced his constant efforts to improve the place and to lighten her tasks. And she knew he was totally dedicated to his child. But there was something to the adage that adversity bonds.

Her gaze strayed to him, busily getting Jade into her coat and gloves. Jesse Slater's love had changed her. Something she'd never thought possible had happened. She trusted this good man with her life.

Most important of all, she trusted him with her heart.

A short time later in Mena, Jesse remained mildly surprised that he'd not only agreed to this trip, he'd suggested it. But Lindsey had that effect on him. He'd do anything in his power to see her smile. So here he was, in a crowded store where cashiers wore red Santa hats, Bing Crosby crooned "White Christmas" over the intercom, and he was almost enjoying himself.

Almost.

He would rather be on the farm or at a quiet little restaurant somewhere, but observing Lindsey's pleasure in such a simple outing made up for the discomfort on his part.

He let his gaze roam over the stacks of cologne sets, gloves, wallets, candy and back massagers. From floor to ceiling the place reeked of Christmas.

With a wry shake of his head, he realized how far he'd come—from a Scrooge who hated Christmas to a man in love who wanted to please his woman. And he couldn't think of anything in the world good enough to give her.

"What do you think, Jesse?" Lindsey held some kind of computer software box in one hand. "Would a boy like this?"

From the looks of her basket, Lindsey was buying for every kid in her church. "Depends on the boy. I always wanted sports stuff."

He'd gotten that kind of thing too before his mother had become ill. Those last two years before she died, he'd received nothing. Les Finch wasn't much of a shopper. Reason enough for him to do better.

A disembodied voice interrupted the music to remind kids that Santa was available in the toy department for picture-taking.

Jade, who'd been examining every baby doll on the shelf, tugged at his hand and requested for the fourth time, "Let's go see Santa."

Jesse was about to refuse when Lindsey caught his eye. "That might be a good idea, Dad," she said. "You two go back there while I do a little bit of *special* shopping."

She put enough emphasis on the word special that Jesse got the idea. She wanted to shop for Jade.

A frisson of energy passed between them. Maybe she wanted to shop for him too. His stomach lifted at the notion.

On the other hand, maybe the sensation was hunger pains. Dinner was beginning to sound good.

"Will you be ready to have dinner by then?"

Fingers curled around the handle of the shopping cart, she questioned pointedly, "Don't you have some shopping of your own to do?"

Jesse suppressed a shudder. Walking around in a huge department store, he could handle. But the pleasure in hassling through the jammed check-outs evaded him. He'd planned to buy Jade's gifts in Winding Stair. Run in the store, grab the doll, pay for it and run out. His way seemed much less trying.

"I don't suppose I could convince you to pick up a couple of things for me," he said hopefully.

Her cart was already littered with items. What would a few more matter? She knew what he wanted to buy Jade because they'd discussed it this morning over the phone.

A knowing twinkle lit her eyes. "Have we pushed you beyond the limits any male can endure?"

With a tilt of his head, he grinned. "Getting close."

Pushing up the sleeve of her blue sweater, Lindsey looked at her watch. "Okay. Tell you what. I'll gather up those last things and meet you back at the truck in thirty minutes. I'm starting to get antsy about leaving the farm for so long anyway."

He frowned. "Tom and Jeff will do fine."

"I know, but I don't want to impose on their kindness forever." She took a box of candy canes from the shelf and placed them in the basket, never mentioning the fact that she was paying her friends good money to run the tree lot. "Besides, shopping does me in, too. I'm always anxious to get back home to my peaceful little farm."

He studied her face, noticing the softness that appeared whenever she talked of her home. Guilt tugged at him. He'd been doing a lot of thinking about his claim on that place.

Looking around to see if anyone was listening, he leaned toward her and whispered, "I love you."

With a parting wink at her blushing face, he and Jade jostled their way toward the back of the store.

He did love Lindsey. And she loved him. And he hoped the words just now hadn't been spoken out of guilt. The farm was an issue that could tear them apart and change her loving to loathing. He couldn't bear that, not now that he'd recaptured the joy sorely missing in his life for so long.

Over the last few days, he'd spent a lot of time praying for answers about the Christmas Tree Farm, but the continual nag of doubt and worry plagued him yet. He had a right to that farm. He must have said that to the Lord a hundred times. Then he'd remember what Clarence said about rights, and how sometimes there was a big difference between being right and doing right.

Hurting Lindsey was wrong, regardless of his true claim to the land. She trusted him—a huge leap of faith on her part. She put a lot of stock in loyalty and truth. If she discovered his original motive had been to repossess her land, would she reject him? Would her heart be broken at his deceit?

A lady elf, garbed in form-fitting tights and a short skirt greeted him with an interested smile as he and Jade joined the line waiting for Santa. Jesse barely noticed her. There was only one woman for him. And she wore flannel and denim and smelled as fresh as the pine trees.

In that moment, he knew the answer he'd been seeking. Loving Lindsey, in the way God intended man to love woman, meant doing what was best for her. *As Christ loved the church, so man should love his wife.* Jesse wasn't sure why he remembered the verse, but he was sure it came from the Bible. To the best of his ability, he wanted always to love Lindsey that way.

The farm belonged to her. She was the heart and soul of that place. He'd wondered what to give her for Christmas and now he knew. Even though she would never be aware of the secret gift, relinquishing his quest for the farm was the best present he could give. From this moment forward, the farm was hers. And he would no longer seek revenge for the wrongs done to him.

As if the shutters were opened and sunlight flooded in, Jesse saw the truth clearly. Jade had not been his motive. His rightful claim had not been his motive. He had wanted someone to suffer as much as he had—and that was wrong.

He would never again harass the pathetic old lawyer, Stuart Hardwick, to confess. And most of all, he would never hurt Lindsey by telling her of his original reasons for coming to the farm. She didn't ever need to know that the Christmas Tree Farm legally belonged to him.

He would find another way to provide well for Jade— and for Lindsey, if she'd have him. He had skills. He could work for any electric outfit in the area.

The final weight of his past lifted off his shoulders. Lindsey was his heart. Doing right *did* feel much better than being right.

Lindsey was in the house, wrapping all the gifts she and Jesse had purchased the day before. In exchange for her gift-wrapping favors, Jesse had agreed to man the tree lot. With only two days left until Christmas, business at the farm had begun to slack off. Only a few procrastinators waited this late to purchase a tree.

The grind and whine of a pickup coming up the drive rose above the television, where Jimmy Stewart serenaded Donna Reed in "It's a Wonderful Life."

"Must be another of those procrastinators," she said to Sushi. The dog perked one ear, then rose and trotted to the door, whining.

"Need out, girl?" Lindsey put aside the silvery roll of foil paper and followed the dog.

The sheriff's SUV was parked in her drive, and Sheriff Kemp came across the yard.

Lindsey opened the door as he stomped up onto the porch. "Hi, Sheriff. Forget to buy your Christmas tree?"

Ben Kemp had been county sheriff for as long as Lindsey could remember, but he was still tall and strong and fit with barely a hint of paunch beneath his wide silver belt buckle. His trademark gray Stetson and cowboy boots made him even taller. In the pleasant December sunshine, he shifted from one boot to the next, looking decidedly uncomfortable.

Worrying a toothpick to one corner of his mouth, he said, "Wish that was the situation, Lindsey, but I'm afraid I have bad news."

Pulse leaping in sudden fear, Lindsey gripped the doorpost. "My folks? Kim? Has something happened?"

"No, no." He took off his cowboy hat and studied the inside. "Mind if I come in for a minute? Got something here I need to show you."

He pulled a file folder from inside his zip-up jacket.

"Of course not. Please." She stepped back to let him in, relieved that her family was all right but troubled about the purpose of his visit. Sheriff Kemp was too busy to make unnecessary calls.

While the lawman made himself at home on the edge of her couch, Lindsey turned down the TV.

"Would you like some coffee, Sheriff?"

"Nothing, thanks." He placed the Stetson on the couch beside him. "A real odd situation has arisen, Lindsey."

She tilted her head. "That concerns me?"

"In a way. It's about this farm."

Now she was really puzzled. A butterfly fluttered up into her chest. "My farm?"

"Well, you see now, there's the trouble." Opening the manila file folder, he removed a sheet of paper and handed it to her. "When your granddaddy bought this place—in good faith, I'm sure—something was sorely amiss."

Lindsey read the paper and then looked up. "This is the deed to my farm."

"Yep. Now take a look at that signature." He took another paper from the folder. "And then have a look at this one."

She did as he asked, but what she read made no sense. Another butterfly joined the first.

"I don't understand."

Sheriff Kemp rubbed at his forehead, clearly disturbed with the news his job forced him to share. "Here's the upshot, Lindsey. This eighty acres belonged to a woman name of Madelyn Finch. She inherited it from her grandparents. When she died, her husband, Les Finch, hired a lawyer name of Hardwick to help him gain ownership of the place. I remember Hardwick. He was dirty to the core but so smart he always got away with his shenanigans."

Lindsey's pulse accelerated. The butterflies were in full flight by now. "Are you telling me that Mr. Finch illegally sold this farm to my grandfather?"

"I'm afraid so. The woman's will was clear. The farm was to go to her son. Somehow Hardwick and Finch forged the boy's name on the sale papers."

Dropping into the nearest chair, Lindsey covered her mouth with her hand to keep from crying out. A dozen questions crowded her mind. "They cheated a child out of his home?"

Suddenly the truth hit her. That child, whoever he was, owned the tree farm—her tree farm.

"The boy must be grown by now. Does he know about this? Is that why you're here? He's filed a claim to regain possession?"

"Yes, ma'am. He's the one stirred things up after all this time. Seems Stuart Hardwick got himself a conscience after Jesse went to visit him. Hardwick brought all this information to my office this morning. Now, I don't know all the ins and outs. I figure the courts will have to look this over and hear some testimony from Hardwick and Jesse, but the evidence looks pretty clear to me."

"Jesse?" Her hands began to tremble. What did Jesse have to do with this? "Why do you keep saying Jesse?"

Sheriff Kemp blew out a gusty sigh. "Your hired man should have told you this himself, Lindsey. He's Madelyn Finch's son, the rightful owner of this land."

Blood thundered in her temples. She, who'd never fainted in her life, thought she might keel over on the coffee table and scatter gift wrap and ribbon everywhere.

She remembered, then, the times he'd taken off work to attend to personal business and the times someone had told her they'd seen Jesse at the courthouse. He'd been searching for proof that he, not she, owned this place.

Her voice, when she managed to speak, sounded small and faraway. "So that's the real reason Jesse came here."

She ached with the realization that his profession of love had been a lie.

"'Fraid so. Not that you can blame a man for trying to reclaim what was stolen from him. Especially since he has a little girl to care for. But he should have told you."

"Yes. He should have told me."

Her face felt hot enough to combust. Her whole body shook. Jesse had lied to her. She'd trusted him. Loved him.

Jesse had even gone as far as pretending to love her. There was always the chance he wouldn't find proof, but by marrying her, he could still take over the farm. Jesse had romanced her in order to regain the land any way he could.

Her heart shattered like a fragile Christmas ornament. Once more she'd been fooled by a handsome face.

Jimmy Stewart flickered across the silent television screen. He was sitting at a bar, tears in his eyes as he prayed in desperation.

Understanding perfectly, she stared bleakly at the screen, lost and broken.

"Could I get you something, Lindsey?" Sheriff Kemp's kind voice broke into her tumultuous thoughts. His weathered face studied her with concern.

Pulling the reins on her emotions, she shook her head. "I'll be okay, but I need to be alone right now, if you don't mind."

"Understandable. Do you want to tell Jesse about this, or should I?"

Her pulse stumbled.

Jesse, no doubt, would be ecstatic.

"He'll have to come by my office," the sheriff went on. "He'll need to sign papers and such to get the ball rolling."

Lindsey gripped the edge of her chair, trying not to break down in front of the sheriff. She licked her lips, her mouth gone suddenly dry. "You tell him, please. He's down in the lot."

She'd trusted him. Oh, dear Lord, why had she trusted him?

"Maybe you should call a lawyer. There might be some way to fight this thing."

"I'll do that." Suddenly, she needed him gone. She needed to pray. And most of all, she needed Jesse to stay away from her until she could get her emotions under control. "Please, go talk to Jesse before he comes to the house." She despised the quaver in her voice. "I don't want to see him right now."

The poor sheriff was worried about her losing her farm. He didn't understand that she was losing that and a great deal more.

Jesse was halfway to the house when the sheriff came out onto the porch. His curiosity had been piqued from the moment the SUV pulled into the yard. But after the sheriff had stayed inside the house so long, Jesse got a bad feeling in the pit of his stomach. Something was up.

Jesse broke into a lope. If Lindsey needed him…

"What's up?" he asked as soon as he reached the policeman. His heart pounded oddly, not only from the jog, but from some inner voice of warning.

Expression serious, Sheriff Kemp handed him a file folder. "Stuart Hardwick came to see me this morning and confessed his part in swindling you out of your inheritance."

Jesse's head swung toward the house. "Lindsey."

"I told her."

"Oh, no." He had to get to her, make her understand. Spinning away, he started that direction. The sheriff's big hand stopped him.

"Leave her be, Jesse. She doesn't want to see you right now. Give her some time alone."

"But I have to explain."

"Explain what? That you came here under false pretenses, looking for information that would take this farm from her and return it to you? That you've been dishonest with her from the start?"

Jesse relented. Remorse pinned his boots to the ground. The sheriff was right. He hadn't lied to her directly, but his silence had been as dishonest as his reasons for taking this job. Lindsey had trusted him with everything, and all the while, he'd gone right on with his devious plans.

No wonder she didn't want to see him now—or possibly ever. How could he expect her to forgive him for worming his way into her heart under such deceitful circumstances? She had been hurt before, betrayed by a man she loved. And now he had hurt her again. He didn't deserve a woman like Lindsey Mitchell.

Sadness shuddered through him.

His arms fell limply to his sides. "I don't know what to do."

Misunderstanding, the sheriff took the file folder from him and said, "Come by the office later today or tomorrow, and we'll get the ball rolling with the legal system."

With an aura of resigned disapproval, the man departed, leaving Jesse standing in the yard of his rightful home. The afternoon air was cool, but sweat covered his body.

He stared around at the quiet little farm that he'd coveted since he was fourteen. All his adult life he'd longed for this moment.

And now, instead of the exultant victory he'd expected, Jesse suffered a heartbreak so profound he nearly went to his knees.

Lindsey was hurting. She needed comfort. But as much as he longed to go to her, he resisted. Lindsey didn't want him. She'd told the sheriff as much. Going to her now, after what he'd done, would only compound the hurt. Nothing he could say would change the truth. Regardless of his good intentions, of his decision not to pursue ownership, he had betrayed her trust.

After one long last look toward the house and the woman who held his heart, he headed for his truck and the trailer park. He didn't know where he would go, but he'd done all the damage any one man should do in this quiet, loving little town.

At last he knew what to give Lindsey for Christmas. This farm wasn't enough, though he'd certainly leave that behind. What she deserved was a return to her peaceful life without him to bring her any more pain or humiliation.

Packing wouldn't take long. The Slaters traveled light. He'd have the truck loaded in time to pick Jade up from school.

The thought of his little girl gave him pause. She'd changed so much here on Winding Stair Mountain. She was happier, healthier and free from many of her fears, thanks mostly to Lindsey's love and care.

His poor baby. She'd be as heartbroken as he was.

But he had no choice now. Better to get out of Lindsey's life and leave her alone.

With a deep sigh of sadness, Jesse drove through the picturesque old town. The cheerful decorations mocked him.

Once more Christmas had brought him heartbreak, but this time, the fault was his own.

Chapter Fifteen

"You can fight this, Miss Mitchell."

Stan Wright, a forty-something lawyer with a soothing baritone voice and intelligent brown eyes, regarded her across his littered desk. Having called the offices of Wright and Banks as quickly as she'd regained her equilibrium, Lindsey was relieved when he'd offered to see her within the hour.

"I don't want to fight it, Mr. Wright." She drew in a deep, steadying breath, determined to do the hardest thing she'd ever had to do. "The farm belongs to Jesse Slater and his daughter. They were cheated out of it through no fault of their own."

She didn't admit that the decision wasn't her original choice. Her first instinct had been anger and hurt and bitter resentment. She'd wanted to rail at Jesse and send him away. She'd wanted to keep the land to pay him back for lying to her, for making her believe he loved her when, all the while, he was plotting to evict her.

But as soon as the first rush of emotion passed, she'd prayed. And as hard as the decision was, she'd seen that Jesse was as much a victim as she. The land was rightfully his, and she wouldn't rest until he'd legally re-gained ownership.

"I understand the circumstances. But you've lived there in good faith and made the land productive. Even if the courts decide in his favor, he could be forced to pay you for all the improvements you've made, for the tree stock, etc."

She held out a hand to stop him. "No, sir. I want you to do whatever paperwork is required for me to sign away any claim to the entire eighty acres. I want Jesse Slater to take possession."

Shaking his head, Mr. Wright leaned back in his ex-ecutive chair and rubbed a hand across his chin. Brown eyes studied her thoughtfully. "I wish you would take more time to think about this."

"I've had all the time I needed." Standing, she shook his hand, and if hers trembled the slightest bit, the at-torney didn't comment. "Call me as soon as you have the papers drawn up."

With a final word of thanks, she left his office and went to her truck. She had a great deal to do between now and the first of the year. A job. A place to live. Maybe she'd go to Colorado and stay with her sister, Kim, for a while.

But for all her bravado, the ache in her chest grew to the exploding point. The Christmas Tree Farm was not only her home, it was her dream. Leaving would tear her in two. But more terrible than losing the farm, was the loss of Jesse and Jade and the sweet plans they'd begun to weave together.

"Why, Jesse?" she whispered to the windshield. But she knew why. He'd done what he'd had to do in order to retake the farm. And pretending to love her had been part of the plan.

Heading the Dakota through town, she let the tears come. As hard as talking to him would be, Jesse needed to know her decision. Harboring unforgiveness would destroy her relationship with Jesus. So she'd take the first, painful step and tell Jesse the farm was his—and that she bore him no ill.

And that was the truth. She wasn't angry. But oh, the hurt was far worse than anything she'd suffered before.

The palms of her hands were moist with sweat by the time her Dakota crunched over the narrow gravel lane leading into the mobile-home park. All the trailers looked sad and a little run-down, but strings of lights and green wreaths spread the joy of Christmas here as everywhere.

Lindsey wasn't feeling much joy at the moment. Swiping at her soggy face, she blew her nose and composed herself. The next few minutes would be hard, but she'd get through them.

As she neared his trailer, she spotted Jesse outside, and her pulse leaped. Foolish heart, she loved him even though he'd betrayed her so terribly.

Jean jacket unbuttoned in the cold air, he was loading boxes into the back of his Silverado. Her stomach twisted at the implication. Was he planning to push her out of the house today?

As she pulled in to his parking area and killed the motor, Jesse looked up. Expression serious, his silver eyes bored into her like laser beams.

Stilling the awful trembling in her knees, Lindsey breathed a prayer for help and climbed out of the cab.

She stood on one side of the pickup bed. Jesse waited on the other.

"Lindsey." A muscle worked in his cheek. She recognized the movement as stress and longed to smooth her fingers over the spot and reassure him. No doubt he thought she hated him. But she couldn't.

From what she understood of the situation, Jesse was the victim of two unscrupulous men who'd stolen his birthright and left him to fend for himself. Thinking of a teenage Jesse scared and alone filled her with sadness.

Resisting the need to touch him, to feel his arms around her once more, she said what she'd come to say.

She hitched her chin up, struggling for control. "I would never keep something that isn't rightfully mine, Jesse. You didn't have to pretend to love me in order to get the farm back."

Her voice cracked the slightest bit on the last words. She bit her lip to keep from breaking down again.

Deep furrows appeared in Jesse's forehead. "What are you talking about? I never pretended—" He stopped, his expression incredulous. "You thought—?" He stopped again, dropped the box he carried into the bed of the truck and started around to her side.

He strode toward her with the strangest look on his face. Lindsey wasn't sure whether to run or stand her ground. Her heart clattered against her rib cage.

Never a coward, she stood her ground.

Lindsey's words lit a spark of hope inside Jesse. The crazy woman thought he didn't love her?

Stalking around the truck, he jabbed a finger at the air. "Let's get one thing straight, Miss Mitchell. I didn't *pretend* to love you. I do love you. I didn't want to, never intended to, but you were too amazing to resist. When Erin died, I thought my capacity to love died with her, but you, with your sweet, caring, decent ways proved me wrong."

A curtain in the next trailer twitched, letting Jesse know his voice had carried and he'd attracted an audience. Across the road, in the other row of trailers, a woman came out on her porch and pretended to adjust the wreath on her front door. All the while, she cast surreptitious peeks toward Jesse and Lindsey. He heard the squeak and swish of windows being raised.

Jesse didn't care if the whole world listened in. All that mattered was the mystified, suffering expression in Lindsey's red-rimmed eyes. She'd been crying—because of him.

He reached for her hand, aching to touch her, but afraid at the same time. When she didn't yank away, he celebrated a small victory. At least, they could part on speaking terms.

"The one constant in all this mess is right here." He placed her hand over his heart. "My love for you is real and true. It has nothing to do with the farm."

She blinked, shaking her head in denial. Her tawny mane tossed around her shoulders and Jesse itched to smooth it, to comfort her somehow.

"I don't understand. I thought you purposely moved here to reclaim the land."

"I did."

She shrank away, forcing him to release her. How he longed to change the past, to take back his devious intentions. But it was too late for that. He'd hurt her too much to expect forgiveness.

Arms falling helplessly to his sides, Jesse knew defeat. He stared up into the tree growing behind the trailer. His insides felt as bare and empty as the naked, reaching limbs of the sycamore.

"Someday, sweet Lindsey, I hope you will try to forgive me." His gaze found her beloved face and soaked in every feature, storing the memory. "But whether you do or not, I will always be grateful for our time together. I'll leave Winding Stair a better man for having known you."

Tears gathered in her eyes, and Jesse despised himself for causing them. "The farm is yours, Jesse. I'm the one who will be leaving. I only ask that you wait until after the holidays so I'll have time to make some arrangements."

The idea of Lindsey moving away from the home she loved cut through him like a chain saw. He stepped toward her again, desperately wanting to hold her, but the distrust in her expression stopped him. He shoved his hands in his jacket pockets instead.

"You're not going anywhere. I'm packed and ready. I'll inform the sheriff of my decision to renounce any claim to your land. As soon as I go by the school and get Jade, we'll be on our way."

Lindsey stared at him in disbelief. "After everything that's happened, you're leaving? You're giving up a home that's rightfully yours?"

"The place means nothing to me without you there."

Tears shoved at the back of his eyelids. If he didn't escape soon, he'd shame himself more than he already had. Spinning on his boot heel, he grabbed for the truck door and bounded inside. He cranked the engine, slammed the gear shift into Reverse and started to back out. One last glance at Lindsey's face stopped him.

Without understanding his new propensity for rejection, he rolled down the window and said, "Remember this much. I loved you. I still do."

Her sorrow turned to bewilderment. After a pregnant pause while time seemed to stand still and the nosy neighbors appeared to hold their collective breath, a trembling smile broke through her tears. In her flannel and denim, she looked radiant.

"Jesse," she said. "Oh, Jesse."

In the next minute, Lindsey yanked open the passenger door and bounded into the seat next to him.

He watched her, hoping, praying and utterly terrified to believe. "What are you doing?"

"I'm going with you," she said, alternately laughing and wiping tears. "To get Jade."

"You are?" Please say yes. Please say yes.

"And then we are all three going home, to *our* farm, where we belong." She gave him another of those tremulous smiles. "We have Christmas presents to wrap."

Understanding, pure and lovely, dawned. Jesse slammed the truck out of gear and did what he'd been yearning to do since her arrival. He pulled her into his arms. This time, she came willingly.

"I'm sorry, sweetheart. So sorry." Showering her face with kisses, he muttered apologies and professions of love. "I should have told you from the beginning, but I didn't know you. I didn't know I'd love you so much. I was wrong, so wrong."

"I'm sorry, too." She took his face between her palms, her golden eyes boring into him with a love so strong he felt humbled. "For all that happened to you as a boy. For my unwitting part in forcing you to take such drastic measures."

With a laugh of joy, Jesse hugged her to his happy heart. God had forgiven him and now Lindsey had too.

After years of searching, he had completely and finally come home. To his faith, to his farm, and to the woman who healed him in a thousand ways.

He was the luckiest man alive.

Epilogue

Lindsey was sure she would never be happier than she was this Christmas morning. She sat on the edge of an ottoman next to the Christmas tree, surveying her world like a queen.

The farmhouse smelled toasty warm with pumpkin bread and spiced cider and the promise of baked ham for dinner. Presents littered the living-room floor, some already unwrapped and exclaimed over while others still waited for their treasures to be discovered. And though these pleased her, the real joy came from the two people beneath her Christmas tree—Jesse and Jade—the loves of her life.

They'd arrived early, almost as soon as Lindsey was dressed in her Christmas best—an outfit she'd purchased especially for today—a silky emerald blouse, long black skirt, and matching dress boots. From Jesse's expression and brow-pumping compliments, she concluded she'd chosen well. She even felt pretty this morning.

"You open one now, Lindsey." Jade pushed a package at her.

Lindsey shook her head. She needed no other presents

than the ones she'd already received. After considerable discussion during which each had tried to give the other everything, she and Jesse had agreed to share ownership of the farm. More importantly, she could spend this special Christmas Day with the man and child she'd come to love so deeply.

The Virginia pine in the living room had long since given up its stately status. Laden with ornaments and tinsel, popcorn strings and lights, homemade angels and clay-dough cookies, Lindsey's Christmas tree was loaded to the breaking point—thanks to Jade's daily additions. She thought it was the gaudiest, most beautiful tree ever.

"I want to see you open all of yours first." She lifted the camera from her lap and aimed.

Dressed in dark red velvet, her black hair pulled away from her face with a matching bow, the little girl was exquisite. With typical six-year-old exuberance, she hugged a stuffed dog to her white lace collar.

"This is my Sushi. I love her."

The real Sushi, watching from her spot next to the furnace, lifted her head and woofed once.

"She loves you too," Jesse said, his beloved mouth kicking up at the corners.

Snapping the ribbons from a box with one quick jerk, he opened a gift from Lindsey.

She held her breath as he lifted the sweater from the tissue.

"Wow." He held the rich blue garment beneath his chin. "Now I'll look decent enough to accompany you beautiful ladies to church this morning."

Lindsey snapped a picture, happiness bubbling inside her. Jesse was as eager as she to spend this holy day together in God's house.

"Do you like it?" She thought the blue looked stunning with his mysterious silver eyes.

"Love it." He leaned across the pile of discarded wrapping paper and grabbed her hand, charming her with a wink. "But I love you more."

Heart somersaulting in delight, she tapped him lightly on the head. "You'd better."

With a gentle tug, he pulled her off the ottoman onto her knees in front of him. "No problem there. But I do have another problem."

The sea-breeze scent of his cologne was almost as heady as the teasing, tender glint in his eyes. "What is it?"

"Some stubborn woman I know won't open her presents."

She'd been too busy relishing Jade's reaction to everything. "Christmas isn't about presents to me, Jesse. It's about loving and giving, the way God gave us Jesus."

"I couldn't agree more. And that's what I'm trying to do here."

Jade lay aside the gift she'd been about to unwrap and scooted toward the two adults. "Now, Daddy? Now?"

Her jittery behavior and dancing eyes told Lindsey something was up.

"Now, Jade. I don't think I can stand the suspense."

"Me either, me either, me either." Jade bounced like a rubber ball.

Lindsey laughed. "What are the two of you up to?"

Jesse left her long enough to go to his jacket and return with a small, gold-wrapped box. "This."

Her heart stuttered, stopped and then went crazy inside her chest. Mouth dry as August sand, she took the gift.

"Go on. Open it. It won't bite." Jesse tried to joke, but his eyes were serious and the muscle below those eyes quivered. Jade appeared excited enough to explode.

With trembling fingers, Lindsey removed the wrapping to find, as she'd suspected, a black velvet ring box.

"Oh, Jesse." Such a silly thing to say, but her mind was frozen.

Gently, he took the box from her fingers and flipped it open.

"Come on, Jade," he said. "Let's do this right."

He went down on one knee in front of her, and to Lindsey's great delight, Jade did the same. The sweetness of the picture overwhelmed her.

Jesse cleared his throat. "We've rehearsed this, so bear with us."

When he took her hand in his, she felt him tremble, and loved him all the more. "Lindsey Mitchell, I love you."

"I love you, Lindsey," Jade echoed.

The lump in Lindsey's throat thickened.

"I love you too," she whispered.

"We don't have much, but we can give you the most important things we own."

Jade touched her own chest. "Our hearts."

Tears welled in Lindsey's eyes. "You have mine too."

"Then, will you make our family complete and marry us? Will you be my wife?" Jesse slid the dainty solitaire onto her finger.

"And will you be my other mommy?"

"Yes. Oh, yes." Lindsey could contain her joy no longer. She tumbled forward, grabbing both her loves into a giant hug.

First, she kissed Jade's cheek. "I promise to be the best mom I can."

And then while Jade giggled, Jesse took his turn, sealing the proposal with a kiss that promised a lifetime of love and honesty.

When at last they parted and sat smiling into one another's eyes, Jesse said, "Glad that's over. I didn't sleep a wink last night."

"Did you actually think I'd refuse?"

"I was afraid if I went to sleep, I'd wake up and discover you were a dream." His words melted her. "You are a dream. And I want to get married as soon as possible. Like tomorrow."

"Tomorrow?" Lindsey burst out in surprised laughter. In truth, she wanted the same thing. "Sorry, Mister Slater, but I've always dreamed of a Christmas wedding, and since it's too late for that this year, we'll have to wait until next Christmas."

"No way," Jesse howled.

"No way," Jade echoed, carefully sorting gifts into neat little piles.

Jesse thrust out a palm. "Hold it. I feel an idea coming on." An ornery twinkle lit the silvery eyes that had once been so wary and sad. "Not every place in the world celebrates Christmas on December twenty-fifth. Right?"

"Right." Lindsey agreed, unsure where he was heading. Not that she cared. She'd follow Jesse anywhere.

Suddenly, he clapped his hands together in victory. "Problem solved. According to a very famous song, there are really twelve days of Christmas. So there you have it. Christmas begins today and won't end until we're married twelve days from now." He squinted hopefully. "Okay?"

Happiness danced through Lindsey's veins. She'd only been teasing about waiting until next Christmas. She wanted to be Jesse's wife now.

"We'll talk to Pastor Cliff today and if he agrees, we'll be married among the trees on the twelfth day of Christmas. Just don't bring me any partridges or maids a-milking."

With a whoop of joy, Jesse grabbed her and twirled her around in a circle. "This is the best Christmas of my life."

"Mine too."

He stilled and grew serious. "No kidding?"

"All my adult life, I've wanted my home filled with love and laughter. With a husband and children. This year, God has granted me those gifts."

"Do you think the people at church will be surprised? About our engagement, I mean."

"I don't know," she admitted. "But I'm eager to find out. Let's go early and tell everyone as they come in."

Jesse surveyed the disarrayed living room. "What about this mess and the unwrapped gifts?"

She slipped into the long wool coat she'd laid out earlier along with her purse and Bible. "They'll wait."

Jesse disappeared and came back wearing his new sweater. He was so handsome, he took her breath away. With a wide grin, he shrugged into his jacket and then helped Jade into hers.

Watching her two loves, Lindsey rejoiced. God was good. And on this glorious Christmas morning, He had blessed her exceedingly abundantly above all she could ever have thought or asked.

Jesse had come to Winding Stair with wrongful intent, but God had turned the bad to good. Only the Lord could have foreseen that the two of them, both with claims to the Christmas Tree Farm, needed each other to make their life circles complete. Only God could have made everything turn out so beautifully.

"Thank You, Jesus," she said, her cup overflowing.

"Amen to that." Jesse held out a hand and she took it. Jade clasped the other.

Then, together as a family, the trio headed out into the bright sunny morning, eager to celebrate the birth of their Savior and to announce their best Christmas present ever.

* * * * *

Dear Reader,

Ah, the memories Christmas evokes in me. I can almost hear my son's voice coming through the darkness at 5:00 a.m. as he stands at my bedroom door asking if it's time to open the presents. I think of the smells, too. Of cedar boughs and roasted turkey. Of orange slices and cinnamon cookies. And the beautiful sights. Colored lights and silver tinsel. My little girl dressed in red velvet with bows in her hair.

Christmas is truly a time of wonder and joy. A time to celebrate all that's good and right. Most of all, it's a time for memories of past Christmases. For Jesse Slater, bad memories outweighed the good ones. If that's the case with you, I hope you'll do what Jesse did. Let the unsurpassed love of God restore and heal you this holiday season.

Wishing you an especially joyous Christmas,

Linda Goodnight

A SEASON FOR GRACE

A father to the fatherless,
defender of widows, is God in His holy dwelling.
God sets the lonely in families.
—*Psalms* 68:5–6

Special thanks to former DHS caseworker
Tammy Potter for answering my social services
questions, and to my buddy Maggie Price for
helping me keep my cop in the realm of reality.
Any mistakes or literary license are my own.
I would also like to acknowledge the legion of
foster and adoptive parents and children
who have shared their insight into
the painful world of social orphans.

Prologue

The worst was happening again. And there was nothing he could do about it.

Collin Grace was only ten years old but he'd seen it all and then some. One thing he'd seen too much of was social workers. He hated them. The sweet-talking women with their briefcases and straight skirts and fancy fingernails. They always meant trouble.

Arms stiff, he stood in front of the school counselor's desk and stared at the office wall. His insides shook so hard he thought he might puke. But he wouldn't ask to be excused. No way he'd let them know how scared he was. Wouldn't do no good anyhow.

Betrayal, painful as a stick in the eye, settled low in his belly. He had thought Mr. James liked him, but the counselor had called the social worker.

Didn't matter. Collin wasn't going to cry. Not like his brother Drew. Stupid kid was fighting and kicking and screaming like he could stop what was happening.

"Now, Drew." The social worker tried to soothe the wild brother. Tried to brush his too-long, dark hair out of his furious blue eyes. Drew snarled like a wounded wolf. "Settle down. Everything will be all right."

That was a lie. And all three of the brothers knew it. Nothing was ever all right. They'd leave this school and go into foster care again. New people to live with, new school, new town, all of them strange and unfriendly. They'd be cleaned up and fattened up, but after a few months Mama would get them back. Then they'd be living under bridges or with some drugged-out old guy who liked to party with Mama. Then she'd disappear. Collin would take charge. Things would be better for a while. The whole mess would start all over again.

People should just leave them alone. He could take care of his brothers.

Drew howled again and slammed his seven-year-old fist into the social worker. "I hate you. Leave me alone!"

He broke for the door.

Collin bit the inside of his lip. Drew hadn't figured out yet that he couldn't escape.

A ruckus broke out. The athletic counselor grabbed Drew and held him down in a chair even though he bucked and spat and growled like a mad tomcat. Drew was a wiry little twerp; Collin gave him credit for that. And he had guts. For what good it would do him, he might as well save his energy. Grown-ups would win. They always did.

People passed the partially open office door and peered around the edge, curious about all the commotion. Collin tried to pretend he couldn't see them, couldn't hear them. But he could.

"Poor little things," one of the teachers murmured. "Living in a burned-out trailer all by themselves. No wonder they're filthy."

Collin swallowed the cry of humiliation rising up in his stomach like the bad oranges he'd eaten from the convenience-store trash. He did the best he could to keep Drew and Ian clean and fed. It wasn't easy without water or electricity. He'd tried washing them off in the rest-room before school, but he guessed he hadn't done too good a job.

"Collin." The fancy-looking social worker had a hand on her stomach where Drew had punched her. "You've been through this before. You know it's for the best. Why don't you help me get your brothers in the car?"

Collin didn't look at her. Instead he focused on his brothers, sick that he couldn't help them. Sick with dread. Who knew what would happen this time? Somehow he had to find a way to keep them all together. That was the important thing. Together, they could survive.

Ian, only four, looked so little sitting in a big brown plastic chair against the wall. His scrawny legs stuck straight out and the oversize tennis shoes threatened to fall off. No shoestrings. They stunk, too. Collin could smell them clean over here.

Like Collin, baby Ian didn't say a word; he didn't fight. He just cried. Silent, broken tears streamed down his cheeks and left tracks like a bicycle through mud. Clad in a plaid flannel shirt with only two buttons and a pair of Drew's tattered jeans pulled together at the belt loops with a piece of electrical cord, his skinny body trembled. Collin could hardly stand that.

They shouldn't have come to school today; then none of this would have happened. But they were hungry and he was fresh out of places to look. School lunch was free, all you could eat.

Seething against an injustice he couldn't name or

defend against, he crossed the room to his brother. He didn't say a word; just put his hand on Ian's head. The little one, quivering like a scared puppy, relaxed the tiniest bit. He looked up, eyes saying he trusted his big brother to take care of everything the way he always did.

Collin hoped he could.

The social worker knelt in front of Ian and took his hand. "I know you're scared, honey, but you're going to be fine. You'll have plenty to eat and a nice, safe place to sleep." She tapped his tennis shoes. "And a new pair of shoes, just your size. Things will be better, I promise."

Ian sniffed and dragged a buttonless sleeve across his nose. When he looked at her, he had hope in his eyes. Poor little kid.

Collin ignored the hype. He'd heard it all before and it was a lie. Things were never better. Different, but not better.

The tall counselor, still holding Drew in the chair, slid to his knees just like the social worker and said, "Boys, sometimes life throws us a curveball. But no matter what happens, I want you to remember one thing. Jesus cares about you. If you let him, He'll take care of you. No matter where you go from here, God will never walk off and leave you."

A funny thing happened then. Drew sort of quieted down and looked as if he was listening. Ian was still sniffin' and snubbin', but watching Mr. James, too. None of them could imagine *anybody* who wouldn't leave them at some point.

"Collin?" The counselor, who Collin used to like a lot, twisted around and stretched an open palm toward him. Collin wanted to take hold. But he couldn't.

After a minute, Mr. James dropped his hand, laid it

on Collin's shoe. Something about that big, strong hand on his old tennis shoe bothered Collin. He didn't know if he liked it or hated it.

The room got real quiet then. Too quiet. Mr. James bowed his bald head and whispered something. A prayer, Collin thought, though he didn't know much about such things. He stared at the wall, trying hard not to listen. He didn't dare hope, but the counselor's words made him want to.

Then Mr. James reached into his pocket. Drew and Ian watched him, silent. Collin watched his brothers.

"I want you to have one of these," the counselor said as he placed something in each of the younger boys' hands. It looked like a fish on a tiny chain. "It's a reminder of what I said, that God will watch over you."

Collin's curiosity made his palm itch to reach out, but he didn't. Instead, Mr. James had to pry his fingers apart and slide the fish-shaped piece of metal into the hollow of his hand.

Much as he wanted to, Collin refused to look at it. Better to cut to the chase and quit all this hype. "Where are we going this time?"

His stupid voice shook. He clenched his fists to still the trembling. The metal fish, warm from Mr. James's skin, bit into his flesh.

The pretty social worker looked up, startled that he'd spoken. Collin wondered if she could see the fury, red and hot, that pushed against the back of his eyes.

"We already have foster placements for Drew and Ian."

But not for him. The anger turned to fear. "Together?"

As long as they were together, they'd be okay.

"No. I'm sorry. Not this time."

He knew what she meant. He knew the system probably better than she did. Only certain people would take boys like Drew who expressed their anger. And nobody would take him. He was too old. People liked little and cute like Ian, not fighters, not runaways, not big boys with an attitude.

Panic shot through him, made his heart pound wildly. "They have to stay with me. Ian gets scared."

The social worker rose and touched his shoulder. "He'll be fine, Collin."

Collin shrugged away to glare at the brown paneled wall behind the counselor's desk. Helpless fury seethed inside him.

The worst had finally happened.

He and Drew and Ian were about to be separated.

Chapter One

Twenty-three years later, Oklahoma City

Sweat burned his eyes, but Collin Grace didn't move. He couldn't. One wrong flinch and somebody died.

Totally focused on the life-and-death scenario playing out on the ground below, he hardly noticed the sun scalding the back of his neck or the sweat soaking through his protective vest.

The Tac-team leader's voice came through the earphone inside his Fritz helmet. "Hostage freed. Suspect in custody. Get down here for debrief."

Collin relaxed and lowered the .308 caliber marksman rifle, a SWAT sniper's best friend, and rose from his prone position on top of the River Street Savings and Loan. Below him, the rest of the team exited a training house and headed toward Sergeant Gerrara.

Frequent training was essential and Collin welcomed every drill. Theirs wasn't a full-time SWAT unit, so they had to stay sharp for those times when the callout would come and they'd have to act. Normally a patrol cop, he'd spent all morning on the firing range, requalifying with every weapon known to mankind. He was good. Real good, with the steadiest hands anyone on the force had ever seen. A fact that made him proud.

"You headed for the gym after this?" His buddy, fellow police officer and teammate Maurice Johnson shared his propensity for exercise. Stay in shape, stay alive. Most special tactics cops agreed.

Collin peeled his helmet off and swiped a hand over his sweating brow. "Yeah. You?"

"For a few reps. I told Shanita I'd be home early. Bible study at our place tonight." Maurice sliced a sneaky grin in Collin's direction. Sweat dripped from his high ebony cheeks and rolled down a neck the size of a linebacker's. "Wanna come?"

Collin returned the grin with a shake of his head. Maurice wouldn't give up. He extended the same invitation every Thursday.

Collin liked Maurice and his family, but he couldn't see a loner like himself spouting Bible verses and singing in a choir. It puzzled him, too, that a cop as tough and smart as Maurice would feel the need for God. To Collin's way of thinking there was only one person he trusted enough to lean on. And that was himself.

"Phone call for you, Grace," Sergeant Gerrara hollered. "Probably some cutie after your money."

The other cops hooted as Collin shot Maurice an exasperated look and took off in a trot. He received plenty of teasing about his single status. Some of the guys tried to fix him up, but when a woman started pushing him or trying to get inside his head, she was history. He didn't need the grief.

The heavy tactics gear rattled and bounced against his

body as he grabbed the cell phone from Sergeant Gerrara's oversize fist, trading it for his rifle.

"Grace."

"Sergeant Collin Grace?" A feminine voice, light and sweet, hummed against his ear.

"Yeah." He shoved his helmet under one arm and stepped away from the gaggle of cops who listened in unabashedly. "Who's this?"

"Mia Carano. I'm with the Cleveland County Department of Child Welfare."

A cord of tension stretched through Collin's chest. Adrenaline, just now receding from the training scenario, ratcheted up a notch. Child welfare, a department he both loathed and longed to hear from. Could it finally be news?

He struggled to keep his voice cool and detached. "Is this about my brothers?"

"Your brothers?"

Envisioning her puzzled frown, Collin realized she had no idea he'd spent years trying to find Ian and Drew. The spurt of energy drained out of him. "Never mind. What can I do for you, Ms. Carano?"

"Do you recall the young boy you picked up last week behind the pawn shop?"

"The runaway?" He could still picture the kid. "Angry, scared, but too proud to admit it?"

"Yes. Mitchell Perez. He's eleven. Going on thirty."

The kid hadn't looked a day over nine. Skinny. Black hair too long and hanging in his eyes. A pack of cigarettes crushed and crammed down in his jeans' pocket. He'd reminded Collin too much of Drew.

"You still got him? Or did he go home?"

"Home for now, but he's giving his mother fits."

From what the kid had told him, she deserved fits. "He'll run again."

"I know. That's why I'm calling you."

Around him the debrief was breaking up. He lifted a hand to the departing team.

"Nothing I can do until he runs."

He leaned an elbow against somebody's black pickup truck and watched cars pull up to a stop sign adjacent to the parking lot. Across the street, shoppers came and went in a strip mall. Normal, common occurrences in the city on a peaceful, sunny afternoon. Ever alert, he filed them away, only half listening to the caller.

"This isn't my first encounter with Mitch. He's a troubled boy, but his mother said you impressed him. He talks about you. Wants to be a cop."

Collin felt a con coming on. Social workers were good at that. He stayed quiet, let her ramble on in that sugary voice.

"He has no father. No male role model."

Big surprise. He switched the phone to the other ear.

"I thought you might be willing to spend some time with the boy. Perhaps through CAPS, our child advocate program. It's sort of like Big Brothers only through the court system."

He was already a big brother and he'd done a sorry job of that. Some of the other officers did that sort of outreach, but not him.

"I don't think so."

"At least give me a chance to talk with you about it. I have some other ideas if CAPS doesn't appeal."

He was sure she did. Her type always had ideas. "This isn't my kind of thing. Call the precinct. They might know somebody."

"Tell you what," she said as if he hadn't just turned her down. "Meet me at Chick's Place in fifteen minutes. I'll buy you a cup of coffee."

She didn't give up easy. She even knew the cops' favorite hamburger joint.

He didn't know why, but he said, "Make it forty-five minutes and a hamburger, onions fried."

She laughed and the sound was light, musical. He liked it. It was her occupation that turned him off.

"I'll even throw in some cheese fries," she added.

"Be still my heart." He couldn't believe he'd said that. Regardless of her sweet voice, he didn't know this woman and didn't particularly want to.

"I'll sit in the first booth so you'll recognize me."

"What if it's occupied?"

"I'll buy them a burger, too." She laughed again. The sound ran over him like fresh summer rain. "See you in forty-five minutes."

The phone went dead and Collin stared down at it, puzzled that a woman—a social worker, no less—had conned him into meeting her for what was, no doubt, even more of a con.

Well, he had news for Mia Carano with the sweet voice. Collin Grace didn't con easy. Regardless of what she wanted, the answer was already no.

Mia recognized him the minute he walked in the door. No matter that the hamburger café was littered with uniformed police officers hunched over burgers or mega-size soft drinks. Collin Grace stood out in a crowd. Brown eyes full of caution swept the room once, as if calculating escape routes, before coming to rest on her.

She prided herself on being able to read people. Sergeant Grace didn't trust a soul in the place.

"There he is," the middle-aged officer across from her said, nodding toward the entrance. "That's Amazin' Grace."

Mia fixed her attention on the lean, buff policeman coming her way. With spiked dark hair, slashing eyebrows and a permanent five o'clock shadow, he was good-looking in a hard, manly kind of way. His fatigue pants and fitted brown T-shirt with a Tac-team emblem over the heart looked fresh and clean as though he'd recently changed.

Officer Jess Snow pushed out of the booth he'd kindly allowed her to share. In exchange, he had regaled her with stories about the force, his grandkids, and his plan to retire next year. He'd also told her that the other policemen referred to the officer coming her way as Amazin' Grace because of his uncanny cool and precision even under the most intense conditions. "Guess I'll get moving. Sure was nice talking to you."

She smiled up at the older man. "You, too, Jess."

Officer Snow gave her a wink and nodded to the newcomer as he left.

Collin returned a short, curt nod and then jacked an eyebrow at Mia. "Miss Carano?"

A bewildering flutter tickled her stomach. "Yes, but I prefer Mia."

As he slid into the booth across from her the equipment attached to his belt rattled and a faint stir of some warm, tangy aftershave pierced the scent of frying onions. She noted that he did not return the courtesy by asking her to use his given name.

She wasn't surprised. He was every bit the cool, detached cop. Years of looking at the negative side of life did that to some social workers, as well. Mia was thankful she had the Lord and a very supportive family to pour out all her frustrations and sadness upon. Her work was her calling. She was right where God could best use her, and she'd long ago made up her mind not to let the dark side of life burn her out.

Sergeant Grace, on the other hand, might as well be draped in strips of yellow police tape that screamed, Caution: Restricted Area. Getting through his invisible shield wouldn't be as easy as she'd hoped.

He propped his forearms on the tabletop like a barrier between them. His left T-shirt sleeve slid upward to reveal the bottom curve of a tattoo emblazoned with a set of initials she couldn't quite make out.

Though she didn't move or change expressions, a part of her shrank back from him. She'd never understood a man's propensity to mutilate his arms with dye and needles.

"So," he said, voice deep and smooth. "What can I do for you, Mia?"

"Don't you want your hamburger first?"

The tight line of his mouth mocked her. "A spoonful of sugar doesn't really make the medicine go down any easier."

So cynical. And he couldn't be that much older than she was. Early thirties maybe. "You might actually enjoy what I have in mind."

"I doubt it." He raised a hand to signal the waitress. "What would you like?" he asked.

She motioned to her Coke. "This is fine. I'm not hungry."

He studied her for a second before turning his attention to the waitress. "Bring me a Super Burger. Fry the onions, hold the tomatoes, and add a big order of cheese fries and a Mountain Dew."

The waitress poised with pen over pad and said in a droll voice, "What's the occasion? Shoot somebody today?"

One side of the policeman's mouth softened. He didn't smile, but he was close. "Only a smart-mouthed waitress. Nobody will miss her."

The waitress chuckled and said to Mia, "I never thought I'd see the day grease would cross his lips."

She sauntered away, hollering the order to a guy in the back.

"I thought all cops were junk-food junkies."

"It's the hours. Guys don't always have time to eat right."

"But you do?"

"Sometimes."

If he was a health food nut he wasn't going to talk to her about it. Curious the way he avoided small talk. Was he this way with everyone? Or just her?

Maybe it was her propensity for nosiness. Maybe it was her talkative Italian heritage. But Mia couldn't resist pushing a little to see what he would do. "So what *do* you eat? Bean sprouts and yogurt?"

"Is that why you're here? To talk about my diet?"

So cold. So empty. Had she made a mistake in thinking this ice man might help a troubled boy?

On the other hand, Grandma Carano said still waters run deep. Gran had been talking about Uncle Vitorio, the only quiet Carano in the giant, noisy family, and she'd been right. Uncle Vitorio was a thinker, an inventor. Granted he mostly invented useless gadgets to amuse himself, but the family considered him brilliant and deep.

Perhaps Collin was the same. Or maybe he just needed some encouragement to loosen up.

She pushed her Coke to one side and got down to business.

"For some reason, Mitchell Perez has developed a heavy case of hero worship for you."

The boy was one of those difficult cases who didn't respond well to any of the case workers, the counselors or anybody else for that matter, but something inside Mia wouldn't give up. Last night, when she'd prayed for the boy, this idea to contact Collin Grace had come into her mind. She'd believed it was God-sent, but now she wondered.

"More and more in the social system we're seeing boys like Mitchell who don't have a clue how to become responsible, caring men. They need real men to teach them and to believe in them. Men they can relate to and admire."

The waitress slid a soda and a paper-covered straw in front of Sergeant Grace.

"How do you know I'm that kind of man?"

"I checked you out."

He tilted his head. "Just because I'm a good cop doesn't mean I'd be a suitable role model to some street kid."

"I'm normally a good judge of character and I think you would be. The thing here is need. We have so many needy kids, and few men willing to spend a few hours a week to make a difference. Don't you see, Officer? In the long run, your job will be easier if someone intercedes on behalf of these kids now. Maybe they won't end up in trouble later on down the road."

"And maybe they will."

Frustration made her want to pound the table. "You know the statistics. Mentored kids are less likely to get into drugs and crime. They're more likely to go to college. More likely to hold jobs and be responsible citizens. Don't you get it, Officer? A few hours a week of your time can change a boy's life."

He pointed his straw at her. "You haven't been at this long, have you?"

She blinked, leaned back in the booth and tried to calm down. "Seven years."

"Longer than I thought."

"Why? Because I care? Because I'm not burned out?"

"It happens." The shrug in his voice annoyed her.

"Is that what's happened to you?"

A pained look came and went on his face, but he kept silent—again.

Mia leaned forward, her passionate Italian nature taking control. "Look, this may not make any sense to you. Or it may sound idealistic, but I believe what I do makes a difference in these kids' lives."

"Maybe they don't want you to make a difference. Maybe they want to be left alone."

"Left alone? To be abused?"

"Not all of them are mistreated."

"Or neglected. Or cold and hungry, eating out of garbage cans."

Collin's face closed up tighter than a miser's fist. Had the man no compassion?

"There are a lot of troubled kids out there. Why are you so focused on this particular one?"

"I'm concerned about all of them."

"But?"

So he'd heard the hesitation.

"There's something special about Mitch." Something about the boy pulled at her, kept her going back to check on him. Kept her trying. "He wants to make it, but he doesn't know how."

Collin's expression shifted ever so slightly. The change was subtle, but Mia felt him softening. His eyes flicked sideways and, as if glad for the interruption, he said, "Food's coming."

The waitress slid the steaming burger and fries onto the table. "There you go. A year's worth of fat and cholesterol."

"No wonder Chick keeps you around, Millie. You're such a great salesman."

"Saleslady, thank you."

He took a giant bite of the burger and sighed. "Perfect. Just like you."

Millie rolled her eyes and moved on. Collin turned his attention back to Mia. "You were saying?"

"Were you even listening?"

"To every word. The kid is special. Why?"

Mia experienced a twinge of pleasure. Collin Grace confused her, but there was something about him…

"Beneath Mitch's hard layer is a gentleness. A sweet little boy who doesn't know who to trust or where to turn."

"Imagine that. The world screws him over from birth and he stops trusting it. What a concept."

The man was cool to the point of frostbite and had a shell harder than any of the street kids she dealt with. If she could crack this tough nut perhaps other cops would follow suit. She was already pursuing the idea of mentor groups through her church, but cops-as-mentors could make an impact like no other.

She took a big sip of Coke and then said, "At least talk to Mitch."

The pager at Collin's waist went off. He slipped the device from his belt, glanced at the display, and pushed out of the booth, leaving a half-eaten burger and a nearly full basket of cheese fries.

Mia looked up at the tall and dark and distant cop. "Is that your job?"

He nodded curtly. "Gotta go. Thanks for the dinner."

"Could I call you about this later?"

"No point. The answer will still be no." He whipped around with the precision of a marine and strode out of the café before Mia could argue further.

Disappointment curled in her belly. When she could close her surprised mouth, she did so with a huff.

The basket of leftover fries beckoned. She crammed a handful in her mouth. No use wasting perfectly good cheese fries. Even if they did end up on her hips.

Sergeant Collin Grace may have said no, but no didn't always mean absolutely no.

And Mia wasn't quite ready to give up on Mitchell Perez...or Collin Grace.

Chapter Two

"Hey, Grace, you spending the night here or something?"

Eyes glued to the computer screen, Collin lifted a finger to silence the other cop. "Gotta check one more thing."

His shift was long over, and the sun drifted toward the west, but at least once a week he checked and rechecked, just in case he'd missed something the other five thousand times he'd searched.

Somewhere out there he had two brothers, and with the explosion of information on the internet he would find them—eventually. After all this time, though, he wasn't expecting a miracle.

His cell phone played the University of Oklahoma fight song and he glanced down at the caller ID. Her again. Mia Carano. She'd left no less than ten messages over the past three days. He hadn't bothered to return her phone calls. Eventually she'd get the message.

The rollicking strains of "Boomer Sooner" faded away as his voice mail picked up. Collin kept his attention on the computer screen.

Over the years, he'd amassed quite a list of names and addresses. One by one, he'd checked them out and moved them to an inactive file. He typed several more names into the file on his computer and hit Save.

The welfare office suggested he should hire a private search agency, but Collin never planned to do that. The idea of letting someone else poke into his troubled background made him nervous. He'd done a good job of leaving that life behind and didn't want the bones of his childhood dug up by some stranger.

Part of the frustration in this search, though, lay with his own limited memory. Given what he knew of his mother, he wasn't even sure he and his brothers shared a last name. And even if they once had, either or both could have been changed through adoption.

Maurice Johnson, staying late to finish a report, bent over Collin's desk. "Any luck?"

He kept his voice low, and Collin appreciated his discretion. It was one of the reasons he'd confided in his coworker and friend about the missing brothers. It was also one of the reasons the man was one of his few close friends. Maurice knew how to keep his mouth shut.

"Same old thing. I added a few more men with the last names of Grace and Stotz, my mother's maiden name, to the list, but I'm convinced the boys were moved out of Oklahoma after we were separated."

Their home state had been a dead end from the get-go.

"Any luck in the Texas system?"

"Not yet. But it's huge. Finding the names is easy. Matching ages and plundering records isn't quite as simple."

"Even for a cop."

A lot of the old files were not even computerized yet.

And even if he could find them, there were plenty of re-cords he couldn't access.

"Yeah. If only most adoption records weren't sealed. Or there was a centralized listing of some sort."

"Twenty years ago record-keeping wasn't the art it is today."

"Tell me about it."

He'd stuck his name and information on a number of legit sibling searches. He'd even placed a letter in his old welfare file in case one of the boys was also searching.

Apparently, his brothers weren't all that eager to make contact. Either that or something had happened to them. His gut clenched. Better not travel that line of thinking.

"Did you ever consider that you might have other fam-ily out there? A grandma, an aunt. Somebody."

He shook his head. "Hard as I've tried, I don't remem-ber anyone. If we ever had any family, Mama had long since alienated them."

He'd had stepdads and "uncles" aplenty. He even re-membered Ian's dad as a pretty good guy, but the only name he'd ever called the man was Rob.

A few years back he'd tracked his mother down in Seminole County—in jail for public intoxication. His lips twisted at the memory. She'd been too toasted to give false information and for once one of her real names, anyway a name Collin remembered, appeared on the police bulletin.

Their subsequent visit had not been a joyous reunion of mother and son. And, to his great disappointment, she knew less about his brothers' whereabouts than he did.

After that, she had disappeared off the radar screen again. Probably moved in with her latest party man and changed her name for the tenth or hundredth time. Not that Collin cared. It was his brothers he wanted to find. Karen Stotz-Grace-Whatever had given them birth, but if she'd ever been a mother he didn't remember it.

"Do you think they're together?"

"Ian and Drew? No." He remembered that last day too clearly. "They were headed to different foster homes. Chances are they weren't reunited, either."

His mother hadn't bothered to jump through the welfare hoops anymore after that. She'd let the state have custody of all three of them. Collin, who ended up in a group home, had failed in his promise to take care of his brothers. He hoped they had been adopted. He hoped they'd found decent, loving families to give them what he hadn't been able to. Even though they were grown men, he needed to know if they were all right.

And if they weren't...

He got that heavy, sick feeling in the pit of his stomach and logged out of the search engine.

Leaning back in the office chair, he scraped a hand over his face and said, "Think I'll call it a night."

Maurice clapped him on the shoulder. "Come by the house. Shanita will make you a fruit smoothie, and Thomas will harangue you for a game of catch."

"Thanks. But I can't. Gotta get out to the farm." He rose to his feet, stretching to relieve the ache across his midback. "The vet's coming by to check that new pup."

"How's he doing?" The other cops were suckers for animals just as he was. They just didn't take their concern quite as far.

"Still in the danger zone." Fury sizzled his blood every time he thought of the abused pup. "Even after what happened, he likes people."

"Animals are very forgiving," Maurice said.

Collin pushed the glass door open with one hand, holding it for his friend to pass through. Together they left the station and walked through the soft evening breeze to the parking garage.

"Unlike me. If I find out who tied that little fella's legs with wire and left him to die, I'll be tempted to return the favor."

Another police officer had found the collie mix, but not before one foot was amputated and another badly infected. And yet, the animal craved human attention and affection.

They entered the parking garage, footsteps echoing on the concrete, the shady interior cool and welcome. Exhaust fumes hovered in the dimness like smelly ghosts.

Maurice dug in his pocket, keys rattling. "Did your social worker call again today?"

Collin slowed, eyes narrowing. "How did you know?"

His buddy lifted a shoulder. "She has friends in high places."

Great. "The department can't force me to do something like that."

"You take in wounded animals. Why not wounded kids?"

"Not my thing."

"Because it hits too close to home?"

Collin stopped next to his Bronco, pushed the lock release, and listened for the snick.

"I don't need reminders." Enough memories plagued him without that. "You like kids. You do it."

"Someday you're going to have to forgive the past, Collin. Lay it to rest. I know Someone who can help you with that."

Collin recognized the subtle reference to God and let

it slide. Though he admired the steadfast faith he saw in Maurice, he wasn't sure what he believed when it came to religion. He fingered the small metal fish in his pocket, rubbing the ever-present scripture that was his one and only connection to God. And to his brothers.

"Nothing to forgive. I just don't like thinking about it."

Maurice looked doubtful but he didn't argue. The quiet acceptance was another part of the man's character Collin appreciated. He said his piece and then shut up.

"This social worker. Her name's Carano, right?"

Collin glanced up, surprised. His grip tightened on the metal door handle. "Yeah."

"She goes to my church."

Collin suppressed a groan. "Don't turn on me, man."

He'd had enough trouble getting Mia Carano out of his head without Maurice weighing in on the deal. The social worker was about the prettiest thing he'd seen in a long time. She emanated a sincere decency that left him unsettled about turning her down, but hearing her smooth, sweet voice on his voice mail a dozen times a day was starting to irritate him.

"Single. Nice family." White teeth flashed in Maurice's dark face. "Easy on the eyes."

Was she ever! Like an ad for an Italian restaurant. Heavy red-brown hair that swirled around her shoulders. Huge, almond-shaped gray-green eyes. A wide, happy mouth. Not too skinny, either. He never had gone for ultra-thin women. Made him think they were hungry.

"I didn't notice."

"You're cool, Grace, but you ain't dead."

"Don't start, Johnson. I'm not interested. A woman

like that would talk a man to pieces." Wasn't she already doing as much?

Maurice chuckled and moseyed off toward his car. His deep voice echoed through the concrete dungeon. "Sooner or later, boy, one of them's gonna get you."

Collin waved him off, climbed into his SUV, and cranked the gas-guzzling engine to life. Nobody was going to "get" him. Way he figured, nobody wanted a hard case like him. And that was fine. The only people he really wanted in his life were his brothers. Wherever they were.

Pulling out of the dark underground, he headed west toward the waning sun. The acreage five miles out of the city was a refuge, both for the animals and for him.

His cell phone rang again. Sure enough, it was the social worker. He shook his head and kept driving.

The veterinarian's dually turned down the short dirt driveway directly behind Collin. The six-wheeled pickup, essential for the rugged places a vet had to traverse, churned up dust and gravel.

"Good timing," Collin muttered to the rearview mirror, glad not to be in back of Doc White's mini dust storm, but also glad to see the dependable animal doctor.

If Paige White said she'd be here, she was. With her busy practice, sometimes she didn't arrive until well after dark, but she always arrived. Collin figured the woman worked more hours than anyone he knew.

The vet followed Collin past the half-built house he called home to the bare patches of grass that served as parking spots in front of a weathered old barn.

A string of fenced pens, divided according to species, dotted the space behind the barn. In one, a pair of neglected and starved horses was slowly regaining strength. In another, a deer healed from an arrow wound.

To one side, a rabbit hutch held a raccoon. And inside the small barn were five dogs, three cats and ten kittens. He was near capacity. As usual. He needed to add on again, but he also needed to continue the work on his house. The bank wouldn't loan money on two rooms, a bathroom and a concrete slab framed in wood.

Booted feet first, the vet leaped from the high cab of her truck with a whoop for a greeting.

"Hey there, ornery. How's business?" she hollered as Collin came around the front of his SUV.

"Which one?"

"The only one that counts." She waved a gloved hand toward the barn, and Collin nearly smiled. Paige White, a fortysomething cowgirl with a heart as big and warm as the sun, joked that animals liked her faster, better and longer than humans ever had.

One thing Collin knew for sure, animals responded to her treatment. He fell in step with the short, sturdy blonde and headed inside the barn.

Without preliminary, he said, "The pup's leg smells funny."

"You been cleaning those wounds the way I showed you?"

"Every day." He remembered the first time he'd poured antiseptic cleaner on the pup's foot and listened to its pitiful cries.

Doc stopped, stared at him for a minute and then said, "We'll have a look at him first."

Paige White could always read his concern, though he had a poker face. Her uncanny sixth sense would have bothered him under other circumstances.

The scent of fresh straw and warm-blooded animals astir beneath their feet, they reached the stall where the collie was confined.

From a large, custom-cut cardboard box, the pup gazed at them with dark, moist, delighted eyes. His shaggy tail thumped madly at the side of the box.

As always, Collin marveled at the pup's adoring welcome. He'd been cruelly treated by humans and yet his love didn't falter.

Doc knelt down, crooning. "How's my pal today? Huh? How ya doin', boy?"

"I call him Happy."

"Well, Happy." The dog licked her extended hand, the tail thumping faster. "Let me see those legs of yours." She jerked her chin at Collin, who'd hunkered down beside her. "Make sure this guy over here's looking after you."

With exquisite tenderness, she inspected one limb and then the other. Her pale eyebrows slammed together as she examined the deep, ugly wound.

Collin watched, anxious, when she took a hypodermic from her long, leather bag and filled it with medication.

"What's that?"

"More antibiotic." She held the syringe at eye level and flicked the plastic several times. "I don't like the way this looks, Collin. There's not enough tissue left to debride."

"Meaning?"

"We may have to take this foot off, too."

"Ah, man." He scrubbed a hand over his face, heard his whiskers. He knew Paige would fight hard to avoid another amputation, so if she brought up the subject, she wasn't blowing smoke. "Any hope?"

"Where there's life, there's hope. But if he doesn't respond to treatment soon, we'll have to remove the foot to save him. Infection like this can spread to the entire body in a hurry."

"I know. But a dog with two amputated feet..."

He let the thought go. Doc knew the odds of the pup having any quality of life. Finding a home for him would be close to impossible, and Collin only kept the animals until they were healthy and adoptable or ready to return to the wild. He didn't keep pets. Just animals in need.

Doc dropped the empty syringe into a plastic container, then patted his shoulder. "Don't fret. I'll run out again tomorrow. Got Jenner's Feed Store to donate their broken bags of feed to you and I want to be here to see them delivered. Clovis Jenner owes me."

Warmth spread through Collin's chest. "So do I."

Doc was constantly on the look-out for feed, money, any kind of support she could round up for his farm. And she only charged him for supplies or medications, never for her expertise.

"Nonsense. If it wasn't for me and my soft heart, you wouldn't have all these critters. I just can't put them down without trying."

"I know." He felt the same way. Whenever she called with a stray animal in need of a place to heal, Collin took it if he had room. He was stretched to the limit on space and funds, but he had to keep going. "Let's go check on the others."

Together they made the rounds. She checked the cats and dogs first, redressing wounds, giving shots, poking pills down resistant throats, instructing Collin on the next phase of care.

At the horses' pen, she nodded her approval and

pushed a tube of medication down each scrawny throat. "They're more alert. See how this one lifts her head now to watch us? That's a very good sign."

One of the mares, Daisy, leaned her velvety nose against Collin's shirtfront and snuffled. In return for her affection, he stroked her neck, relishing the warm, soft feel against his fingers.

The first few days after the horses had arrived, Collin had come out to the barn every four hours to follow the strict refeeding program Doc had put them on. Seeing the horses slowly come back from the brink of death made the sleepless nights and interrupted days worth the effort.

Sometimes the local Future Farmers of America kids helped out. The other cops occasionally did the same. Most of the time, Collin preferred to work alone.

At the raccoon's hutch, Paige declared the hissing creature fit and ready to release. And finally, she stood at the fence and watched the young buck limp listlessly around the pen.

"He's depressed."

"Deer get depressed?"

"Mmm. Trauma, pain, fear lead to depression in any species." She squinted into the gathering darkness, intelligent eyes studying every move the deer made. "The wound looks good though."

"You do good work."

Some bow hunter had shot the buck. He had escaped with an arrow protruding from his hip, finally collapsing near enough to a house that dogs had alerted the owner. Paige had operated on the badly infected hip.

"I do, don't I?" The vet smiled smugly before sobering. "Only time will tell if enough muscle remains for him to survive in the wild, though."

She turned and started back around the barn to her truck. Collin took her bag and followed.

Headlights sliced the dusk and came steadily toward them, the hum of a motor loud against the quiet country evening.

Collin tensed. "Company," he said.

"Who is it?"

"My favorite neighbor," he said, sarcasm thicker than the cloud of dust billowing around the car. "Cecil Slokum."

Collin and his farm were located a half mile from the nearest house, but Slokum harassed him on a regular basis with some complaint about the animals.

The late-model brown sedan pulled to a stop. A man the size and shape of Danny DeVito put the engine in Park and rolled down a window. His face was red with anger.

"I'm not putting up with this anymore, Grace."

The sixth sense that made Collin a good cop kicked in. He made a quick survey of the car's interior, saw no weapons and relaxed a little.

"What's the problem, Mr. Slokum?" He sounded way more polite than he felt.

"One of them dogs of yours took down my daughter's prize ewe last night."

"Didn't happen." All his animals were sick and in pens.

"Just 'cause you're a big shot cop don't make you right. I know what I saw."

"Wasn't one of mine."

"Tell it to the judge." The man shoved a brown envelope out the window.

Collin took it, puzzled. "What is this?"

"See for yourself." With that, Slokum crammed the car into gear and backed out, disappearing down the gravel road much more quickly than he'd come.

Collin stared down at the envelope.

"Might as well open it," Doc said.

With a shrug, Collin tore the seal, pulled out a legal-looking sheet of vellum and read. When he finished, he slammed a fist against the offending form.

Just what he needed right now. Someone else besides the annoying social worker on his back.

"Collin?" Doc said.

Jaw rigid, he handed her the paper and said, "Nothing like good neighbors. The jerk is suing me for damages."

Chapter Three

Mia perched on a high kitchen stool, swiveling back and forth, her mind a million miles away from her mother's noisy kitchen as she sliced boiled zucchini for stuffing.

At the stove, Grandma Maria Celestina stirred her special marinara sauce while Mama prepared the sausages for baked ziti.

The rich scents of tomato and basil and sausages had the whole family prowling in and out of the kitchen.

"Church was good today, huh, Mia?"

"Good, Mama."

At fifty-six, Rosalie Carano was still a pretty woman. People said Mia favored her and she hoped so. She'd always thought Mama looked like Sophia Loren. Flowered apron around her generous hips, Rosalie sailed around the large family kitchen with the efficient energy that had successfully raised five kids.

The whole clan gathered every Sunday after church for a late-afternoon meal of Mama's traditional Italian cooking, which always included breads and pastries from the family bakery. In the living room, her dad,

Leo, argued basketball with her eldest brother, Gabe, and Grandpa Salvatore. Gabe's wife, Abby, had taken their two kids outside to swim in the above-ground pool accompanied by Mia's pregnant sister, Anna Maria. The other brothers, Adam and Nic, roamed in and out of the kitchen like starving ten-year-olds.

Mia was blessed with a good family. Not perfect by any means, but close and caring. She appreciated that, especially on days like today when she felt inexplicably down in the dumps. Even church service, which usually buoyed her spirits, had left her uncharacteristically quiet.

Collin Grace had not returned one of her phone calls in the past three days, and she'd practically promised Mitchell that he would. She disliked pulling in favors, tried not to use her eldest brother's influence as a city councilman, but Sergeant Grace was a tough nut to crack.

Nic, her baby brother, snitched a handful of grated mozzarella from the bowl at her elbow. Out of habit, she whacked his hand then listened to the expected howl of protest.

"Go away," she muttered.

His grin was unrepentant. At twenty, dark and athletic Nic was a chick magnet. He knew his charms, though they had never worked on either of his sisters.

"You're grumpy."

Brother Adam hooked an elbow around her neck and yanked back. She tilted her head to look up at him. Adam Carano, dark and tall, was eleven months older than Mia. From childhood, they'd been best friends, and he could read her like the Sunday comics.

"What's eating you, sis? You're too quiet. It scares me." He usually complained that she talked too much.

Gabe stuck his head around the edge of the door. "Last time she was quiet, Nic and Adam ended up with strange new haircuts."

Mia rolled her eyes. "I was eight."

"And we've not had a moment of peace and quiet from you since," Adam joked.

"And I," Nic put in, "was scarred for life at the ripe old age of one."

"I should have cut off your tongue."

"Mom," Nic called in a whiney little-boy voice. "Mia's picking on me."

Mia ignored him and set to work stuffing the zucchini boats.

"What is it, Mia?" Mama asked. "Adam's right. You are not yourself."

"It's a kid," Adam replied before she could. "It's always one of her kids."

Mia pulled a face. He knew her so well. "Smarty."

Mama shushed him. "Let her tell us. Maybe we can help."

It was Mama's way. If one of her chicks had a problem, the mother hen rushed in to fix it—bringing with her lasagna or cookies. So Mia told them about Mitch.

"He's salvageable, Mama. There is a lot of good in him, but he needs a man's influence and guidance. I tried getting him into the Big Brothers program but he refuses."

"One of the boys will talk to him. Won't you, boys?" Rosalie eyed her three sons with a look that brooked no argument.

"Sure. Of course we would." All three men nodded in unison like bobble toys in the back window of a car.

Heart filling with love for these overgrown macho

teddy bears she called brothers, Mia shook her head. "Thanks, guys. You're the best. But Mitch is distrustful of most people. He'd never agree. For some reason, he zeroed in on one of the street patrolmen and will only talk to him. The cop is perfect, but—"

"Whoo-oo, Mia found her a perfect man. Go, sis." The brothers started in with the catcalls and bad jokes.

When the noise subsided, she said, "Not that kind of perfect, unfortunately. I don't even like the guy."

But she couldn't get him out of her mind, either.

"Mia!"

"Oh, Mama." Mia plopped the last zucchini boat on a pan and sprinkled parmesan on top. "Our first meeting was disastrous. I bought the man a hamburger to soften him up a little, and he didn't even stick around long enough to eat it. And now he doesn't bother to return my phone calls."

"You've lost your charm, sis. Need some lessons?" Nic flexed both arms and preened around the kitchen, bumping into Grandma, who, in turn, shook a gnarled finger in his laughing face.

Rosalie whirled and flapped her apron at the men. "Out. Shoo. We'll never get dinner on."

Gabe and Nic disappeared, still laughing. Adam stayed behind, pulled a stool around the bar with one foot, and perched beside Mia.

The most Italian-looking of the Carano brothers, Adam was swarthy and handsome and a tad more serious than his siblings.

"Want me to beat him up?"

"Who? Mitch or the cop?"

He lifted a wide shoulder. "Either. Say the word."

"Maybe later."

They both grinned at the familiar joke. All through high school Adam had threatened to beat up any guy who made her unhappy. Though he'd never done it, the boys in her class had thought he would.

"If I could only convince Sergeant Grace to spend one day with Mitch, I think he'd be hooked. He comes off as cold and uncaring, but I don't think he is."

"Some people aren't kid-crazy like you are. Especially us men types."

"All I want is a few hours a week of his time to save a kid from an almost certain future of crime and drugs." Mama swished by and took the pan of zucchini boats. "The couple of times I managed to get him on the phone, he barely said three words."

Adam swiveled her stool so that her back was to him. Strong hands massaged her shoulders.

"The guy was short and to the point. *No.* The least he could do is explain *why* he refuses, but he clams up like Uncle Vitorio."

Adam chuckled. "And that drives you nuts in a hurry."

"Yes, it does. Human beings have the gift of language. They should use it." She let her head go lax. "That feels good."

"You're tight as a drum."

"I didn't sleep much last night. I couldn't get Mitch off my mind so I got up to pray. And then, the next thing I know I'm praying for Collin Grace, too."

"The cop?"

"Yes. There's something about him…sort of an aloneness, I guess, that bothers me. I can't figure him out."

Adam squeezed her shoulders hard. "There's your trouble, sis. You always want to talk and analyze and dig until you know everything. Some people like to keep their books closed."

"You think so?" She swiveled back around to face him. "You think I'm too nosey? That I talk too much?"

"Yep. Pushy, too."

"Gabe thinks I'm too soft."

"That's because he's the pushiest lawyer in three states."

Didn't she know it? She'd lost her first job because of Gabe, and though he'd done everything in his power to make it up to her in the years since, Mia would never forget the humiliation of having her professional ethics compromised.

Nic stuck his head into the kitchen, then ducked when his mother threw a tea towel at him. "Mia, your purse is ringing. Should I get it?"

Mia slid off the stool and started toward the living room. She might be pushy, but she played fair.

A large masculine hand attached to a hairy arm—Nic's—appeared around the door, holding out the cell phone.

Taking it, Mia pushed the button and said, "Hello."

"Miss Carano, this is Monica Perez."

"Mrs. Perez, is something wrong?" Mia tensed. Today was Sunday. A strange time for calls from a client. "Is it Mitchell?"

The woman's voice sounded more weary than worried. "He's run away again. This time the worthless little creep stole money out of my purse."

Collin kicked back the roller chair and plopped down at his desk. He'd just returned from transporting a prisoner and had to complete the proper paperwork.

Paperwork. Blah. Most Sundays he spent at the farm or crashed out on his couch watching ballgames. But this was his weekend to work.

"I need to see Sergeant Grace, please."

Collin recognized the cool, sweet voice immediately. Mia Carano, social worker to the world and nag of the first order, was in the outer office.

"Dandy," he muttered. "Make my day."

Tossing down the pen, he rose and strode toward the door just as she sailed through it. She looked fresh and young in tropical-print capris and an orange T-shirt, a far cry from the business suit and heels of their first meeting.

"Mitch has run away again," she blurted without preliminary.

"Nothing the police can do for twenty-four hours."

"We have to find him. I'm afraid he'll get into trouble again."

"Probably will."

Her gray-green eyes snapped with fire. "I want you to go with me to find him right now. I have some ideas where he might go, but he won't listen to me. He'll listen to you."

The woman was unbelievable. Like a bulldog, she never gave up.

"It's not police business."

"Can't you do something just because it's right? Because a kid out there needs you?"

Collin felt himself softening. Had any social worker ever worked this hard for him or his brothers?

"If I take a drive around, have a look in a couple places, will you leave me alone?"

"Probably not." Her pretty smile stretched wide beneath a pair of twinkling eyes.

She was a pest. An annoying, pretty, sweet, aggravating pest who would probably go right on driving him nuts until he gave in.

Against his better judgment, he reached into a file cabinet and yanked out a form. "Sign this."

"What is it?"

"Department policy. If you're riding in my car, you gotta sign."

The pretty smile grew wider—and warmer.

He was an idiot to do this. Her kind never stopped at one favor.

Without bothering to read the forms that released the police department of liability in case of injury, Mia scribbled her name on the line and then beat him out of the station house. At the curb, she stopped to look at him. He motioned toward his patrol car and she jumped into the passenger's seat. A gentle floral scent wafted on the breeze when she slammed the door. He never noticed things like that and it bugged him.

He also noticed that the inside of his black-and-white was a mess. A clipboard, ticket pad, a travel mug and various other junk littered the floorboards. Usually a neat freak, he wanted to apologize for the mess, but he kept stubbornly silent. Let her think what she liked. Let her think he was a slob. Why should he care what Mia Carano thought of him?

If she was bothered, she didn't say so. But she did talk. And talk. She filled him in on Mitch's likes and dislikes, his grades in school, the places he hung out. And then she started in on the child advocate thing. She told him how desperately the kid needed a strong male in his life.

That he was a good kid, smart, funny and kind. A computer whiz at school.

This time there was no Delete button to silence her. Trapped inside the car, Collin had to listen.

He put on his signal, made a smooth turn onto Tenth Street and headed east toward the boy's neighborhood. "How do you know so much about this one kid?"

"His mom, his classmates, his teachers."

"Why?"

"It's my job."

"To come out on Sunday afternoon looking for a runaway?"

"His mother called me."

"Bleeding heart," he muttered.

"Better than being heartless."

He glanced sideways. "You think I'm heartless?"

She glared back. "Aren't you?"

No, he wasn't. But let her think what she would. He wasn't getting involved with anything to do with the social welfare system.

His radio crackled to life. A juvenile shoplifter.

Mia sucked in a distressed breath, the first moment of quiet they'd had.

Collin radioed his location and took the call.

"It's Mitchell," Mia said after hearing the details. "The description and area fit perfectly."

Heading toward the complainant's convenience store, Collin asked, "You got a picture of him?"

"Of course." She rummaged in a glittery silver handbag and stuck a photo under his nose.

Collin spotted the 7-Eleven up ahead. This woman surely did vex him.

He pulled into the concrete drive and parked in the fire lane.

"Stay here. I'll talk to the owner, get what information I can, and then we'll go from there."

The obstinate social worker pushed open her door and followed him inside the convenience store. She whipped out her picture of the Perez kid and showed it to the store owner.

"That's him. Comes in here all the time. I been suspicious of him. Got him on tape this time."

Collin filled out the mandatory paperwork, jotting down all the pertinent information. "What did he take?"

The owner got a funny look on his face. "He took weird stuff. Made me wonder."

Mia paced back and forth in front of the counter. "What kind of weird stuff?"

Collin silenced her with a stare. She widened rebellious eyes at him, but hushed—for the moment.

"Peroxide, cotton balls, a roll of bandage."

Mia's eyes widened even further. "Was he hurt?"

The owner shrugged. "What do I care? He stole from me."

"He's hurt. I just know it. We have to find him."

Collin shot her another look before saying to the clerk, "Anything else we should know?"

"Well, he did pay for the cat food." The man shifted uncomfortably and Collin suspected there was more to the story, but he wouldn't get it from this guy. He motioned to Mia and they left.

Once in the car, he said, "Any ideas?"

She crossed her arms. "You mean, I have permission to talk now?"

Collin stifled a grin. The annoying woman was also cute. "Be my guest."

"I know several places around here where kids hang out."

He knew a few himself. "I doubt he'll be in plain sight, but we can try."

He put the car in gear and drove east. They tried all the usual spots, the parks, the parking lots. They showed the kid's picture in video stores and to other kids on the streets, but soon ran out of places to look.

"We have to find him before he gets into more trouble."

"I doubt he'd come this far. We're nearly to the city dump."

As soon as he said the words, Collin knew. A garbage dump was exactly the kind of place he would have hidden when he was eleven.

With a spurt of adrenaline, he kicked the patrol car up and sped along the mostly deserted stretch of highway on the outskirts of the city.

When he turned onto the road leading to the landfill, Mia said incredulously, "You think he's here? In the city dump?"

He shot her an exasperated look. "Got a better idea?"

"No."

Collin slammed out of the car and climbed to the top of the enormous cavity. The stench rolled over him in waves.

"Ew." Beside him, Mia clapped a hand over her nose.

"Wait in the car. I'll look around."

Collin wasn't the least surprised when she ignored him.

"You go that way." She pointed left. "I'll take the right side."

Determination in her stride, she took off through the trash heap apparently unconcerned about her white shoes or clean clothes. Collin watched her go. A pinch of admiration tugged at him. He'd say one thing for Miss Social Worker, she wasn't a quitter.

His boots slid on loose dirt as he carefully picked his way down the incline. Some of the trash had been recently buried, but much more lay scattered about.

He watched his step, aware that among the discarded furniture and trash bags, danger and disease lurked. This was not a place for a boy. Unless that boy had no place else to turn.

His chest constricted. He'd been here and done this. Maybe not in this dump, but he understood what the kid was going through. He hated the memories. Hated the heavy pull of dread and hurt they brought.

This was why he didn't want to get involved with Mia's project. And now here he was, knee-deep in trash and recollections, moving toward what appeared to be a shelter of some sort.

Plastic trash bags that stretched across a pair of ragged-out couches were anchored in place by rocks, car parts, a busted TV set. An old refrigerator clogged one end and a cardboard box the other.

Mia was right. The kid had smarts. He'd built his hideout in an area unlikely to be buried for a while and had made the spot blend in with the rest of the junk.

As quietly as he could, Collin leaned down and slid the cardboard box away. What he saw inside made his chest ache.

The kid had tried to make a home inside the shelter. An old blanket and a sack of clothes were piled on one end of a ragged couch. A flashlight lay on an up-turned crate. Beneath the crate, the kid had stored the canned milk, a jar of water, cat food and a box of cereal.

In the dim confines Mitchell knelt over a cardboard box, cotton ball and peroxide in hand.

Collin had a pretty good idea what was inside the box.

At the sudden inflow of light, the kid's head whipped around. A mix of fear and resentment widened his dark eyes.

"Nice place you got here," Collin said, stooping to enter.

"I'm not doing anything wrong."

"Stealing from convenience stores isn't wrong?"

"I had to. Panda—" Mitchell glanced down at the box "—she's hurt."

Curiosity aroused, Collin moved to the boy's side. A mother cat with three tiny kittens mewed up at him. Mitchell stroked the top of her head and she began to purr.

Collin's heart slammed against his ribs.

Oh, man. Déjà vu all over again.

"Mind if I take a look?"

The kid scooted sideways but hovered protectively.

Collin frowned. The cat was speckled with round burns, several of them clearly infected. "What happened?"

"Some kids had her. Mean kids who like to hurt things. She was their cat, but I took her when they started—"

Collin held up a hand. He didn't need the ugly details to visualize what the kid had saved the cat from.

"You can't stay here, Mitchell. Your mother is worried."

"She's just worried about her ten bucks."

"You shouldn't have taken it."

The kid shrugged, didn't answer, but Collin's own eyes told him where the money had gone. And if his nose was an indicator, the kid had scavenged a pack of cigarettes somewhere too which would explain the store owner's guilty behavior. He'd probably sold cigarettes to a minor.

"I'm not going back to her house."

"You have to."

"I can't. Panda and her babies will die if I don't take care of her. Archie, too."

"Archie?"

The kid reached behind them to the other couch and gently lifted a turtle out of a shoe box. A piece of silver duct tape ran along a fracture in the green shell.

Emotions swamped Collin. He felt as if he was being sucked under a whirlpool. Memories flashed through his head so fast he thought he was going blind.

At that moment, little Miss Social Worker poked her head through the opening. "I thought I heard voices."

Mitchell shrank away from her, blocking the box of cats with his body.

"I won't leave her," he said belligerently. "You can't make me."

"Maybe your mother will let you keep them," Collin said, hoping Mitchell's mother was better than he suspected.

"I'm not going back there, I said. Never."

"Why not?"

The boy's face closed up tight, a look Collin recognized all too well. Something ugly needed to be said and the kid wasn't ready to deal with it.

As the inevitability of the situation descended upon him, Collin pulled a hand down his face.

After a minute of pulling himself together, he spoke. "Nothing's going to happen to your cat. You have my word."

Mitch's face lightened, though distrust continued to ooze out of him. "How can you be sure?"

"Because," Collin said, wishing there was a way he could avoid involvement and knowing he couldn't, "I'll take her home with me."

The boy's face crumpled, incredulous. The belligerent attitude fled, replaced by the awful yearning of hope. "You will?"

"I know a good vet. Panda will be okay."

Mia ducked under the black plastic and came inside. Her eyes glowed with pleasure. "That's really nice of you, Sergeant Grace."

"Yeah. That's me. Real nice." Stupid, too.

He was a cop. Tough. Hardened to the ugliness of humanity. He could resist about anything. Anything, that is, except looking at Mitch's face and seeing his own reflection.

Like it or not, he was about to become a big brother— again.

He only hoped he didn't mess it up this time around.

Chapter Four

Mitchell sat huddled in the backseat of the patrol car, tense and suspicious. The cardboard carton containing cat, kittens and turtle rested on the seat beside him. The rest of his property was in a battered paint bucket on the floor.

"I told you I'm not going back there."

Mia turned in her seat, antennae going up. "Why not? Is something wrong at home?"

The boy ignored her.

Ever the cop, Collin spoke up. "Juvie Hall is the other alternative."

"Better than home."

The adults exchanged glances.

Collin hadn't said two complete sentences since they'd left Mitch's lean-to. He'd simply gathered up the animals and the rag-tag assortment of supplies and led the way to the cruiser. Mitchell had followed along without a fuss, his only concern for the animals. For some reason that Mia could not fathom, the two silent males seemed to communicate without words.

Right now, though, Collin's words were not helping.

Mia stifled the urge to shush him. Something was amiss with the child and he was either too scared or too proud to say so.

She pressed a little harder. "I wish you'd talk to me, Mitch. I can help. It's what I do. If there is a problem at home I can help get it resolved."

Dirt spewed up over the windshield as they bumped and jostled down the dusty road out of the landfill. Once on the highway, Collin flipped on the windshield washers.

"How do you and your mother get along? Any problems there?"

Mitch turned his profile toward her and stared at the spattering water.

Mia softened her voice. "Mitch, if there's abuse, you need to tell me."

His head whipped around, expression fierce. "Leave my mom out of this."

Whoa! "Okay. What about your stepdad?"

Collin gave her a sideways glance that said he wished she'd shut up. She didn't plan on doing that any time soon. Something was wrong in this boy's life. Otherwise, he wouldn't be running away. He wouldn't be shoplifting, and he wouldn't dread going home. She would be a lousy social worker and an even worse human being if she didn't investigate the very real possibility of abuse.

"Mitchell," she urged softly. "You can trust me. I want to help."

The cruiser slowed to a turn, pulled through a concrete drive and stopped. Mitchell jerked upright. His eyes widened in fright.

"Hey. What are we doing here?"

The green-and-red sign of the 7-Eleven convenience

store loomed above the gas pumps. Mia recognized it as the store from which Mitch had shoplifted. Facing consequences was an important part of teaching a child right from wrong, but Mia still felt sorry for him. And she felt frustrated to be getting nowhere in their conversation.

Collin shifted into Park and got out of the car.

Mitchell shrank back against the seat. "I ain't going in there."

Mia braced for a strong-armed confrontation between the cop and the kid, prepared to intervene if necessary. But the cop surprised her.

He opened the back door, hunkered down beside the car and spoke quietly, almost gently, to the scared boy. "Everybody messes up sometime, Mitch. Part of being a man means facing up to your mistakes. Are you willing to be a man about it?"

Although Mia was dying to offer to go inside with the boy and talk to the owner, she knew Collin was right. For once, she had to bite her tongue and let the cop do the talking.

Several long seconds passed while Mia thought she would burst. The need to blurt out reassurances and promises swelled like yeast bread on a hot day. Would Mitchell go on his own? Would Sergeant Grace drag him inside if he didn't?

As if in answer to her unasked question, Collin placed one wide hand on the knee of the boy's dirty blue jeans and patiently waited.

The gesture brought a lump to Mia's throat. Her brothers would laugh at her if they knew, but she couldn't help it. There was something moving about the sight of a tough, taciturn cop conveying his trustworthiness with a gentle touch.

The boy's shoulders were so tense, Mia thought his collarbone might snap. Finally, he drew in a shuddering breath and reached for his seat-belt clasp.

"Will you go with me?" Mouth tight and straight, he directed the question to Collin.

The policeman pushed to his feet. "Every step."

And then, as if the social worker in the front seat was invisible, the two males, one tall and buff and immaculate, the other small and thin and tattered, crossed the concrete space and went inside.

The kittens in the backseat made mewing sounds as Panda shifted positions. Mia glanced around to be sure they were staying put. Yellow eyes blinked back.

"Hang tight, Mama," she said. "The abandonment is only temporary."

The poor, bedraggled cat seemed satisfied to stay with her babies and the hapless turtle. So, Mia tilted her forehead against the cool side glass and watched the people inside the store. There were a few customers coming and going, an occasional car door slammed, though the area was reasonably quiet.

She could see Collin and Mitchell moving around inside, see the clerk. Although frustrated at being left behind, for once, she didn't charge into the situation. But she did use her time to pray that somehow the angry shop owner would give the child a break without letting him off scot-free.

Ten minutes later, Collin and Mitch emerged from the building. Collin wore his usual bland expression that gave nothing away. Mitch looked pale, but relieved as he slammed into the backseat.

Mia could hardly contain herself. "How did it go?"

"Okay." Collin started the cruiser and pulled into the lane of slow Sunday-afternoon traffic.

Mia rolled her eyes. That wasn't the answer she was asking for. But since the cop wasn't willing to elaborate, she asked Mitchell, "What was decided? Is he going to press charges?"

Mitch trailed a finger over one of the kittens. "I don't know yet. But he said he'd think about it."

The quiet, gentle boy she usually encountered had returned. The belligerence, most likely posturing brought on by fear, had dissipated. He looked young and small and lost.

Collin spoke up—finally. "We worked out a deal."

"And is this a secret all-male deal? Or can the nosy, female social worker be let in on it?"

Collin glanced her way, eyes sparkling. At least she'd badgered a smile out of him. Sort of.

"Didn't like being left in the car?"

The rat. He had already figured out that she needed to be in the middle of a situation. "This is the sort of thing I'm trained to do. I might have been useful in there."

He didn't argue the point. "We're asking for twenty hours of community service."

That was something she could help with.

"I'll talk to the DA if you'd like." She did that all the time, working deals for the juveniles she encountered. "He's a friend."

"Figures."

"Having friends is not a bad thing, Sergeant."

"It is when you use them to harass people."

Ah, the phone calls to the chief had not pleased him. "I did not harass you."

He lifted an eyebrow at her.

"Well, okay. Maybe I did. But just a little to get your attention."

"You got it."

"Was that a good thing or a bad thing?"

"Time will tell."

Was that a smile she saw? Or a grimace? He was the hardest man in the world to read.

The cruiser pulled to a stop in front of an older frame house in a rundown area of the city. Paint had peeled until the place was more gray than white, and the yard was overgrown. A rusted lawnmower with grass shooting up over the motor looked as though it hadn't been used all summer.

Mia knew the house. She'd been here more than once at the request of the school system, but never could find out anything that justified removing the boy from the home.

"I thought Mitch opted for Juvenile Hall?" she asked.

Collin shut off the engine and opened the car door. "He changed his mind."

A dark-haired woman who was far too thin came out into the yard and stood with her arms folded around her waist.

"Where's my ten bucks?" she asked as soon as Mitch was out of the car.

To Mia's surprise, Mitch reached in his jeans and withdrew a crumpled bill. She looked at Sergeant Grace, suspicious, but the man's poker face gave away nothing. The idea that the tough cop might have bailed the boy out with his mother touched her. Maybe he wasn't so heartless after all.

She listened without comment as Collin apprised Mitchell's mother about the situation. Mrs. Perez didn't seem too pleased with her son, as expected, but her fidgety behavior raised Mia's suspicions. She didn't invite them into the house and seemed anxious to have them gone.

"What's going to happen to him?" she asked. "I don't have no money for lawyers and courts."

"He broke the law, Mrs. Perez. Miss Carano will talk to the DA for him, but at the least he'll do some community service to pay for the things he took from the store."

"He stole from me, too."

Collin's nostrils flared. "You want to press charges?"

Said aloud, the idea seemed harsh even to the fidgety mother. "I don't want him stealing from me anymore. That's all. He'll end up in jail like his old man."

Conversation halted as an old car, the chassis nearly dragging on the street, mufflers missing or altered, rumbled slowly past. Loud hip-hop music pulsed from the interior, overriding every other sound.

Collin turned and stared hard-eyed at the vehicle, garnering a rude gesture in return. Mia had a feeling the car's inhabitants hadn't seen the last of Sergeant Grace.

When the racket subsided, Mia picked up the conversation. "Have you considered counseling?"

Monica Perez rolled her eyes. "Mitchell don't need no shrink. He needs a new set of friends. Them Walters boys down the street get into everything. You oughta go arrest them."

"I could help him meet some new friends if you'd like," Mia said and received a sideways glance from Collin for her efforts.

"Fine with me."

"My church has a basketball league for kids. He could sign up to play."

"I wouldn't mind that, but I ain't got a car. Is it far from here?"

"I'll pick him up. Saturday morning at nine, if he wants to go." She looked at Mitch, stuck like a wood tick to Collin's side. "Mitch?"

"Sure. I guess so."

Collin dropped a hand on the boy's shoulder. "Miss Carano's going out on a limb for you."

Mitch gazed up at the tall cop, his expression a mix of frightened child and troubled youth. "I know."

Mia glimpsed his bewilderment, his failure to understand his own behavior. And as always, something about this kid got to her. A good person was inside there. With God's help, she'd find a way to bring him out.

"Someone will give you a call next week and let you know the DA's decision," Collin was telling Mrs. Perez.

And then with a curt nod, he turned and started back toward the police car. Mia, who preferred long goodbyes with lots of conversation and closure, felt off balance.

Mitch didn't seem to be finished either because he darted after the departing figure.

"Sergeant Grace."

Collin stopped, one hand on the car door.

Suddenly, every vestige of the tough street kid was gone. Mitch looked like what he was, a little boy with nothing and no one to cling to. "You'll take care of Panda?"

"I will."

"Can I come see her sometime?"

The hardened cop studied the small, intense face, his own face intense as if the answer would cost him too much. "She'd be sad if you didn't."

Mia said a quick goodbye to Mrs. Perez and hurried

across the overgrown lawn. Now was her chance. Now that Collin had softened just the tiniest bit.

"I could bring Mitch out to your place. Anytime that's convenient for you."

Collin looked from Mitchell to Mia and back again. Mia was certain she must be imagining things because the strong, hardened cop looked more helpless than the boy. Helpless…and scared.

Mia shoved away from the mile-high stack of file folders on her desk and scrounged in the bottom desk drawer for her stash of miniature Snickers. A day like today required chocolate and plenty of it. She took two.

Her case load grew exponentially every day to the point that she was overwhelmed at times. Looking out for the interests of kids was her calling, but on days like today, the calling was a tough one.

She'd made a school visit and six home visits. At the last one, she'd done what every social worker dreads. She'd pulled the two neglected babies and taken them to a foster home. Even now, though she knew she'd made the right choice, she could hear the youngest one crying for his mama. Poor little guy was too young to comprehend that he lived in a crack house.

She nipped the corner of Snickers number one and turned to the computer on her desk. All the reports from today had to be typed up and stored in the master files before she could go home.

"See ya tomorrow, Mia," one of the other workers called as she passed by the open office door.

Mia waved without lifting her eyes from the computer screen. "Have a good evening, Allie."

She reached for another bite of candy. Over the tick-

tick-tick of the keyboard, she heard another voice. This one wasn't her coworker.

"Mind if I interrupt for a minute?"

Her head snapped up.

"Collin?" she blurted before remembering he'd never given her permission to call him by his first name. But she had to face the fact. She thought about him, even prayed for him, by his first name.

During the three days since he'd helped her find Mitchell, she'd prayed about him and thought about him a lot. The fact that she didn't know him that well didn't get him out of her mind. She was intrigued. And attracted. More than once, she'd wondered if he was a Christian, but she was afraid she might already know the answer.

Now he stood before her in his blue uniform, patches on each sleeve, shiny metal pins on each collar point and above his name tag. He looked as crisp and clean as new money.

Great. And she looked like a worn-out, overworked social worker whose white blouse was wrinkled and pulling loose from her red skirt. She hoped like crazy there was no chocolate on her teeth.

"Can we talk?"

Collin Grace wanted to talk? Now there was a novel concept.

"Do you know how?" She softened the teasing jab with a smile.

Those brown eyes twinkled but he didn't return the smile. "I want to make a deal with you."

He scraped a client chair away from her desk a little. He might want to talk, but he was still keeping his distance.

Mia rolled back in her own chair to study his solemn

face. Whatever was on his mind was serious business. "A deal?"

"In exchange for your help, I'll mentor the kid."

The wonderful thrill of victory shot much-needed energy into her bloodstream. After the day she'd had, this was great news.

"Mitchell Perez? Collin, that's marvelous. He told me on the phone last night that you stopped by after school yesterday. That was so nice of you, and it really made his day. He tried to act all tough about your visit, but he was thrilled. I could tell. And when I told him the DA agreed to community service, he asked if he could work for you. But I had no idea how to answer that without talking to you first and I've just been so busy today...."

Collin lifted one hand to slow her down. "The deal first."

Once she got on a roll, stopping was difficult. But that halted her in her tracks. "Am I going to like this deal?"

"This is confidential. Okay?"

Now her interest was piqued. Very. "Most of my work is confidential. Believe it or not, I can keep my mouth shut when necessary."

He made a huffing noise that sounded remarkably close to a laugh. She got up and moved around the desk past him to close the door even though the office was probably empty by now.

When she sat down again, she had to ask, "Do I have chocolate on my teeth?"

This time he *did* laugh.

"No. You look great."

"Such a smooth liar," she said, and then reached in the file drawer and took out another candy bar. "Want one?"

"No, thanks."

"Oh, yeah. You're the health-food cop. Poor guy. You don't know what you're missing." She unwrapped a Snickers, nibbled the end and shifted into social-worker mode.

"You said you needed my help. What can I do for you, Officer?"

"Collin's okay."

Another thrill, this one as sweet as the caramel, and completely uncalled for, raced through her. Before she could wipe the smile off her face, he did it for her.

"I want you to help me find my brothers."

She blinked, uncomprehending. "Your brothers?"

"Yeah." Collin leaned forward, muscled forearms on his thighs as he clasped his hands in front of him. Steel intensity radiated from him as though the coming confidence was very difficult for him to share. "My little brothers, Drew and Ian, though neither of them are little now."

She got a sinking feeling in the pit of her stomach. "When did you last see them?"

His answer hurt her heart. "More than twenty years ago."

"Tell me," she said simply, knowing for once when to keep quiet and let the other person do the talking. Whatever he had to share, in confidence, about his brothers was important to him.

Over the next fifteen minutes, during which Mia went through three more Snickers bars, Collin told a story all too familiar to a seasoned social worker. Oh, he spoke in vague, simplistic terms about his childhood, but Mia had worked in social services long enough to fill in the blanks. Collin and his brothers had been separated by the social system because of major issues in his family.

"What happened after that day in the principal's office? Where did you go? Foster care?" she asked, hearing the compassion in her voice and wondering if he would resent it. But she had brothers she adored, too. She knew how devastated she would be if she couldn't find one of them.

"Foster care never worked out for me. I went into a group home," he said simply, and she heard the hurt through the cold retelling. "Ian was so little, not even five. Foster care, maybe even adoption, would be my best guess for him. He was small and sweet and cute. He could have made the adjustment, I think." His nostrils flared. "I hope."

"And your middle brother? Drew? What do you think happened to him?"

He shook his head. The skin over his high, handsome cheekbones drew tight, casting deep hollows in his face. Clearly, talking about the loss of his brothers distressed him. "Drew was a fighter. He would have had a harder time than I did. I remember the social worker that day saying he was headed to a special place or something like that."

"A therapeutic home?"

"Maybe. I don't remember." He pinched at his upper lip, frustrated. "See? That's the problem. I was a kid, too. My memories are more feelings than facts."

And those feelings still cut into him with the power of a chain saw.

"Did you ever see or hear anything at all about them? Anything that could help us find them?" She didn't know why she'd said *us*. She hadn't agreed to do anything yet.

"The summer after we were separated, we both ended up at one of those summer-camp things they do for kids in the system. We immediately started making plans to run away together. But, like I said, Drew was a fighter. He got kicked out the second day. I didn't even know about the trouble until he was gone."

"And no one told you anything about him?"

"No more than I've told you. Twenty years of searching, of sticking my name in files and on search boards and registries hasn't found them." The skin on his knuckles alternated white and brown as he flexed and unflexed his clenched fists. "I've had leads, good ones, but they were always dead ends."

And it's killing you. All the things she'd wondered about him now made sense. His chilly reserve. The way he seemed isolated, a man alone.

Collin Grace *had* been alone most of his life. He'd been a child alone. Now he was a man alone.

To a woman surrounded by the warmth and noise and love of a big family, Collin's situation was not only sad, it was tragic.

"Somewhere out there I have two brothers. I want them back." And then as if the words came out without his permission, he murmured gruffly, "I need to know they're okay."

Of course he needed that. Mia's training clicked through her head. As the oldest of the three boys, he'd been responsible for the others. Or at least, he'd thought he was. Having them taken away without a word left him believing he'd failed them.

Now she understood why he'd been so reluctant to take Mitchell under his wing. He was afraid of failing him, too.

The sudden insight almost brought tears to her eyes. Mia tilted back her chair and drew in a breath, study-

ing the poster on the far wall. The slogan, Social Work
Is Love Made Visible, reminded her why she did what
she did. The love of Christ in her, and through her, min-
istered to people like Collin, to kids like Mitchell. If she
could help, she would.

"Twenty years is forever in the social services system. Do you really think I can find them if you haven't
had any success?"

"You know the system better than I do. You have access to records that I don't even know exist. Records that
I'm not allowed to see."

Warning hackles rose on Mia's back. She tried not to
let them show. "You aren't asking me to go into sealed
records without permission, are you?"

"Would you?" Dark eyes studied her. He wasn't pressing, just asking.

"No." She'd done that once for her oldest brother,
Gabe. The favor had cost her a job she loved and a certain amount of credibility with her peers. The bad decision had also cost her a great deal emotionally and
spiritually. God had forgiven her, but she'd always felt
as if she'd let Him down. "I will never compromise my
professional or my Christian ethics."

Again.

"Okay, then. Do what you can. You still have access
to a lot of records, even the unsealed ones. I've looked
everywhere I know, but that's the problem. I don't know
how to navigate the system the way you would. I can't
seem to find much when it comes to child welfare records of twenty years ago."

"Records from back then aren't computerized."

"I finally figured that one out. But where are they?"

"If they exist, they're still in file cabinets somewhere or they could be piled in boxes in a storage warehouse."

"Like police records."

"Exactly." She crumpled the half-dozen Snickers wrappers into a wad, dismayed to have consumed so many.

"Are you willing to try?"

"Are you willing to be Mitchell's CAP? That's what we call adults who volunteer through our Child Advocate Partners Program." She would help Collin in his search no matter what, but Mitch might as well get a good mentor out of the deal.

"What do I have to do?"

"Some initial paperwork. Being a police officer simplifies the procedure since you already have clearances."

"How much is the welfare office involved?"

"You don't like us much, do you?"

He made a face that said he had good reason.

"Things are different now, Collin. We understand things about children today that we didn't know then."

He didn't buy a word of it. "Yeah. Well."

"If I help you and you become Mitch's CAP, you're going to be stuck with me probably more than you want to be."

"As long as it's you. And only you."

Now why did that make her feel so good? "But you think I talk too much."

The corner of his mouth hiked up. "You do."

"But you're willing to sacrifice?"

"Finding my brothers is worth anything."

Ouch. "Sorry. I was teasing, but maybe I shouldn't have. Finding your brothers *is* serious business."

"No apology necessary." He rose with athletic ease,

bringing with him the vague scent of woodsy cologne and starched uniform. "I was teasing, too."

He was? Nice to know he could. "I'll need all the information you can give me about your brothers. Ages, names, dates you can remember, people you remember, places. Any little detail."

From his shirt pocket, he withdrew a small spiral notebook, the kind all cops seemed to carry. "The basics are in here. But I have more information on my computer."

"What kind of information?"

"The research I've done. Names and places I've already eliminated. Group homes, foster parents. I know a lot of places my brothers never were. I just can't find where they are."

He made the admission easily, but Mia read the hopelessness behind such a long and fruitless search. Twenty years was a long time to keep at it. But Collin Grace didn't seem the kind that would ever give up.

And that was exactly the type of person she was, too.

"Everything you've investigated will be useful. Knowing where *not* to look is just as important as knowing where *to* look. The files and the computer will be helpful, but we may have to do some legwork, as well." Now, why did the prospect of going somewhere with Collin sound so very, very appealing? "People are more comfortable with face-to-face questions about these kinds of things."

"Whatever it takes."

"I can't make promises, but I'll do what I can."

"Fair enough."

"Then I guess we have a deal. Will you go out and talk to Mitchell or do you want me to?"

Reluctance radiated from him in waves, but he'd made a deal and he was the kind of man who would keep it. Wasn't he still trying to keep a promise he'd made when he was ten years old? A man like that didn't back off from responsibility.

"I can contact him tomorrow," she offered.

"We could both tell him now. You know what's involved more than I do."

She shook her head, more disappointed than was wise, considering how little she knew about Collin as a person.

"I'm slammed with extra work tonight. I'll be here until seven at least." And Mitch was a lot more interested in Collin than he was in Mia.

"Too bad," he said. His expression was unreadable as usual so Mia didn't know what to make of his comment. Too bad she couldn't go with him? Or too bad she had so much work to do?

Either way, she watched him turn and stride out of her office and suffered a twinge of regret that she hadn't gone along anyway. She could be dishonest and say she wanted another look at Mitchell's living situation or that she needed to explain the program in more detail. But Mia was not dishonest. Even with herself. She had wanted to spend time with her enigmatic policeman.

And the notion was disturbing to say the least. She hadn't dated anyone in a while. To find her interest piqued by a man who didn't even seem to like her was a real puzzle.

He was a good cop, had a good reputation, and she'd had a sneak peek at the kindness he kept safely hidden. But he also carried a personal history that sometimes meant major emotional issues. Issues that might require counseling and work and, most importantly, healing from God.

And that was the big issue for Mia. Was Collin Grace a believer?

She reached for another Snickers.

Chapter Five

Sometimes Collin felt as if he spent his life inside a vehicle. He'd driven from Mia's office directly to Mitch's place, only to find the little twerp wasn't there. After driving through the neighborhood, he'd spotted him in a park shooting hoops with three other boys.

When Collin got out of the cruiser, Mitchell passed the ball off and headed toward him. The other boys quickly faded into the twilight and disappeared.

"Why are your friends in such a rush?" Collin leaned against the side of the car and folded his arms, watching the shadowy figures with a mixture of amusement and suspicion.

"You scared them off."

"They have reason to be scared of a cop?"

"Maybe."

Which meant yes in eleven-year-old talk.

"It's getting dark. Come on. I'll take you home."

"Am I in trouble?" Mitch asked, climbing readily into the front seat of the cruiser.

"No more than usual."

Streetlights had come on but made little dent in the

shadowy time between day and night. This part of town was a haven for the unsavory. Gang types, thugs, druggies, thieves all came sneaking out like cockroaches as soon as the sun went down. No place at all for a young boy.

Collin had to admit Mia was right about one thing. This kid needed a mentor before he fell into the cesspool that surrounded him. Though he still wasn't sure he wanted to be the one, Collin had begun to feel a certain responsibility toward Mitchell. He hated that, but he did. Who better than him to understand what this kid was going through? And that was all he planned to do. Understand and guide. He wasn't letting the kid get to him.

"Why're you here?" Mitch slouched down into the seat and stared out the window at the passing cars with studied disinterest.

"Miss Carano sent me."

Mitch sat up. "No kidding? You gonna be my CAP?"

So, she'd already prepared the kid for this. How had she known he would agree? He hadn't even known himself.

"What do you think about that?"

The kid hitched a shoulder. "I got plenty of other stuff to do."

"Yeah. Including a lot of community service. At least ten hours at the store where you jacked the stuff. The rest is up to you and me and Miss Carano."

"I guess I could come out to your place. Help with the animals. I'm good at that."

"Up to you." Mitch had to make the decision. Otherwise, he'd only resent Collin's interference.

"Panda probably misses me a lot. She doesn't trust many people."

"With good reason." A lot of people had let the cat—and the kid—down. The cruiser eased to a stop at the light. "You work for me, you'll have to lose the cigarettes."

The denial came fast. "I don't smoke."

One hand draped over the steering wheel, Collin just looked at him, long and steady. The boy's eyes shifted sideways. He swallowed and hitched a shoulder. "How'd you know?"

"I have a nose." The light changed. "Gonna lose them or not?"

"Whatever."

"Your choice."

"Why do you care?"

"The animals at my place depend on me."

"What's that got to do with anything?"

"You think about it and let me know which is more important. The animals or the smokes."

Collin slowed and turned into the drive-through of a Mickey D's. "Want a burger?"

He rolled down his window. The smell of hot vegetable oil surrounded the place.

"Miss Carano said you didn't eat junk food."

"She did?" The fact that she'd mentioned him to the boy in any way other than as a court-appointed advocate sent a warm feeling through him. Warm, like her sunny smile.

That warmth, that genuine caring both drew and repelled him. He didn't understand it. But he couldn't deny how good it had felt to dump his burden on her desk and to believe she would do exactly what she promised. Maybe she'd have no better luck than he'd had in finding Drew and Ian. But for the first time in years, he felt renewed hope.

Hanging out with a social worker might not be so bad after all.

Little more than a week later, Collin considered changing his mind.

He stood in the last stall of his barn showing Mitchell how to measure horse feed. The smell of hay and horses circled around his head.

The kid was all right most of the time. The social worker was a different matter.

He did okay on the days Mia dropped Mitch off as planned, said hello and goodbye and drove away in her power suit and speedy little yellow Mustang. The days she climbed out of that Mustang wearing blue jeans and a T-shirt gave him trouble. Regardless that she was here on business to assess the CAP arrangement, dressed like that, she was a woman, not a social worker. It was hard to dislike one and like the other, so he tried to keep his distance.

Trouble was, Mia didn't understand the concept of personal space. She was in his, talking a mile a minute, smile warm, attitude sweet. The more he retreated, the more she advanced.

Over the clatter of horse pellets hitting metal, he could hear her talking in soft, soothing tones to Happy, the pup with the lousy luck and the cheerful outlook.

"How much feed does Smokey get?" Mitch's question pulled Collin back to the horse feed.

"None of the pellets. Just some of this alfalfa."

Mitch frowned, dubious. "He's awful skinny."

"Too much at first can kill him."

"How come somebody let him get like that? I can see his ribs."

The buckskin colt stood quivering in the stall, head down, so depressed Collin wondered if he'd survive.

"Some people don't care."

It was a cold, hard fact that both he and the boy knew all too well. "Yeah."

In the few days Mitch had been here, Collin had ferreted out a few unsavory facts about his home life. The stepdad wasn't exactly father-of-the-year material. And mom wouldn't win any prizes, either, although the kid was loyal to her anyway. Collin didn't press him about his mother. He'd been the same once, until the woman who'd birthed him walked away and never looked back. He hoped that never happened to Mitchell.

Hand full of green, scented hay, the kid knelt in front of the little horse. "Come on, Smokey. It's okay."

The colt nuzzled the outstretched fingers, then nibbled a bit of grass.

Mitch had a way with all the creatures on the farm. Even Doc had commented on that. Like a magnet, he was drawn to the sickest ones, the most wounded, the near-hopeless. Street-kid wariness melted into incredible tenderness when he approached the animals. Not one of them shied away from the boy's tenacious determination to make them all well.

"I promised Happy I'd soak his foot later. Is that okay?" Mitchell was on a mission to save the crippled little collie. Every day, he went to Happy's stall first and last with some extra time in between.

"What did Doc say?"

"She said extra soaks can't hurt nothing."

She was right about that. Happy's foot had reached the

point when hope was all but gone. Soaking couldn't make the wound any worse, and any action at all made them feel as if they were doing something. "All right, then."

Collin moved down the corridor, taking care of the menial tasks so necessary for the survival of these wounded creatures who depended on him. Cleaning pens, scooping waste, lining stalls and boxes with fresh straw.

Mia was inside the cat pen.

He frowned at her. "I thought you left." He hadn't really, but he didn't know what else to say.

"You wish." With a laugh, she lifted one of Panda's kittens from the box and draped the fur ball over her shoulder. "What's wrong? Rough day?"

Yeah, he'd had a lousy day, but how did she know? He didn't like having some woman, a social worker at that, inside his head.

"I'm all right." He ducked into Happy's stall to escape her. She followed, but didn't press him about his gray mood.

"Mitch seems to be doing a good job for you, don't you agree?"

"Yeah." The dog wobbled up from his straw bed, tail wagging. The smell of antiseptic and dying flesh was hard to ignore.

"Has he opened up at all about why he runs away so much?"

"A little."

"But you're not going to tell me."

"Confidential."

She rolled her big eyes at him. She had interesting eyes. Huge and almond-shaped, soft and sparkly. He didn't know how a person made her eyes sparkly, but she did.

Mia knelt to stroke the pup while still holding the kitten against her shoulder. Happy, tail thumping a mile a minute, didn't seem to mind having a cat invade his territory. Dumb dog didn't seem to mind much of anything.

"What's going to happen to him?"

"Happy? Or Mitch?"

She gave him another of her wide-eyed looks. He wanted to laugh. "The dog."

"If things don't improve this week, Doc's going to amputate the other foot on Monday."

"Oh, Collin." Her face was stricken. She glanced toward the stall door. "Does Mitch know?"

"No."

"No wonder you're in a bad mood tonight. I thought maybe you'd had to shoot somebody today."

"That would have made me feel better."

She looked up. "Not funny."

"Sorry. Bad cop joke." Using force was the last thing he ever wanted.

"How do you cops do that, anyway? Shoot somebody, I mean."

"We pretend they're lawyers." He shook kibble into Happy's bowl. "Or social workers."

"Ha-ha. I'm laughing." But she did giggle. "When are you going to tell him?"

He crumpled an empty feed sack into an oversize ball. "I don't know."

"Want me to do it?"

"My responsibility." He tossed the sack into a trash bin and knelt beside the pup. "I wish I knew who did this to him."

The little dog licked his outstretched hand, liquid brown eyes delighted by the attention. Anger and helplessness pushed inside Collin's chest. He hated feeling helpless.

"I ran a computer search of the system today on you and your brothers."

His pulse quickened though he told himself to expect nothing. "And came up empty?"

"Mostly."

"Figures." Refusing to be disappointed, he stood and took the kitten from her. The soft, warm body wiggled in protest. As many years as he'd searched he couldn't expect miracles from Mia in a week.

"There's some information about you, but the facts on Drew and Ian seem to be the same that you already have. A couple of foster placements. Some medical records."

He wanted to ask what she'd found on him, but didn't bother. She'd probably tell him anyway. Mia already knew too much about him and she was likely to learn more. Opening his sordid background to anyone always made him feel vulnerable, and nothing scared him like vulnerability.

He led the way out of Happy's stall to take the kitten back to Panda. A glance toward the horses told him Mitch was busy mucking out stalls. A perverse part of him figured that particular job was adequate punishment for shoplifting.

"Collin."

He lowered the tiny tabby to her mother. Panda's burns were healing, but she didn't let anyone except Mitch touch her. Even Doc had had to sedate the cat before treating the wounds, an unusual turn of events.

"Collin," she said again, this time from beneath his elbow.

With a sigh, he turned. "What?"

She wrinkled her nose at him, fully aware her chatter bothered him. She looked cute, and he didn't like it. Social workers weren't supposed to be cute.

"I brought the file of information with me. Do you want to see it?"

"Might as well."

Nothing like cold, hard welfare facts to make a man stop thinking about a pretty woman.

Inside Collin's house for the first time, Mia thought the interior of the unfinished, basically unfurnished house was exactly what she expected of him. Neat and tidy to a fault, one long room served as kitchen, living room, and dining room. The furniture consisted of an easy chair, a TV and a small dining-room set. There were no pictures on the walls, no curtains on the shaded windows, no plants or other decorating touches. Collin lived a neatly Spartan lifestyle.

To Mia, who lived in a veritable jungle of plants, terra-cotta pots and pieces of Tuscan decor jammed into a tiny apartment, the house was sadly bare but filled with potential. A pot here. A plant there.

"I live simply," he said when he caught her looking.

"The place has great potential."

"It's not even finished."

"That's why it has great potential."

He shook his head and pulled out two chairs. "Sit. I'll move the laptop."

She eyed the animated screen saver. "Did Mitchell do that?"

"Yeah. He loves the thing."

Mia knew the boy didn't have a computer at home. "His teacher says he's a regular whiz kid."

"He knows keystroke shortcuts I didn't know existed and can navigate sites I can't get into. I'm afraid to ask if he's ever tried hacking."

"The answer is probably yes."

"I know." With a self-deprecating laugh that surprised her, Collin admitted, "He even offered to teach me keyboarding."

"You should let him. Teaching you would be good for his self-esteem."

"It wouldn't be too good for mine." He wiggled his two index fingers. "Old habits die hard."

A large brown envelope lay on the table beside the computer. She reached for it. "Is that more information about your brothers?"

"No. Just another problem I'm working on."

"Anything I can help with?"

"Not unless you're a lawyer. My neighbor," he said, his lips twisted, "is suing me."

"What for?" She couldn't imagine Collin Grace ever being intrusive enough for any neighbor even to know him, much less be at cross-purposes.

"He claims one of my animals has attacked his prize sheep on more than one occasion."

"They couldn't." All the animals here were both too sick and too well-confined to bother anything.

"Cecil Slokum has found something to complain about ever since I bought this place."

"Why?"

"Don't know. This time though—" he waved the envelope in the air "—I ran a background check on him."

"Oooh, suspicious. Remind me never to tick you off."

"Too late."

There was that wicked sense of humor again, coming out of nowhere.

"Have you hired an attorney?"

"No."

"You should."

"And I suppose you just happen to know one. Or two. Maybe you even know the judge."

"Well…" She cupped her hands under her chin and leaned toward him. "As a matter of fact, one of my brothers is an attorney. He's also a city councilman."

Collin leaned back his chair. "So he's the one."

"Don't look like that. If my brother hadn't spoken to the chief, you might never have agreed to mentor Mitch. And you like having him out here. You know you do."

"The kid's all right. He's good for the animals."

She laughed. If Collin wanted to pretend he cared nothing about the boy, fine. But he did.

"You've made more progress with Mitchell in a week than anyone else has made in a year."

The boy basked in the policeman's attention, eager to please him, ready to listen to his few, terse words. According to his fifth-grade teacher, Mitch had even turned in all his homework this week, a first.

Collin set the laptop and the brown envelope on an empty chair. "So, you gonna show me that file you brought or talk me to death?"

"Both." She handed over the manila folder.

His eyes twinkled. "Figures."

"You won't die from a little conversation, Collin. Talking things out might do you some good."

She liked listening to his quiet, manly voice as much

as she enjoyed looking at him. He was an attractive man. Mia squelched a stomach flutter. Very attractive.

Less intimidating in street attire, tonight he wore a Tac-team T-shirt neatly tucked into well-worn blue jeans. Muscular biceps, fine-cut by exercise and work, stretched the sleeves snug.

"I keep noticing your tattoo." Among other things. "What is it?"

He looked up from studying the file. For a moment, she thought he wouldn't tell her, but then he pushed the sleeve higher and rotated toward her.

Her heart stutter-stepped. Each leaf of a small shamrock bore, not initials as she'd thought, but a name. "Drew, Ian, Collin," she read.

"I didn't want to forget," he said simply. "Not even for a day."

All her preconceived ideas about tattoos went flying out the door. Without forethought, Mia placed her fingers on his arm just beneath the clover. His dark skin was warm and firm and strong with leashed power.

"What an incredibly loving thing to do."

He slid away from her and stood, closing the file. "Mitch should be up here by now. He has homework."

Helping Mitchell with his homework hadn't been part of the court order but Collin didn't let that deter him.

He crossed the few steps to the door and stood gazing out, his back to her. She felt the uncertainty in him, the discomfort that she'd generated with her comment. Or maybe with her touch. One thing was clear. Collin had a hard time expressing emotions. He might feel them. He just couldn't let them show.

She held back a smile. To an Italian, Collin Grace was a red flag waved in front of a bull. Expression was what she and her family did best. She would either drive Collin crazy or help him heal. She hoped it was the latter. Collin had a lot to offer people if he would only open up and trust a little more.

"Collin?"

He tensed but didn't turn around. "What?"

"My family's having a birthday party on Saturday for Nic, my youngest brother. He's turning twenty-one. If you'll come, I'll introduce you to Adam. He might be able to help with the lawsuit."

He looked at her over one shoulder. "How many brothers do you have?"

"Three bros, one sister and a lot of cousins, aunts and uncles."

"You're lucky."

"Yes. Incredibly blessed. You'll like them, Collin. They're great people."

He turned all the way around, tilting his head so she would know he teased. "Do they all talk as much as you?"

She grinned. "All but Uncle Vitorio. Come on, Collin. Say you'll be there."

"I wouldn't want to intrude." Which meant he wanted to come.

"No such thing at a Carano gathering. We have a motto. The more the merrier."

"Not too original."

She shrugged. "Who cares? It fits. So what do you say?" She really, really wanted him to come. For professional reasons, of course.

Cocoa-colored eyes holding hers, he considered the invitation for a minute but finally said, "Better not."

Disappointment seeped into her, but disappeared as

quickly as the next thought arrived. "You could bring Mitch. He needs to interact with a strong family unit, and even if I do say so myself, mine fits the bill."

Hanging out with the Caranos would be good for Collin, too, but she couldn't say that.

"Proud of them, are you?"

"They're a little crazy, and none of us is perfect by any stretch of the imagination, but yeah, I have a great family."

"Taking Mitch is a good idea, but you don't need me along."

"He won't go without you." And she was glad. Collin needed the warm circle of family around him as much as the child did. A man who'd grown up in the system wouldn't have had too many opportunities to witness healthy family relationships. Besides, the Caranos were a lot of fun and if anyone could melt the ice shield from Collin and Mitchell, her family could.

"Here he comes now," she said at the sound of feet tromping on the porch. "Why don't we ask him?"

Collin held the door open as Mitch, Archie the turtle in hand, came inside. To everyone's astonishment, the turtle with the cracked shell was thriving.

"Ask me what?" The little turtle's claws scratched at the air and found purchase when Mitchell placed him on the table.

"You want to go to a party at my house on Saturday?"

Mitch squinted at Mia and then up at Collin. "You going?"

Mia giggled. Collin slanted his eyes at her in silent warning. She laughed out loud.

"It'll be a great party. Lots of food and games and

craziness. My folks have a swimming pool." She let that little bit of enticement dangle.

Scooping Archie against his chest, Mitch plopped into a chair. "A real pool? Or one of them kiddie things?"

"Above-ground, but it's big. Has a slide and everything."

"Are your parents rich?"

Mia laughed. "No. They've run a little family bakery forever, but they know how to save money for the things that matter."

Mitch eyeballed Collin, who had gone to the fridge for boxes of juice. Mia knew avoidance behaviors when she saw them.

"They probably wouldn't want me to come." The boy's voice held a longing that neither adult could miss. "I don't have any trunks."

Collin slammed a straw through the top of a juice box with such force the plastic bent.

"We'll get some," he said gruffly.

"You're going too?" Mitch sat up straight and punched the air. "All right. This will be awesome!"

Collin sent Mia a look that would have quelled anyone but a determined social worker.

And she knew she'd won.

Chapter Six

By the time Saturday afternoon rolled around, the knot in Collin's stomach had grown from the size of a pea to that of a watermelon. Mitchell wasn't in any better shape. The kid, usually mouthy as Mia, had barely said two words on the drive to the Carano place.

Collin knew how the kid felt. Out of place. A misfit. The uncertainty was one of the reasons he avoided hanging out with his police buddy, Maurice. How did a person fit into a family when they didn't know what a family should be?

But Collin had learned about and yearned for the kind of relationships Mia bragged about. Even if he might never have them for himself, he wanted them for Mitch. The kid needed to know there was better out there than a stepdad who knocked your mom around and hung out with thugs. Mitchell needed this, which was exactly why Collin had swallowed his reluctance and put on a show about wanting to meet the Caranos.

When they pulled up in front of the sprawling home in a nice older neighborhood in northwest Oklahoma City, a half-dozen other cars already lined the street out front. Collin did his usual scan of the premises, committing the vehicle descriptions and the entrances and exits to memory, the police officer in him never off duty.

Mitch fidgeted with his seat belt. "You think they'll like me?"

The question bothered Collin but he didn't let his feelings show. The kid already knew that people would judge him by his rough clothes and poor grammar. He might as well have White Trash tattooed on his forehead.

"If Mia likes you, they will, too."

"She likes me because she has to. It's her job."

Collin squeezed the back of Mitch's neck. "You know better."

"Yeah." The boy pumped his eyebrows in silliness. "She likes me 'cause I'm cute."

Collin made a rude noise. Mitch's laughter relaxed them both.

As they started up the hedge-lined walkway, squeals and laughter echoed from the backyard. A football came flying over a wooden privacy fence and landed at Collin's feet. He picked it up just as the gate opened. He expected a kid to come charging after the ball. Instead, a grown man, probably near his age, trotted toward him. His maroon T-shirt was sweat-plastered to his upper body.

Collin held up the ball. "This belong to you?"

"Coulda had a touchdown if I'd been taller." The man stopped in front of them and bent forward, hands on knees to catch his breath. "You must be Collin and Mitch. Glad you're here. Mia's wearing a hole in the carpet."

She was?

"I'm Adam, Mia's favorite brother." He laughed, smile

bright in a dark face, and extended his hand to Mitch and then to Collin. "You must be the cop Mia's been telling us about."

She talked about him? "I hope it's good."

"So far."

The man was friendly enough, but Collin knew when he was being checked out. He didn't miss the subtle warning. Mess with a Carano and you have to answer to the whole clan. He admired that. He had been that way with his own brothers, though he was surprised that Adam would feel the need to warn him about anything. He'd come here to help a troubled kid, not because of Mia.

Adam tossed the ball back and forth from one hand to the other. "You play football?" he said to Mitchell.

"I stink at it."

"Awesome." Adam gently shoved the ball into the boy's midsection. "You can be on my team. We all stink at it, too. How about you, Collin?"

"Yeah. I stink at it, too."

Adam laughed and slapped him on the back. "Come on. I'll take you inside to find Mia. We'll get a game going later."

Adam's friendly greeting took some of the tension out of Collin's jaw. Maybe he could get through this afternoon with a minimum amount of stress.

Collin's first impression of the Carano house was the noise, good noise that came from talk and laughter and activity. Several conversations bounced around the large, crowded living room in competition with a big-screen TV blasting a game between the Texas Longhorns and the Oklahoma State Cowboys. There were kitchen noises too, of pots and pans and cabinets opening and closing.

Through patio doors at the opposite end, the pool was visible, along with the remnants of the touch football game they'd interrupted. He glanced down at Mitch, saw the boy scanning the backyard with typical kid radar. He figured Mitch would be fine as soon as he worked his way outside.

The incredible smell of home-cooked food issued from the enormous area to his left. The kitchen was exactly the kind he had envisioned for Mia, though she no longer lived here. Washed warm with sunlight and the rich earthy colors of brick-red flooring, the room was dappled with overflowing fruit baskets, clear jars of colorful pasta, and copper pots dangling above a center island. He located Mia at the island arranging cheese and fruit on a platter.

The knot in his stomach reacted oddly. He was glad to see her, whether because she was the only familiar face in the crowd or otherwise, he didn't know. And he wasn't bothering to go there. Two weeks ago, she was a pain in his neck.

She looked so natural here, so much more real than she did in her office and business suits. Home was her element.

She said something to a pretty older woman who could only be her mother. They both had the same large, almond eyes and full mouths. And like her mother, Mia tended to be more rounded and womanly than was currently the trend—a look Collin appreciated.

Today her long hair was down, flowing in soft red-brown waves around her shoulders. Her red T-shirt fitted her to perfection and topped off a pair of white, loose-fitting cropped pants and sandals.

She was talking—no big surprise—as she popped

a piece of cheese in her mouth. Suddenly she laughed, clapping one hand over her lips.

"Hey, Mia," Adam hollered over the noise. "You got company."

When she caught sight of him, her face brightened. Hurriedly, she said something over her shoulder, wiped her hands on a towel and rushed in their direction.

"You're here!" For a minute, Collin thought she might hug him. Instead, she grabbed his elbow with one hand, dropped the other arm over Mitch's shoulder, and drew them into the melee.

"I see you've already met Adam, so follow me and we'll try to forge a path to the others."

Adam disappeared into the mix as Mia introduced the newcomers to her sister, parents, grandparents and a number of other people whose connection escaped him.

"I don't expect you to remember everyone the first time," Mia said.

The first time? Collin wasn't sure he could survive a second go-round. Though everyone was as friendly as Mia, he felt like a bug under a microscope.

"This is my baby brother, Nic," Mia was saying. "The birthday boy."

"That's birthday *man* to you, big sister." Across Nic's T-shirt were the words, *What if the Hokey Pokey really is what it's all about?*

Mia laughed and rolled her eyes. "He's twenty-one today and I suspect he will be impossible to live with now that he thinks he's become one of the grown-ups."

Collin shook the younger man's hand. "Good to meet you, Nic. Happy birthday."

"Thanks," Nic answered, his grin wide as he looked from Collin to Mia. Speculation, totally unwarranted, was rife. Just what exactly had Mia told them about him anyway? "You want to hear some secrets about my evil big sister?"

Mia poked a teasing finger in Nic's chest. "No, he doesn't. Not if you want to live to be twenty-two."

Speculation or not, Collin enjoyed the joking exchange between brother and sister.

He leaned toward Nic and spoke in a low voice. "Maybe we should talk later. When Mia isn't around."

Mia pretended horror. "Don't you dare. Nic tells lies about how mean I was to him when he was small."

"They're not lies. Just ask Adam." Nic whipped around. "Hey, Adam. Come help me out."

Adam, the football player in the maroon shirt, popped up from the couch, where he was surrounded by kids who fell away like brushed-off dust. Collin was startled to see Mitchell in the mix. At some point the kid had wandered off toward the big-screen TV, and Collin hadn't even noticed. Chalk up one demerit for the Big Brother.

"What's up?" Adam asked, his sweaty T-shirt still damp and dark. "The birthday boy already showing off?"

"Of course," Mia said. "I'm leaving Collin in your mature company so I can help Mom and Grandma get dinner on the table. Do not allow Nic to tell horror stories."

Nic guffawed and Adam struggled to keep a straight face. "Sure, sis. Whatever you say."

"I mean it," she warned with a wagging finger. "Collin, I'll be back to rescue you in five minutes."

Then she returned to the oregano-scented kitchen, leaving Collin with Adam again. The feeling of abandonment came with startling swiftness, that emptiness he despised. Collin bit down on his back teeth, annoyed.

He was a grown-up. He didn't need a babysitter. In fact, he didn't need to be here. He didn't fit.

He shifted uncomfortably and wished for a quiet corner where he could watch and listen without being noticed. Mitchell was probably miserable, too. But one look in the living room told him he was wrong. Mitch was deep in conversation with Mr. Carano and they were both fiddling with a laptop chess game. Give the kid a computer and he was at home anywhere. Collin envied that ease and wondered if he'd ever had it as a kid. If he had, it had been very early in his life. He sure didn't remember.

"You have that shell-shocked look that says Mia didn't warn you about us." Adam's voice broke into his thoughts.

"What? Sorry, my mind strayed."

"No wonder. The noise level in here could rival a landing strip."

"No problem." The noise wasn't what bothered him, though it *was* loud. Loud and enthusiastic. He could see where Mia got her positive energy and upbeat attitude.

"From the look on your face, I'd say your family isn't as big or rowdy as the Carano bunch."

"You'd be right about that." If he had a family.

Adam grabbed a bowl of chips from the coffee table. "Come on, let's head out to the backyard, where there's some relative peace. There could be a football game in your future. How about you, Nic? Ready to rumble?"

"Not now. Dana Rozier just pulled up out front with a carload of babes." He cranked his eyebrows up and down a few times. "Can't disappoint the ladies."

Nic rubbed his hands together and then bounded for the front door.

"Ask them if they want to play football," Adam called

and was rewarded with a hyena laugh from the birthday boy. "Oh, well, it was worth a try." He shook his head. "Nic and his girls. I don't see the attraction, do you?"

The Carano brothers were fun. He'd say that for them.

Adam shrugged, hollered at Gabe to organize a team, and then led the way through the sea of people and at least one large dog. The backyard was filled with kids, some swimming, two shooting hoops, and a couple of little ones just running in circles squealing for the joy of it.

Adam set the bowl of chips on the ground and collapsed into a lawn chair. "Grab a chair."

Collin did.

"Man, is this a gorgeous day or what?"

"Yeah." He thought of all the work he could be doing on his house on a day like this. Winter would come soon and he wouldn't be any closer to finishing than he'd been at the beginning of summer.

"Mia says you run a rescue ranch for hurt animals."

"That's right."

"She told me about your problem."

Collin stiffened. Mia had promised to keep his search for Drew and Ian confidential. "Why would she do that?"

"Mia doesn't keep much from her family. But in this case she thought I could help."

He should have known he couldn't trust a social worker. "I can handle it."

"Sometimes lawsuits, even frivolous ones, can be tricky."

A truckload of tension rushed out of Collin. The lawsuit.

"Mia told me her brother was a lawyer. I didn't realize she meant you."

"I hope you didn't think she meant Nic."

They both chuckled. "Seeing him in a courtroom might be entertaining."

"What about in the operating room?"

"Excuse me?"

"He's applying for medical school. There really is a brain beneath that happy-go-lucky personality."

"I'm impressed."

"Don't be. He hasn't been accepted yet." Adam reached for another handful of tortilla chips and offered the bowl to Collin. "So how can I help you with this lawsuit?"

"I don't want to impose."

"No imposition. A friend of Mia's is a friend of mine."

Were they friends? He hadn't wanted to be, hadn't really thought about it until now. "She's a nice girl."

"A very nice girl." Adam shifted around in the lawn chair so they were face-to-face.

"Sometimes she pushes too hard, comes on too strong, but don't hold that against her. Gabe and I call her a coconut. Tough on the outside, a little nutty when she gets on one of her crusades to change the world, but soft and sweet on the inside."

Collin had seen the sweet side at the ranch. He'd also wrestled with her talkative, pushy side.

"She hounded me for days until I agreed to mentor Mitchell."

"See what I mean? She's so sure she can change the world with love and faith that she never gives up. Sometimes she gets hurt in the process. I wouldn't want to see that happen again."

Mia had been hurt? How? Why? And, most importantly, by whom? Collin, who seldom ate chips, took a handful.

"She's in a tough profession," was all he could think of. "The ugliness burns out a lot of strong people."

"Not Mia. She'll never let that happen. There's too much of God in her. She'll always stay tender and vulnerable to hurt. That's just the way she's made." Adam tossed a chip into the air, caught it in his mouth and crunched. "You know why she's not married?"

He'd wondered. Mia was smart, pretty, personable… though he wondered more that Adam would bring up the subject with a stranger like him. "I figure she's had her chances."

"She has. But Mia is waiting for the right guy. Not just any guy, but the one God sends."

Well, that left him out for sure. Not that it mattered. He wasn't in the market for a woman. Especially a nosey social worker who talked too much and made him think about things and feel things he'd kept buried most of his life.

Adam could relax. Neither he nor his sister had anything to fear from Collin Grace.

Chapter Seven

"He's out in the backyard." Adam jerked a thumb in that direction. "The guy looked like he could use a breather from all of us."

Mia took a fresh glass of tea, sugarless the way she'd seen Collin take it during the meal, and pushed open the patio doors.

The glorious blue sky hung over a perfect early-autumn afternoon. She breathed in a happy breath of fresh air. What a great day this had been. Collin and Mitchell had seemed to have a good time. And her family had risen to the occasion as they always did, wrapping the two newcomers in a welcome of genuine friendliness. Nic had been his usual wild and crazy self, celebrating his twenty-first birthday by shooting videos of all the attendees wearing the Groucho glasses he'd bought for party favors.

This kind of gathering was good for Mitchell. He could learn here, interact with real men and motherly women, learn how to have fun in a clean and healthy way. Though she knew Collin would argue the fact, he needed this kind of thing, too. The protective shell around him kept away hurt, but it also kept away the good emotions.

When he'd walked in the door this afternoon, she'd been almost giddy with pleasure. Later, she'd have to examine that reaction.

In the shady overhang of the house, he leaned against the sun-warmed siding to watch Mitchell splash around in the pool. Was it her imagination or did Collin look isolated, maybe even lonely, standing there apart from the bustle of people? She'd thought a lot about him lately, about his upbringing, about how awful he must feel to be alone in the world, not knowing where his family was, or even if they were alive.

Yes, he was on her mind a great deal.

"You look like you could use this." Ice tinkled against the glass as she held the tea out to him.

"Thanks."

Mia wiped her hand, damp from condensation, down her pant leg. "Overwhelmed?"

He sipped at the tea and swallowed before answering. "A little."

"If a person survives their first dose of Caranos, they're a shoo-in for navy SEALs training or a trip to the funny farm."

He smiled his appreciation of the joke. A day with her family showed him where she derived her great sense of humor.

"My experience with family gatherings is pretty limited."

"Well, you're a hit. You officially passed inspection by the Carano brothers."

"Carano brothers." He held up his Groucho glasses. "Sounds like a family of mobsters."

"Shh. Don't say that too loud. We are Italian, remember."

They grinned into each other's eyes. From inside the house came a shout of "Touchdown."

The Cowboys must have scored. Here in the yard, the sounds were quieter, the splash of kids sliding into the pool, the occasional yip of the dog.

Though he'd felt out of place all afternoon, Collin liked Mia and her family. A couple of times he'd seen Mrs. Carano, who insisted on being called Rosalie, pat Mitchell's back and ply him with goodies from the family bakery. The kid must be ready to explode, but he'd soaked up the attention like Happy did, as though starved for positive reinforcement.

Had he been like that? He couldn't recall. He'd spent so much time keeping Drew out of trouble and Ian fed and safe that he really didn't remember ever being a child.

Mia swirled the melting ice round and round in her own glass, then pressed the coldness to the side of her neck. Collin's belly reacted to the feminine sight. Mia, with her nice family, her chatterbox ways and her honest concern for people was putting holes in his arguments against social workers. Except for the title and the business suits, she didn't fit the stereotype. Adam hadn't helped any with his innuendoes.

"You won Gabe over when your phone played 'Boomer Sooner.'" A soft smile lifted her pretty mouth, setting a single tiny dimple into relief. He'd never noticed that dimple before.

"I saw the Oklahoma Sooner tag on a couple of cars out there." He didn't bother to say Adam had grilled him about his intentions. No point in embarrassing Mia about a simple misunderstanding. Adam was a good guy. He'd meant well. Even if he was badly misguided.

"We all attended OU. Adam played a little baseball, so we're pretty hard-core Sooner fans. Gabe even has season tickets to the football games."

Collin had never made it to college. "I'm a big football fan myself." Which had made conversation with the Caranos a little easier.

"But not of the Dallas Cowboys. Nic is a little miffed about that, though he thinks he can convert you."

"Want me to lie to him since it's his birthday?"

She punched his arm. "Silly."

"Bully." He rubbed the spot just over his shamrock. A lot of people had asked him about the tattoo before and he'd told them nothing. But Mia was different. She had a way of slipping under his guard, catching him unawares, and the next thing he knew he was telling her way too much.

"I never liked tattoos before. But I like yours," she said as if reading his mind. "When did you have it done?"

"When I was seventeen." He wasn't about to tell her the shape he'd been in when he'd gone to the tattoo parlor.

"Isn't it illegal to get one at that age?"

"I wasn't a cop then."

He'd made the remark to encourage a smile. She didn't disappoint him.

"Well, even if it was illegal, you were very insightful to choose a tattoo that represents so much."

"Yeah. Real insightful." To him the tattoo represented a man, a cop at that, who couldn't find the brothers he'd promised to look after. It represented years of failure. He made a wry face. "I chose a shamrock because I needed space for three words and I like the color green."

Undaunted by his dry tone, she studied the figure. "Three leaves, three brothers. Your names are Irish. And green means everlasting, like the evergreen trees. Everlasting devotion."

He blinked down at the tattoo. Then at her.

She came to his shoulders and he could see the top of her hair. In the bright sunlight, the soft waves gleamed more red than brown. He defeated the sudden and unusual urge to touch her hair.

The tattoo had come about on what would have been Ian's twelfth birthday. Collin had been fighting a terrible depression, and the tattoo seemed like a grown-up, proactive thing to do at the time. Now he looked back on the day with a sense of chagrin and failure.

That had been a tough time for him. His days of being cared for in the foster system had been coming to an end, and he was scared out of his mind. He had no place to go, no training, no family, no money. Only a dim memory of two brothers to cling to and the fish keychain that somehow bound the three of them together. Then as now, every time he smoothed his fingers over the darkening metal, he felt closer to Drew and Ian.

"I can't say I was all that deep and symbolic about a tattoo, Mia. I think I was just hoping for a little good luck." He'd needed all the help he could get in the days following his eighteenth birthday.

"Did it work?"

She tilted her head back against the white siding and stared out at the pool, where Mitch splashed with Gabe's ten-year-old son. Abby, Gabe's wife, watched from a lawn chair.

"Nah. Mostly, I think we make our own luck. What about you? Got a rabbit's foot in your purse?"

She smiled, but her eyes remained serious.

"I don't put much stock in luck, either. God, on the other hand, is a different matter. I truly believe He, not luck or coincidence, controls my destiny."

"Like a robot?"

She laughed and shook her head. The reddish waves danced back from her pretty face. "Not like that. People have free will. But if we let Him, God will guide our lives and work everything out for our good."

"You really think that?"

"Yes. I really do."

Well, he didn't. He thought you had to claw and fight and struggle uphill, hoping like mad that some crumb of good would fall in your lap.

"I always figured God was out there somewhere, but He was probably too busy to bother with one person."

"God's not like that, Collin. He's very personal. He cares about the smallest, simplest things in our lives."

"If that's so, why is there so much trouble in the world? Why do kids go hungry and parents mistreat and abandon them?" And why couldn't he find his brothers?

The seed of bitterness he tried to hide rose up like a sickness in his throat.

Mia placed a hand on his arm, a gentle, reassuring touch much like the ones he'd seen Rosalie give to Mitchell. He wanted her to stop. "I hear what you're not saying."

Of course she would. She dealt with people in his shoes all the time. She was trained to read behind the mask, a scary prospect if ever there was one. He didn't want anybody messing around inside his mind.

While his insides churned and he wondered what he was doing here, Collin tossed the remaining ice cubes onto a small bush growing beside the house. When the movement dislodged Mia's hand from his arm, he suffered a pang of loss. Talk about messed up. One minute he wanted her to stop touching him, and the next he was disappointed because she did.

"God can help you find your brothers," she said. "Or at least find out what happened to them."

He kept quiet. Mia had a right to her faith even if he had never witnessed anything much from God.

He rolled the empty glass back and forth between his palms. "Like I said, I don't know much about religion."

"That's okay. Faith's not about religion anyway."

She was losing him again.

"Faith is about having a relationship with the most perfect friend you could ever have. Jesus is a friend who promises to stick closer than a brother."

"Closer than a brother," he murmured softly. And then for some reason, he slid a hand into his pocket, found the tiny fish. The metal was warm from his body heat. "For me that wouldn't be too close."

"Then why can't you stop looking for them? And why is your arm tattooed with their names?"

She had a point there. "I guess I'm trying to keep them close even though they're lost." He pulled the tiny ichthus from his pocket. "See this?"

Her expressive face couldn't hide her surprise. "A Jesus fish?"

"I suppose you want to know why I carry it if I'm not a believer?"

"Yes."

He started to tease and say he carried the fish for luck.

But that wasn't true. His feelings were deeper than that though he wasn't sure he had the words to express them.

"The day my brothers and I were separated the school counselor gave us each one of these." He turned the fish over. The bright sunlight caught the faded engraving, *Jesus will never leave you nor forsake you.* He'd thought of that scripture often and hoped it was true. He hoped there was somebody in this world looking after Ian and Drew.

"I wonder if they still have theirs," she murmured quietly.

"Why would they keep a cheap little keychain?" But he hoped they had.

"You kept yours."

He rubbed a finger over the darkened engraving as he'd done dozens of times. This was his link, his connection to Drew and Ian. That link, religion aside, gave him comfort. And if he'd tried to pray a few times as a boy, asking the distant God for help, well, he'd been a kid who just didn't understand the facts of life.

He wished that God could do something about his lost brothers, but he didn't know how to believe in anything but himself. His own strength and determination had gotten him where he was today. He knew better than to rely on anyone or anything else.

Before he could say more, Nic came sprinting around from the opposite side of the house, an orange plastic water pistol in one hand.

Gabe was right behind him, squirting his own water pistol like mad.

"You're gonna pay, birthday boy," he roared. And from the looks of Gabe's soaked shirtfront, Nic had started the trouble.

With a wild hyena laugh, Nic turned and fired, squirting Gabe as well as the two innocent bystanders. Mia jumped aside with a squeal of laughter.

Oddly disappointed to have his strange conversation with Mia interrupted, Collin brushed a water droplet from his arm.

"And you said your family was functional."

They both laughed as Adam came running past, wearing the Groucho glasses and carrying two squirt guns with another stuck in his shirt pocket.

"Defend yourself," he yelled and tossed a purple plastic pistol in their general direction.

With quick reflexes, Collin caught the squirt gun. As soon as the toy hit his hand, a sudden flashback hit Collin square in the heart.

Drew and Ian armed with water guns they'd gotten somewhere chased him around the trailer. He'd hidden under the house, behind the dangling insulation, and unloaded on them when they'd discovered his whereabouts.

They had all squirted and yelled and chased until the night grew too dark to see each other. As they often did, they'd spent that night without adults, but for once they'd gone to bed smiling.

"Collin?" Mia said, touching the hand that held the water pistol. "What's wrong?"

Even the good memories hurt. All those years he'd missed. All the good times he and his brothers had deserved to have. Though he recognized the irrationality of his emotions, he envied the Caranos. They had what he wanted and would never have. The missing years could not ever be recaptured.

"I gotta go." He handed her the squirt gun and abruptly strode to the pool. "Time to roll, Mitchell."

He felt Mia's gaze on his back.

Mitchell was instantly protesting. "I don't wanna leave yet."

"Sorry. I have to work tomorrow." He did have to work. On his house.

Water sluicing off his hair and shoulders, body language screaming in protest, Mitchell pulled himself slowly out of the pool. He grumbled, "It's not fair."

"Yeah, well, life isn't fair, kid. Get used to it."

Mitch stopped and tilted his head back to look into Collin's face. "Are you mad at me?"

Collin relented the slightest bit. The kid had behaved himself today. No use making Mitch pay for his lousy mood. He hooked an elbow around the boy's wet head.

"I'm not mad."

Trailed by an unusually quiet Mia, they went into the house to bid a civil goodbye to all the Carano clan. Mitchell dragged through the house like a man condemned, gathered his clothes and shoes for departure. Rosalie bustled into the kitchen and came back with two foil-wrapped plates.

"Leftovers. You two could use a little meat on your bones."

A funny lump formed inside Collin's chest. Was this what a mother did? Just like on television? Did normal mothers fret over the children and make huge family dinners and nag everyone to eat more?

"Take them, Collin," Mia murmured. "Make her happy." She'd protested their departure with all the usual niceties, but his mind was made up. He couldn't be here among this family any longer. It was killing him.

"I hope you'll come back soon, Collin," Rosalie was saying. "And bring this boy." She patted Mitchell's head.

"You come anytime you want to, Mitchell. A friend of Mia's is our friend, too."

Finally, when he could bear no more of their kindness, he worked his way out to the sidewalk.

Mia stood in the doorway. She looked uncertain, worried. "Thank you for coming, Collin."

"Our pleasure, huh, Mitch?"

"Yeah." Mitch's bottom lip was dragging the ground. He looped a towel around his neck and sawed the rough terry cloth back and forth.

Collin didn't want to answer the questions in Mia's eyes, so he turned and started toward his truck. The door behind him didn't close for several more seconds.

He'd gotten himself into this mess with Mia. He'd known from the beginning that a social worker only brought trouble. Now he was knee-deep in this big-brother thing with Mitch and stuck with the constant reminders of everything he and his brothers had missed out on. He knew that sounded selfish and envious. Maybe he was.

Long ago, he'd made peace with who he was as well as who he wasn't. He'd made a decent life for himself and, except for his fruitless search for Drew and Ian, he was happy most of the time.

There was an old adage that said you don't miss what you've never had. He'd always thought it was a lie. Today confirmed his suspicion.

He wished he'd never come here.

Halfway down the sidewalk, Mitch asked, "Can I have Miss Carano bring me out to your house tomorrow afternoon?"

"Miss Carano goes to church. She's not your personal chauffeur."

"I can walk, then. No big deal."

"Five miles?"

"I could borrow a bike."

When Collin didn't answer, Mitchell said, "I guess you don't want me to. That's cool. It's okay. I got plenty of stuff to do."

They walked in silence, Collin feeling like a major jerk. He didn't want the kid around right now. He wanted to be alone, to sort out whatever was eating a hole in him.

One hand on the truck door, Mitchell said, "Will you soak Happy's foot for me? I promised him, ya know."

That clinched it. The little dog *was* making progress with Mitch's tender, relentless care. "Be ready at one. I'll pick you up."

He was in over his head. He had agreed to mentor Mitchell indefinitely, and he wasn't a man to go back on his word. But Mia's brothers with their camaraderie and craziness stirred up a nest of hornets inside him. The reminders were there, too strong to ignore.

He'd have to set up some ground rules if he was to keep his sanity. Working with Mia was part of the deal but mentoring didn't have to include her family. If she wanted Mitch to experience family relationships she could bring him here herself. He was never coming back to this place again.

Mia sat on the floor of her office surrounded by bent, bedraggled cardboard boxes filled with old files dating back more than twenty years. Three weeks ago she'd hauled these files over from the storage room and had been going through them a few at a time whenever she could break away from her caseload.

So far, dust and an occasional spider were the only

things she'd found. The task was, after all, a daunting one that could take years to turn up something. If it ever did.

With the back of her hand she scratched her nose, itchy from the stale smell and dust mites. The Lord had sent Collin Grace her way, and she wouldn't let a little thing like twenty years and a mountain of dusty files stop her from trying to show him that God cared enough to help him find his brothers.

"You busy?"

She looked up to find Adam standing in the doorway. He held out a tall paper cup. "Could you use a break?"

"I hope that's a cherry icy." She took the cup, peeked under the lid and said, "You are the best brother on the planet."

"Does that mean you'll help me clean my apartment this weekend?"

"I knew there was a catch." She sipped the cold drink, let the cool, clean sweetness wash away some of the dust. "New girlfriend coming over?"

He grinned sheepishly. "How did you know?"

Mia chuckled. Every time Adam started dating someone new he went into a cleaning frenzy. Only he wanted Mia to do the cleaning. And the redecorating. And the cooking.

"As long as I don't have to repaint this time."

"We only repainted last time because Mandy isn't a big sports fan."

And Adam's living room had been painted in red and white with a Red Sox insignia emblazoned on the ceiling. "I knew she wouldn't last long."

"If only I were as wise…." He toasted her with his fountain drink. "Which reminds me, I brought some information by for you to take to your new guy."

She eyed him from beneath a piece of floppy hair. "Excuse me? I haven't had a date in four months. There is no new guy."

"Collin. The cop." He made himself comfortable on the floor beside her. From inside his jacket he extracted an envelope, handing it to her.

"He's a friend, Adam." She read Collin's name on the front of the envelope. "Is this about that lawsuit?"

Adam nodded, but wouldn't be deterred from his original intent of matchmaking. "A few weeks ago you didn't even like the guy. The relationship is progressing pretty fast if you ask me."

"There is no relationship." Even if she wanted there to be, Collin had an invisible shield around him that held others at arm's length. "Ever since the birthday party he's been different. Cooler than usual." And for someone like Collin, that was as cool as this slush.

"He left soon after we started the water fight. Do you think we scared him off somehow?"

She'd wondered the same thing, though she couldn't imagine anything scaring a tough cop like Collin. "I don't know. Collin's hard to read sometimes. He holds a lot of himself in reserve."

From the bare-bones information Collin had shared about his childhood, he had every reason to distrust other human beings. But Mia didn't like the idea that he distrusted her, which accounted for her redoubled efforts to find some bit of information for him in these files. Trust had to be earned. And she wanted his.

"I keep wondering if we offended him somehow." He'd been fine while they were talking.

"Anyone who listens to Grandpa tell that story about the nanny goat and doesn't run at the first opportunity is not easily offended. Did he mention anything about why they left so early?"

She'd been out to his farm on a regular basis since the party, but their conversations had mostly been about Mitchell's latest truancy from school and the rescued animals. Once they'd talked about his search and another time he'd shocked her to no end by asking a question about God. She'd been frustrated to have no answer, but thrilled to know he was thinking about spiritual matters.

She rifled through another file, saw nothing related to Collin or his brothers and reached for another.

"Only that he appreciated our hospitality, thought we were a great family. You know, the usual polite stuff. And he thought the afternoon had been good for Mitchell."

Adam took the file folder from her hand and stuck it back in the box. "The boy needs a lot of attention. Did you see Mama plying him with cookies and questions?"

"Mama thinks food is the answer to everyone's problems."

"Isn't it?"

"My hips seem to think so." Every time Mia decided to do something about her few extra pounds, Mama invited her over for pasta and bread or asked her to work a few hours at the bakery. Or she went through a mini-crisis and baked some marvelous creation for herself. Having a family in the bakery business was both a blessing and a terrible temptation.

"So, do you like him?"

"Mitchell? Sure. He's basically a good boy, but he needs a firm hand and a strong role model. He went to Sunday School with me last week."

Adam gave her a look reserved for thick-headed sisters. "I'm talking about Collin."

"And I'm not." Every time a new man appeared on the horizon, her brothers zeroed in like stealth missiles.

"I can hope, can't I?"

"Not in this case." Though there was something about Collin that kept him on her mind all the time, she knew better than to let her feelings take over. She wanted God to choose the right man for her.

"Want me to beat him up? Get things moving?"

She laughed. "You know how I feel about the whole husband-hunting thing. God's timing is always perfect."

"If God is going to send you a husband, He needs to hurry."

"Adam," she admonished. But she had to admit to a certain restlessness lately. Though her job and her community and church activities kept her life more than busy, she had always planned to be married with a big house filled with kids by now. "You're a fine one to talk. When are you going to find Miss Right and settle down?"

He shrugged a pair of shoulders that had plenty of women interested. "I want what Mom and Dad have. I'm willing to wait as long as it takes to get it."

And she was willing to wait, as well. She only hoped she didn't have to wait forever.

Chapter Eight

An excited Mia jumped out of her Mustang, leaving her jacket behind and hurrying through the cool, windy evening to Collin's front door. In the west the sun was setting, a testament to the shorter days of late autumn.

The hollow sound of a hammer rang through the otherwise quiet countryside. Not once in the months since meeting him had she come to this house and found Collin idle. He was either working on the house, with the animals or helping Mitchell do something. Didn't the man ever lie around on the couch like a slob the way her brothers did?

She waited for a pause in the hammering and then pounded hard on the door. She'd finally found something and she couldn't wait to share the news with Collin.

"Collin, hello."

The hammering ceased. After a minute, she saw movement from the corner of her eye and heard Collin's voice. She spotted him near the side of the house, the area still mostly in skeleton form.

In the fading light, Collin raised the hammer in greeting, a smile lifting the corners of his mouth. Dressed in jeans and a denim shirt, he wore a tool belt slung low on his hips.

"Hey," he said.

She started toward him, her heart doing a weird kerthumping action. Okay, so she was glad to see him. And yes, he was good-looking enough to make any woman's heart beat a little faster. But she was excited because of the news she had, not because Collin had smiled as if he was glad to see her, too. Mostly.

Adam and his insinuations were getting to her.

"Watch your step." Collin gestured at the pile of tools strewn about on the concrete pad, and then reached out to put a hand under her elbow.

His was a simple act of courtesy, but her silly heart did that ker-thump thing again. Come to think of it, this was the first time Collin had ever intentionally touched her.

A naked lightbulb dangled from an extension cord in one corner to illuminate the work space. The smell and fog of sawdust hung cloudlike above a pile of pale new boards propped beside a table saw.

"I finally have the decking on top," he said with some satisfaction, unmindful of her sudden awareness of him as a man. "Even if the room won't be completely in the dry before the really cold weather sets in, I'll be able to work out here."

Usually Mitchell was under foot, pounding and sawing under Collin's close supervision. She looked around, saw no sign of the boy. "Where's Mitchell?"

Collin placed the hammer on a makeshift table, his welcoming expression going dark. "I caught him smoking in the barn. Took him home early."

"Oh, no. I thought you'd made him see the senselessness of cigarettes."

"Yeah, well that was a big failure, I guess." He sighed, a heavy sound, and ran both hands up the back of his head. "He's been acting up again. Mouthy. Moody. Maybe I'm not doing him any good after all."

"Don't think that, Collin. All kids mess up, regress. But he's come a long way in a short time. The school says he's only missed two days since you spoke to his class on careers in law enforcement. His discipline referrals for fighting are down, too."

He squinted at her. "You know what he's been fighting about?"

"No. Do you?"

"I've got a clue." He turned to the closed door leading into the living area. "Come on in. You're getting cold."

Pleasure bloomed. He'd noticed.

Inside the kitchen, he motioned toward a half-full Mr. Coffee. "Coffee?"

"Sure." She took the offered cup, wrapping her hands around the warmth. "Are you going to share your insights with me?"

Collin leaned a hip against the clean white counter. If she was a betting woman, she'd bet he'd laid the tile himself. "I think Mitch is under a lot of pressure from some of the other boys."

"What kind of pressure?"

"I haven't figured that part out. There's something though. I have a feeling it has to do with his stepdad. That's a very sore subject lately."

Her caseworker antennae went up. "Anything I need to investigate on a professional basis?"

Over the rim of his coffee cup, Collin gave her the strangest look, a look she'd come to recognize each time she mentioned her job. He took a long time in answering such a simple question.

"I guess it wouldn't hurt to keep your eyes and ears open."

She was already doing that.

"How's Happy?"

"Still happy." He grinned at his own joke and pulled a chair around from the table to straddle the seat. "Doc says the foot is still in danger. It'll kill Mitchell if she has to amputate."

She could tell Collin wouldn't be too happy either, but he wasn't about to say so.

"He's attached."

"Very." Arms folded over the back of the chair, the coffee mug dangled from his fingers.

"You are, too."

He made a face. "Yeah."

And she was glad to know he could form bonds this way, even though they saddened him. Some kids who grew up in the system were never able to love and bond.

"I have a bit of news for you." She laid her purse on the table and pulled out a slip of paper.

"I could use some today. Shoot."

"This may turn out to be nothing, but—" she handed him the note "—this is the address of foster parents who took care of one of your brothers shortly after you were separated. They're not on your list."

The expression on his face went from mildly interested to intense. "Seriously?"

"The address hasn't been updated and there was no telephone, so we may not find anything."

He shoved out of the chair and grabbed a jacket. "Let's go see."

"Collin, wait."

He paused, face impassive.

Suddenly, she regretted her impulsive action to come here first before checking out the address herself.

"I haven't made contact. We don't know if anything will come from this. Don't get your hopes up, okay?"

"It's worth a shot." He shrugged the rest of the way into his jacket. "We'll take my truck."

She had known he'd react this way, pretending not to hope, but grasping at anything. If the foster parents were still around, they might not remember one little boy who passed through their lives so long ago. And if they did, they probably wouldn't remember where the child had gone from there.

"This is the first new piece of the puzzle I've had in a long time," Collin admitted as he smoothly guided the truck around the orange barrels and flashing lights of the ever-present road construction that plagued Oklahoma City. "Dartmouth Drive is back in one of these additions. I've been out here on calls. Not the best part of town."

A bad feeling came over her. She felt the need to say one more time, "Remember, now. This address comes from a very old file."

"I heard you." But she could tell that he didn't want to think that the trip might be futile.

Night had fallen and the wind picked up even more. An enormous harvest moon rose in the east. Mia had a sense of trepidation about approaching a strange house at night.

"Maybe we should have waited until tomorrow."

"I've waited twenty years." The lights of his vehicle swept over a wind-wobbled sign proclaiming Dartmouth

Drive. He turned onto a residential street. "Should be right down here on the left."

She could feel the tension emanating from him like heat from a stove. He wanted to find out something new about his brothers so badly. And now that they were nearing the place, Mia was scared. If the trip proved futile, would he be devastated?

"Here's the address." He pulled the truck to a stop along the curb.

She squinted into the darkness. "I don't think anyone is at home, Collin."

"Maybe they watch TV with the lights off."

They made their way up the cracked sidewalk. In the moonlight Mia observed that the grass was overgrown, a possibility only if no one had been here for a long time. Growing season had been over for more than a month.

She shouldn't have let him come here and be disappointed. But she'd been so excited that she hadn't thought everything through in advance. She'd only wanted to give him hope. Now, Collin could be hurt again because of her.

He banged on the front door.

"Collin," she said softly, wanting to touch him, to comfort him.

He ignored her and banged again, harder. "Hello. Anybody home?"

"Collin." This time she did touch him. His arm was like granite.

He stared at the empty, long-abandoned house. In the moonlight, his jaw worked. She heard him swallow and knew he swallowed a load of disappointment.

Abruptly, he did an about-face. "Dry run."

Inside the truck, Mia said, "This was my fault. I'm so sorry."

He gripped the steering wheel and stared at the empty house. "I should be used to it by now."

That small admission, that no matter how many times he came up empty he still hurt, broke Mia's heart. She couldn't imagine the pain and loneliness he'd suffered in his life. She couldn't imagine the pain of being separated from her loved ones the way Collin had been.

When they'd first met, she'd thought him cold and heartless. Now she realized what a foolish judgment she'd made.

Because she didn't know what else to do, Mia closed her eyes and prayed. Prayed for God to help them find Drew and Ian. Prayed that Collin could someday release all his heartache to the only One who could heal him. Prayed that she would somehow find the words to compensate for her bad judgment.

In silence they drove out of the residential area and headed toward Collin's place and her vehicle. Mia was glad she'd left her car at the farm. Collin didn't need to be alone even if he thought he did.

"Are you okay?" she finally asked.

In the dim dash lights he glanced her way, his cop face expressionless. "Sure. You hungry?"

The question had her turning in her seat. "Hungry?"

"As in food. I haven't had dinner."

"Neither have I." She felt out of balance. He had shoved aside what had to be, at least, a disappointment. Was this the way he handled his emotions? By ignoring them?

They parked behind a popular steak house and went inside.

They passed a buffet loaded with steaming vegetables and a variety of meats that had her mouth watering.

"You look confused," Collin said as he held a chair for her.

She was. In more ways than one. "I was expecting a tofu bar with bean sprouts and seaweed."

"I eat what I like."

There went another assumption she shouldn't have made about him.

They filled their plates from the hot bar and found a table. Collin had ordered a steak, as well.

"Comfort food?" she asked gently after the waitress brought their drinks and departed.

He shrugged. "Just hungry. This place makes great steaks."

She squeezed the lemon slice into her tea.

"Want mine?" Collin said, removing the slice from the edge of his glass.

"You're giving up vitamin C?" She teased, but took the offered fruit. "Do you eat out like this all the time?"

"Not that much. Mostly I cook for myself."

She should have figured as much. He'd been self-reliant of necessity all of his life, a notion that made her heart hurt. But that strength had made him good at about anything he set his mind to. She wondered if he knew that about himself and decided that he didn't.

"What's your specialty?" she asked.

"Meat loaf and mashed potatoes. How about you? You live alone, too. Do you eat at your folks' or cook for yourself?"

"For myself most of the time. Although I sneak over to the bakery a little more often than I should."

"You any good?"

"Look at this body." With a self-deprecating twist of her mouth, she held her hands out to the side. "What do you think?"

"I think you look great." His brown eyes sparkled with appreciation.

"That wasn't what I meant." A rush of heat flooded her neck. "I meant—"

He laughed and let her off the hook. "I know what you meant." He pointed a fork at her. "But you still look good."

"Well." She wasn't sure what to say. She got her share of compliments, but she'd never expected one from Collin. He was full of surprises tonight. "Thank you."

The waitress brought his steak and they settled in to eat, making comments now and then about the food. After a bit the conversation lagged and all she could think about was the night's failed trip. Collin might want to ignore the subject, but Mia would explode if she didn't get her feelings out in the open.

"Will you let me apologize for not checking out that address before telling you about it?"

"No use talking the subject to death."

"We haven't talked about it at all." Which was driving her nuts.

"Just as well." He laid aside his fork and took a man-size drink of tea.

"Not really. Talking helps you sort out your feelings, weigh your options." And made her feel a whole lot better.

Collin looked at her, steady and silent. If anyone was going to talk, she would have to be the one.

"I'll keep looking. The information has to be there somewhere. We'll find them."

"You could check the adoption files. See if either of my brothers was adopted."

"I'm checking those."

Attention riveted to his plate, he casually asked, "The sealed ones?"

Her breath froze in her throat. "I won't do that."

He looked up. The naked emotion in his eyes stunned her. "Why not?"

Shoulders instantly tense, she had to remind him, "I told you from the beginning I wouldn't go into sealed files."

"That was before you knew me. Before we were friends."

Friends? "Is that what the compliment was about? To soften me up?"

His jaw tightened. "Is that what you think?"

She leaned back in her chair, miserable to be at odds with him over this. "No. Not really, but I can't believe you'd ask me to do such a thing."

Anger flared in the normally composed face. His fork clattered against his plate. "Wanting to find my brothers is not a crime. I'm not some do-wrong trying to ferret out information for evil purposes. This is my life we're talking about."

"I know that, Collin. But the files are closed for a reason. Parents requested and were given sealed records because they wanted the promise of privacy. And until those people request a change, those files have to stay sealed."

He crammed a frustrated hand over his head, spiking the hair up in front. "Nearly twenty-five years of my life is down the drain, Mia. I need to find them. They're men now. Opening those files won't hurt them or anybody else."

She shook her head, sick at heart. "I can't. It's wrong. Please understand."

Back rigid, he pushed away from the table and stood. The cold mask she'd encountered the first time they'd met was back in place.

Chapter Nine

Collin was not having a good day. In fact, the last two had been lousy.

He pushed the barn door open, stopping in the entrance to breathe in the warm scents of animals, feed and the ever-present smell of disinfectant. He went through gallons of the stuff trying to protect the sick animals from each other.

Since the night he'd let himself hope, only to be slapped down again, he'd battled a growing sense of emptiness.

After work tonight he'd gone to the gym with Maurice and true to form, his buddy had invited him home for dinner and Bible study. For the first time, he'd wanted to go. But he always felt so out of place in a crowd. And a Bible study was a whole different universe.

Not that he hadn't given God a lot of thought lately. Every time he showered or changed shirts and noticed his shamrock, Mia's words rang in his memory. She had something in her life that he didn't. And that something was more than a big, noisy family. Maurice had the same thing, so Collin figured the difference must be God.

One of the horses nickered as Collin moved down the dirt-packed corridor. These animals depended on him, regardless of the kind of day he'd had. He could take care of himself. They couldn't.

As was his habit, he headed to Happy's pen first. The little dog's attitude could lighten him up no matter what.

Mitchell, whom he hadn't seen since the smoking incident, was already inside the stall.

Irritation flared. The little twerp had some nerve coming back around the animals without permission.

Collin was all prepared to give him a tongue-lashing and send him home when the boy looked up.

What he saw punched him in the gut.

The kid's face was bruised from the eyebrow to below the cheekbone. A sliver of bloodshot eye showed through the swelling.

"What happened?" He heard his own voice, hard and angry.

Mitchell dropped his head, fidgeting with the dog brush in his hands. "I won't smoke anymore, Collin."

"Not what I asked."

Mitchell jerked one narrow shoulder. "Nothing."

With effort, Collin forced a calm he didn't feel. "Home or school?"

The boy was silent for a minute. Then he blew out a gust of air as if he'd been holding his breath, afraid Collin would send him away. "Not my mom."

The stepdad, then. Collin had run a check on Teddy Shipley. He had a rap sheet longer than the road from here to California, where he'd spent a year in the pen for assault with a deadly weapon and manufacturing an illegal substance. A real honey of a guy.

Collin hunkered down beside the boy, rested one hand lightly on the skinny back. "You can tell me anything."

Mitchell developed a sudden fascination with the bristles of Happy's brush. He flicked them back and forth against his palm. "I can't."

And then he dropped the brush and buried his face in Happy's thick fur. Happy, true to his name, moaned in ecstatic joy and licked at the air.

The kid was either scared or he knew something that would incriminate someone he cared about. And the cop in Collin suspected who.

He sighed wearily. Life could be so stinking ugly.

"If he hits you again, I'm all over him."

Mitch's head jerked up. His one good eye widened. "I never told you that. Don't be saying I did."

Compassion, mixed with frustration, pushed at the back of Collin's throat. He clamped down on his back teeth, hating the feelings.

"Did you go to school like this?"

Mitch shook his head. "No."

So that's why he'd shown up here this evening. Things were out of hand at home.

"Does he hit your mom, too?"

Tears welled in the boy's eyes. "She'd be real mad if she knew I told."

"Why?"

"She just would."

What Mitch wasn't saying spoke volumes. Collin had seen this scenario before. He'd also lived it.

Violence. Codependence. Drugs. A mother who preferred the drugs and a violent man to the safety and well-being of herself and her child. He wouldn't be a bit surprised if Teddy was cooking meth again, a suspicion that deserved checking into.

The sound of a car engine had Mitchell scrubbing frantically at his face. Collin turned toward the interruption. He'd know that Mustang purr anywhere. Mia. Just who he did not want to see. A social worker who'd stick her nose into something she couldn't fix. He was a cop. He could handle the situation far better than she could.

Mitch leaped up, recognizing the car, as well. His one good eye widened in panic. "Don't say anything, huh, Collin?"

Like she wouldn't notice an eye swollen shut.

"Go brush down the colt and give him a block of hay," he said, giving the kid an out. If Mia didn't see him, she wouldn't ask questions, and no one would have to lie.

Mitch shot out of the pen, disappearing into the far stall.

Collin picked up an empty feed sack and crushed it into a ball.

His world had been orderly and uneventful until Mia had come barging into it, hounding him, talking until he'd said yes to shut her up. And then her family had gotten in on the deal. First the birthday party. Then Adam's help with the lawsuit. And now Leo, Mia's father, found daily reasons why Collin had to stop by the bakery. Try as he might, Collin couldn't seem to say no.

Man. What had he gotten himself into?

The colt whickered. One of the dogs started barking. And the whole menagerie began moving restlessly.

Collin didn't rush out to greet his visitor. He needed some time to think. Still baffled by Mia's stubbornness over something as simple as looking into a file, he wasn't sure what to say to her.

They didn't share the same sense of justice. He believed in obeying the law, but there was a difference in the spirit of the law and the letter of the law. To him, opening his own brothers' adoption files, if they existed, would fall under the spirit of the law. It was the right and just thing to do.

But he had to be fair to Mia, too. She'd gone above and beyond the call of duty in searching those moldy old files in the first place. And even if she was a pain in the backside sometimes, having her around lightened him somehow, as if the goodness in her could rub off.

After a minute's struggle, Collin decided to wait her out. Mia knew where he was if she had something to say. He'd known from the start he didn't want the grief of some woman trying to get inside his head. He had enough trouble inside there himself.

He went to work scrubbing down a newly emptied pen. The last stray, hit by a car, hadn't made it. He'd been hungry too long to have the strength to fight.

Fifteen minutes later, when Mia hadn't come storming inside the barn, smiling and rattling off at the mouth, Collin began to wonder if he'd heard her car at all. He dumped the last of the bleach water over the metal security cage and went to find out.

Sure enough, Mia's yellow Mustang sat in his driveway but she was nowhere to be seen.

Mitch came to stand beside him, one of Panda's adolescent kittens against his chest. "Where is she?"

"Beats me."

At that very moment, she flounced around the side of the house, her sweater flapping open in the stiff wind.

She wasn't wearing her usual smile. Almond eyes shooting sparks, she marched right up to Collin.

"I don't stop being a friend because of a disagreement."

That didn't surprise him. The sudden lift in his mood did. Renewed energy shot through his tired muscles. He hid a smile. Mia was pretty cute when she got all wound up.

She slapped a wooden spoon against his chest.

"I brought food. Home-cooked." She tilted her head in a smug look. "And you are going to love it."

He fought the temptation to laugh. Normally, when a woman pushed too hard, she was history, but with Mia he couldn't stay upset. That fact troubled him, but there it was.

Unmindful of the sparks flying between the adults, Mitch stepped between them. "Food. Cool."

Mia started to say something then stopped. Her mouth dropped open. She stared at Mitchell's bruised face, expression horrified. "What happened to you?"

Mitchell shot Collin a silent plea and then hung his head, averting his battered face.

"I got in a fight."

"Oh, Mitch." And then her fingers gently grazed the boy's cheekbone in a motherly gesture. The tension in Mitch's shoulders visibly relaxed, but his eyes never met Mia's.

Collin let the lie pass for now. Whether Mitch liked the idea or not, a cop was mandated by law to share his suspicions with the proper authorities, and that was Mia. If there was any possibility that a child was in danger, welfare had a right to know. The policeman in him accepted that regardless of his personal aversion.

"I'm starved," he said, knowing his statement would be an effective diversion. Mia's respondent smile washed through him warm and sweet, like a spring wind through a field of flowers. "Cleaning pens can wait until after dinner."

"Not mad at me anymore?" she asked.

Quirking one brow, he started toward the house and left her to figure that out for herself. He wasn't sure he knew the answer anyway.

The early sunsets of November were upon them and the wind blew from the north promising a change in weather. Leaves loosened their tree-grip and tumbled like tiny, colorful gymnasts across the neatly fenced lots housing the grazers. The deer with the bad hip had healed and now roamed restlessly up and down the fence line longing to run free. Collin and Doc had decided to wait until after hunting season ended to give the young buck a fighting chance.

When they reached the house, Collin opened the door and let Mia and Mitchell enter first. The smell of Italian seasoning rushed out and swirled around his nose.

"Smells great. What is it?" Not that he cared—a home-cooked Italian dinner was too good to pass up. Especially one cooked by Mia.

"Lasagna. Wash your hands. Both of you." She shooed them toward the sink. "Food's still hot."

Along with Mitchell, he meekly did as he was told, scrubbing at the kitchen sink. If anyone else came into his house issuing orders and rummaging in his cabinets, he would be furious. Weird that he wasn't bothered much at all.

While Mia rattled forks and thumped plates onto his

tiny table, he murmured to Mitch, "A lie will always come back to bite you. Better tell her."

Mitchell darted a quick glance at Mia and gave his head a slight shake, his too-long hair flopping forward to hide his expression. Collin let the subject drop. For now.

Moments later, they dug into the meal. Collin could barely contain a moan of pleasure.

Lifting a forkful of steaming noodles and melted mozzarella, he said, "If this is your idea of a peace offering, I'll get mad at you more often."

Mia sliced a loaf of bread and pushed the platter toward him. Steam curled upward, bringing the scent of garlic and yeast.

"There are still things I can do to help, Collin. Unlike foster-care files, many of the adoption files have been computerized. I started searching the open ones today."

He took a chunk of the bread and slathered on a pat of real butter. "Are the sealed files on computer, too?"

There was a beat of silence, and then, "It doesn't matter."

She wasn't budging from her hard-nosed stand.

"After all the years I've searched and come up empty, I think the adoption files are the answer. They have to be."

Mitchell was already digging in for seconds. "Why are you trying to get into adoption files?"

Collin started. He never spoke openly about his brothers or his past. He'd never before said a word about them in front of Mitchell. Was this what hanging around with a chatterbox did for a guy? He started to lie to the boy, and then remembered his words only moments before. A lie would always come back to haunt you.

"I'm looking for my brothers," he said honestly. "We were separated in foster care as kids."

Saying the words aloud didn't seem so hard this time.

"No kidding?" Mitch backhanded a string of cheese from his mouth. "You were a foster kid?"

"Yeah. I was." He held his breath. Would the knowledge lessen him in Mitchell's eyes?

Mitch's one unblemished eye, brown and serious, studied him in awe. "But you became a cop. How'd you do that?"

And just that simply, Collin experienced a frisson of pride instead of shame. Mia had been right all along. Mitch needed to know that the two of them shared some commonalities.

"A lousy childhood doesn't have to hold you back."

By now, the boy's mouth was jammed full again, so he just nodded and chewed. He chased the food with a gulp of iced tea and then said, "So where are your brothers? Can Miss Carano find them? Can't the police find them? I'll help you look for them. How many do you have?"

His words tumbled out, eager and naive.

Collin filled him in on the bare facts. "And Miss Carano's helping me search, too. Even though I've been a pain about it."

He gave her his version of an apologetic look. He wasn't sorry for asking her to bend the rules a little, but he was glad to be back on comfortable footing with her. The last couple of days had been lousy without her.

"I've started a hand search of the old records in the storage room of the municipal building," Mia told him. "That's where I found that address the other day."

The police records were warehoused the same way,

and he knew from experience that hand searches were tedious and time-consuming. And often fruitless.

"I appreciate all you're doing, Mia. Honestly. But you can't blame me for wanting to investigate every available option."

"I don't blame you." She pushed her plate aside and said, "Anyone for dessert?"

"Dessert?" Both males moaned at the same time.

"You should have warned us." Collin put a hand over his full belly. He looked around the tiny kitchen, spotted a covered container on the bar. "What is it?"

Mia laughed. "My own made-from-scratch cherry chocolate bundt cake. But we can save dessert for later."

"You made it yourself?"

"Yep. The bread and lasagna, too."

The sweet Italian bread *must* have come from her parents' bakery. "No way."

"Way. I didn't grow up a baker's daughter for nothing. All of us kids cut our teeth on the old butcher-block table in the back of the bakery where Mom and Dad hand-mixed the dough for all kinds of cakes and breads and cookies."

She got up and started clearing the table. Collin grabbed the glasses.

"Let me help with this."

"I can get the dishes. Didn't you say you still have work in the barn?"

"Work can wait."

Mitchell, who looked as if he'd rather be anywhere but in a kitchen with unwashed dishes, piped up. "I'll do the rest of the chores outside. I don't mind."

With a knowing chuckle, Collin gave him instructions and let him go.

"Did you see the look on his face?"

"And to think he prefers mucking out stalls to our esteemed company." Mia feigned hurt.

In the tiny kitchen area, they bumped elbows at the sink. Collin didn't usually enjoy company that much, but over the weeks and months he'd known Mia, she'd become a part of his life. Sometimes an annoying part, but if he was honest, even when they disagreed he depended upon her to see through his anger to the frustration and still be his friend.

He'd never expected to call a social worker "friend."

At times, he could be brooding and moody, and admittedly, he wore a protective armor around his heart. Trouble was, Miss Mia had slipped beneath it at some point and discovered the softer side of him. The idea unhinged him.

"Thanksgiving's coming soon," she said, her voice coming from above a sink of soapy hot water. "We always have a big to-do at Mama's. Turkey, dressing, pecan pie. The works. The Macy's Thanksgiving Day parade on TV and then a veritable marathon of football games afterward."

He knew what was coming and didn't know what to do. Nic's birthday party had stirred up something inside him, a hunger for the things missing in his own life, and he wasn't sure he could go there again.

Mia rinsed a plate under the hot tap. As he reached to take the dish, she held on, forcing him to look down at her.

Green eyes, honey-sweet and honest, held his. "We'd love for you to come. Please say you will."

Steam rose up between them, moist and warm. Her eyes, her tone indicated more than an invitation of kindness to a man who had nowhere else to go. She really wanted him there.

Like most holidays, Thanksgiving was a family occasion. The time or two he'd accepted an invitation, he'd felt like an intruder. "I usually volunteer to work so the officers with families can be off that day."

"Then I'd say you're due a day off this year. Wouldn't you?"

"I'd better not."

Disappointment flashed across her face. Unlike him, she could never hide her feelings. They were there for the whole world to see. And what he saw both troubled and pleased him. Mia liked him. As more than a friend.

She let go of the plate and went back to washing. The air in the kitchen hung heavy with his refusal and her reaction. He didn't want to hurt her. In fact, he couldn't believe she was disappointed. Couldn't believe she'd be interested in him. He didn't belong with her all-American perfect family.

Mia, true to form, rushed in to the fill the quiet, and if he hadn't known better, her chatter would have convinced him that she didn't really care one way or the other. But now he knew her chatter sometimes covered her unease.

Then she mentioned some guy she'd met during the 10-K charity walk last weekend, and his mood turned from thoughtful to sour. If she was attracted to him, why was she having Starbucks with some runner?

He interrupted. "Wonder what's keeping Mitchell?"

Mia stopped in midsentence and gave him a funny look. "He hasn't been gone that long."

"Long enough." He tossed his dish towel over the back of a chair that served as a towel rack, coat rack, whatever.

The water gurgled out of the sink. Mia dried her hands. "If you'll stop scowling, I'll go check. I need to get something out of my car anyway."

"I can go. He's my responsibility."

"Mine, too. You stay here and slice the cake. I have a book in the car for you."

"A Bible?" he asked suspiciously.

Tossing on her sweater, she laughed and opened the door. "You'll see."

Halfway out, she stopped and looked over her shoulder. "I want coffee with my cake."

The door banged shut and Collin found himself grinning into the empty space. Tonight Mia had made this half-finished, scantily furnished, poor excuse for a house feel like a home.

He turned that thought over in his head and went to make the lady's coffee.

Four scoops into the pot, a scream shattered the quiet. Coffee grounds went everywhere. His heart stopped.

"Mia."

He was out the door, running toward the barn before he realized the previously dark sky was lit with bright light. Fire light.

"Mitchell!"

He heard Mia's cry once more and this time he spotted her, running toward the burning barn. Before he could yell for her to stop, to turn back, she disappeared inside.

Collin thought he would die on the spot. Adrenaline ripped through his veins with enough force to knock him down. He broke into a run, pounding over the hard, dry ground.

Flames licked the sky. Sparks shot fifty feet up, fueled by the still wind. The horses screamed in terror.

Dogs barked and howled. Several had managed to escape somehow and now scrambled toward him. A kitten streaked past, her fur smoking.

A horrible sense of doom slammed into him, overwhelming. Mia and Mitchell were inside a burning barn along with more than a dozen helpless, trapped, sick and injured animals.

He darted toward the outside water faucet, thankful for the burlap feed sack wrapped around the pipes to prevent freezing. Yanking the sack free, he dipped the rough cloth into the freshly filled trough then rushed into the barn just as Mitchell came stumbling out.

Collin caught him by the shoulders. "Where's Mia?"

Mitchell shook his head, coughing. "I don't know."

With no time to waste, he shoved Mitchell out into the fresh air. "Call 911."

He could only hope the boy obeyed.

And then he charged into the burning building.

Smoke, thick and blinding, wrapped him in a terrifying embrace.

"Mia!" he yelled as he slung the wet sack around his face and head.

Eyes streaming, lungs screaming, he traversed the interior by instinct, throwing open stalls and pens as he called out, over and over again. The animals would at least have a chance this way. Locked in, they would surely die.

He stumbled over something soft and pitched forward, slamming his elbow painfully into a wall. A familiar whine greeted him. When he reached down, the dog licked his hand. Happy.

With more joy than he had time to feel, he scooped the little dog up and headed him in the direction of the open doorway. Even a crippled dog would instinctively move toward the fresh air.

A timber above his head cracked. Honed reflexes moved him to one side as the flaming board thundered to the barn floor. If he stayed too long, he'd never make it out.

Another board fell behind him and then another. Common sense said for him to escape now. His heart wouldn't let him.

"Mia." His voice, hoarse and raspy, made barely a sound against the roaring, crackling fire. Heat seared the back of his hands. His head swam.

If something happened to her. If something happened to Mia.

Suddenly, he heard her coughing. And praying.

Renewed energy propelled him forward.

"I'm coming."

Keep praying, Mia, so I can find you.

With his free hand, he felt along the corridor wall. No longer could he hear animal sounds, but Mia's prayers grew louder.

In the dense darkness he never saw her, but he heard her and reached out, made contact. She frantically clawed at his arm.

"I've got you."

"Thank God. Thank God." A fit of harsh coughing wracked her. "Mitch," she managed.

"He's safe."

Without a thought, Collin stripped the covering from his face and pressed the rough fabric against Mia's mouth and nose. Her breath puffed hot and dry against his fingers.

"This way."

With his knowledge of the barn, he guided them away from the falling center toward the feed room. There, a small window would provide escape.

Though the seconds seemed to drag, Collin knew by the size of the fire that they'd been inside only a few minutes. Thankfully, the flames had not reached this section of the barn yet, but they were fast approaching.

"Hurry," he said needlessly, pushing and pulling her stumbling form.

Inside the feed room, he felt for the window, shoved the sash upward, then easily lifted Mia over the threshold and to safety on the ground.

A roar erupted behind him. The flames, as if enraged by Mia's escape, chased him. Licking along the wall, they found the empty paper sacks and swooshed into the room.

Collin scrambled up and out the window, falling to the ground below. What little air he had left was knocked out in the fall.

Mia grabbed his hand and tugged. "Get up. We have to get away."

Hands clasped, they stumbled around the side of the barn to an area several yards out from the flames. Mia fell to her knees, noisily sucking in the fresh air.

Collin went down beside her, filling his lungs with the sweet, precious oxygen.

"You okay?" he asked when he could breathe again.

"Fine."

But he couldn't take her word for it. By the flickering light of the fire that had nearly stolen her, he searched her face for signs of injury and found none.

"If anything had happened to you—"

And then before his reasonable side could stop him, he pulled her into his arms and kissed her.

She tasted smoky and sweet and wonderful. Emotion as foreign as an elephant and every bit as powerful coursed through him. His world tilted, spun, shimmered with warning.

He pulled back, suddenly afraid of what was happening to him. It was only a kiss, wasn't it? Given out of fear and relief. That was all. Only a kiss.

But he knew better. He'd kissed other women before, but not like this. The others he'd kept at a distance, outside of the armor. Mia was different. Way different.

And the truth of that scared him more than the barn fire.

Chapter Ten

"Here Mitch, take this end down to Adam."

Mia stood in the yard of her parents' home surrounded by large plastic containers filled with Christmas lights and decorations. Twined around her shoulders and across her arms was a tangled strand of frosty icicle lights. Adam worked at the opposite end of the fence attaching the strands as she unraveled them.

The other Caranos were scattered about in the yard and over the exterior of the house in similar activity. Each year on a given Saturday, Rosalie commandeered all available family members to set up outside Christmas decorations while the weather was decent. Today was the day.

Mitch, eager for a promised turkey hunt with Mia's dad, was trying to hurry the process.

"Why are you putting up Christmas lights so early? We haven't even had Thanksgiving yet."

He took the proffered end of the lights and trudged toward Adam.

Mia squinted at him, the November sun bright, the wind light but sharp. "That's the whole point. At the

Caranos, turning the lights on for the first time on Thanksgiving night is a big deal. You *are* still coming, aren't you?"

One narrow shoulder jerked. "I guess. Nothing else to do."

Mia recognized Mitch's unique method of saving face. Holidays at his house, from what he'd told her and from what she'd seen, were not festive occasions. And from the latest information Collin had shared, Mia was more concerned than ever. Life at the Perez house grew more troubled with each passing week, and Mitchell spent most of his time on the streets, or with her or her mother and dad to avoid going home. His was a worrisome situation indeed, especially with the added tension between Collin and Mitch since the fire.

"Sure he's coming," Adam hollered. "We're going to finish that computer chess tournament, and I'm going to beat the socks off him."

Mitch handed him the light cord and grinned. "Wanna bet?"

"If I win, you have to wash my car inside and out."

"When *I* win, I get to wear your OU jersey to school."

"No betting around here, boys," Rosalie called from her spot on the front porch. She was winding greenery around the columns.

"Yes, ma'am," Adam replied, his swarthy face wreathed in ornery laughter. He loved to get Mama riled up.

"Yes, ma'am," Mitchell echoed, grinning at Adam.

Mia's dad came around the corner of the house, carrying the last of the nativity pieces that would grace their front yard. "As soon as I put this with the others, I'm going out to Collin's place."

Mia looked up in surprise, her pulse doing the usual flip-flop at Collin's name. "What for?"

Leo, like the other Caranos, had worked overtime to draw Collin into the fold. Though they'd yet to get him back to a large family gathering, he'd started hanging out with regularity at the Carano Bakery—at Leo's insistent invitation.

"Cops and doughnuts. They're a natural," her dad had said, but she knew he liked the quiet cop.

So did she.

"We need a couple of bales of hay to make the stable scene look authentic," Leo said. "I figured Collin might have some extra."

"Dad," Mia said, stricken at the memory. "Collin won't have any hay."

"Sure he will." He stopped and set the manger down with a thud. "What was I thinking? All his hay went up with the barn."

"Yeah." Mitch scuffed a toe against the brown grass.

After their escape, while the firefighters drenched the glowing remains of the animal refuge, Collin had asked Mitch if he'd been smoking in the barn again. The question had devastated the boy. He hadn't been to the farm in the days since.

"He doesn't want me out there anymore."

"That's not true. He's upset right now because of the lost animals, but he's not upset with you."

"I could hear the puppies crying."

A heaviness tugged at Mia. They'd discussed this before, but the dying animals haunted him. "I know."

"I tried to find them, but the smoke was so bad."

She slid the lights from her shoulder and signaled Adam with a glance. He touched a finger to his eyebrow in silent agreement, understanding her need to counsel with Mitch. "Let's go sit on the porch and talk."

He followed her, slumping onto the step of the long concrete porch. Rosalie had moved down to the end post to add a red bow to the greenery.

"The investigators are still checking into the fire, but if you say you weren't smoking, I believe you."

"But Collin doesn't."

"I think he does, Mitchell, and he's sorry he hurt your feelings. He just has a hard time saying so."

"He's mad because of the puppies."

"No. He's sad. The same way you and I are."

The young boy stared morosely across the street where two squirrels gathered nuts beneath a pecan tree. "Do you think God cares about animals? Strays, I mean?"

She'd wondered when he'd ask something like that. Her faith was an open topic with anyone who knew her and the two of them had had more than one deep discussion.

"Sparrows aren't worth much in our eyes, but the Bible says God feeds them and watches over them." She pointed toward the squirrels. "And just look at those guys. God provided all the nuts they could ever want in that one tree. And they don't even have to buy them!"

Her attempt at humor fell flat. Mitchell wasn't in a joking mood.

"I'm going to miss them. Rascal and Slick and Milly and her kittens." Mitchell had named them all, something that had bothered Collin at first.

He gathered a handful of dead grass and tossed the blades one at a time.

"There would be something wrong with us if we didn't grieve over what we care about. But remember this one good thing—God allowed us to love them and give them a nice home in their last days. They hadn't had that before."

"Yeah. That's true." He tossed the remaining grass and wiped a hand down his jeans' leg. "I guess God is okay."

Mia draped an arm across Mitch's shoulders. "God is the best friend you could ever have, Mitchell."

"Is Collin a Christian?"

Something sharp pinched at her heart. "You'll have to ask him about that."

She wanted to believe that Collin would eventually accept Christ. Especially now. And not just because of Mitch's adoration, though that certainly loomed large. Mitch admired her Christian dad and brothers, too, but he shared a bond with Collin.

"You miss him, don't you?"

"Yeah."

"He misses you, too."

Mitch looked at her, hope as rich as the coffee-colored eyes. "You think?"

"I know. He told me on the phone last night." A phone call she'd instigated. Since the fire, he'd drawn back somewhat, as though he couldn't deal with all the emotions that had come pouring out that night. She was still puzzled and exhilarated by that unexpected kiss. Puzzled even more at how he had seemed to develop amnesia afterward.

"He needs your help out there to get things going again. Let's call him later, huh?"

She would keep on calling until he opened up again.

"I guess so."

"Hey, Mitchell," Mia's dad called. "Are you going to

sit around on the porch and suntan or are we going to that turkey shoot?"

"I'm ready." Mitchell leaped up, then caught himself and looked back at Mia. "Okay, Mia?"

After the fire she'd become Mia instead of Miss Carano. That kind of familiarity had never happened before with one of her clients, and she prayed she wouldn't lose perspective. Somehow Mitchell had wound his scruffy self around her heart and that of her family.

"Have fun."

Mitch was gone in a flash.

"You can depend on Dad to interrupt an important conversation," Rosalie murmured, coming to join Mia in Mitch's now-abandoned spot.

"Mitch needs the distraction. He's been pretty down since the fire."

"So have you. Maybe not down so much as too quiet. Want to talk about it?"

"I have a lot on my mind, Mama. That's all. Work, Mitch." She shrugged.

"Collin," Mama concluded.

"Yes. Him, too." She picked at a thread on her knit jacket. "He kissed me the night of the fire."

"Who could blame him? You're beautiful."

Mia laughed. "Oh, Mama, no wonder I love you so."

"You like him?"

"Maybe more than I should. I don't date guys who aren't Christians, Mom. You know that. You taught me that."

"But you're falling for him anyway."

Mia stared morosely at the crystal lights Adam and Nic were tacking in place along the board fence. The brothers argued happily as they worked, the sound of frequent laughs punctuating the air. Two big ol' macho men with marshmallow hearts. How she loved them.

No wonder Collin Grace appealed to her. For all his outward toughness, he was a softie on the inside just like her brothers.

Two nights ago, he'd lost his hard facade, both with her and then later when he'd found the first of several dead animals. Happy, the little survivor, had saved himself. Mitchell had freed Panda and her remaining kittens, and the large animals were safe in outside pens. But one litter of new kittens and an old sickly dog and her pup hadn't made it out alive. Mia couldn't forget the look on Collin's face: stricken, haunted, guilty.

He'd looked the same in those seconds before he had kissed her. She couldn't get that look or that kiss off her mind.

A kiss shouldn't be such a big deal. She wasn't a teenager. But she had already been fighting her growing emotions and when he'd looked at her, fear and firelight in his eyes, and wrapped her in a hard, protective hug, she'd faced the hard truth. Christian or not, she had strong feelings for Collin Grace. And even if he never admitted it, Collin felt something for her, too. Maybe that's why he was running scared. Collin didn't like to feel.

The wind blew a lock of hair across her face. She pushed the curl behind one ear.

"At first, I thought I was helping Collin. You know, doing the Christian thing, being a witness, going the extra mile, trying to draw him out to a place where he can heal. Collin's a good man, Mama. But he's had so much heartache that he's afraid to trust anybody. Even God."

Mama took Mia's chilled hands in her warm ones. "Then our job is to show him that he can. That God is trustworthy. And so are we. Dad's trying to do that at the bakery."

"I know. After the fire I gave him a book to read, the one about finding your purpose through Christ. We talked about the Lord a little then, but I felt so inadequate in the face of what had happened. I'm not sure I said the right things. I wanted him to know that God cared about him and his animals and his losses."

She yearned to tell Mama about Collin's lost brothers and lean on her wisdom. But she'd promised confidentiality even though telling her mother would help both of them. Rosalie was a prayer warrior who never stopped praying for something until the answer came. Mia wasn't having much success on her own, but God knew where Ian and Drew were.

"How is he handling the fire?"

"The usual way—by pretending he isn't bothered." The fact that he'd retreated into his shell again told her the tough cop with the marshmallow center was mourning the animals and the uninsured barn.

If only she could find some trace of his brothers to cheer him. Some bit of good news. She gripped her mother's hands tighter, giving them a quick bounce.

"Mama. I need you to help me pray about something." Rosalie's eyes lit up. "Of course. What is it?"

"Well, that's the trouble. I need you to pray. But I can't tell you why."

Her mama looked at her for one beat of time, then smiled a mother's knowing smile. And Mia felt better than she'd felt since the night of the barn fire.

"Thank you, Lord," Mia said as she hung up the telephone. After going through dozens of boxes and hundreds of old records, she'd hit pay dirt two days after the conversation with her mama.

This time, she'd tempered her excitement long enough to make some phone calls and verify that a foster mother named Maxine Fielding not only still lived in Oklahoma City, but also remembered caring for a rowdy eleven-year-old named Drew Grace.

She glanced at the clock. Another two hours before she could head for Collin's place with her news. She thought about calling his cell, but found that unsatisfactory. She wanted to see his face, to watch him smile again. The past week had been a rough one.

A desk laden with paperwork needed her attention anyway, so she went to work there, weeding through files, making calls, setting up appointments. She phoned Mitchell's school to check on his attendance and discipline referrals and to inquire about any further indication of abuse.

Even with the barn fire setback, the boy had held his ground. And after the turkey shoot last Saturday, he'd let her take him out to Collin's, where the three of them had spent hours putting together makeshift pens for the remaining animals.

The problems with the stepfather were accumulating though, and all her praying hadn't changed that one bit. The man had been furious when she'd interviewed him about Mitch's black eye, and Mitch hadn't helped by claiming he'd gotten into a fight at school. She wanted to get Mitch out of that house, though she couldn't without substantiated evidence. But now, both she and Collin were watching. Collin had even alerted the drug unit to be aware of possible illegal activities, though nothing had surfaced yet.

At ten after five she rotated her head from side to side, stretching tired muscles. Time to go. She tossed three Snickers wrappers into the trash and then dialed Collin's cell number.

"Grace."

She smiled at the short bark he substituted for a simple hello. And she couldn't deny that her heart jumped at the sound of that strong, masculine voice.

"Your name always makes me think of a song."

"Oh. Hi, Mia," he said. "I didn't recognize the number."

"My office."

"How does my name remind you of a song?"

She'd known he wouldn't let that one pass. With a smile in her voice, she said, "*Amazing grace, how sweet the sound, that saved a wretch like me.*' It's a song about God's incredible love for us."

"The guys call me Amazing Grace sometimes. I never quite got that."

"Do you know what grace actually means?"

"I'm sure you're going to tell me." She heard the humor behind the gentle jab.

"Unmerited favor. God chooses to love and accept us, not because of what we do or don't do, but all because of His amazing grace."

A moment of silence hummed through the line. Though she hadn't planned to talk about her faith just now, she wanted Collin to understand how much Jesus loved him. She prayed that the truth of amazing grace would soak into his spirit and draw him to the Lord. She also hoped she hadn't just turned him ice-cold to the whole idea.

Finally, his voice soft, Collin said, "I'll never let the guys call me that again."

"Oh, Collin." He'd understood.

"So what's up?" he asked, sidestepping the emotion they both heard in her voice.

"I'm about to leave the office. Are you home?"

"Not yet. Why?"

"I want to talk to you in person."

"News?"

"Maybe." She didn't want to get his hopes up again and have them shattered.

"I'm off duty. Meet me at Braums on Penn. I'll buy you a grilled chicken salad."

"Throw in a hot chocolate and you've got yourself a date."

A soft masculine laugh flowed through the wires and straight into her heart. The memory of their kiss flared to life, unspoken but most definitely not forgotten. Oh, dear.

Mia bit down on the inside of her lip. Why couldn't she ever keep her big mouth shut?

Maxine Fielding had a great memory. The silver-haired woman regaled Collin with the good, the bad and the ugly about his brother's behavior. And the pleasure in Collin's face served as a reward for the lunch hours Mia had spent in the spooky, smelly basement of the municipal building.

"You don't by any chance have some pictures from that time, do you?" she asked the older woman. "Anything that could lead us to some of the boys who might have known Drew?"

"Sorry, hon," Maxine said, her fleshy face sorrowful. "I used to have a lot of pictures of my kids. That's what I always called them. Every one of them that came through here was mine for a while." She gestured with one hand. The knuckles were twisted with arthritis. "Anyways, while I was in the hospital a while back, my daughters decided to clean my house. Threw out all my mementos." She shook her head. "I'm still peeved about that."

Mia wished she hadn't asked, though Collin, sitting on an old velvet couch with his elbows on his knees, showed no emotion. His uniform was still neat after a day's work. And even with a five-o'clock shadow on his normally clean-shaven face, he looked good. A woman could get distracted with him around.

In fact, she *was* distracted. She let Collin do most of the talking, a strange turn of events. She was falling for him, all right, and didn't quite know what to do about it.

In the end, the foster mother recalled two other families that had cared for troubled boys during the same time period as well as a couple of group homes no longer in operation. That information alone gave Mia more names to plug into the computer, some specific files to dig through, and more chances to come up with something solid.

"So what do you think?" she asked when she and Collin were back inside his truck. He cranked the engine and pushed the heat lever to high. As night had fallen, so had the temperatures, and now a light rain spat at the windshield.

"Nice lady. I'm glad Drew was here for a while."

She could hear the unspoken wish that he'd been here, too. "Doesn't that give you hope that your brothers did okay in the system? That maybe they even found a family?"

"Wanna look into those locked files and find out?" A ghost of a smile reflected in the dashboard lights.

"No."

"I knew you'd say that." But his reply held humor instead of animosity, and she hoped he finally understood. There were some things she wouldn't do, even for him.

"Mrs. Fielding liked Drew."

"I've worried about him for so long, thought the worst." He shifted into Reverse and backed the truck onto the street. "Hearing that someone cared about him, even temporarily, felt good."

She was glad. More than glad, she was thankful. Collin had needed this news. He'd needed to leave the tragedy of the barn fire behind for a while. He'd needed to believe something positive had happened to his brothers. As he'd talked with Mrs. Fielding, he'd smiled, even laughed at her fond memories.

Collin's love for his lost brothers was fierce and steadfast, a powerful testament to the way he might someday love a woman. Mia refused to dwell on the lovely thought.

"We're going to find them, Collin."

He reached across the seat and touched her hand. "After tonight, I'm starting to believe you."

Three days before Thanksgiving the weather turned sunny and mild. Collin felt pretty sunny himself as he left the gym with his partner, Maurice, along with Adam Carano. The other two men argued amiably over which sit-ups worked best, straight knee or bent.

Adam had first come to the gym to discuss the lawsuit, but now he'd become a permanent member along with the two cops. Collin liked the guy. And he also admired the way Adam was handling the lawsuit. When he took on a case, he was a real bulldog. Like his sister.

Collin's smile widened. Thinking about Mia did that to him lately.

"What are you grinning about, Grace?" Adam slapped him on the back. Collin's sweat-damp sweatshirt stuck to his shoulder.

"You talk as much as your sister."

"That's a terrible thing to say to your lawyer."

"When are you going to quit torturing me and get that problem solved?"

"I'm getting close. Did you know your neighbor has a real problem with cops? Especially you?"

Collin sawed a towel back and forth behind his neck. "Tell me something I don't already know."

"Okay, I will." Adam looked pleased with himself. "You remember busting a kid named Joey Stapleton a few years back for breaking and entering?"

"No, but the fire inspector suspects my barn was arson. Not B and E." His good mood evaporated at the memory of the animals Mia, Mitch and he had buried beneath the harvest moon.

Adam held up a hand. "Collin, my man. Lesson one about attorney-client privileges. Never interrupt your lawyer when he's on a roll. You disappoint me. You didn't even ask how Stapleton was connected."

"Okay, I'll bite. Who is he?"

"First of all, Stapleton didn't burn down your barn. He's still serving time. However, his half-brother, who mortgaged his land to defend Stapleton, lives down the road from you. His name is Cecil Slokum."

Now that *was* interesting. But there were plenty of do-wrongs out there with a grudge against him. "You think Slokum could be responsible?" Collin asked.

"Maybe. If Slokum can force you to pay damages for his daughter's ewe and destroy your barn at the same time, he not only gets revenge, he gets back some of the money he spent on his so-called innocent brother."

Collin had entertained the thought before, but a man didn't accuse his neighbor of arson without some kind of evidence. He'd also suspected Mitch of the fire and had lived to regret that mistake. Though his young friend was hanging around the farm once more, Collin could feel a hesitancy in the relationship, as though Mitch feared Collin would turn on him again.

"You got evidence?"

"Circumstantial, but enough to strongly suspect."

Collin's jaw tightened. Though he wanted to grab Cecil Slokum by the neck and shake the truth out of him, he wouldn't. He wasn't that kind of cop.

"Where do we go from here? Anything we can bust him on?"

"I've turned my findings over to the fire marshal and the DA. If I'm right—" Adam's grin was cocky "—and I usually am, an arrest could come at any time."

"I appreciate it." Although sincere, Collin heard the gruffness in the thanks. He wasn't a lawyer and couldn't do the job Adam could, but he didn't like needing anyone's help either. More and more lately, Adam and Mia and the whole Carano clan made him feel needy. Inside and out. It kept him off balance, edgy, vulnerable.

"I can't believe I didn't figure out Cecil's grudge myself." In fact, he was annoyed that he hadn't dug deeper when the suspicion first sprouted. But work and Mitchell and rebuilding, not to mention Mia and his search, had kept him too busy to think straight.

"That's what friends are for, Collin. To lighten the load."

The words *unmerited favor* flitted through his mind. Was that what Mia meant? He'd thought a lot about that conversation, and the idea that anyone would do something for him without expecting anything in return never would jibe.

"How much do I owe you?" he asked.

Adam looked at him, an odd smile on his face. "My sister would hurt me if I took your money."

A cord of tension wound around inside him. Cool from drying sweat and November air, he shrugged into his hoodie. "I pay my debts."

"There are some debts you can't pay, Collin. The sooner you learn that the better off you'll be. The better off my sister will be, too."

Collin had no clue what Adam meant. And he didn't think he wanted to ask. Especially about the reference to Mia.

They were nearing his truck, and he needed this settled now. "How much, Carano?"

Adam rubbed a hand over his chin as if in deep thought. "Tell you what, Grace. If you really want to repay me, you can do me a favor."

"Name it."

Too late, Collin saw the ornery twinkle.

"Come to Mama's house for Thanksgiving dinner."

Maurice started to laugh. His partner knew his aversion to large family gatherings. He'd also been on Collin's case about Mia.

"I think he blindsided you, partner."

Adam shrugged his wide shoulders and didn't look the least bit sorry. "What do you expect? Lawyers are supposed to be sneaky." He pointed a finger at Collin. "You're going to show up, aren't you?"

"Do I have a choice?"

"Actually, no." Then, with a laugh and a wave, Adam hopped into a sleek SUV and left him standing in the parking lot. To make matters worse, Maurice was still laughing.

Chapter Eleven

Anticipation, sweeter than Christmas morning, filled Mia. She'd had so many failures, but today she felt sure something new would turn up in this stack of records.

With Mrs. Fielding's information, she had located the placement files of the family that had taken Drew after he'd run away from the Fielding home. Surely some mention of Collin's brother would be inside this folder.

She rummaged in her desk for a Snickers, but after a glance at her dusty hands, changed her mind. With the holidays coming up, she'd be fighting more than five pounds if she wasn't careful.

She flipped through page after page, eyes straining at the faded typewritten print until some of her excitement began to fade. The records seemed jumbled, bits and pieces of several files that might or might not relate to Collin's brothers. Then, as if lit by a neon sign, Drew's name leaped out at her.

"Yes!" she whispered, barely able to contain her excitement.

Collin knew she and Mama were praying for a breakthrough, and he'd been politely receptive, but Mia was ready for God to show off a little and prove to Collin that prayer really worked.

She quickly perused the document, found nothing of significance and decided to put the sheet aside while she searched for others. If there was one page about him, perhaps there would be more.

But when she reached the bottom of a rather thick file, two yellowing forms was all she had found. Disappointed, but not disheartened, she settled back to read, hoping for any tidbit to share with Collin.

One was a general report concerning the reasons Drew continued to live in foster care. There was a chronicle of his psycho-social problems, his habit of skipping school, and numerous reports for fighting. He'd been removed from any number of places because of the chip on his shoulder and his propensity for running away.

The other was a social worker's report indicating a placement in a therapeutic group home with six other teenage boys. Her heart fell into her high heels. Drew was fifteen at that point and had been in foster care since age seven. Gone was any hope that he had found a forever family.

She stopped to rub her tired eyes. Thirty was creeping closer and she'd always heard the eyes were the first to go. She needed to schedule a checkup with her optometrist—soon.

After jotting down names and addresses that might prove useful she started to replace the folder in the appropriate box when a newspaper clipping slipped out and filtered to the floor.

The word *fire* caught her attention. Her heart thumped once, hard. The reaction was silly, she told herself. A newspaper article about a fire wasn't necessarily about Drew.

But the clipping *had* been in the same file.

Unable to shake the foreboding, Mia picked up the two-inch column and read. A fire had broken out in a foster home claiming the lives of several teens, though no names were mentioned.

Dread, heavy as a grand piano, came over her. The address matched one of the homes that had cared for Drew. And the timing was perfect.

She rifled through the box, hoping to find something more about the tragedy but came up empty. Finally, she rested her chin in her hand and stared at the clipping, unsure of what to do with this new information. Should she tell Collin right away? Or keep the clipping to herself until she could verify whether Drew had been in that fire?

She rubbed at her eyes again. This time they were moist.

Collin stood in the doorway watching Mia. Deeply focused on her work, she hadn't heard him come in.

Her dark auburn hair swung forward, brushing her cheek, grazing the top of her desk. He studied her, remembering the silkiness of that hair, the softness of her skin.

He couldn't escape the memory of that night. Especially that insane moment when he'd kissed her and she'd kissed him back. More than once, he'd been tempted to repeat the performance, but caution won out. She pretended nothing incredible had happened. So would he. But that didn't stop him thinking about it.

Her mouth was turned down tonight, unusual for Mia.

She rubbed at the corner of one eye and sighed. She was tired.

Her regular workload was always heavy and she was involved in church and the community, but for the past few months, she had been committed to helping him and Mitch. In her spare time, if there was such a thing, she searched the records for his brothers. In the evenings, she was now an active participant, along with Mitch, in rebuilding the barn. He'd asked too much of her.

He was suddenly overcome with a fierce need to take the load off her shoulders. To cheer her up. To make her laugh. Mia had a great laugh.

"Got a minute?"

Mia jumped and slapped one hand over her heart. Her red-rimmed eyes widened. "Collin."

"Didn't mean to scare you." He stepped inside the small office.

"What's wrong?" She didn't smile her usual wide, happy welcome.

"Why does anything have to be wrong?" Man, she was pretty, even with her hair mussed and her eyes red and every bit of makeup rubbed away.

"Because you hate this place. You never come here." She didn't look all that happy to see him.

He frowned. What was going on with her tonight? "Want me to leave?"

She rotated her head from side to side, stretching tight muscles. Collin thought about offering a neck rub, but decided against it. Last time he'd touched her, he'd gone nuts and kissed her, too.

"Don't be silly."

Which was no answer at all. He shifted from one foot to the other and checked out the messy office. Boxes,

bent and aging, lined one wall and stacks of manila folders with glaring white typewritten labels were spread
here and there.

"Are these the old records you've been searching for
me?"

A funny expression flitted across her face. For a second, he wondered if she'd found something. But if she
had, wouldn't she be shouting from the rooftops and
talking a mile a minute? Instead, she was abnormally
quiet tonight.

"These are only a few of the hundreds and hundreds
of boxes in that basement," she said.

"Maybe I could help." His offer should have come
long before now, but he suspected the files were confidential.

Mia shook her head, long hair swishing over the
shoulders of a bright-blue sweater. Blue was definitely
her color.

"I was about to stop for the night anyway." She slid
some papers into a folder and looked up at him. "So are
you going to tell me why you're here or can I assume
I'm under arrest?"

This time she offered a smile.

This was the Mia he knew and…appreciated.

"I came with some news." He scraped a straight-
backed chair up closer to her desk and sat down. "Unless Adam beat me to it."

Her smile disappeared and she tensed again. "What
kind of news? Did something happen?"

Collin waved away her concern. "Nothing bad. At
least, I hope you don't think so. Adam invited me to
your Mom's for Thanksgiving."

She studied him for two beats. "So did I, but you said no."

That wasn't the reaction he'd anticipated.

"I'm coming now."

"What changed your mind?"

"Your brother is a devious man."

He expected her to laugh and agree. She didn't. She seemed distracted, not really into the conversation. Earlier he'd felt unwanted, but now he saw what he hadn't before. Something was wrong.

He leaned across the desk to tug at her hand. The bones felt small and fine, and her skin was smoother and softer than Happy's fur. "Let's get out of here. You're exhausted."

"It's not that, Collin. Oh, I am tired, but I'm also upset about something I found in an old file. I need to tell you and I'm not sure how."

That got his attention. The desire to tease her about Thanksgiving dinner disappeared. "Whose old files are we talking about?"

"Drew's. Or at least files associated with Drew. There's some confusion in them. Several files seem to be jumbled together with parts missing. Maybe a box was spilled somehow and hastily repacked. I don't know. But I did find some information that may or may not involve Drew."

He saw the pinched skin around her mouth, the worry around her eyes. And he knew beyond a shadow of a doubt, the news was not going to make him happy.

The day before Thanksgiving Collin unearthed an ancient police report which identified the cause of the Carter Home fire as an electrical short. Better yet, the report listed several witnesses, one of whom turned out to be another former foster kid, Billy Johnson. Collin needed less than thirty minutes to track down the man's name, address and place of employment.

"I'm going with you," Mia said, when he called to tell her of the discovery.

"This is your day off. I thought you and your mom were cooking."

"We are. We still can. But I'm going with you. Don't argue. Come pick me up."

Collin hid a smile. Deep down, he was glad that the bulldog in Mia insisted on going along. Something in him worried that the interview might produce bad news. And though Mia couldn't stop bad news, she was a dandy with moral support and comforting prayers. He'd come to respect that about her. He'd even tried praying a few times himself lately.

Someone had died in that house fire. That's when he'd started praying in earnest. Praying that Drew wasn't the one. He'd even taken to bargaining with God. If Drew was alive, he would believe. If Drew was okay, God must care. He knew such prayers were selfish and unfruitful, but he was a desperate man.

Billy Johnson met them in the grease bay of an auto repair shop on the east side of town, a rag in hand. His blue service uniform was streaked with oil and grease and his fingernails would never see clean, but when he offered his hand, Collin shook it gratefully. This man had known Drew at age fifteen.

"Kinda cold out here," Billy said. "Y'all come inside the office. My boss won't care. I told him you were coming."

They followed the mechanic inside the tiny office

stacked with tools and papers and red rags and reeking of grease. A small space heater kept the room pleasantly warm.

"Y'all have a seat." He shoved a car-repair manual off one chair and swiped the red rag over the seat for Mia. Collin settled onto a canvas camp stool. No one sat around this place much.

"I remember Drew." Billy rolled a stool from beneath the desk and balanced on it, pushing himself back and forth with one extended foot. "He was a wiry rascal. Liked to fight."

Collin shot Mia a wry glance. "Sounds like my brother."

"He was okay, though. Me and him, we only punched each other once. After that, we was kinda buddies, ya might say." He grinned. "Foster kids, ya know. We sneaked smokes together. Raided the kitchen. Tormented the house parents. The usual."

"What do you remember about the night of the fire?" Mia asked, and Collin was grateful. His shoulder muscles were as tight as security at the White House. He wanted to get this over with.

"More than I want to," Billy said, scratching at the back of his head. The metal rollers on his stool made an annoying screech against the cement floor. "The house was full, seven or eight boys, I think, so I was asleep in the living room on the couch when the fire broke out."

"But you woke in time to escape?"

"Yes, ma'am. Me and this one other kid." He rolled the stool in and out, in and out, oblivious to the screech.

"Was it Drew?"

"No, ma'am." *Screech. Screech.* "A kid named Jerry. I think he's in the pen now."

Blood pulsing against his temples, Collin leaned forward. "What about Drew?"

Billy hesitated. Collin got a real bad feeling, worse than the time he'd walked into a dark alley and come face to face with a double-barrelled shotgun.

The screeching stopped. "Drew slept in the attic. I'm sorry, officer. Your brother never made it out."

Mia wanted Collin to get angry. She wanted him to cry. She wanted him to react in some way, to show some emotion. But he didn't.

With his cop face on, he thanked Billy Johnson and quietly led the way to the car. The drive back to Mia's apartment was unbearable. She talked, muttered maddeningly useless platitudes, said she was sorry a million times, reminded him that Ian was still out there somewhere, but Collin said nothing in response.

"Why don't you come inside for a while?" she asked when he stopped outside her apartment. "I'll make us something to eat. Better yet, my tiramisu brownies are already baked for tomorrow's dinner. We can sneak one with some fresh coffee. I know brownies and coffee won't change things, but comfort food always makes me feel better."

"I don't think so."

Her heart broke for him. Lord, hasn't he had enough sorrow in his life? Why this?

She pushed the door open, hesitant to leave him alone. "Will you call me later if you need to talk?"

For a minute, she thought he might respond, might even smile. He'd teased her so many times about her tendency to rattle on, but this time he was hurting too much even to tease.

"I'll come out to your place later if you want me to. Or you can come back here. You really shouldn't be alone."

He looked at her and what she read there was clearer than words and so terribly sad she wanted to cry. He'd always been alone.

"I'm here for you, Collin. If you need anything at all, please call me. Let me help. I don't know what to do, either, but I want to do something."

Feeling helpless, she slid out of the truck and stood with one hand holding the door open. Wind swirled around her legs, chilling her. Someone slammed an apartment door and pounded down the metal stairs outside her complex.

"I'm praying for you, Collin. God cares. I care. My family cares. Please know that."

This time he answered, his voice low, and Mia thought she saw a crack in the hard veneer. "I do know."

She couldn't help herself. She reached back inside the cab and touched his cheek. Her heart was full of sorrow and love and the desire to help him heal, but this time she was the one with no words.

Collin reached up and took her hand from his whisker-rough face, gave it a squeeze and let go. "Better get inside. You'll freeze."

She backed away, reluctant to let him leave, but having no other choice.

"We'll see you tomorrow at Mama's, won't we?"

"I don't know, Mia," he said. "I probably wouldn't be very good company."

And then he drove away.

Chapter Twelve

*D*ead.

The word clattered round and round in Collin's head like a rock in an empty pop can.

Drew, his full-of-energy-and-orneriness brother, was dead. Long dead.

All the years of searching, hoping, gone up in smoke in a house where the kids were throwaways that nobody wanted anyway. Nobody missed them. Nobody mourned them.

He lay on his bed in the darkness, staring up at the shadows cast by the wind-tossed maple outside his window. He had used all the energy in him to drive home and care for the animals. By the time he'd dragged his heavy heart inside, he hadn't had the energy to undress except for his boots.

He'd been alone for years, but tonight he felt empty as if part of him had disappeared. In a way, he supposed it had. The search for his brothers had sustained him since he was ten years old. The hope of reunion had kept him moving forward, kept him fighting upstream when he'd been ready to give up on life in general. The search had given him purpose, made him a cop. Now, half of that hope was gone forever. And with it, half of himself.

He heard the soft shuffle of animal feet on wood floors. The familiar limp and thump that could only belong to Happy.

After the fire, Collin hadn't had the heart to leave the little guy outside with the others. So Happy had moved into a box in the living room, quietly filling Collin's evenings with his sweet presence.

But now, he whined at the bedside, an unusual turn of events.

"What do you want, boy?" Collin said to the dark ceiling.

Happy whined again.

Though his body weighed a thousand pounds and moving took effort he didn't have, Collin rolled to his side and peered down at the shadowy form. The collie lifted one footless leg and pawed at him. When Collin didn't pick him up, Happy tried to jump, a pitiful sight that sent the dog tumbling backward.

Collin swooped him up onto the bed. "Here now."

With a contented sigh, Happy buried his nose under his master's arm and settled down. Collin had never had a dog. Not as a pet. But Happy was getting real close. Both his legs had finally healed after the second amputation, but a dog with two missing feet wasn't likely ever to be adopted.

He smoothed his hand over the shaggy fur, glad for the company of another creature, especially one that didn't talk.

No, that wasn't fair. He liked Mia to talk. He loved her soothing, sweet voice. He loved her enthusiasm for life, her positive take on everything, her belief in the ultimate goodness. She was a light in a dark place.

Mia had been so upset for him. He'd wanted to talk to her, wanted to let her help, but he couldn't. He didn't know how.

Burrowing one hand deep into Happy's thick fur, Collin drew comfort from the warm, loving dog.

A lot of good prayer had done. Not that he expected God to pay any attention to him. But Mia had prayed. And if God was going to listen to anybody, wouldn't He hear someone like her?

With his free hand, Collin dug down into his pants' pocket, felt the metal fish. All this time he'd carried the keychain as a reminder of his brothers. Of that last day together. Of the counselor who'd prayed for them and shown them kindness, given them hope. Had Drew still carried his that fateful night?

A fire. Another fire. He squeezed his eyes shut, but quickly opened them when flames shot up behind his imagination. Drew in a fire. Helpless. Just like the animals in his barn.

All night, he lay there, unable to sleep, unable to stop picturing the burned animals he'd had to bury. Unable to stop his imagination from making the terrible comparison.

When at last the sun broke above the horizon, heralding the new day, Collin rolled onto his belly and pulled the pillow over his head.

Today was Thanksgiving.

And he wasn't feeling too thankful.

At noon Collin awakened, cold and depressed, to a very urgent demand from Happy to be let outside.

Amazed to have slept at all, he stumbled to the front door, bleary-eyed and heavy-headed. The house was cold and the wood floors chilled his bare feet. He'd forgotten to turn on the heat last night.

After cranking the thermostat, he stood at the door to watch the collie hobble around the front yard, tail in motion, sniffing the scent of the resident squirrel as if he had the legs to catch it. Collin had to admit, the little dog's attitude had a positive effect on his own.

When Happy made the choice to stay outside and play, Collin closed the door and went to make coffee.

He felt bad about backing out of dinner at the Caranos'. He didn't like disappointing Mia—or any of the others for that matter. They were a great family. The best. The kind he would have loved to have grown up in. But he didn't belong, especially not today when negative energy was all he had to share.

He hoped Mitch was there, though, instead of at home. The boy needed the Caranos.

While the coffee brewed, the kitchen grew warmer, but Collin's feet didn't. He headed for the bedroom in search of clean socks.

As he opened the dresser drawer, his attention fell to the book Mia had given to him the night of the barn fire. She'd said the contents would encourage him, help him understand his purpose. Until yesterday he'd believed his purpose was to find his brothers. Now he wondered if there had to be more to life than a single-minded effort to accomplish only one thing. He'd found Drew, for what-ever good that had done him. What would he do after he found Ian? Once his only purpose was fulfilled, then what? Would his life be over?

Without giving the decision too much thought, he

grabbed the book along with a pair of socks and headed for the kitchen and that much-needed cup of coffee. The smell alone was waking him up.

He poured a cup and sat down at the table, flipped the book to a random page, and began to read.

Late that afternoon Happy's excited yip warned Collin that he was not alone. He jammed his hammer into the loop on his tool belt and walked around to the front of the house. For the last few hours, he'd sweated out his depression on the house-in-progress while mulling over the things he'd read in Mia's book.

As he stood in the front yard, chilled by winter wind on sweat, a caravan of familiar-looking vehicles wound down his driveway, stirred dry leaves and dust and elicited a cacophony of barking from the penned dogs. Happy danced on two feet and a pair of stubs, furry tail in overdrive, mouth stretched into a wide smile.

One fist propped on his hip, Collin blinked in bewilderment at the incoming traffic. Mia's yellow Mustang led the pack, an entire invasion of Caranos.

"Hi, Collin." Mitch jumped out of Mia's barely stopped car, wearing new jeans and an oversize OU jersey. Happy was all over him like honey glaze on ham, wiggling and whining, eyes aglow with love. Mitch laughed in delight and fell to the ground, pulling the dog onto his chest.

Adam bolted out of his red SUV and came charging across the yard, a mock scowl on his face. "Hey, squirt. Don't be desecrating my OU jersey like that."

Mitch leaped up, brushing away the dust. "Sorry, Adam."

Mitchell had come a long way from the defiant kid Collin had picked up for shoplifting.

Adam ruffled his head. "Joking. The jersey is yours. I told you that." He stuck a hand out toward Collin, his dark eyes sparking with the Carano humor. "As your lawyer, I have an obligation to tell you something." He jerked his head toward the rest of the laughing, jabbering group who came toward the house loaded with boxes and dishes. "These women cooked a mega-meal. And any invited man who doesn't show up to eat it could be in serious danger."

"What is all this?"

"You know the old saying. If Mohammed won't come to the mountain, the mountain will come to him. So, the Caranos have moved Thanksgiving to your place."

"You're kidding." Collin stared in amazement as the whole group trouped inside his house. A waft of incredibly delicious smells trailed them.

Adam clapped him on the back. "Caranos take their food seriously. Especially Thanksgiving food."

The old feelings of inadequacy crowded in with the unexpected company. His house was tiny and his table impossibly small. How would they have a dinner inside there? How would they all even get inside?

But the undaunted Carano clan had thought of everything. From the back of a pickup came folding tables and chairs. He watched, unmoving for several long, bewildered minutes while all around him people laughed and joked and juggled boxes and covered dishes. Why had they done this? Why would Mia and her family go to so much trouble to bring Thanksgiving to a guy who was accustomed to having no holidays at all? Why did they care?

"Close your mouth, Collin," Mia said as she swished past him smelling like sunshine and banana nut bread. "And take this into the house."

Her smile warmed a cold place inside him.

He accepted the foil-wrapped package, still warm from the oven. "You didn't have to do this."

She pointed a finger at him. "Don't say that to Mama."

He didn't understand this kind of family bond. He didn't understand these people. They scared him and nurtured him and made him long to be someone he wasn't. He didn't know whether to run away from them or to them.

For today, he figured he didn't have much say in the matter either way. If this was a game of tag, you're it, he was it. Might as well make the best of the situation.

The twenty-odd people were a tight fit inside Collin's home-in-progress, requiring some creative arrangement, but in no time at all his house smelled of the huge Thanksgiving dinner spread out before them on folding tables. Someone, Mia, he figured, had even thought of brown-and-orange tablecloths and a perky tissue-turkey centerpiece.

Around him, conversation ebbed and flowed. Nic, wearing a sweatshirt that proclaimed *I'm going to graduate on time no matter how long it takes,* wielded a carving knife and fork with a maniacal laugh that had the girls squealing.

As he watched the interaction of people who loved each other, some of the heavy sorrow lifted from Collin. Every time he hung out with the Caranos, he was overwhelmed with both yearning and fear. Yearning to be a part. Fear that he didn't have what it took.

He removed a stack of plates from Mia's hands and began to set them out in long rows.

"I hope you aren't upset with our invasion," Mia said, her sweet eyes seriously concerned that he was angry with her. "I couldn't stand to think of you out here alone on Thanksgiving."

He'd figured Mia was the instigator. She had wanted to be here—with him—and the idea gave him a happy little buzz. Maybe he had it in him after all.

Dinner was over, but the pleasant zing of having Mia and her family in his house didn't go away. The television blared a game between the Lions and the Cowboys which brought occasional shouts of victory from Adam and Nic. Gabe and his wife were deep into a game of Go Fish with their oldest child while the youngest was fast asleep in Collin's bedroom. Mitchell was sprawled with his back against Leo's knees, Happy in his lap. They all looked as full and drowsy and content as Collin felt.

Contentment was not a word he used very often. But something had happened to him today when Mia's family had come onto his turf to draw him into their midst with food and love. If he dwelled on the idea, he'd probably get nervous and back off, so he chose to enjoy. His mind needed their exuberant distraction.

"I'm on KP," he said, gently nudging Rosalie out from in front of his shiny stainless-steel sink. "Cleaning up is the least I can do."

A chorus of groans issued from the Carano men.

"Traitor," Nic grumbled.

"You're starting a terrible precedent," Adam called. "Next year, they'll expect us to cook."

This time the women hooted.

"Anna and I will help Collin, Mama. There's really not room for more than three, anyway. You go sit down. You've cooked for three days."

"Sounds good. I wanted to watch this game anyway." Rosalie untied her apron and hung the starched poplin over the back of a chair. "When these tables are cleared, you boys get them folded and put out in the truck so we have room to play charades or something."

"Will do, Mama."

Rosalie bustled around the tables and squeezed a chair into a tiny space between the wall and Leo. Collin leaned toward Mia and murmured, "Your mom likes football?"

Mia looked up from scraping leftover yams into a container and grinned. He loved the way she always had a smile ready to share. "Mama doesn't know a touchdown from a field goal, but she treasures the time with her boys."

"Your family's lucky to have her."

Mia studied him, expression soft and understanding. "We're very blessed."

Blessed. Yeah, he could see that. But they worked at being a family, too. At this whole togetherness thing. They were a clear picture of how functional families made it happen. Sacrifice, commitment, overlooking each other's quirks. He understood that now in a way he hadn't before.

"I'll wash. You dry. Dish towels in that top drawer." He took a heavy ceramic dish from her and dumped the empty bowl into the soapy water. "You Caranos are great cooks. I can't believe I ate two pieces of pie."

Mia reached for a rinsed glass and their arms brushed. Suddenly, he was remembering that disconcerting kiss.

"There's more for later."

He'd like that a lot. And he didn't mean pie.

They made short work of the kitchen, Anna and Mia whisking dishes and leftovers from the tables while he scrubbed away. While the women carried on most of the conversation Collin listened, comfortable with their chatter.

"I think that's the last one," Mia said, taking a huge stainless pot from his drippy hands.

Collin looked around, saw the tables cleared, and pulled the plug. "Good. The animals are probably thinking I've abandoned them. Can you take over from here?"

"I can," Anna said, her smile a mirror of Mia's. "You two go on. I'll finish up and make some fresh coffee, too."

"I'm not arguing with a deal like that," Mia said.

Nic popped up from his folding chair as Collin and Mia donned their coats. "Need any help?"

"We've got it. Thanks, anyway." As much as he liked Nic and the other Caranos, he was ready to be alone. Well, almost alone.

Collin pushed the storm door open and waited for Mia to pass through. Her companionship no longer felt like an intrusion. He figured he should worry about that. Later.

Once outside he was tempted, if only for a split second, to take her hand. He settled for a hand under her elbow instead. A man had to form some kind of boundaries with a woman like Mia.

As they fell into step toward the lean-to that now served as shelter for the remaining animals, she glanced over at him. "You didn't get much sleep last night."

"Perceptive." Beneath a narrow slice of silver moon, the air had grown frosty. Collin's breath puffed out beneath the bright yard light. Last night had been one of the worst nights of his life.

"The bags under your eyes gave you away." She slowed her steps to rest one hand on his upper arm. Whether imagined or real, Mia's warmth penetrated the sleeve of his thick coat. "How are you? Really."

"Better now." That surprised him. To know that family not his own could lift his spirits this much.

"I'm so sorry. Deeply, truly sorry. You have every right to be angry and hurt and grief-stricken. I wish I knew what to do to make things better."

She already had. She and her rambunctious family with their big hearts and their open arms.

"Every holiday for more than twenty years, I've wondered about my brothers. I know what happened to Drew now, but what about Ian? Does he have a family to go home to? A wife and kids? Is he having turkey and dressing and pumpkin pie right this minute with a loving family?"

Or is he as lonely and messed up as me?

"We're going to keep on believing and praying that he's okay and that we are going to locate him. If we found information about Drew, we can find Ian."

"I hope you're right." Maybe then the hole inside him would heal a little.

As they approached the pens, the animals moved restlessly, eager for their own Thanksgiving dinner. The colt whinnied a greeting. A cat meowed, followed by a chorus of kitten mews.

Even after losing six animals to the fire and making the decision to take no more until the barn was rebuilt, he still had too many animals. Caged up this way was no life for them and he hated the arrangement, though there was no other place for the strays to go. He'd ruled out the animal shelter knowing that sick animals wouldn't be adopted and the alternative was euthanasia. Better with him than there. Some were well enough to move around inside a stall but not well enough to be safe from coyotes and other predators if he left them loose. The puppies and kittens were in borrowed cages that opened out to short, makeshift runs. The larger dogs were on chains next to borrowed dog houses. The grazing animals were the lucky ones, unaffected by the fire except for the loss of stall space.

He went to the row of barrels that contained a variety of animal feed. "I have to find a way to get this barn up faster."

At the rate he was going, the barn wouldn't be finished for a year. He had only one stall completed to house the sickest, and a chain-link run for the dogs.

Mia began to distribute dry dog food, stopping to give each animal an ear rub. "I'll feed everyone while you take care of the medications."

He gave her a grateful look. "Good idea."

Panda, who had survived the fire and recovered sufficiently to be adopted, had yet to find a home, though her kittens had. Collin figured he'd never find a place for her. The mama cat allowed Collin or Mia to feed her, but otherwise she feared humans except for Mitchell.

"I thought this was Mitchell's job," Mia said, coming around the shadowy side of the lean-to.

Collin knelt on the ground dabbing antibiotic cream onto a pup's stitches. "He's through serving his time."

"I know. But the responsibility has been good for him."

"He's changed a lot."

"Thanks to you." She handed him a roll of adhesive tape.

"And your family. Sometimes I wonder what will happen to him."

"His stepdad scares me."

Collin looked at her sharply. She'd shoved her hands into her pockets. "Do you mean personally or professionally?"

Even in the halflight, he saw her frown. "Both. Since you told me of your suspicions, I want Mitch out of there, but…"

"But Mitch won't tell you the truth." He put the finishing touches on the bandage and stood. He was as frustrated as Mia over Mitch's reluctance to give them a reason to move him to safety. And for all his watchfulness, Collin couldn't find reasonable cause to pay Teddy Shipley an unexpected official visit.

"I think Mitch won't talk because his mother is using, too. He's afraid of what will happen to her."

In his entire life, including twelve years on the force, Collin had seen nothing but horror come from drugs. He was lucky. Mia would say blessed. And maybe he was. Whichever, he'd somehow escaped the trap of drugs. Too many of the boys he'd known in the group homes were dead, in jail, or living lives of unspeakable despair because of drugs.

"If a meth lab is operating in that house, it's only a matter of time until something bad goes down."

Her voice was stunned. "Do you think that's the case?"

"Maybe." Probably. They were gathering more evidence daily.

A chill of fear trickled down his backbone. "Stay out of there, Mia. You hear me?"

"I'm afraid for him, Collin."

"Me, too," he admitted grimly. Collin knew the reality of Mitchell's situation. Mia was an experienced professional, but she hadn't lived the life. He had.

In silence, his thoughts churning, he put the medical supply box away and doubled-checked the cage latches for security. He couldn't keep the whole world safe, but he could take care of these animals. And Mitchell, too, if the kid would only let him.

Mia tugged on the front of his coat. Her hair blew softly back from her face as she looked up at him. "Stop fretting. You can't always be with him. But Jesus is."

"'He'll never leave you nor forsake you,'" he quoted softly, the words of his keychain making more sense at that moment than they ever had.

"Exactly."

If he was indeed blessed to have avoided the curse of drugs, was Jesus the reason? Had God been with him through everything? "Do you think it's true?"

"I know it is." She pulled her hood up and shivered against a sudden gust of wind.

Collin draped an arm around her shoulders and drew her against his side. She fitted beneath his arm as if curved in exactly the right places for that purpose.

They started back toward the house. Collin reined in his long stride to accommodate her shorter one.

"Mind if I ask you something?" His words were deep and thoughtful.

"Anything." And she meant it.

"I can't believe how much I've laughed tonight."

She bumped him with her hip. "That's not a question."

"After hearing about Drew—" He stopped. Talking about his brother's death was still too fresh and cut too deep.

Mia slipped an arm around his waist and squeezed. She prayed he could feel her compassion and somehow gain comfort. From the time she and Adam had come up with the idea to bring Thanksgiving to him, she'd prayed. Thankfully, he'd responded well to their invasion and had even seemed to enjoy himself in spite of the awful sorrow in his heart.

"I want to ask you something," he said, stopping in a wind break next to the front porch. From inside the house Mia could hear one of the first Christmas commercials of the season.

"Sounds serious."

"It is. I've spent most of my adult life coming to terms with my crazy life, but I'll never understand Drew's death. That's where I'm confused about God. I want to believe He cares but the evidence isn't too strong. I don't mean I'm angry at Him or that I blame Him. But He doesn't seem too involved in my life so far."

His words were not bitter. Instead, they held a yearning, a seeking to understand. Somehow in all the past rejections, Collin had come to see himself as unlovable.

Mia looked up at him, at the strong, manly profile illuminated by the moon. She admired so much about Collin Grace that he didn't even recognize as good. He'd overcome some incredible odds to become a man with so much depth of character, so much rich emotion that he didn't know how to express all that was inside him.

She shifted against the wall and gazed off into the darkness, praying for wisdom. She'd been a Christian since she was twelve years old. She had a strong, healthy family and many friends. Though she'd had hurts and struggles, nothing in her experience could compare to what this good and decent man had lived through. How could she make him understand that God was here, caring? How could she make him understand that he was loved and loveable?

Her heart filled with realization. Tonight was the night he needed to know.

"I don't have any easy answers. I wish I did. But there's something I want to share with you. Actually, three somethings."

Collin peered down at her, his expression sincere and curious. She saw a trust there that gave her courage.

"First of all, I don't pretend to understand why terrible things happen to innocent people, especially kids. But I do know that God cares. So much that He sent His son to give us hope of a better place than this. A perfect place called Heaven.

"Secondly, He knew Drew's death would devastate you. He kept the news from you until you were ready to handle it. Until you had met a crazy bunch of Caranos who would try their best to help you through the grief."

"Why didn't he just give me back my brother? That's the only thing I've ever wanted."

"I don't know, Collin. I wish He had. But God has a plan for you. And even if Drew isn't a part of your future, he'll always be a part of who you are and what you've become—a good cop, a caring man, a dear and trusted friend."

A gust of wind whipped her hood back. Collin caught each side and tugged the hood up around her face. When she thanked him with a half smile, he moved a fraction closer.

Mia's skin tingled from his nearness. As hard as this was going to be, she had to tell him the truth—all of it.

In the narrow space between them, her breath mingled with his, moist and warm. They really should go inside.

She could see he wanted to kiss her again. And she wanted that too, but she wouldn't follow through. The first time had been unplanned reflex, completely understandable and forgivable. This time would be premeditated.

"Wasn't there a third thing you wanted to tell me?" he murmured, wonderfully, painfully near.

She wasn't scared of the truth, but she didn't know how to predict Collin's reaction. Was she doing the right thing by telling him? She fidgeted with the string on her hood but held Collin's gaze with hers. His expression might not change, but his eyes would tell her what he wouldn't.

"Yes. There is. Something very important. Something that I hope will make you realize how special and valuable you are. At least to me."

Inside the house, Nic's voice shouted "Touchdown!" Neither she nor Collin reacted.

She had his full attention now.

Throat thick with emotion, Mia bracketed Collin's face in her gloved hands. And then, her voice sure, she said, "The third thing is this—I'm in love with you, Collin."

Chapter Thirteen

Collin blinked into her eyes, stunned. She loved him?

A thousand responses thundered through him as wild as mustangs. He didn't know what she expected him to say. He had feelings for her, wanted to kiss her, to be with her, but love? He wasn't even sure what that was.

"You don't have to respond to that." She gave his jaws a final caress and dropped her hands. "I just wanted you to know."

She started to slip under his arm and move away, but he caught her. "No, you don't. You don't drop a bomb like that and walk off."

She stopped and looked up at him, her gaze as clear and honest as a baby's. Something dangerous turned over inside Collin's chest. She was serious. She loved him.

Oh, man. How did he deal with that? And why had she chosen to tell him now in the midst of a conversation about God and Drew?

If her intention was to distract him, she'd succeeded. The idea of kissing her had been on his mind since she'd bopped out of that yellow Mustang and sashayed across his front yard with her family in tow.

Ah, what was he talking about? He'd wanted to kiss her a lot longer than that.

Now that he knew she loved him, he wasn't quite so hesitant to follow through.

Drawing her closer, he lowered his face to hers.

She shrank back against the house and placed a hand on his chest. "I'm sorry, Collin. As much as I'd like to kiss you, I won't."

He frowned. "You love me? But you won't let me kiss you?"

Her eyes filled with tears, confusing him more. He'd made her cry, though he had no idea what he'd done. "I'm sorry. Let me explain."

Reluctantly, he dropped his hands and backed off. Everything in him wanted to hold her more than ever now.

The wind circled in between them. Mia shivered and hugged herself, and he had to fight to keep from taking her in his arms again.

"I could do that for you," he said with a half smile.

But they both knew he wouldn't push the issue.

She rubbed her hands up and down her arms, eyes focused on some distant point in the darkness. "Tonight, I understood something about you, Collin."

"Yeah?" He wished she'd tell him because right now he didn't understand much of anything.

"I realized that you don't know how to receive love. From God or anybody else. You've been hurt and rejected so much in your life that you think you're unlovable."

He didn't much like the idea of anyone poking around inside his head, and he liked it even less when someone thought they knew what made him tick. But he had to admit, there was validity to her words. Normally, he didn't listen to psychobabble, but from Mia—well, Mia was different.

"Love is a gift, Collin, and unless a gift is given away, it has no value. You're valuable to me. I wanted you to understand that. I wanted to give that to you."

"Then why—?" He left the question hanging. She loved him, but she wouldn't kiss him?

He shoved his hands into his jacket pockets.

Her logic didn't make sense.

"Because as much as I love you, I love God more. And I trust Him to know what's best and right for me even when His rules hurt."

Her words were a splash of cold water in the face. One minute she declared her love and the next she shut him out. "And God says I'm not good enough for you?"

"That's not what I mean."

She closed the distance between them and rested her head against his chest. He didn't yield. He'd never let a woman get this close. And now she was telling him she loved him but he wasn't good enough?

But in his heart, he knew she was right. A foster kid from questionable bloodlines could never be good enough for a woman like Mia.

"Will you hear me out?" she asked softly. "This has nothing to do with being good enough."

He relented then, letting her tug one hand from his pocket. He couldn't seem to say no to Mia.

"You have a lot of baggage from the past to deal with, Collin. None of that scares me off. God can heal anything. But that's the key. You have to let Him."

"What does any of that have to do with me kissing you? Does God have rules against a man kissing a woman he cares about?"

Okay, so he cared about her. Maybe a lot, though love wasn't a word in his vocabulary.

Mia's full mouth widened in a characteristic smile. "God's all for kissing. He probably invented it. But he has rules about Christians kissing non-Christians. That's hard for me to accept, but I have to. I'll be your friend. And I won't stop loving you even for a second, but that's as far as we go."

"You mean if I was a Christian, I could kiss you?"

"Yes." She tilted her head to one side and gave him a lopsided smile. "But don't be thinking I go around kissing just anybody, Christian or not."

He already knew that about her.

"Okay, then. Friends. I can do that." Friendship was all he'd ever expected anyway. Just knowing she was in love with him was burden enough.

Yes, friendship was far better anyway.

Mia dropped the last gaily wrapped gift into her shopping bag and headed out of the mall. The Christmas crowd was thicker than Grandma Carano's spaghetti sauce.

She had met her best girlfriend for a late lunch and they'd talked about Collin. Sharing her concerns with a praying friend had helped. She was thinking about her cop far too much lately and though convinced she'd done the right thing by admitting her love for him, holding to the friendship rule was harder than she'd imagined.

Collin had the uncanny ability to move right on as if nothing had happened. But with a subtle difference. Last night, he'd come to her apartment, bearing a glorious red poinsettia and asked her out to dinner. When she'd refused, he'd wanted to stay and talk about the book she'd loaned him.

Not knowing if she was playing with fire or trying to be a good witness for the Lord, she'd made microwave popcorn and spent the next two hours in an interesting discussion about her faith. Collin was a bright man with a lot of questions and misconceptions about God. He was stuck on the idea that God had abandoned him along with everyone else in his childhood, and nothing she said seemed to help.

But he was seeking the truth, and that alone was a big step.

Upon leaving the crowded mall, Mia picked Mitchell up from school and took him back to her office. They had some things to discuss that couldn't be said at his home. Later, she had his mother's permission to take him Christmas shopping with the money Collin had paid him for working with the animals. No matter that she'd already spent two hours at the mall, shopping was something Mia could always do.

Mitchell looked scruffy and smelled worse. She hoped the odor was normal boy sweat and not cigarette smoke. He'd come too far these six months to regress now.

Once inside her small office, she handed him a stick of beef jerky and motioned to a chair. "Sit down. We need to talk."

He ripped into the jerky. "About Collin?"

That surprised her. "Why do you think this is about Collin?"

One shoulder hitched. He flopped into the chair. "Since we didn't go out to his place, I figure something's up. He said I don't have to come anymore."

"You don't."

"I guess he's tired of me hanging around."

Mia rounded her desk and sat down. "You know that's not true. Your official community service time is completed so nobody will force you to work on the farm anymore. Now the decision to go or not is yours to make."

"Did he and Adam find the guy who started the fire?"

"They think so."

He chewed thoughtfully, then spoke around a wad of jerky. "I don't."

Mia frowned. "What do you mean?"

Mitchell took a sudden interest in the tip of his beef stick. "Nothing."

"Is there something you want to tell me?"

He slouched a little lower in the chair. "No."

Which meant there was.

She sighed and let the subject drop. Mitchell shared confidences according to his timetable, not hers. "Collin needs your help now more than ever."

"It really stinks about his brother. I wish I could do something."

"You already do. You help with the animals. Keep him company. Cheer him up. He depends on you." The boy *was* good for Collin, and the cop was finally at a place where he could realize as much.

Mitchell sat up straighter. "Yeah. I guess he does. He hates mucking out stalls." One tennis-shoed foot banged the front of her desk. "But I meant about his brother."

"We can't do anything about Drew's death, Mitch."

"I meant the other one."

She smiled. "Sooner or later, we'll find Ian."

She let a couple of seconds pass. The subject she needed to broach wasn't a good one. Muffled voices came and went outside her closed door.

"You want a Coke?" she asked to soften him up.

"Nah."

"Later, then. We'll go to that Mexican place you like."

"Cool." His toe tapped the front of her metal desk over and over again.

Mia picked up a pen. Put it down. Took it up again. "We need to discuss your stepdad."

Mitchell stiffened. The thudding against her desk ceased. He didn't look up.

"I know you're scared of him."

No answer.

"I talked to your mother about going to a women's shelter, but she refuses. She says there's nothing wrong. Frankly, I don't believe her, and I'm worried about both of you." When he didn't respond, she dropped the pen and leaned toward him. She was getting nowhere with this one-sided conversation.

"Mitch, if something should happen, anything at all, if you should ever be afraid, will you call me? Or Collin?"

He thought about her question for several seconds while a telephone rang in another office and a door down the hall slammed shut. Finally, he nodded. "Yeah."

That was the best she was going to get. She rubbed the back of her neck and stretched. "I'll trust you on that."

Her office door opened and another social worker peeked inside. "Mia, could I see you for a minute?"

"Of course." She stood and said to Mitch, "Stay put, okay?" She glanced at the clock. "When I get back we'll head for the mall."

"Can I play on your computer?"

"Sure. And have another beef jerky. I'll be back in a few minutes."

* * *

Three days later, Collin bounded up the stairs to the second floor of the Department of Human Services. Mia had said she loved him, but he'd never believed she'd do this.

She looked up from a stack of paperwork, the kind of overwhelming mountain he understood too well. Jammed into one corner of her office, a miniature Christmas tree blinked multicolored lights. A whimsical Santa waved from the wall behind her desk, and Christmas carols issued from her computer speakers.

"Oh, hi, Collin." Mia's face lit up. "I got your note."

"Sorry I missed you." More than sorry. Every day since she'd said those shocking words he'd found an excuse to talk to her, either in person or on the phone. The last couple of days she'd been out of contact and he'd missed her. He'd wanted to surprise her with a special offer that was sure to make her happy. Instead, she'd surprised him.

Somehow the knowledge that she loved him had changed him. He wasn't sure what was happening inside him, but he liked the difference. He felt lighter, happier, freer, which made no sense at all considering the news of Drew's death.

But then today in his mailbox… He slapped the brown envelope down onto her desk. He could never repay her for this.

"This is the best news I've had in a long time."

She grinned at his unusual enthusiasm. "You could use some good news."

He didn't want to think she'd done this out of pity, but if he told the truth, he didn't really care why she'd done it.

"I think this is Ian, don't you?"

She blinked, puzzled. "Excuse me?"

He slid a sheet of paper from the envelope and laid the all-important document in front of her. "I think this is my Ian. I think this is the agency that handled his adoption."

And he hadn't even known Ian was adopted. Part of him rejoiced. At least one brother had found a family.

"Collin, I don't know what you're talking about—" She froze in midsentence as her eyes moved across the confidential document.

All the color drained from her face. Disbelief mixed with hurt, she shot to her feet. Rollers clattered as her chair thunked against the wall behind her. "I can't believe this, Collin. How could you?"

Now he was confused. "How could I what?"

"Break into these confidential files. Compromise me this way. I thought we were at least friends."

They were friends. A lot more than friends. "What are you talking about?"

"You were here in my office while I was gone."

He rocked back, stunned at the unspoken accusation. "You think I broke into your files?"

"What else can I think? This document is from a sealed adoption file. No one, not even me, is supposed to look at those files without express permission or a court order."

He knew how important her professional integrity was. He'd never even considered such a thing. "I wouldn't do that."

"Somebody did."

His jaw grew hard enough to bite through concrete as her accusation hit home. "And you think it was me."

She stared at the twinkling Christmas tree. He sensed a battle going on behind those warm gray-green eyes, but her silence was an affirmation. Finally she said, "Who else would want to?"

He had an idea but if she couldn't figure that one out on her own, he wasn't about to toss out accusations. Not like she'd done. "You'll have to trust me on this, Mia."

She pushed the sheet of paper back into the envelope and handed the packet across the desk. Her hands trembled. "I hope you find him."

"Will you help me?" He needed her. And he wanted her there beside him when Ian was found.

She shook her head, expression bleak. "I'm sorry, Collin. I can't."

She didn't believe him.

All his joy shriveled into a dusty wad. He'd finally let a woman into his heart and she couldn't even give him her trust. Some love that was.

Fine. Dandy. He should have known.

He yanked the envelope from the desk and stalked out.

Mia locked the door of her office and cried. From her computer radio, Karen Carpenter's lush voice sang "Merry Christmas, Darling." She clicked Mute.

How could Collin have done such a thing? He'd been in here two days ago, at her desk while she was at lunch. He'd even left a note. She'd wanted to believe he wouldn't do this to her, but how could she? Hadn't he pressured her more than once to open those files?

Over and over she remembered when Gabe had badgered confidential information from her. Just like Collin he'd said, "Trust me, Mia. You know I wouldn't do anything that could hurt you."

But in the end, her actions on his behalf had hurt her plenty. She'd lost her job and her credibility. And though

Gabe had worked hard to make the loss up to her, she couldn't forget the awful sense of betrayal and shame.

Her own flesh-and-blood brother had compromised her for his own gain. How could she believe that Collin wouldn't do the same for a much more worthwhile reason?

Not that she wasn't glad he had the information about Ian. She only wished he'd come by it more honestly.

Collin stewed for two days, hammering away his anger on the barn that didn't seem to be getting any larger.

He hadn't broken into Mia's computer, but even if he had, he wouldn't lie about it. Why couldn't she see that? He'd considered questioning Mitch, but why bother? The deed was done and Mia blamed him.

If he'd known falling for a Christian was this much trouble, he would have run even harder the day she'd bought him a hamburger.

His cell phone rang and he slapped the device from his belt loop. "Grace."

"Mr. Grace, this is the Loving Homes Adoption Agency in Baton Rouge. I think I may have some information for you."

His heart slammed against his rib cage. His hammer dropped to the ground. Happy gazed up at him, puzzled as he grappled in his shirt pocket for a pencil. With shaking fingers, he scribbled the information on a piece of plywood.

His brother's name might be Ian Carpenter.

Everything in him wanted to call Mia, to share the excitement of finally having a concrete lead.

But he wouldn't. She wouldn't want him to.

Chapter Fourteen

The call came in at ten minutes to nine in the morning. A hostage situation. The suspect a convicted felon, armed and dangerous. And probably high on drugs.

Collin donned his gear along with the rest of the Tac-team members as the captain drilled them on the situation. During the serving of a warrant, the suspect had gone ballistic and taken a woman hostage, probably the common-law wife.

Collin exchanged glances with Maurice. He knew his buddy was already praying and he was glad. In situations like this, they needed all the help they could get. The Christmas holidays were high-stress periods. If anyone was going off the deep end, this time of year seemed to bring it on.

As the van approached the neighborhood, Collin grew uneasy. He knew this area.

"This is the Perez house," he said.

Captain Gonzales nodded. "Isn't that the name of the kid you've been mentoring?"

"Yeah. Is he in there?"

"Not anymore. We just got a call from Shipley on

somebody's cell phone. There's a social worker inside with him. Not the wife."

Collin's blood ran cold. "Who's the social worker?"

He already knew before the captain spoke. "Adam Carano's sister, Mia. You know her?"

He and Maurice exchanged quick glances.

"We've met." What was Mia doing in there? Hadn't he told her to stay away?

The captain gave him a strange look. He'd told no one except Maurice about his friendship with Mia. If the captain knew he was personally involved he'd send him back to the station. No way Collin was going to leave Mia at the mercy of some doped-up maniac whose last address was the state penitentiary.

Keeping his face passive, he readied his equipment, mind racing with the possibilities. Anything could go down in a situation like this. Anything.

"Why's the social worker involved? Was she there to grab the kid?"

"Bad timing, I think. She was inside when an arrest warrant was served. Shipley flipped out when he saw the cops approaching, and took her hostage."

Dandy.

"Anyone else in the house?"

"We don't know that yet, either. Jeff is working on getting the floor plans from the rental company that owns the house. Gomez is talking to neighbors to see what they know."

They set up a command post in the parking lot of an apartment complex across the street. Team members quietly dispersed around the property while uniformed officers blocked off the streets and cleared the surrounding area of bystanders.

Collin climbed to the second floor of the apartment building, seeking an advantageous position from which to view the Perez place. Adrenaline raced through his bloodstream at a far greater rate than usual in a callout. He'd practiced this scenario a thousand times. Had even executed it. But no one he loved had ever been inside the premises.

He squeezed his eyes shut and rubbed a hand over his forehead. Of all the times to realize he was in love, he'd sure picked a doozy.

Through the earpiece in his helmet he heard the captain. They'd made contact with Teddy Shipley. The guy was spewing all kinds of irrationalities, blaming the cops for harassing him, for his inability to get a job, asking for money, a car, amnesty from prosecution.

For the next hour and a half, the negotiator tried to soothe the frenzied suspect. Collin wished like crazy he could hear the conversation but all his information was filtered through the commander. He could hear the other officers, and from his vantage point above the scene he watched the stealth movement of Tac members maneuvering closer to the house, hoping for a chance.

After a while, the suspect moved the hostage into the living room, though even through his scope, Collin could see only their shadowy forms. One of those shadows belonged to Mia. The other much larger form definitely brandished a weapon. And as much as Collin wanted to charge the place and take the guy out with his own hands, right now all he could do was wait.

By noon, the tension hung as thick as L.A. fog. Shipley grew angrier and more demanding by the minute.

Collin, jaw tight, spoke into his mouthpiece. "Has anyone talked to the hostage?"

The answer crackled back. "Yes. She sounded okay. Scared, but pretty calm under the circumstances. We gathered from her subtle answers that Shipley is popping pills on top of meth. He's seriously messed up."

No big surprise there. Collin ground his teeth. No surprise but a really big problem.

At one o'clock, food was brought in. No one bothered to eat it.

At two o'clock, the negotiator still had not established a rapport. The suspect was spewing vitriol with the frequency and strength of a geyser. He was sick of being harassed. He wasn't taking it anymore. He wasn't going back to the pen. And scariest of all, they'd never take him alive.

By three in the afternoon, hope for a peaceful resolution was fading. Shipley came to the dirty window, dragging Mia with him, a nine millimeter at her temple. Collin saw her expression through his scope. Saw the fear in her eyes, the bruises on her face. Hot fury ripped through him.

Collin knew the minute Shipley spotted an officer outside the house. Wild-eyed and crazed, he fired one shot through the picture window. Glass shattered. Shipley shoved Mia toward the opening, screaming threats.

They had an active shooter with a hostage. Things could go south fast. Real fast.

The question came through his earpiece, terse but strong. "Have you got a visual?"

"Yeah." For a man whose knees had turned to water, his voice sounded eerily calm.

He slid down onto his belly, the rough shingles scraping against his vest. He had a visual, but Mia was in the way.

"If you have the shot, take it."

The surge of adrenaline prickled his scalp. His mouth went dry. To his horror, his hands, renowned for their steadiness, began to shake.

In twelve years on the force, he'd never missed, never been scared, not even when he took down a cop killer. But Mia had never been the hostage. Her bright red Christmas sweater and frightened eyes were imprinted in his brain.

What if he hit the woman he loved more than his own life? What if the ice-water-in-his-veins sniper they called Amazing Grace missed?

The December temperature was in the thirties, but sweat broke out all over Collin.

He was the only person standing between Mia and the maniac, and he was terrified.

He couldn't do this. But there was no one else. The other sniper had no shot. Mia's life was in his hands— hands that wouldn't stop shaking.

He needed help. And there was only one place to get it.

Intent on the house, he was afraid to blink and too focused to move. Under the circumstances, he figured God would understand if his prayers weren't too formal. There was no time to close his eyes and bow his head.

"Help me, Lord. I can't handle this one. Steady me. Give me the perfect shot. For Mia."

Then as if God had actually heard him, the strangest thing happened. His hands and guts stopped trembling. The usual cool detachment settled over him. Only the feeling wasn't cool. It was warm, comforting. Something incredible had just happened to him, but he had no time to dwell on it.

"Thanks," he whispered. Later, he'd do a lot better.

His gaze flicked from the felon to Mia. Eyes wide, she stared outward toward the invisible cops. As if in slow motion, Collin saw her mouth move. For a second, he thought she was praying, too, but then through his scope, he read her lips.

"Do it."

She knew he was out here. She knew he was the sniper on duty. And she trusted him to take care of her. Mia trusted him.

And he wasn't about to let her down.

With exacting skill, he trained the sights on the suspect and waited for the precise moment. No muscle quivered. Not an eyelash blinked.

Suddenly, Mia slumped in a faint.

Collin pulled the trigger. The crack ripped the air, and the suspect crumpled.

In the next few milliseconds that seemed like hours, the Tac-team swarmed the house. Voices screamed in his earpiece.

"Suspect down. Suspect down."

Collin pushed up from the roof. A minute ago, he'd been deadly calm. Now his legs wobbled with such force he wasn't sure he could walk. Rifle in hand, he started down. He made it to the first-floor stairwell and collapsed, sliding down with his back against the hard, block wall.

He could have killed her. He could have hit Mia.

"I will never leave you nor forsake you."

The words entered his head unbidden and he knew they didn't come from him. He shoved one hand into his pocket and withdrew the little keychain.

"Thank you," he muttered. Keychain in his fisted

hand, he pressed the little fish to his mouth, dropped his head to his elevated knees, and did something he hadn't done since he was ten years old.

He wept.

"I don't need an ambulance. I'm okay. Really." Mia struggled against the strong arms of too many paramedics and police officers who wanted her to get into the ambulance. There was only one cop she wanted to see and he was nowhere around.

"Humor us, Mia." Maurice Johnson's familiar face materialized from the crowd. "You're in shock."

Maybe she was in shock. Except for an overriding sense of relief, she felt numb.

A paramedic wrapped a blood pressure cuff around her arm. As she started to resist, her knees buckled. Maurice grabbed her slumping form and helped the paramedic lift her into the back of the ambulance.

"Where's Collin?" she asked. The bruise on her cheekbone started to throb and her head swam.

"Right here."

A tall, lean officer in SWAT uniform pushed through the crowd. His handsome face exhausted, he was the most wonderful thing she'd ever seen.

"Collin," she said, and heard the wobble in her voice, felt the tears in her eyes. She dove out of the ambulance into the strongest arms imaginable. Collin wouldn't let her fall.

"I'm sorry. I was so wrong. I do trust you. I do." The tears came in earnest then.

"I know." His lips brushed her ear. "It's okay. Everything is okay now."

She searched his face and saw something new. A peace she hadn't seen before.

He was still strong and solid and every bit the confident police officer, but something about him had changed.

Later, she'd have to ask. Yes, later, she thought, as she snuggled against his chest and the world went dark.

Collin didn't bother to clean up. Still in uniform, he made one stop before heading to the hospital.

When he walked into the room, Mia was sitting in a hospital bed, chattering at mach speed to convince a young doctor to let her go home.

"Might as well say yes," Collin said.

The blond resident gave him a weary smile. "Persistent, is she?"

"Like a terrier. She'll yap until you give in."

"You sound like a man of experience."

Collin looked at the smiling Mia and his heart wrenched. Her pretty face was swollen and bruised from eye to chin. But that didn't keep her from talking.

"Just trust me on this." He winked at Mia. "And let her go. She'll be well taken care of. I can promise you that."

The doctor scribbled something on the chart and dropped the clipboard into a slot at the foot of the bed. "I'll see what I can do."

As he left, Collin scraped a heavy green chair up to the bedside. "How ya doin'?"

"Better. How are you?"

No one had ever asked him that before except the force psychologist.

"It's part of the job."

"I didn't ask you that." She took the single red rose

from him and pressed the bud to her nose. "I knew you were out there today. And I knew you and God would take care of me."

"How?"

She tapped her heart. "I felt you. In here. Just the way I felt God's presence. You saved my life."

Just thinking about what could have happened made Collin want to crush her to him and never let her go. "I've never been that scared."

"You?"

"Terrified," he admitted. "I prayed, Mia. And the strangest thing happened. My hands were shaking and I couldn't do my job. One prayer later, I'm a changed man."

"Oh, Collin." Hope flared in her sweet eyes.

He smiled, the tenderness inside him a scary thing. He had to tell her. He had to say the words no matter how difficult. With Mia, he could be vulnerable.

"I realized that I need God in my life even more than I need you. And I need you more than my next breath. I love you, Mia. Please say you haven't given up on me."

Collin had never seen an angel, but he couldn't imagine anything more beautiful than the expression on Mia's face.

"I don't ever give up, Collin. Don't you know that by now?" She shifted on the bed, grimaced at the IV in her arm. "Mitchell came by with another social worker. He wanted to tell me not to be mad at you anymore."

"He broke into your confidential files?"

"How did you guess?"

"I figured as much all along."

"And said nothing."

"Now don't get your back up. I wanted him to be man enough to own up to mistakes on his own."

"He told us something else, too. Shipley set your barn on fire. Revenge for messing in his business, as he put it. He's just a mean man."

Now that was a stunner. "I guess I owe my neighbor an apology on that at least."

"What about the lawsuit?"

"You brother convinced Mr. Slokum to play nice. He dropped the case when Adam brought up the half brother."

"Adam's a good lawyer."

"What's going to happen to Mitch now?" He hated to ask the obvious. "Foster care?"

She offered a smug smile. "Yes, but I have a plan."

"Which means someone is about to be hit by a bull-dozer named Mia."

"The people I have in mind are used to it."

"If you're thinking who I'm thinking, I approve."

"Mom and Dad love him. He's crazy about them. They're starting the paperwork and foster-care classes, but I think I can pull a few strings so he can live with them now while his mom is in treatment."

"Miss Carano, I love you. Even if you are a social worker."

With a relieved and happy heart, he leaned across the metal rail and kissed her. When she didn't protest, he kissed her again. This time she kissed him back.

Epilogue

The halls were decked with tinsel and garland and rows and rows of white lights. Christmas carols played softly, and the stockings really were hung by the chimney with care.

The Carano Christmas was in full swing. Mia had managed to spirit Collin away from the prying eyes and teasing brothers to give him her gift in private.

"Open your present."

"I don't need presents. I have you, your awesome family and an even more awesome relationship with Christ. What more could a man want?"

He was different since accepting the Lord into his life. Not that his quiet personality had changed, but he was less tense, warmer, freer.

She pressed a small box, wrapped in shiny blue paper and topped with silver ribbon, into his hands. "Don't argue with me, mister. You know I'll win."

Mia watched him, her heart in her throat. He took his time sliding the ribbon over the corners. Turning the box over and over, he slowly caressed the slick, smooth foil with his fingertips.

Mia bubbled with impatience, but she didn't interfere. He grinned up at her. "I haven't done this many times. Let me enjoy the moment."

The notion that his Christmases weren't filled with good memories stabbed at her. She was determined to make up for lost time, and her family felt the same. They'd finally managed to draw him into the fold and he had begun giving back the banter, though his was still far more reserved than Nic's or Adam's.

Finally, when Mia thought she'd have to rip the gift from his hands and open the box herself, he pulled away the last bit of tape. Tissue paper crinkled as he lifted out the blue-and-white Christmas ornament.

The fragile bulb, held gently in his palm, glimmered beneath the bright light. The old black-and-white photo of three small boys was perfectly centered amidst a snowy Christmas scene. Collin, Drew and Ian in a photo she'd found stuck in a file.

"How did you—?"

The expression on his face was one she would never forget. The cop who hid his feelings couldn't hide them now.

Awe. Yearning. Joy.

With exquisite care, he replaced the bulb and set the box aside to wrap his arms around Mia.

She knew him. Knew he would struggle with the right words to express his feelings. His heart thundered against her ear. She heard him swallow once. Twice.

"I knew you'd love it."

"Yeah." His chest rose and fell as he continued to press back a tide of emotion. This was one of the things she'd learned to love the most about him. He was so deeply emotional. He felt things so intensely, but all his life he'd stuffed them deeper to avoid hurt.

Finally, he sighed and then with the same sweet tenderness kissed the top of her head. "It's the best present I've ever had."

"Want to hang it on the tree?"

He cast a sideways glance toward the noisy living room. "Dare we go back in there?"

"Actually, I'd rather stay right here with you forever."

"But your brothers would never allow that to happen."

As if on cue, Adam's voice yelled down the hallway. "What's taking you two so long? We got a party going on in here."

"Yeah," Nic hollered. "And I wanna open my presents."

Mia giggled and took Collin's hand. "Be brave."

Such a silly thing to say to a man who had never been anything else in his entire life.

As they entered the living room, everyone quieted. Mitchell stood by the enormous Christmas tree with Nic, Adam and Gabe. Each male wore a Cheshire grin.

"Now you've corrupted Mitchell," she said to them. "What are you up to?"

They all looked at Collin. He, in turn, flicked at glance at her dad who gave a slight nod. Her mother and grandmother, each holding one of Gabe's kids, beamed from the couch. Her very pregnant sister, Anna Maria, waddled across the room and handed Collin a beautiful maroon velvet box topped with a gold plaid bow.

He cleared his throat. "Your present," he said.

Mia got a fluttery feeling in the pit of her stomach. Her gaze ran around the room, saw the intense, excited faces of all the people who loved her best. Gabe aimed the video camera in her direction.

They knew something she didn't.

She lifted the lid and frowned in puzzlement. Lavender rose petals sprang out of the box and fluttered to the floor. She plunged her hands into the velvety petals, releasing the rich spicy scent as she pulled out yet another box. A velvet jeweler's box.

She gasped and looked up at Collin, her mouth open in surprise.

"Look, guys," Nic muttered. "Mia's speechless."

She was too stunned and thrilled to react to the titter of amusement circling the warm, festive room.

"Mia." Collin took the final box from her shaking fingers and went down on one knee in front of her. "I'm not too good with words." He cleared his throat again.

One of the brothers guffawed. Collin slanted him a look. "Give me a break, Nic."

"Want me to ask her for you?"

"Shut up, Adam," Mia said good-naturedly. She touched a trembling palm to Collin's cheek. "You were saying?"

"I love you."

"I love you, too."

"All my life I've distrusted other people. I've kept them on the outside. But you wouldn't let me do that. You forced me to open up, to feel. And I'm so glad you did. To love and know that I'm loved back is an awesome thing."

Mia's heart was about to burst with love. She knew how hard this was for him. For a man of few words, he'd just said a mouthful.

In the background came the soft strains of "I'll Be Home for Christmas."

"Mia." A quiver ran from Collin's hand into hers. He bent his head and placed a whisper of a kiss upon her hand, then slid the ring onto her finger. "Will you marry me?"

Tears sprang into her eyes.

"Yes, I will," was all she could manage as she collapsed against him. Sure and strong, he absorbed the impact and rocked her back and forth, laughing and laughing while she sobbed into his shoulder.

Much later, after Mia's brothers and dad had pounded his back in congratulations and the ladies had kissed his cheek declaring this the most romantic proposal they'd ever witnessed, Collin finally stopped shaking. He'd known how important Mia's family was to her and proposing this way would make her happy. He just hadn't known how nervous he'd be.

Then as if to overwhelm him to the point of no return, Mia's brothers had pledged their time and talents along with that of their church—now his church, too—to help rebuild and expand his animal rehab facility. Their Christmas gift to him and the animals, they'd said. And he was too moved to speak.

"Spiced cider, anyone?" Rosalie manned the large urn that emitted the rich scents of cinnamon and apple.

Standing with his back against the cold patio doors, his new fiancée leaning into him, the fragrance of her perfume embracing him, Collin felt more content than he could remember. He didn't need or want anything else.

Well, perhaps one other thing. "Could I tell you something?" he murmured against Mia's hair.

"Anything." She twisted around to smile at him and he couldn't resist another kiss.

"I followed up on that information Mitchell found."

She was quiet for a moment and he hoped he hadn't rekindled her anger over the unfortunate incident. "I'm glad."

"You are?"

"God turned Mitchell's mistake into something good. How could I be upset about that?"

He should have known she'd say that. "I have a phone number and a name. Someone who may be Ian."

She whirled around, sliding her arms around his waist, her expression joyous. "Collin, that's wonderful! Have you called? What did he say? When are you going to meet him?"

He swallowed a laugh. "Whoa, Miss Bulldog. I have the name and number but I haven't called yet."

"Why not?" But being Mia, she answered her own question. "You're nervous."

"Scared spitless. What if it isn't him?"

"What if it is?" She grabbed his arms and shook him a little. "Collin, you may have found Ian. Come on. Let's call right now. Where is that number?"

He took the slip of paper from his shirt pocket and shared the bits of information. "Ian Carpenter. The dates match. The age matches. I think it's him, but I've had hope before."

"This time, my love, you have something else. You have a family who will always love you and stand with you no matter what. And best of all you have the Lord. He'll—"

"Never leave me nor forsake me," Collin finished with a smile, feeling the truth of her words. He was full to the brim with the kind of love he'd craved all his life. Finding Ian would be icing on his very sweet cake.

He reached into his pocket and took out the small fish keychain, now polished to a pewter gleam.

Mia smiled gently, her face full of love, and stretched out a palm. Instead of handing her the keychain, he took her hand. "I love you, Mia."

"I love you, Collin."

"Good." He drew in a breath, feeling the strength of his faith urging him on. "Let's go make that call."

* * * * *

Dear Reader,

In my other career, I'm an elementary school teacher. Some years ago my principal asked me to remain in the hallway after school for a few minutes. Social Services was on the way to pick up three of our students. My job was to meet the caseworker and direct her to the office. As long as I live, I will remember the scene inside that room. The three children, one stoic and accepting, one furious and fighting and the last one silently crying, are imprinted on my memory forever. I've never been able to forget them. I've often wondered what happened to them, where they are now. They haunted me until the only way I could find closure was to create a story for each one, and of course, to give them the happy endings every child deserves. I'm so pleased to bring this heartfelt series, The Brothers' Bond, to you. I hope you fall in love with each one of "my boys."

I love hearing from readers. Please visit my website at lindagoodnight.com or send an email to linda@lindagoodnight.com.

Blessings to you and yours this Christmas,

Linda Goodnight

A DOCTOR FOR THE NANNY

Lone Star Cowboy League • by Leigh Bale

When Eva Brooks finds a baby on Stillwater Ranch's doorstep, she'll have to go from kitchen cook to temporary nanny. Working with Dr. Tyler Grainger to take care of the infant could bring her closer to her happily-ever-after.

THE AMISH MIDWIFE

Lancaster Courtships • by Patricia Davids

Sparks fly when Joseph Lapp is forced to ask midwife Anne Stoltzfus for help in taking care of his infant niece. Will they be able to put their neighborly quarrels behind and realize that they're a perfect fit?

THE CHRISTMAS FAMILY

The Buchanons • by Linda Goodnight

Contractor Brady Buchanon loves Christmas—especially the home makeover his construction company awards each year. When single mom Abby Webster becomes the next recipient, can they see past their differences and build a love to last a lifetime?

YULETIDE COWBOYS

by Deb Kastner and Arlene James

In these two brand-new novellas, Christmas brings a pair of ruggedly charming cowboy brothers a chance to start over—and find love and family on their journey.

HER CHRISTMAS HERO

Home to Dover • by Lorraine Beatty

Single mom Gemma Butler is intent on revamping Dover's Christmas celebrations—despite Linc Montgomery's protests. But just as a storm threatens the town, they'll join forces to save the holiday—and to find a future together.

RANCHER FOR THE HOLIDAYS

by Myra Johnson

Seeking a fresh start at his uncle's ranch, Ben Fisher is drawn to help local girl Marley Sanders with her mission work—and finds himself falling for the pretty photographer. But could a secret from Marley's past derail their chance at happiness?

LICNM1015

We hope you enjoyed reading
this special collection.

If you liked reading these stories,
then you will love **Love Inspired**® books!

You believe hearts can heal. **Love Inspired**
stories show that faith, forgiveness and hope
have the power to lift spirits and change
lives—always.

Enjoy six new stories from
Love Inspired every month!

Available wherever books and
ebooks are sold.

**Uplifting romances of faith,
forgiveness and hope.**

STEPLI

SPECIAL EXCERPT FROM

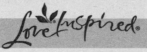
Love Inspired.

*When an Amish bachelor suddenly must care for a baby,
will his beautiful next-door neighbor rush to his aid?*

Read on for a sneak preview of
THE AMISH MIDWIFE,
the final book in the brand-new trilogy
LANCASTER COURTSHIPS

"I know I can't raise a baby. I can't! You know what to do. You take her! You raise her." Joseph thrust Leah toward Anne. The baby started crying.

"Don't say that. She is your niece, your blood. You will find the strength you need to care for her."

"She needs more than my strength. She needs a mother's love. I can't give her that."

Joseph had no idea what a precious gift he was trying to give away. He didn't understand the grief he would feel when his panic subsided. She had to make him see that.

Anne stared into his eyes. "I can help you, Joseph, but I can't raise Leah for you. Your sister Fannie has wounded you deeply, but she must have enormous faith in you. Think about it. She could have given her child away. She didn't. She wanted Leah to be raised by you, in our Amish ways. Don't you see that?"

He rubbed a hand over his face. "I don't know what to think."

"You haven't had much sleep in the past four days. If you truly feel you can't raise Leah, you must go to Bishop Andy. He will know what to do."

"He will tell me it is my duty to raise her. Did you mean it when you said you would help me?" His voice held a desperate edge.

"Of course. Before you make any rash decisions, let's see if we can get this fussy child to eat something. Nothing wears on the nerves faster than a crying *bubbel* that can't be consoled."

She took the baby from him.

He raked his hands through his thick blond hair again. "I must milk my goats and get them fed."

"That's fine, Joseph. Go and do what you must. Leah can stay with me until you're done."

"*Danki*, Anne Stoltzfus. You have proven you are a good neighbor. Something I have not been to you." He went out the door with hunched shoulders, as if he carried the weight of the world upon them.

Anne looked down at little Leah with a smile. "He'd better come back for you. I know where he lives."

Don't miss
THE AMISH MIDWIFE
by USA TODAY *bestselling author Patricia Davids.*
Available November 2015 wherever
Love Inspired® books and ebooks are sold.

LIEXP1015

Turn your love of reading into rewards you'll love with
Harlequin My Rewards

**Join for FREE today at
www.HarlequinMyRewards.com**

Earn **FREE BOOKS** of your choice.

Experience **EXCLUSIVE OFFERS** and contests.

Enjoy **BOOK RECOMMENDATIONS**
selected just for you.

PLUS! Sign up now
and get **500** points
right away!

Earn
FREE
REWARDS
Join
Today!
HarlequinMyRewards.com

MYR16R